In Blood We Lust

Depraved Sexual Fantasies for Vampires

Edited by Louisianax E. M. Caliban & Louis Ravensfield

DARK ANGEL PRESS
London, England

To Francesca,

From

Rupert.

xx

First Published 1999 by Dark Angel Press
BCM Box 3475, London, WC1N 3XX

http://www.darkangelprod.demon.co.uk

ISBN 0 9536566 0 8

Typeset in 9.5 Garamond Book

Cover photography by Debbi Clark
Cover design by Colin Chester & Louis Ravensfield

This book is dedicated to
Holly Flaxton
and
Sylve Swinborne
whose support for this
project was an inspiration

Blessed Be

For Vampires everywhere

Contents

Introduction

'In Blood We Lust' has been several years in the making. The idea was originally conceived in the mind of co-editor Louis Ravensfield many years before Dark Angel Press was ever even dreamed of.

One of the earliest contributors to the book was Louisianax Caliban, who became by dint of destiny, coincidence or sheer good fortune, joint co-editor of the book and a major player in the new direction the book took after the success of 'Bloodstone:The Magazine for Vampires', Dark Angel Press' first publishing sensation.

And it was through the pages of 'Bloodstone' that 'In Blood We Lust' really came into being in the form in which you now hold it in your hands. After advertising within these hallowed pages, writers previously unknown to either editor came forward offering their work gratis, and the resulting 33 stories are evidence of the wide range of imaginative talents which abound in the world of underground Vampire authorship. (With a couple of choice pieces from both editors!)

'In Blood We Lust' is intended to be a collection of Vampire erotica set within an immortal framework. For many years the mainstream market has been virtually flooded with collections of erotic Vampire stories written by mortals and for mortals. 'In

Blood We Lust' is different. Coming from a unique, distinctly pro-Vampire stance - in only one story does the Vampire not ultimately triumph over the mortals surrounding him - these stories are proffered as an example of how Vampires would write erotica for their own kind.

A broad spectrum of writing styles, and indeed subject matter, is here covered. There are no final taboos, no sexual depravities to which the Undead beings in these pages will not descend. And there is surely something here to suit everyone's palate - bondage, incest, torture, bisexuality, bestiality, crucifixion and necrophilia, we have it all here! Historical erotic classics with conventional Vampires sit comfortably alongside modern and futurist tales of excess, perversion and distinctly kinky blood-lovers. From the gently seductive to the brutally pornographic, no holds are barred in this compelling and exciting new tome. Sex and death have never seemed so perfectly blended as they are within this pages.

This book is essentially a product of the underground Vampire scene in the UK, although we are proud to have two European contributors amidst the largely British contingent. There are few 'known' names in this book, and this is a reflection of the nature of the scene. Most of the authors you will find within these pages have never been published before, whilst for some this is their only written testament to their fascination with the Vampire.

We are privileged to have the opportunity to offer a forum such as this to those who otherwise might never have seen their work in print (ourselves included!) For some contributors, 'In Blood We Lust' is seen as a possible launching stage for a new career in professional writing, and as the biographies attest, several authors have full-length writing projects in hand which their exposure in the pages of 'In Blood We Lust' will hopefully encourage and promote.

We are delighted to welcome every one of the people who have donated their work to this ambitious project, even those whose stories we were unable on this occasion to use, and we thank them each and every one for their support and patience during the lengthy process of getting this book into print.

Thanks must also go to some invaluable people without whom this book would never have happened. Colin Chester for his advice and for his excellent job of making the cover look as good as it does. Debbi Clark for taking the front cover photograph, and Emily Bouffanté and Kirsty Smith for modelling in very sticky circumstances. Duncan Gutteridge for his superb internal artwork and the back cover picture. Bishops Printers for printing this tome. Harvey Fenton for his example of how a small scale publisher can produce something stunning with a lot of hard work, dedication and inspiration. Ian Dowler at Books in the Belfry for all his help, assistance and advice. Brian Dineen, whose support for everything that we at Dark Angel Productions have ever done is eternally gratefully received. Walter at VCD for UK distribution and for his help in promoting the book. And to every Vampire who has ever walked on page, screen or reality, without whom the desire to do this would never have been born in the first place!

And so here you are, on the verge of turning the page into a new dimension of erotic horror. We hope that, whatever your passion, you'll find something within this book to satiate your darkest immortal cravings.

Yours in Blood,

Louisianax E. M. Caliban & Louis Ravensfield
London, England, 1999 CE

Final Stab

D. K. Korps

They were all gone. The cursed crusaders had crushed them from existence, sending the Vampires the way of so many endangered species, hunting them to the brink of extinction and beyond. Who the hell did they think they were, riding across the globe like some putrid Apocalypse, destroying the world's most magnificent creatures? The Champions of Light they had called themselves.

The vile light.

All Karysa had ever wanted was to be taken by a Vampire, to know what it was like to feel his penetration from whichever part of his anatomy he deemed fit to use upon her. For her it would have represented the pinnacle of her sexual explorations. She had devoted years of her life to becoming a Vampire's victim, following up leads, watching the news and gleaning through papers, acting on every sighting that seemed valid. She had travelled thousands of miles, city to city, endless circles, trying to become a morsel of prey. But always the damned Champions of Light, there to thwart her, to stake out the Vampires and incinerate the remains.

And so, eventually, there had been but one Vampire remaining. Just one. The final one. And she had found him. By the eyes of Empusa, she had found him, tracked him down, sought him out, attracted him like a bee to sweet honey.

That night he'd been coming for her, his clear footsteps approaching down the dark alleyway behind. What had once seemed like no more than simple vagary on her part had suddenly developed into a real, happening situation. Her heartbeat had been frantic, disjointed, her head pounding to the beat of wanton thrill. She had been able to smell him; a surprisingly compatible combination of sophistication and base, male whorishness. The scent's seething proximity had made her shudder with painful expectancy.

But they had followed her. They had shadowed her. They had known of her game and her desire. As the Vampire was upon her, his pungent aura wrapping a strong embrace around her, the villainous Champions of Light had struck. Stake after stake had showered down upon the magnificent creature, seeking out his heart and finding deadly penetration. And then they had hauled him off for incineration, carrying him high like hunters with a deer. In their cold-blooded eyes there could be no redemption for the crime of being Vampire.

Karysa had been left there, powerless to prevent the destruction of the Vampire in the face of such overwhelming odds. She had fallen to her knees in that dark alleyway, sobbing, screaming, keening out her grief and anger. But then she had seen it, glistening on the ground; the Vampire's blood, shed as the wooden shafts had been hammered home.

Quickly she had scraped it into a discarded bottle and absconded into the night.

Now she was looking at that very blood, as fresh as the night it had spilled from the dying Vampire and spattered to the ground. There wasn't a lot; maybe as much as a shot of vodka. Maybe a little more.

But, she hoped, enough.

Ownership of such a treasure had presented her with a whole honeycomb of options, and it had taken her weeks, months, to decide what to do for the best. But, at last, she had settled for the one avenue that she deemed best.

The blood was in a syringe now, waiting for her to select a suitable candidate for the honour of being the only Vampire in the world. She slipped the syringe back into her purse and sipped her drink. She was sitting alone at a table in The Carnivian Womb. She had pulled in the club before, and she hoped that she would pull again. But it had to be the right man, a man worthy of being enhanced by the last remaining essence of Vampiric manhood.

The night's entertainment was arriving on the stage, shambling out like the ragtag outfit that they were. No wonder there had been no extra charge on the door for the live entertainment. The singer approached his mike while the other band members took up their positions.

"Fee fi fo fum, I smell the blood of a Christian," growled the singer. "Be she alive or be she dead, I'll grind her bones to give me head."

The band thundered into their first track and Karysa cringed at the lack of talent they displayed as the music splattered out like cold vomit.

But, for her, tonight wasn't about the music.

She looked around at the clientele of The Carnivian Womb. She knew some, not many. There were plenty of males, plenty of good looking males. But she had to ensure that she selected the right one. The lucky recipient of the vital Vampiric infusion of full-bodied blood would have to be someone who could fulfil her desires and expectations. If the blood was endowed to somebody unworthy, then it would have been wasted.

But nothing was happening. As she sat at the table nobody approached. And, she supposed, if a man did approach, there wasn't much chance of him being the right person. She would have to go looking. She had managed to find the last Vampire by hunting him down. She would have to hunt now, through the ranks of the club. But in a moment. She wanted to sit for a minute longer.

She began to play with the silver ring in her bottom lip. It hadn't been there long and she still found it mildly uncomfortable, hard not to be aware of at any time. She was continually trying to thread the tip of her tongue through the small hoop. But, annoyingly, she was never able to succeed.

"Hey girl," came a voice at her side, and Karysa turned to see her friend Veronica pulling up a pew. "On your own?"

"Not now."

Veronica grinned, her cast fangs dimpling her bottom lip.

Karysa just had the one ring in her lower lip, and a couple in each ear. Veronica could have opened a small jewellery shop with the metalwork she had fused into her facial flesh. Each of her ears was circumscribed by stainless steel rings. There were crescents of silver rings where eyebrows used to grow, and she had more barbells than the local gym. Her tongue was twice its natural weight, dotted with metallic modifications, and when she danced she played her own bizarre jingle. There were so many different metals, some recommended, some not.

"You alone?" asked Karysa.

Veronica shook her head and Karysa thought of a slinky spring walking downstairs. But her friend really was beautiful under all that metal - a steel-clad Vampire Venus.

"Who then?"

"You don't know him," said Veronica. "He's at the bar, so he might take a while."

Karysa scrutinised her friend's face. "Any new ones?" she asked. She was waiting for the day that Veronica had her eyelids linked by silver. It would probably come.

"Oh no, I've got all the metal I need."

"I'm pleased to hear it."

"It's brands now."

"What?!" exclaimed Karysa, almost spitting out her drink.

"Brands."

Veronica lifted up the rubber sleeve of her dress to reveal a fresh burn on her arm. It was a rough representation of a cross, but all sore and inflamed. Karysa grimaced. Thinking of some of her friend's more sensitively placed piercings made her toes curl. They offered the wrong kind of sensation. But this was madness at a new level. Pain for pain's sake. She could accept the sexual elements in some of Veronica's rings. But branding! Where was the sexual element in that? It seemed that Veronica was moving on to other things.

"Who did it?" asked Karysa.

"I did," replied Veronica with another grin. "There's nothing more compatible than flame and flesh."

"You're insane." Karysa decided that it had to be some kind of fetishistic onanism.

"Probably."

It was then that Veronica's man approached, complaining that the bar was packed and that he'd try later. Karysa eyed him up and down and, had he not been with her friend, then he still would not have been the one. Even as a Vampire he'd be able to do little for her.

He took hold of one of Veronica's nose rings and led away the branded Venus as she squealed with happy delight.

"See ya," she giggled, and then was gone.

Karysa wasn't sorry to see her go. She loved her friend dearly. But there were limits. Still, the girl had no trouble attracting men. Sometimes it seemed that all that metal made her magnetic so far as males were concerned.

And here she was, alone and without a sniff of interest. And she was just as hot as her friend. Was it really the metal?

It was time to move, to go on the prowl and hunt down the man who would make her his victim. She rose and began to circulate through the bloodstream of the crowd, entering the swirl of scents: the Vampiress perfumes, the leather and rubber, sweat fresh and stale, the smell of arousal, the smell of smokes.

She took it all in, and she blew it all out.

Karysa loved to be within the creature of the crowd, assimilating it and being assimilated by it.

In the bloodstream.

The crowd was loud, but the band was louder. At least the stage was a good distance from where she was. She slipped between people, making physical contact with all that she passed. She felt her pulse tumbling through her like a runaway train. A face loomed up in front of her, all drunken leer and spots. The lad had a ring in each eyebrow. From one hung a silver cross on a short chain. From the other dangled an inverted cross on a slightly shorter chain. He obviously thought that it was cool.

"Hi," said the cocksure boy. "Can I get you a drink?"

"If you want to," purred Karysa. "But don't expect anything for it."

The boy quickly blended into the roil around them.

Karysa continued to weave her way through the club's clientele, seemingly always against the flow of the bloodstream. The band was really beginning to piss her off. So abrasive. So musically obstreperous. But at least there was only the devoted few thrashing along the front of the stage. Most people just milled.

But still, she wasn't exactly attracting much attention, just when she really wanted to. Men should have been gravitating about her - moths to light, flies to a corpse, demons to the desirability of darkness. She knew that she looked good. The black fabric of her dress was tight enough to accentuate her smooth curves, and the taut laces up the right side latticed her soft skin, allowing pale, pearlescent flesh to bulge slightly between the black criss-crosses. The outfit wasn't as striking as some of her House of Harlot garments that she often wore to The Womb, but it should have been enough.

Condensation dripped from metal pipes that traversed the ceiling. The cold drips occasionally struck her exposed shoulders; sharp stabs of sudden iciness that only added to her irritation as the night rolled on.

Then, suddenly, she was facing a real beauty.

Karysa's attention was momentarily snared by the girl before her. From the neck down she was wrapped up snug in PVC – every square inch of skin save for brash breasts that protruded forth, untouched by fabric. Karysa had toyed with the idea before. Did it have to be a man? Why not a woman? And, if a woman, then surely this beauty would be perfect. The creature leaned forward, bared breasts flattened against Karysa's own in a head-on collision of curvaceous flesh. Karysa felt warm breath in her ear. What was said wasn't important. It was only for the proximity. And what wonderful proximity. Karysa didn't notice the icy stabs from above while the vixen was close, moist tongue squirming in her ear. She reached up to one of those brash breasts, feeling its bud swell pleasurably in her hand as though spring had arrived.

There was heat between them, a seductive heat. But this creature would not have the Vampire's blood in her veins. These feelings just were not enough. It had to be a man.

Karysa turned her head and kissed the oil black creature on the lips, letting her hands slip over the slick garment. And there, in the mingling crowd of The Carnivian Womb, they responded to one another's ever more insistent moves until Karysa had to pull away before she succumbed to the maelstrom of desires that swirled within her.

She was so tempted, and the encounter had fuelled the imbroglio in her mind. But she yearned for the force, the brutish intrusiveness of a man. The purity of it.

As Karysa moved away she felt swells of heat erupting all over her body, centred on certain places. She looked back once, but already the creature had moved on to her next encounter.

It just wasn't going to plan and frustration was setting in like a rainy day. Things that didn't usually annoy her were really pissing her off now. The damned band babbled on, thinking that volume equalled talent. She still seemed to be continually fighting the flow of people, and those cold stabs still came from above, ever more regular. Even the lights in the club were annoying her, flashing on and off. They were never right; either blindingly bright or simply non-existent.

She hated the light.

The vulgar light.

The ring in her lip was beginning to cause her pain now. Damn Veronica for talking her into getting it one drunken night when shaggable men had been thin on the ground. And they had been to such an insalubrious place where the guy hadn't had a bloody clue.

"Anaesthetic?" he'd asked. "What's that then?"

She'd known that she should have gone to somewhere reputable and had the job done safely, cleanly. But oh no, Veronica had known best. Some friend she was. Most of hers had been done professionally. Who knew what this ring was made of? If it was silver, as the guy had promised, it would probably tarnish. But Karysa wouldn't have been at all surprised if it went rusty over the winter. The guy would have threaded a rusty chain link through her lip if the price had been right.

It all added to her current irritation. She found herself looking for the PVCed vixen, just to see if she was around. Just to see if there was somebody to fall back on. She couldn't believe that she was actually thinking about making do. She had set off looking for the most suitable man she could find. After all, the elixir she held was the last essence of Vampire in existence. She'd been right to look for the very best.

But now she was considering second best. Seventh best. And even that wasn't available. Karysa caught sight of shining black PVC exiting The Womb with another siren in tow. She was an option no longer.

Karysa could see Veronica in a passionate embrace with her bloke in some non-secluded corner of the club. Her spangled face glittered in the light, and Karysa had to hand it to her. She was outrageous, but men loved her. And, with all that body piercing, she was following in illustrious footsteps - Egyptian royalty, Roman centurions, and now Veronica.

Karysa often envied her.

"For the love of Empusa," she hissed when a venal guy with vulpine eyes came scurrying up to meet her. "Fuck off."

He did.

Was there nobody good enough? Karysa could feel her frustration boiling up into a full blown bout of exasperated rage. The night in The Womb was almost over and she needed another drink. So she turned and made for the bar, still fighting the flow of the bloodstream. Whichever way she turned, everybody was always oncoming.

The bar was packed, like a trough at feeding time on a farm, animals everywhere, jostling for position. Except jostling was too mild a word to describe the way these people fought for a front row position. Wrestling maybe. Wrangling. Writhing. Seething.

As Karysa struggled through the hot pack of people she could feel her tight dress rucking up, which only added to her annoyance. At one stage she felt an errant hand find its way up between her legs. She hoped that her stiletto found its target; the yelp from behind suggested that it had.

At least the terrible singer had announced that the band were performing their final track of the night – 'Visigothic Vice'. Karysa prayed that there would be no encore.

She was glossy with sweat by the time she reached the bar, hot, uncomfortable, prickly and pissed off. But the tedious journey – 8 feet in 15 minutes – had been worth it. Because, in the mirror behind the bar, as the dreadful music finally faded, she saw the perfect subject. Her eyes met with those of his reflection, and she knew that he was the one.

The night was crisp and clear, a startling and welcome contrast to the atmosphere inside the club. But a wonderful coupling had surely been conceived within the walls of The Carnivian Womb. Karysa's body glowed in the chill with fresh-kindled flames of anticipation, and she oozed with a sense of satisfaction as she looked at her prize. Abe was his name, and he was gorgeous, perfect, everything she had hoped for physically. He was lean, muscles defined. He wore his thick, black locks long and, she had to confess, he looked like a Vampire even now. If not for his reflection at the bar she would have thought that the Champions of Light had let one slip through their contemptible fingers.

At the bar she had slipped a brazen hand into his pants as he'd whispered honey-tongued lilts in her ear. And she'd gasped when she'd felt the size of the fleshy fang in there, already drooling with sexual fervour and eager to bury itself deep. All that pent-up potential, awaiting release. Just like the Vampire's blood, sitting patiently in the syringe.

But there was some commotion at the front of the club. Sometimes unenlightened boneheads would show up, just to cause trouble with The Womb's clientele. They just couldn't let them mind their own business and have a good time. They were too small-minded for that.

Let's go and kick a freak's head in. That was their attitude. They were as bad as the Champions of Light. Karysa saw one of the bastards break a half-full beer bottle against a lamppost and thrust it at some lad whose only crime was wanting to get by on the pavement without taking out his studs. The jagged spurs of glass sunk into the boy's neck, drawing blood quickly to the surface, some of the red fluid coming out through the bottleneck and down the thug's arm. Trouble was breaking out and Karysa wanted no part of it, especially not on this night.

As the innocent victim staggered away from his attacker, hand clasped to neck and warm blood seeping between his fingers, Karysa took Abe by the arm and led him away.

Now they walked hand in hand, heading for her flat. There were no lights here. The streets were in darkness and Karysa could remember the alleyway where the last Vampire had been slain so bloodily, so grotesquely at the hands of the Champions of Light. But they weren't around now. Their own efficiency had brought about their end. No need for them when the darkness no longer hid the fanged legions of the night.

"Is it far?" asked Abe.

"No."

He smiled, as smug as she. His hand slipped around her side, rubbing up and down the flesh exposed there. He wove his fingers into the laces of her garment and pulled her close as they walked.

He met with no resistance.

A car came down the street towards them, violating the surrounding darkness. The car's bright eyes penetrated the night like two broad fangs of light, engulfing Karysa and her man, swallowing them up in a voracious maw of radiance before passing on down the street.

Karysa shuddered. The vicious light had chilled her.

But at least she felt at ease in the grasp of he who would soon know what it was to be Vampire.

"You're shivering," he said. "Feeling the cold?"

"No."

"Not even in that outfit?"

"Especially not in this outfit. How could I ever feel cold in this?"

"Impossible."

Abe smiled before kissing her roughly, using his tongue like a thresher, giving her no chance to respond to its Draconian intrusion.

As a human he was forceful.

As a Vampire...

She hardly dared to ponder.

By the time they were in her flat Karysa felt drained, just with the anticipation of it all. On the journey he'd kept on pausing, again and again, just to manhandle her roughly, to take the doses of fulfilment he wanted until they were in the privacy of the flat.

Karysa had trembled under his touch. She loved to be exposed to the kind of contact that others would see as abuse. It wasn't only the thrill of his touch, but also the pleasure of giving him the power that would make his loins heat up like fuel-fed flames. And Abe had seemed ideal, not even waiting for the seclusion of her flat before unleashing a taste of what was to come. As a human he would be the perfect master, as a Vampire the perfect lover. To Karysa it seemed like such a natural progression. And, if that lover took her life on the first contact, then so be it. She had been prepared for that for years. But, if she was to know his brutally assertive love for a lifetime, then all the better. Death wasn't a thrill, but it was a price worth paying.

But Abe looked as though he was going to make himself comfortable in the sitting room, maybe expecting a drink before they got down to business. Karysa didn't even give him a chance to sit, instead whisking him straight through to the bedroom.

"Whoa there," said Abe. "We're in a bit of a hurry, aren't we?"

He reached for the switch by the door and flooded the room with artificial light. Karysa winced and immediately killed the vivid intrusion, not wanting the light to be part of this coupling. She didn't want it to poison this encounter with its presence.

The venomous light.

It would do its best to douse the passion and destroy all the carnal joys that would unfurl in the darkness. It would wrap its scaly, constrictive coils about them and try to squeeze the rapture away.

Karysa pushed Abe down so that he was sitting on the edge of the bed, and then stepped forward to stand before him, as close as she could.

Abe sucked in a sudden breath. "Let me taste some honey."

He stripped off his shirt to reveal a torso every bit as perfect as Karysa had imagined it to be - solid concentrations of muscles, but defined, chiselled, each muscle surrounded by a demarcation zone that set it off from those around it. Karysa wanted to trace every firm contour with her tongue; and she knew that she would be doing so, very soon.

Abe reached out and slid his hands up her sleek thighs, lifting her dress as he went. Seconds later her lace knickers were around her knees and Karysa moaned as he covered her with kisses. It was a little tender, though. She hoped that he would step up the pace. Even when he used his tongue to search out her melliferous cleft, suckling at the honey she yielded, he did so with a delicateness which their earlier contacts had not suggested.

Karysa needed more.

She reached down and ran her hands through his dark locks which rested gently upon his shoulders. And then she tugged at them slightly, as though they were bell ropes, hoping that he would give pain for pain. She cringed at her own assertiveness now that proceedings had begun. But her desire to feel his power drove her actions on.

Abe ran his hands up higher, exposing her mid-section before moving up once more. Karysa's breasts were soon exposed and, as he took them in his firm hands, she could feel her nipples swell like blisters under heat.

But still it wasn't enough.

She pulled harder at his hair, making Abe grunt. And, at last, he responded in the desired way. He began to use his teeth rather than his tongue, biting at her flesh, harder and harder as she continued to yank at his locks. Karysa found herself gasping continually as sharp sensations lanced through her. She wished that he had fangs already, so that he could sink them into her acquiescent flesh like probing prongs, and pepper her with pain.

Abe bit into her with all the fervour of a Viking king devouring beef-on-the-bone at a banquet. He drew blood on occasion, and the pangs were delectable. Once he had fangs digging into her pliant flesh she would not be able to take in all the pleasure. And she would know what it was to live in thralldom, enslaved to the utter baseness of a Vampire's desires.

"Harder," she moaned. "Bite harder."

Abe rewarded her with actions that bordered on brutality, mauling her and tasting her as he saw fit. Karysa shuddered with delight.

Too much arousal.

Too much need.

Too much sheer abandonment.

She wanted him to rape her. Yet how could it be rape if she wanted it? So, if not rape, then let it be violent, uncaring, selfish on the part of the beast. Karysa dribbled and drooled, her desire seeping from her like juice from an over-ripe fruit. She just couldn't hold it in.

She pulled herself completely free of fabric and flung herself onto Abe. He fell back, taking her with him and oh, how he buried himself deep.

Karysa didn't know how many times he'd been inside her, how many times she'd felt the heat of his releases and the pain of his punishment. She was exhausted as she watched him, sleeping soundly after his commendable performance. And, all the time he'd been ravishing her, Karysa had been thinking what it would be like once Vampiric essences were surging through his veins and loins.

She held the syringe now as she looked down at him, lying naked above the sheets. Karysa ran her free hand up and down his body, following the dips and curves, appreciating his compact leanness. And, even in his sleep after such exertions, he became hard once more, responding to her nimble fingers. She began to massage his stiffening manhood as she pondered over where to insert the needle. And what would happen when she did put the blood in him? Would he be a Vampire in that moment, or would it take endless days for the goodness in the blood to work its wonders on his mortal body? Or maybe, just maybe, it would have all been for nothing, the blood unable to convert Abe into what she wanted him to be.

Karysa just didn't know.

But, if he did turn, she prayed that he would have the ability to make others and create a whole new race. Abe would be the ProtoVamp. And if he was to take her, make her into his Vampire bride, then together they could be the progenitors of a brutal new world, the Father and Mother of all Vampires to be. Their union would be a union as fruitful as Eden's tree. Yet how would they breed? Could Vampires give birth to baby Vampires? Or would they have to bite to breed, giving birth to adult offspring who had once been human? She didn't know, but legends would grow from these seemingly inauspicious beginnings in her little flat over an X-rated video shop. At least that was a possibility. But she hardly dared even hope for it.

It was time now.

Time to dispense the blood. And, when she did, she would be calling her last shot. She would be losing any control she still had. And, in a way, it would be good riddance to that control. For that was all that stood between her and total submission to the beast. She would be placing herself completely at his mercy. Yet she didn't falter.

With heart beating like a bodhran she carefully selected a vein in Abe's arm and slid the needle gently through his skin. This was it. He was getting his infusion at last. Karysa was ready for a Vampiric infusion herself, and she hoped that it wouldn't be long.

Slowly she injected the blood into Abe's system and then sat back, breathing heavily as the virus began to burn through the vascular bloodways of his body. And she knew that it was working. She could sense it, turning him, making him into what she craved. Oh, to be loved by a Vampire. To be taken by a Vampire. It would be like having the heat of Vesuvius erupting inside her and, as the Vampire's blood pumped through Abe's veins, so adrenaline and sheer thrill cavorted through her own.

She bent down and kissed him on the cheek. There was a hiss as the silver ring touched his flesh, and Karysa knew for sure that he was turning. So the backstreet piercer had put real silver in after all. It was lucky that Veronica wasn't present. If Karysa's ring had singed his cheek, then a kiss with full tongue from her friend would have probably set the Vampire's head ablaze.

The sting of silvery heat had been enough to awaken the slumbering Abe. His eyes opened and Karysa could tell that they were the eyes of a Vampire.

Abe's eyes with added lust.

Abe's eyes with added intensity.

Abe's eyes with added power.

Sexual furore coursed through every particle of her body as she waited to be taken, to be plundered by the Vampire beast.

Abe rose up before his recreator, seemingly at ease with the metamorphosis that boiled within. As the two of them knelt on the sex-soaked sheets, facing one another, Karysa could smell him. It was that same combination of sophistication and baseness that had come to her in the dark alleyway on that distant night when the last Vampire had been put to an end. The scent was enough to tease out even more need in her, and she could tell that he was ready to rut once more. He had already fucked her raw, but she yearned for him to plunge her into a world of recrudescent pain.

She sucked in a sharp breath as he reached out for her, that scent of Vampiric libido strengthening all the time. But, on the verge of contact, Abe shrieked out in pain as, between them, a band of light like a laser-guided guillotine sliced through his flesh, severing his hand at the wrist. Red freckles appeared on Karysa's breasts as they became bedewed with Vampiric blood, and Abe began to shred his lower lip with virgin fangs.

"No!" screamed Karysa, not knowing what was happening. Her first thought was of the cruel crusaders, here again to thwart her on the brink of hard-earned success. Her blood-boltered breasts heaved with intakes of horror as she saw such sudden violence at close range.

Abe twisted in agony, turning within the sabre of sunlight that sliced through the air. Portions of him were carved away by the light, falling to the sheets as a laser-made pile of ruined flesh, blood and bone, cut cleanly from the body.

Karysa screamed again as realisation dawned upon her.They had been together all night, and now a laser-beam of brightness was cleaving through a chink in her heavy curtains. She just hadn't thought, being too caught up in her own desires.As Abe writhed in agony on the bed Karysa flung herself at the curtains, attempting to pull them closed. But, in her desperation, she pulled too hard, snapping the hooks which popped out from the gliders in a rapid succession of breaks. One of the curtains tumbled to the floor and the room was awash with light.

Without pausing, the brutal sunlight set about vandalising the Vampire's body. It treated him as Karysa had wanted Abe to treat her: roughly and without respect. But the light went so much further, incorporating a stunning amount of violence - pain from which even Veronica would balk. The light was murdering him bloodily and Karysa was unable to stifle its entry into the room as she fumbled with the felled curtain.

The light showed no mercy, this vengeful light, this vindictive light, hating the creature that loved its opposite and resided within that opposing world of shadows. It was performing a savage vivisection upon the helpless creature, eloquently expressing its feelings towards the fledgling Vampire.

Unable to get the curtain back across the window, Karysa tried to throw it over Abe, to protect him from the light that was attacking with Varangian severity. But, in the agony of glaring brightness, he thrashed about too much. Now he was beginning to burn up in the light and stenching, vaporous clouds rose from his stricken flesh.

Karysa was flailing uselessly, unable to do anything to reverse the effects of her fatal blunder. She couldn't believe the violence with which the light was devouring him.

The ultraviolent light.

She knew that it was all over. As she looked on helplessly the thrashing ceased. And soon nothing remained, every ounce of the Vampire burned away into wisps of smoke that dispersed into the sunny dawn.There was nothing left to save. Nothing to build upon. Karysa had been even more efficient that the Champions of Light.

She just knelt on the bed, her breasts spotted with burns where the Vampire's blood had been charred away in the callous blaze of dawn. Thanks to her own stupidity, her own rash need for fulfilment, the world would now be forever Vampireless. That deep-rooted craving to feel the sexual force of a Vampire's desire would never be quenched now. She'd had her opportunity. Her own ingenuity had given her one last stab at knowing what it would be like. And it was all her own damned fault that the chance had gone up in smoke. Her fault, and the fault of that vile light.

Blood-Lust

Louisianax E. M. Caliban

It had been a barren few nights. The city didn't seem to be proffering its usual glut of food, and what there was didn't appeal terribly. For almost a week now there had been nothing but tramps and vagabonds and whores. Nothing very appetising, nothing very exciting. The exhilaration of a drug dealer or a serial killer had long been absent. Food was scarce, and food was starting to become a bore. I longed to rediscover my former passion for this city, but it was looking increasingly unlikely that I would do so. And then I saw her...

Tall and fragile, pale and elusive, hungry and seductive, all at the same time. She was exquisite, in a raw and dangerous way. Right from my first sight of her, I knew she was not all she pretended to be. I read the rage in her dark eyes, the anger that burned as hot and cruel in her heart as it ever had in mine. She was as much a predator as I, finally, despite her delicate appearance and coquettish smiles. When she smiled like that, I could almost see the knives in her mouth, could almost see the blood running down her ivory chin.

Her name was Amaranth; at least that was what she called herself - I stole the name from her unconscious mind as easily as from a child's. I doubted very much that her parents would recognise the title, but it seems customary for young women today to adopt such sobriquets. I followed her around for two consecutive evenings, watching her every move, noting where she went and to whom she spoke. My first impression of her proved correct - she was certainly no innocent. She frequented notorious clubs and bars, mixed in very dubious company and lived in a suspiciously expensive apartment, paid for no doubt by a grateful part-time lover or shady associate. She dressed like a cyber-goth: all leather mini-skirts and slashed tops and plastic boots, her ebony hair crimped and spiked, her face painted a livid white, her eyes dark pits, her mouth a scarlet sneer. She was brittle in her beauty, too harsh to be as hard as she seemed. There was a nervous energy about her that belied the apparent languor of her movements. Within the space of two nights I was infatuated - I had to have her.

My pursuit was assiduous, as steadfast and true as any lover. I followed her wherever she went throughout the entire night, only giving up as she returned to her apartment (fortunately enough for me) at dawn. Her activities seemed confined to the dark hours, as were mine, and it came to be our secret, the shared knowledge that we possessed, something sacred to us like a favourite song. Although she remained oblivious to my existence, I felt that somehow we were kindred spirits, alive with the same destructive fire.

Though a cunning shadow, there would inevitably come a time when she saw me, and at length it happened, fortunately in a crowded club where the two of us were neither out of place nor alien to one another. I had just gone through my rather tedious routine of purchasing a drink, which of course went un-drunk all night, and she had just left the dance-floor in search of refreshment. She bumped into me at the bar, I believe accidentally, and was about to turn away after a brief, compulsive apology, when our eyes met and she hesitated. What was it she saw in me? Did she see what I was? Was I a revelation to her of some terrifying truth she had only half-subscribed to all these years? Whatever it was, it captivated her, and she sat on the stool next to mine and set down her drink. She pulled a battered packet of cigarettes from her jacket and waved them in my direction.

Intimacy was at last established. I could feel the electric heat of her gaze, those large dark eyes dilated with what I assumed was a perverted pleasure of some kind. The way she sat caused her stockinged thigh to brush against my leg, and her flesh was warm and succulent. On this particular night she wore a plastic skirt with a rubber slashed top, and the aroma of her skin was hot and spicy, fragrant with perspiration and musk in the stifling heat of the crowded club. I am fortunate not to be affected by such extremes of temperature any more, but she was clearly discomfited by it at the very least. She sucked vigorously on the cigarette, her cheeks pulling inwards, giving her an emaciated appearance that matched her pallid complexion. Her make-up was starting to run in the heat, but she still looked terrific, even this close up. A dozen erotic thoughts flooded my mind: of she and I dancing naked beneath the moon; of her leading me into her flat, eyes beckoning and wide; of her pressed close to me, her voice breathless and deep; of her lying on a bed of satin, her legs wide and her cunt glistening in the half-light; of her red lips enclosing my cock; of penetrating her slippery hole and pushing so deep inside her that she cried out; of coming inside her, filling her with my spunk – "oh, it's so cold!", her eyes snapping back with the shock of it; of her hot little hands on my spent flesh, rousing it once more to acts of carnal depravity; of shooting off another load all over her beautiful, deathly white face; of sinking my fangs into her throat, the kiss she will never forget; of sharp nails clawing at my back; of making her mine forever...

She had introduced herself by this time – dear girl, I knew your name a lifetime ago! – and I felt compelled to do the same. The danger involved in such a confession only added mystery to our relationship. I only ever confessed my name to the Food just before they died, just so they departed this life with my name upon their bloodied lips, just so I could drink of their fear more deeply. This time, perhaps, I would let her live, or bring her into the Eternal Darkness with me...

"I am Gabriel, Gabriel Koslowski." I felt her drowning in my eyes. My deep, ocean-green eyes that had served me so well in the past. Her pupils were totally dilated now, her dark eyes as black as the grave of earth from which I had risen so many centuries before. "Your servant." I raised her hand to my lips, pressed that soft skin close to me and breathed in its rich mortal scent.

"I've never seen you here before," she said, her voice shrill against the pounding music all around us. "I feel sure I would have noticed you." She licked her scarlet lips, her moist tongue pausing at one corner of her mouth. Her eyes were devouring mine, and I felt a hunger as keen as mine had ever been emanating from her. Witless mortal, to think that you can pretend with me – I, who see everything.

"I am no stranger to this town," I replied. "But its ways are not mine. I move in... unusual circles." Was I sounding too theatrical? She seemed flattered by whatever she imagined me to be, but why should I hide my true nature behind this shroud of lies? I am a predator, I told myself: I kill, I rape, I torture, I sacrifice others to sustain my own evil life. I am the worst of scavengers.

"Would you like... I mean, well, I was just wondering if maybe you wanted to..." She leaned forward, her lips less than inches from my face, her breath hot and tobacco-stained. "I live just around the corner." One white hand descended on my thigh and her long fingers closed gently around the muscle. I caught a whiff suddenly of another perfume above the sweat and the musk and the tobacco - a rich, salty syrup spiked with sugar pearls. I was not the first of her conquests this evening, and she was hot for another to take his place. The thought of another man's cock inside her sent waves of raging blood into my groin and my own cock responded instantaneously. She felt the sudden movement and ran her hand up to enclose my swollen flesh softly. "If you think you can hold it that long..." she whispered, her lips brushing against my ear, her hair on my cheek.

What could I do but follow her? Wherever she led me, it would be no worse than where I could lead her - to the gates of Hell itself. I stepped through the door of that deceptive apartment, and both our fates were sealed. She knew what would happen next; I knew what would happen later.

We were barely through the door before she pounced upon me, her hot hands on my chest, around my waist, holding me tight against her while her mouth devoured mine. My cock was unbearably stiff now, crushed against the flesh of her thighs, those milky thighs between which it would soon be penetrating. The more I thought of her, the fiercer my passion to possess her became. Without a word she began to open my shirt, pulling it out from my waistband and scratching the skin of my stomach gently with her long red nails. She was surprised at how cold my skin was to the touch - "when you're obviously so hot elsewhere" (laying a fiendish emphasis on the 'hot', her eyes widening as she looked at the strident outline of my cock inside my trousers). I thought for a moment that she would push me to the floor right there in the hallway, but it seemed that the desire for comfort outweighed all other impulses in her, and she took my hand and led me into the bedroom.

As she shut the door behind us, she threw off her jacket and unzipped her skirt. It fell to the ground with a silky swish, and she stepped out of it, her long, pale legs encased in seamless black stockings. Her thighs were every bit as soft and milky as I had imagined, their pallor accentuated by the dark stockings and the carefully cultivated triangle of black down on her mound. She stepped towards me again, her hands placed close to that hidden garden of delights, her eyes and mouth provocative and moist.

"You do want me, don't you?" she queried, her voice vibrant with raw passion. "Don't I please you?"

I was momentarily unable to speak: the beauty of her held me spellbound, and I could think of nothing beyond slipping my huge cock inside her and fucking the very life out of her. She must have read my thoughts, for she lay down upon the bed and beckoned me to her. I approached with all haste, throwing my shirt upon the floor and kicking off my shoes, before sinking down into the vast bed at her feet and admiring her delicious skin. Such pallor! It seemed impossible that she could be mortal, she looked so like one of my own kind.

I rained kisses upon her feet and her legs, travelling smoothly and with practiced ease up to her bony hips, bypassing completely that salty, pungent slit to which I should later turn my most eager attention. I had rarely known a mortal woman this crazed, this horny, this desperate to be loved. She seemed to care about none of the precursors which mortal women usually so insist upon. She wanted my cock inside her, and she wanted it now, even if it hurt. I could do nothing but pamper her needs.

At last free of its bondage - her hands expertly removing my trousers with the minimum of fuss - my cock stood up stiff and proud, so hard that it hurt. The hunger for blood had never been as intense as the hunger for sex was at that moment, and I was hard pressed to wait while she offered her admiration of its length, size, texture and so on. She weighed my balls in her hands, again remarking on my coldness, and leaned forward to gently kiss each one. Her hair rubbed against the swollen head of my cock and I could control my passion no longer.

I pushed her down deeper into the bed, tore her rubber top clean in two, watched her small breasts tumble out with a smile of disinterested amusement, and then forced her legs wider apart than she had already spread them, and forced my massive cock inside her. With what delight did I feel her ragged cunt lips part to make way for me, with what undeniable pleasure did I negotiate my way past her pelvic bone to seek the warm, snug, moist passage beyond?! I felt her cunt lips draw up upon me as I entered her, as she pushed her hips off the bed to allow me in deeper still. As I found her full depth, she cried out with pleasure, her voice breathless and excited, thrilled with the size and the force of me.

She begged me to "hold it there just a moment", and I earnestly tried, but the lust in me was too strong to be checked for long. A brief pause, feeling the blood pounding through the length of my cock, feeling my balls tighten with anticipation, feeling the walls of her wet cunt crushing me – and then I had to move.

Moving inside her was unforgettable. She was slick with well-use, but I filled her adequately, and any deficiency in her of being too wet was compensated for by the strength of her internal muscles, and the tenacity with which she gripped my cock inside her. For all intents and purposes, she was snug and close enough to have been a virgin, but with all the obvious advantages of a woman of experience. She was pressing up against me, writhing on the bed beneath me, apparently in ecstasy, her hands clenching coils of satin sheet into tight little balls, her eyelids puckered with concentration, her mouth a wild, vacant O of surprise and confusion. I wondered how long it had been since a man had fucked her – not long, I knew, since I had still been able to smell his scent mingled with hers when I met her – and how long it had been since a man had fulfilled her in the way I seemed in danger of doing – far longer, I imagined, judging from her expression and the way her hands kept fluttering up towards my face, as though she wanted to embrace me but feared the intimacy.

I made no move to embrace her, to kiss her. In one way it felt wrong to show her affection while I was fucking her like a whore; in another it felt almost sacrilegious to try to get close to her because she was so radiantly beautiful, literally untouchable. It was fine to pollute her with my cock, to defile her and rape her and drag her to heights (or depths) of pleasure by screwing her, but if I thought about her in a romantic light I would be sure to lose my will to fuck, and that would never have done. She had made it abundantly clear that any affection she had for me depended solely on my performance here and my ability to use and abuse her naked body.

She was so slippery now, her cunt wet and harder to negotiate while pumping the way I had been – swift, deep descents punctuated by long moments of pulling away from her, almost leaving her completely. When I pulled out, my cock was slick and shiny with her creamy juices; when I plunged back in, she was wider and more welcoming with every stroke. I was losing control fast, and began to pump harder into her, staying close to her and stabbing at her, so that each inward action caused her to moan breathlessly – "ah, ah, ah, ah!". I think she even said my name once or twice, her lips quivering, soft tears in her eyes.

She began to push harder up against me, her hips grinding against mine, her cries becoming louder and sharper and faster as I fucked her deeper and harder and stronger. Building up speed inside her, I felt my orgasm approaching at a rate of knots. I could feel waves of delirium spreading all over my body, tensing for the shock of it. In those final few seconds, I was trembling from head to foot as I felt the hunger cresting inside me - coming as a surprise after the intensity of my carnal desires. My gums were itching, my eye-teeth felt as swollen as my cock, as keen to be plunging into soft flesh as it already was. When the climax finally came - against a symphony of desperate cries from the shaking body beneath me, obviously on the verge of her own climactic release - the growl of passion in my groin merged with the death-snarl of hunger as I threw my head back to prepare for the fatal kiss.

Her mouth was a loose caricature of itself now, the sounds of her pleasure echoing in her throat and in her heaving chest. Her legs were tight around mine, her thighs drenched in sweat and spunk and her own lovely juice. And blood. It was the sight of that which froze me momentarily. It caused the hunger in me to radiate outwards, to burn my stomach and my chest and my throat. The pounding in my cock at last allayed, the smell of my spunk rich in my nostrils, the ache in my balls more poignant and grating than ever, I could give myself over to my true hunger, the one which sustained me. And yet that blood on her thighs was mine, and it seemed at once terrible and hilarious to be shedding hers so soon after she had given me such transitory, potent pleasure. How could I do this to her? How could I think of killing, of sacrificing, so generous a woman, who had made the gift of herself to me, without knowing me, without caring, without fear of recrimination or regret? My little Amaranth, so brittle, so fragile finally, so hard to the outside world, but so gentle and weak inside, so afraid of her own passion, hiding behind the lie of the whore a heart that beat with pure beauty, pure love.

For a predator like me, such romantic notions are fatal. Of course, as is the nature of this particular beast, I killed her.

But I fear I shall never see her like again.

Sexual Deviants

Angélique Bessant

It took a special kind of person to fuck a vampire, a person who was bred to the challenge and denied all mortal diversions. The Cydonia colony had been established at the end of the previous millennium to try to engineer a race of human-vampire hybrids who could cope with the demands of their undead clientele without becoming undead themselves.

Christophe Banadour had been part of that selective breeding program in his youth, and now his sons Philippe, Armand and Léopolde were all participating in the next stage of the procedure. Léopolde as the youngest was still under strict scrutiny in the medical lab, Armand was being put through his paces in the safe area of Cydon city, and Philippe was already a fully-fledged, and fully-qualified, vampire-whore. His genetic make-up had been infected over and over under test conditions with the necrotising bacterium which was now known to be the primary cause of congenital vampirism, but each attempt had been rejected. Philippe's immune system, bolstered by a lifetime of blood-enriching compounds, shrugged off the invasive molecules, suffering at worst a slight fever which passed within days.

Philippe Banadour was one of the greatest triumphs of controlled genetic modification that Cydonia had ever produced. He was popular with the vampires, a rôle model for future generations of mutants, an intelligent and bright young man. In the

hair, scratching his face gently with those nails that could kill as easily as caress.

Philippe placed one finger against the wet lips, pressing firmly against the hard nub of flesh above the welcoming slit. "You're sure you want to be female first?" he asked, meeting the vampire's eyes briefly.

A wider smile, the barest hint of white fang, and the vampire slowly nodded, reaching down to touch the boy's fingers and hold them closer against her body, insistent.

Philippe slid one finger inside the warm slit, pushing apart the delicate lips and probing deeper into the dark hole of the vampire's cunt. Carefully he pushed a second digit inside the widening hole and began to gently excite the already slick tunnel.

The vampire moaned, one hand cupping her breasts alternately as the human's flesh entered her cunt, the other hand caressing her belly and the rising tumescence of her prick. She was well-endowed in both genders, and had a prodigious appetite for both kinds of sex. Despite all vampires having accoutrements for both genders, some were more obviously one or the other. Inbreeding with humans and mutants had done that. As one of the Ancient Race she was more evenly balanced. In all her dealings she referred to herself as a woman, but the male side of her could be just as strong, when it came to sex at least. Her cock swelled thick and long, and she rubbed the foreskin back from the engorged head. The boy's fingers - three now - played at a more aggressive tempo, provoking waves of delicious juice in her female part, and she wanted very much to have his mouth lap up that juice. She pulled at him, tugging him by the hair, trying to make him understand.

Philippe leant eagerly down to the vampire's wet cunt, watching as her pearly liquid oozed from the hole where his fingers pumped in and out. The vampire's cock was rock hard now, standing to stiff attention beneath her slowly moving fingers. He lashed out his tongue to drink her juice, feeling the golden fire of it burn his mouth. The vampire pushed her hips up from the bed, grinding her wet shaven pussy into the mutant's face.

Philippe slipped his remaining finger and thumb inside the convulsing cave of her cunt, squashing his hand to slide it in past the knuckle. The vampire howled in delight, fresh spasms racking her body, tiny beads of pre-come weeping from the crown of her swollen cock.

"Do you like that?" he asked between mouthfuls of her juice.

The vampire gasped, hands like fists at her sides, clutching the folds of her gown. "Where did you learn that?" she marvelled. Four hundred years and you think you've experienced everything!

"One of your kind," he replied. "A trick they showed me once."

The vampire didn't want to think about another vampire's fist penetrating the amber crack of this young boy's body, but the sensation of his fist inside her was incredible in its intensity. "It's good to know there are always new things to discover, even after all this time," mused the vampire, before being swept away on the crest of another shattering orgasm.

Philippe withdrew his hand and began to lick it clean of her juice, his other hand stroking her smooth sex-lips and rubbing her swollen clitoris. Despite his professional detachment, and his knowledge that vampires rarely reciprocated any sexual favours, his own cock was hardening, blood rushing into it so fast that he wanted to pull it out and wank it hard until he came in great wet spurts all over the vampire's hermaphroditic body. He pushed the thought into the back of his mind, but the vampire had seen his flushed face and was reaching for him. She fumbled beneath him, roughly grabbing at the material of his trousers and tearing at it.

Philippe tried to pull away but she was far stronger than him and he had no choice but to be exposed by her insistent fingers. She might punish him for his insolence, but she might just reward him. He groaned, a picture of her red mouth sucking vigorously on his rampant prick coming involuntarily into his head.

She took his cock in her cool hands, making it swell even more. "You're well developed," she noted with a smile all fangs and loose, wet tongue. "Do you use your sex with my kind as a memory to masturbate to?" she asked, licking her fingers then rubbing his engorged cock.

Philippe closed his eyes and groaned. There was no way on this earth he could continue his job of pleasuring her with a hard-on as rampant as this. He had to come, he simply had to.

Suddenly she was on top of him, her legs straddling his hips, her juice dripping onto his thighs. Their two cocks stared sightlessly at one another, aching and red. Before he could question what she wanted of him she sank down onto him, her gaping pussy swallowing his cock, sliding it inside herself so easily, so fast.

He bucked urgently up against her for a moment, his hips jiggling spastic and loose beneath her legs, until he felt a roaring sensation of blinding intensity gushing up through him, searing his groin and sputtering out of his throbbing cock in dense jets of creamy, juddering wetness. He cried out, his voice feral and bewildered, his balls tight, his cock spasming endlessly inside her grasping cunt. "God, oh god, oh god!" he breathed, his body full of perfect ecstasy and delirium.

She withdrew from him, drawing up towards his face, thrusting her dancing cock into his gaping mouth. "Suck it!" she ordered, though his lips were shaking with pleasure, and his eyes looked unfocussed and lost. "Suck it."

Philippe closed his lips around the hard flesh and sucked upon it. His face felt numb with ecstasy but he felt the length of her prick expand to fill him, felt the smooth, salty taste of her juices rising.

The vampire thrust against him, pushing her cock deep into his open, hungry mouth. She felt his spunk cooling against her thighs and the thought of his excitement at the moment of his copious orgasm made her start to spasm. The male part of her responded to the sensation, her voice deepening to a growl, her muscles tensing and contracting to violent centres of pleasure almost pain. "Oh yes!" she breathed, watching the boy's face as he sensed it too, the approaching climax. "Oh god yes!"

Seconds later the rich salty waves of dense vampire spunk flooded Philippe's mouth, spurting out of the vampire's huge cock and gushing down his throat. There was so very much of it that he gagged and it trickled out of his mouth like cream.

The vampire pounded against the boy's face, forcing her swollen cock deep down his throat, forcing him to swallow every drop of her spunk. "Yes, take it, take it all!" she gasped, cataclysmic in her orgasmic delight.

Philippe sucked hard until he could no longer breathe, drowning in the taste of the vampire's rampant sexuality. As sensation fell away in black curtains of unconsciousness, he felt his own cock explode once more, felt the vampire's hungry mouth sucking on his swollen shaft.

The boy awoke to the bright agony of hunger. His eyes shut tight against the sight of the vampire, he felt the coils of desperate thirst rack his body, tearing at his throat and his tongue, filling his mouth with torturous need.

The vampire caressed his lead-heavy body, rubbing his cock into a fresh tumescence, sparking a different hunger deep within his belly. Opening his eyes he saw the vampire's cock and cunt, both beckoning, speaking to both his hungers.

"Yes, this is what you want," said the vampire, her voice like starlight, her hands moving to her cock, her breasts. "Drink from me and sate your thirst."

Philippe tilted his head up to the vampire's cool white flesh and nipped at her breast, licking gently at first, then stronger as the blood burst onto his tongue in brilliant crimson ripples. "Oh god," he whispered through the taste of her.

Her blood flowed swiftly, filling his body, filling his cock with a renewed frenzy for the feel of her sex enveloping him, possessing him. The vampire's cock rose up to the boy's urgent cries of lust, liquid burning once more at its swollen head. She took her cock in one hand and his in the other, and began to play vigorously with both of them. The boy, exhausted by his earlier orgasms, came quickly, a thin fountain of almost clear spunk that arced over the vampire's hand.

The boy reached up to touch the vampire's cock, rubbing it eagerly as his lips still drank from her breast. Recalling his profession he found the vampire's rhythm and quickly brought her to a further climax, slipping his fingers inside her cunt as her spunk gushed out of her raging cock. Blood spilled from her nipple as Philippe fell back from her, spent at last, and satisfied that the vampire was too, feeling the female and the male parts of her spasm in final union together.

The payment from the vampire's estate was as always generous, a reflection of the dual nature of the pleasure and peace given, and as always Philippe found a way of paying a part of it back to his beneficiary's surviving children, a token of thanks for the blood given, and for the secret the vampire took to his or her final grave, the secret truth of what exactly Philippe Banadour had become...

The Mortician's Assistant

Ryan Acheson

Vampires. We've all heard the myths. We all know of the films, books, records, cereals and all the other crap that at the mention of the word springs to mind. Before Kate Dale had even entered into the inner sects of vampirism she had been more than familiar with the myths and legends. Kate had learnt to count with a muppet vampire on Sesame Street. That had lead her to children's versions of Dracula (with Van Helsing completely removed) and Marvel's Tomb of Dracula Comic, so it wasn't really a surprise to anyone when some years later she started reading Anne Rice novels. Kate had, to be truthful, left behind any fascinations with vampires around about the time she went to secondary school, but she did pick up an interest in Beverly Hills 90210. It was because of this that a few days after her eighteenth birthday Kate found herself queuing up outside her local multiplex to see Brad Pitt in 'Interview With The Vampire'. So it came to be that her interest in the myth was reborn and that she stopped at the library the next day, to discover 'Interview' was but the first of many Anne Rice books on the subject. She borrowed the first three, and took them home to read. Kate didn't realise that she was taking the first few steps on a path that would ultimately destroy her soul, as she thumbed through those creased and well read books. Anne Rice's novels struck a chord with her, and Kate became the complete vampire addict. She bribed her dentist to make her a pair of false fangs, she bought a death shroud, a coffin, a whole collection of sun glasses, and started to attend the conventions. She was in effect asking for it, sure, but she was unaware of the dark clouds gradually forming over her.

Conventions. If Kate had realised that quite a number of people's fangs were real, she probably wouldn't have gone. Since although she wouldn't have admitted it to anyone, Kate really enjoyed the simple things in life as much as the more complex, unorthodox ones. She liked shopping. She also liked going out in the full get up during the day to see everyone's reaction, since no-one looked twice after the sun had set. Kate didn't realise how often her fake dentures had saved her life. The dentist had done a fantastic job on them. They were a perfect colour match to her existing teeth and they fixed strongly. She could eat an apple while wearing them. Kate was totally unaware that most of the vampires at the conventions believed her to be one of them. The last night of Kate's mortal life had been one she had been looking forward to for a few weeks. Halloween. A night when anyone with any sense stays in and cuddles up with a loved one in front of the fire. Kate had slipped her teeth in and put on her white face make up and crimson red lipstick and set off to an Anne Rice convention. It was there that she bumped into Katrina Kristian. Kate mistook Katrina for a fellow fan of a similar age to herself and hooked up with her. Katrina mistook Kate for something rather different. Katrina was actually a few centuries Kate's senior, she had lived through a lot of wars, and had reached the point where she partied whenever she could. Which in the generally peaceful nineties was quite a lot. Katrina talked Kate and some guy they picked up into going back to her place.

Katrina's house was one of the coolest things Kate had ever seen. From the hundreds of candles grouped on the floor to the pentagrams on the wall. "Kate darling," Katrina purred. "Do you mind if I have first taste of this one?" Kate shook her head, pointing to the guy. His name may have been Steve, or Shaun, Kate couldn't recall. "No you're welcome to him." Kate smiled a pointed grin. "Just don't completely drain him of all his energy." So, Steve (or whoever) was lead into Katrina's bedroom. The walls were painted black, and the blood red drapes were undulating in the slight breeze. Katrina lay down on her bed and slowly removed the black lace dress from her body. "Man you've overdone it with the body make-up," the poor bastard had uttered as he crawled across the bed towards her slim white body. He undid the belt from around his waist and slid off his trousers, while Katrina unbuttoned his shirt. He slid himself into Katrina and gently started rocking back and forth. Katrina spun him around so he now lay beneath her. She ran her pointed tongue up his chest towards his neck.

Kate had poured herself a glass of wine and raised the glass to her lips. The claret liquid spilled over her lips onto her tongue. It wasn't wine. Kate couldn't quite place the familiar taste, and didn't have time since that was when she heard the screaming. Steve ran out of the bedroom, his hand clasping his neck. The skin was torn and shredded and blood was gurgling between his fingers. Kate took a step towards him, and he reached his other hand out to her. Katrina stepped out of the bedroom. Her teeth were stained with blood, as were her lips, her chin, her breasts... Kate screamed and Katrina's eyes widened. "You aren't..." Katrina began, as it all became too much for Kate. Her knees gave in and she slumped to the ground.

She had woken in Katrina's bed. It was still night and she felt really groggy. Katrina was sat watching her, brushing her hair. She saw Kate had woken. "Kate I'm sorry. I didn't know." Kate's neck hurt. She reached up to massage the pain, but was shocked to find two dried patches of blood, a few centimetres apart. "Kate it's not easy to control the urges. You'll understand." Kate shook her head. How long had she been unconscious? Why did she feel so weak? Katrina almost reading her thoughts told her. "You're probably feeling weak. Drink this." Katrina lifted a crystal cut glass to Kate's lips. Kate drank the pleasantly warm liquid and recognised it as the stuff she had found in Katrina's fridge. She finished the glass and it felt as if all her weariness drained out of her. She felt revitalised, she felt powerful. Then came the awful moment of recognition. As the murkiness slid away, the whole truth came sliding together. She was now a vampire. Katrina had done something to her and she was now a vampire. She placed her hand between her breasts. No heartbeat. Kate picked up Katrina's hairbrush and smashed the handle straight through Katrina's rib cage. Katrina's ribs buckled inwards, as the hairbrush penetrated her right through her heart. There was surprisingly little blood coming from the wound, a few droplets had splattered onto Kate's face, but it was nothing like with that guy, where it had sprayed from his neck, like some crimson fountain... Katrina's eyes slowly shut and she dropped to the floor. Dead. Dead for good. Kate figured the lack of blood was either down to the fact Katrina would have had no heart beat or had little blood inside her. Kate fingered the protruding end of the hairbrush. The hair in the brush had become matted with blood, and some of the bristles had broken off. Kate emptied all the corked bottles, twelve in all, from Katrina's fridge into the bin liner she had found. Kate checked the clock, it was just past one in the morning, as she left. Luckily no-one saw her leave, just as no-one had seen her enter. Dead people don't have finger prints either, since they don't sweat, and no greasy moisture builds up on the fingers. So Kate became a vampire, and walked away from a double murder scene carrying twelve bottles of someone's blood.

The blood had lasted about a fortnight, and it was a further day before Kate killed her first human. She had stood on the corner of the street dressed up in some tarty outfit. The man had thought she was a hooker, her intentions, and had paid her well for the blow job she gave him.

She hadn't actually intended to do anything with him, just kill him. But it took her a long time to get the courage up to commit such an act and she didn't want the man to get suspicious and leave. She had really enjoyed giving him the once over though. Maybe it was to do with the fact she was about to kill him, but something dark stirred inside Kate as she sucked on the man's hard erect penis. His flesh tasted somehow more real, more vivid. As the sense of power built up inside of her, she felt a pain in her gums, but that too gave her pleasure. Pleasure and pain intertwined not just for Kate. Almost absent mindedly Kate bit down strongly, and the man's moans of pleasure turned into screams of pain. Just as he ejaculated Kate tore off the end of his penis. A creamy mixture of blood and semen spat forth from the stump. The man desperately tried to get up, and get out, away from the monster before him, but Kate pinned him down with a single strong arm and continued to suck, only this time sucking the blood welling forth from his butchered crotch. The warm, sticky blood was somehow more powerful than the bottled variety. The man struggled, but since most of his life was draining out of him through his penis, it was a waste of energy. After a few minutes he stopped struggling. As he slipped away he realised that maybe he should have accompanied his wife to the museum, maybe in another life...

Kate, still high from the experience, dragged his naked pale body outside. It was limp, and it seemed light, not the expected deadweight at all. Kate placed the body into the back of her car and drove to the bridge. She opened the boot and dragged him out. He slapped down onto the asphalt and as she dragged him to the roadside his skin tore and flaked. The wounds yielded no blood because there was none left. Hoisting him up onto the safety barrier, Kate stared at the lifeless mannequin before her. She waved his hand at herself, kissed him and wished him a safe voyage. Dropping him over the side, she watched him as he fell towards the black water below, a mass of flailing limbs. She continued to watch until he finally disappeared beneath the surface into the hollow darkness below.

He would wash up on the banks a few miles further down the following day. Another nameless body, causing more paperwork for some poor policeman, but nothing more. His wife had known about his sordid life and was about to divorce him for someone younger anyway. Life goes on.

Luck seemed to be on Kate's side. After her feed she had managed to get some sense back into her head. She figured she'd be okay for at least a week, before she'd need to kill again. Though it had felt so good at the time, Kate felt a strong sense of guilt and remorse for what she had done. When she read about his funeral three days later she visited his grave the same night. She stood, her hair whipping in the wind and sticking to her forehead in the rain, staring at this man's tombstone. He had been forty two. Kate wondered how old she'd be when she died. There were no flowers and the epitaph simply read 'Husband and Father'. Kate looked up at the over-cast sky, the moonlight just breaking through, and tried to picture the sun, shining down on this poor, wretched, man's tombstone. That was when she heard the voice. "You knew him?" Kate turned to see a fifty year old man, wearing a black suit looking at her. "Er... sort of. Not really." The grey haired man nodded, a slight grin on his face. "So you don't mind hanging around graveyards at these sort of hours then?" The grey haired man seemed friendly, not a threat at all, as Kate had first feared. Kate felt her fangs which had instinctively reared up under her lips receding back into her gums. "It's only I'm looking for an assistant. I'm a mortician here at the funeral parlour." Kate scanned the man's face for any sign that he might be lying, but her intuitions told her, rightly, that he was being quite serious. "I'd be grateful for any night work." Kate hazarded. "You see I have this skin condition..."

Two nights later Kate had been shown the ropes. She had been shown how to work the embalming machine and had already started bottling blood, or just drinking it straight from the pipe when a body was being embalmed. The pay wasn't brilliant, but since she had nourishment, she didn't really need all that much money. The mortician was a nice enough fellow, though quite quiet in his work. He had been amazed at how Kate had handled herself around all the dead bodies and hired her immediately.

The blood was adequate. Sometimes some embalming fluid got mixed in with it, making it taste sour, but Kate could cope with that. The mortician had bought her story about the skin condition and was happy for any good help, even if that meant Kate's working hours were dictated by the length of night. Less people died in summer anyway, so it really wasn't that much of a problem. One thing worried Kate though. She still had desires. Violent, dark and deeply sexual. It was as if some primitive part of Kate had been awakened when she was turned. It seemed to be dictated by the moon, though Kate thought it could be more to do with her old menstrual cycle. That had seemed to invert itself. She no longer bled; in fact on those days her desire to kill was even greater.

It was on such a day that the electrocution victim was brought in. Phil, the mortician, had been unwilling to let Kate see him, but it really was busy that night. A gunman had gone mad at a local school a few days earlier giving them a fair few bodies to deal with, so he didn't have any choice.

The man, who now lay on the metal table in front of Kate, had been on his stag night. After twelve Tequila Slammers he had staggered to the underground station in a desperate attempt to get home. Influenced by drink he had thought it would be a good idea to urinate on the tracks. He had unzipped his jeans and got out his dick. As he let rip (twelve tequila slammers had filled his bladder to bursting point), his urine splashed onto the live rail. The high voltage electricity had earthed through him, leaving him a charred mess on a mortician's slab.

It was his penis that Kate couldn't take her eyes off. Like the rest of his body it was charred, twisted and black, with blisters filled with pus rife on the surface of the skin. It was however quite massive. The electricity had caused the muscles in his penis to swell, causing it to become erect, and become the towering black monolith before Kate. Kate's fangs forced their way out of her gums as her libido went into overdrive. Kate slipped off her underwear and slid the scarred mutilated penis inside her. Some of the blisters burst as she moved it back and forth inside her. She leant forwards and plunged her fangs into his neck, draining the somehow pleasingly curdled blood from him. The skin on his penis cracked and flaked with the massaging movements of her vagina as she tore a chunk of his neck off his body and ate the cooked, blistered and seared flesh. Kate didn't stop until his penis had been reduced to dust. She wiped the blood from her chin with her black lace underwear, and slid it back over her legs. Her desire to kill had been exorcised in the midst of this act of pure hate and lust. It was to be the first of many dead bodies that Kate mutilated and used as sex toys. She even started to use children's bodies and after a while the sex, male or female, stopped being relevant.

As Kate rushed home that morning a general sense of well being came over her. What she had done was sick and depraved, she knew that, but it didn't matter. She had found a way to satisfy her primitive urges. A way that didn't involve killing anyone. As Kate climbed into her coffin, just as the sun rose that morning she was still beaming. She was a vampire, and since she didn't have to kill anyone, she could cope with that. So maybe if you die, then Kate Dale may have her decidedly wicked way with your body. Your soul will have passed on to a higher plane, something Kate's never will. Your body, after all is said and done, is just a flesh and bone vessel for your consciousness. So let Kate do what she will. After all it's not as if you can stop her.

Gentle Persuasion

M. E. Warner

This one's new; but they're all the same. Pandering to the dark side. Letting it off the leash to run and play. Paying handsomely for the privilege. On the surface they're the same as the rest of the cattle. Working 24:7 in towers of glass and concrete, going home to prefabricated families. All the time thinking of the few hours of abandon that make it all worthwhile. A fleeting moment in which darkest fantasies become living, breathing reality in an orgy of the forbidden.

He likes to talk. Calling me bitch and whore, he spits in my face. I don't answer back. The hard plastic ball in my mouth, and the tight leather strap around my face, make sure of that. On past nights I would react. Try to inflict some damage, draw first blood, before I am incapacitated.

Tonight I just let it happen.

I slowly rise into languid monochrome cast by the light high above us. My body tenses, skin taut over flesh and muscle, as the ties that bind me at every juncture withdraw into the velvet obscure. Pulleys whimper around the walls of my room, a nest of black metal snakes slither through honey-yellow grease. He gasps. Partly at my pale lines bathed in luminescence, mainly with anticipation of what is to follow.

He surveys the sturdy rack of whips, flails, bludgeons and blades. Selects a nine-foot whip infested with cruel barbs, then gazes up at me suspended in the tendrils of my dark web. Usually they have me dressed in leather or PVC. He wants me ready for business in Versace, complimented with black stockings and fuck-me stilettos.

There's nothing like the classics.

Tentative at first, casting a few practice strikes at the floor, he feels the whip take on a contorting life of its own.

Then the fun begins.

I don't feel the initial strikes as razors shred the pinstriped power dressing from my torso. The wait is short. My body bucks and flails at the first delicious stings. The flex spirals around me, embracing me like a lover. Tearing streams of flesh and blood from my body with each kiss.

The bitter ecstasy makes my body dance and my mind scream.

Undeath plays tricks on the temporal sense. Centuries become floating embers, disappearing in a heartbeat, while a moment can last an eternity. A never-ending re-run. Pain floods poison into my mind. It finds a moment, and I find release.

My skin was dusted by the touch of the rain fresh wood. Outer skins of purple silk and black satin sodden and ragged, I forced my way through glistening shadows and snaking thorns.

The clarion of men and hounds infested my mind; their sweating bodies and adrenaline fuelled vigour filling my senses. A flicker-flash of flame hastened my gait, and I left the cover of the matted tree canopy. In the distance across the valley – perhaps a mile away – I could make out a bonhomie amber star.

Calling me.

I turned back to the dense woodland. Hastily assessing my options. I stumbled backwards in response to a scar-gouged muzzle exploding from the pitch. I gripped the bloodhound's throat; almost snapping its brittle neck without thought. The decision was made. I tore off a piece of skirt closest to my skin, knotting it around the creature's neck. Fixed it with a stare, baring my canines, chilling its blood with my eyes. It bolted back from whence it came.

Keeping low to the ground, I became one with the darkness. The rain soaked earth, the grass and gorse, entered me. Mingling with my blood. I became part of the land as it became part of me.

I emerged in a small farmyard, brimming with rustic quaintness, in the shadow of a great house that seemed to be hewn from the mountainside. It was dark. Dead, save for a low orange light escaping the window of a small stone barn, which dappled the surrounding buildings with hellish silhouettes. My star. I crept around the side of the barn, still fearing my pursuers who were hopefully on their way back to the town.The town, which was five miles away, seemed a lifetime past. Pressing myself to the thick oak door, I could feel the inviting warmth within the heart of stone. I entered.

The air in the barn enveloped me. Scattered hay and straw radiated the low heat from the candles at the far end of the structure. In a pool of light stood a young man, stripped to the waist. In front of him was a canvas to which he was applying careful strokes of paint with his fingers.

The night's excursions compelled me to take him. To tear him open and feast on his blood. Instead I stood captivated by his rough beauty. Watching as sinew and muscle worked beneath flame bronzed skin. Hair, liquid gold, flowing on to broad shoulders from which his sculpted torso fell. His body danced with casual grace. I knew I had to join with it.

As he stepped back, still oblivious to my presence, I saw what he was rendering. A young woman of ethereal bearing. Unparalleled amongst the inhabitants of the earth, living or dead. A captivating beauty with wide pavonian eyes and golden hair that entwined her deiformed body.

"Is she your sweetheart?" I ask him, causing him to turn with a start.

"My sweetheart? No I could never..."

"I'm sorry, have I frightened you?" I enquired, lulling him to my shores.

"No, a little start, that is all," he said. "You look chilled to the bone, my lady. Let me take you to my father's house. I'm certain that he..."

"No, do not trouble him. I assure you that I am quite comfortable. You have a talent," I remarked, looking at the painted paragon. I could feel his ocean eyes, studying my lines.

"Thank you," he replied, his boyish features assuming a look of embarrassment. "You are bleeding." He wiped the paint from his hands with a rag, and began to reach toward me. He drew back.

I took his hand, gently guiding him to the teardrop of blood on my cheek. "Just a scratch." I pressed his finger to his mouth. Delighting as the blood smeared over his lips. His tongue darted out, taking it in.

The sound of his breath ceased for a moment, I moved closer, joining our lips in a tentative embrace. His lips parted, my tongue gliding into him. I could taste my blood. Part of him.

His body was firm beneath my touch. I explored every ridge and crevice of his moistened torso. Breaking from his mouth, I languorously trailed kisses over his jaw, and down his quivering throat. Veins and arteries pulsed, blood racing at my closeness. I could feel him growing, getting harder, and pressing against me. My teeth brushed his skin, I could taste his sweet sea salt, but I wanted to enjoy him first.

I pushed him away, turning from him.

"Help me undress," I ordered. His hands fumbled, unable to concentrate on buttons and bows. "Quickly." I tore my dress from my breast. His fingers locked around my throat, before slipping beneath my high collar. He pulled, tearing my garments from me as if they were dead skin. I felt his anticipation as waves of satin and silk tumbled from my body.

I returned to him, lingering. Letting him admire my curves. The swell of my buttocks, my high firm breasts with hard ruby nipples. His hands mingled with the amber illumination caressing my opalescent flesh. Melting beneath him. Absorbing him. Reaching down, I unfastened his breeches, freeing his blood-engorged penis. He teased me, playfully rubbing against my eager glistening sex. I didn't want to be teased. I wanted him inside me. My limbs ensnared him, and brought him into me. I guided his first strokes, until lust engulfed him, forcing him deeper and deeper inside me. My head fell back, I gasped like a maiden deflowered, as each successive thrust unleashed a storm of ecstasy within.

I met his gaze again, drawing him further. We rediscovered the kiss, more feverish this time, as if we were devouring each other. Biting down I released a stream of blood from the churning sea. Vitae flowed from his mouth to mine. I savoured the taste, rolling it on my refined palate, before allowing it to continue down my throat.

Bracing myself on his taut shoulders, I allowed myself to fall down his body, leaving a snail trail of bloody kisses. Finally I reached his twitching cock, slick with my nectar. Kissed the head, wetting the glans with my saliva and his sweet blood. His hands entered the dewy black forest of my hair, I took him into my mouth.

My tongue wrestled his phallus, encircling it like a serpent. I licked his tip with a fast flicking tongue, making his body tense. Just as he was about to come I raked my teeth beneath his cock-head. I was rewarded with a cocktail of life-force splashing against the back of my throat. I drank for a moment, like a contented calf at the teat, then scaled his body to kiss his neck. Liberating his blood, transferring his youthful energy to me. As it fled him, I cradled him in my arms, and laid him down.

Sensing the rising sun, I extinguished the diminished candles, and buried the night's lover and myself in the hay.

Falling into slumber.

A guttural grunt brings me back. I try to blink through the weeping viscose blanket that envelops me.

His face a sweating mask.

I should be dead now. He's done his bit but this dirty little bitch won't play her part. Of course, I'm not one of the pathetic young things, nullified with heroin or solvent, that he plucks from the street in his company car.

I'm the real deal.

I don't die easy.

My eyes laugh at him. Mocking his inadequacies, his pathetic attempts to snuff me out.The challenge is accepted, he throws his stench-sodden shirt to the ground with the resolve of a matador. I'm sure that there must be muscles working under that jiggling mass of meat and hair. His rhythm is waning.A flash of white spurs him on.

We have an audience. One of the peepholes that pepper my walls slowly slides open.

My captor.

He used to watch my every performance. Hoping that I would yield to his gentle persuasion. These days, after so many bloody years, he rarely descends the 836 spiralling stone steps.

I can sense his desperation.As palpable and sweet as fear.

I give him a sidelong glance, then slip into death.

Hours have passed since I awoke on fire. My flesh and fluids forming an expanding pool beneath me. Drip, drip, dripping with the tortuous regularity of a clock, I was a hanging corpse. Stripped of flesh by absent corax. That which remained glistened, choice cuts in a butcher's window. Through watery swollen eyes I watched dead butterflies falling from me.

A familiar ripping accompanied the slacking of my restraints, and I slumped unceremoniously onto the bloodied stone.

I have fed on the blood of the rats that hide in the dank recesses and flaking crevices of my room.They are a poor source of sustenance but they keep me alive. I feel stronger, though pain still nags at my body like a forgotten dream.

Returning to my rippling lake of blood, I lie down, allowing it to envelop me. I clear my mind.Trying to re-absorb and re-constitute as much of myself as I am able. Swallowing screams, my body slowly reforms and knits itself together. It must be day up above. The process takes hours rather than minutes.

My body is squirming within molten chains of excruciation. I force myself out. Become the voyeur. Watching restless limbs, a body tossing and turning, beneath bedclothes. The wound, my tender lover's kiss, has become a silvery ghost. He writhes in and out of sleep. I watch, savouring the moment, and his troubled lines, before dropping from my perch. Resting in the shadow of the bed's tester, I inhale the wet heat of him into me. His scent is neither one thing nor the other. Man nor beast. Alive nor dead.

Shedding my outer layers, I sneak beneath his covers. Crawl over him. Not touching. Enjoying the electric intimacy that fires between us. Kissing his manhood, making it sit up, an overexcited puppy desperate to play. The journey recommences, licking his stomach, smooth chest and leadshot nipples. Press down. A suffocating night terror. He moans, and my lips join his. I breathe for him as we kiss, then release him. I begin to rub myself against his turgid sex, tracing my clit along his shaft.

I smile as his eyes open. "Hello again."

He grabs my shoulder. Moves from under me, as he hurls me against the bed head.

"This is not the response I had hoped for, lover," I laugh. "Has it been so long that you do not remember me?"

"How could I forget?" he barks. "It has been twelve nights since you... we..."

"Made love?" I offer.

"Since that night I have suffered twelve nights of torment. Of waking nightmares. My body aches night and day, and I am plagued by an insatiable hunger."

"That is perfectly normal," I assure.

"Normal?" he raves.

"Yes, your body pains you because it is dying, that is all. That which you do not need atrophies. It is perfectly natural," I say matter-of-factly.

"There is nothing natural here. What am I becoming?"

"You are becoming part of my family. Of my blood. You may understand it better if we use the term moroi, nosferatu or vampire. It is a simple case of transmutation."

"Damn you, witch," he shouts, throwing himself away from me as if I were his mother's corpse.

"Vampire, remember?" I say, reaching for him. "Let's make love."

"Then this degradation will continue? The hunger?" he asks desperately. "I am unable to go out in the daytime. The sunlight makes me sick."

"Soon its merest touch will kill you. Reduce you to ash. It is a small price to pay for forever." I take his hand. "As for the hunger, I will show you how to satisfy it. Come, I can feel your uncertainty. Your fear. They will fade in time, I promise. We have an eternity."

I lead him down the stairs, like a reticent child, into the night.

834, 835, 836. I am honoured, my captor is paying me a visit. The heavy steel door creaks like his rheumatic bones, then clanks shut behind him. He sniffs the air with disdain, before shuffling deeper into my prison. His body sighs as he comes to a halt six paces from me.

His appearance is even more ridiculous than the last time I laid eyes upon him. A claret velvet frock coat and a dress shirt hang from his withered frame. His riding boots slap embarrassingly against wasted calf muscles. He looks like a grotesque child in his father's clothes.

I cloak myself in my arms.

"Apologies for my tardy appearance, old man," I sneer with a higher sense of superiority than my situation allows. "But it has been an age since I received such esteemed company."

His face remains set in stone.

"You are looking well," I smile, taking in the new fissures and gouges.

"As do you," he rasps.

"What brings you to me after so many years?" I ask, knowing the answer. "Is it in the hope that your gentle persuasion has weakened my resolve?"

"You know that it is," he replies. "I have come to ask you once more, my lady. To implore you one last time to bestow your gift upon me. To bless me with your kiss."

"My gift?" I retort. "You have turned any such gift into a curse during these forty long years. You have subjected me to an endless cycle of cruel torments and degradation. Watched me die a thousand times. I would cast myself into the sun before granting you such pleasures."

"Haven't those same years been torture for me also?" he asks, pressing the small control pad in the palm of his hand, which raises my hands and feet away from temptation. "I have crumbled into decay whilst you have remained as beautiful as ever."

I cast my eyes away from the leathery hand attempting to caress my body, and the withered lips kissing the firm flesh of my breast.

He whispers sweet nothings. "Such delectable flesh. So sweet and unyielding. So young."

"Young?" I mock, ignoring the wet snuffling as he buries his death's-head between my legs. "My flesh is older than your grandmother's grandmother. Although, I have done worse than rob a cradle in my time," I muse.

The truffle-rooting swine raises his head. "Don't you think that it pains me to know that one such as yourself is debased night after night, year after year? Let me end it. Is what I ask so high a price for your liberty?"

I hiss with four decades of hatred. "Far too much."

"At least tell me your name, my lady. It is not right that two people who have become as intimate as we have have not introduced themselves."

"My name?" I laugh. "I have had many. What would telling you serve? You would only use it to barter for my freedom with my family."

"Tell me," he demands, striking me with the back of his hand. He rubs his frailty. He bruises far more easily than I do.

"Come closer," I breathe. "Let me whisper."

He inches warily toward me, a glimmer of hope in his extinct eyes.

"You will know my name," I whisper. "There will come a time when you will call it out in prayer. Begging me to grant you death."

I smile.

Small victories are all I have now.

"Reconsider," he pleads. "As I have told you this is the last time I will request your boon. A cancer is eating away at my brain. I do not have long."

My smile widens.

"Save your smile," he splutters. "For your fate is entwined with mine. When I am gone my servants will seal these chambers, and you will be left alone to wither and perish as I have. A flawless flower deprived of the sun's light."

He lets my bonds fall slack.

"I grow weary," I tell him. "Leave me to enjoy my solitude."

"I'm afraid I must insist," he grins, pressing another button on his control. My skin shivers. I can feel the air in the room slowly rising in temperature. "Before we begin I must confess that it's all done with mirrors." His brow raises wickedly, accompanied by a familiar metal grind. One of the peepholes is opening.

I scream for the first time in years.

Instead of a voyeur's eye, a searing sensation invades my flesh. A brilliant ribbon of powdered sunlight is pouring from the wall onto my shoulder. My skin begins to sizzle and smoke, until I scuttle away.

Rage consumes me. It is an instinctive reaction to sunlight. My body contorts, presenting the smallest possible surface. Then I lunge at the old man's exposed throat like a wild beast.

I should have learnt this lesson long ago. I curse him as he presses his damned control again. The snap of metal cords precedes the cracking of sinew and bone. My arms wrench from their sockets, wrists and ankles fragment, and my head whips back, breaking my neck.

I awake.

Hanging limply. Ball-gag in place again. Joints crackle like an old radio if I attempt to move. The metal grinding again. My head flops around on my shoulders, trying to ascertain which aperture is opening.

Burning gives me my answer. A vehement hiss of smoking flesh. I remain lifeless, an effort at damage limitation. My face contorts, I can feel it discovering new features of pain, as the scorching light, excruciatingly slowly, bores a hole through my hip. The wound cauterises as it passes through.

I try to escape. Force my mind into welcoming darkness.

A maelstrom of light breaks from the dark. For an instant I fear it is the sun. The pounding of drum and bass, and the scent of expensive perfume and meat, brings a club into focus. It is Abaddon, Constantino Brunelli's establishment. Swollen with the beautiful ones. The throng unconsciously parts for me as it, and the rest of my surroundings, becomes sharper. I can feel their eyes. Their desire. I'm not on the menu tonight, which, fortunately for them, means neither are they.

Satanna, Brunelli's chief protector, greets me, with a silent nod. Amazonian in stature, she stands head and shoulders above me. I shudder - a little fear, a little pleasure - when I see the outline of the wooden katana beneath her leather trenchcoat. She searches my body for weapons that are not part of it.

"You shouldn't start something you're not going to finish," I chastise. She ushers me through a disguised steel door.

The door slams shut, and I am alone in a long corridor, cocooned from the sounds and smells of the wildlife. If I needed to breathe I would discover that the air is stale. Like a tomb. The corridor is lined with mirrors and uplights, which suggest a warm sense of sunlight.

I meet my own reflection.

At first I don't recognise the society hunter. I go through a lot of changes. It's in my nature. I am bound in a leather catsuit that looks as if it has been sprayed on to my lissom contours. My arms are bare, consisting of taut slender muscle, which would take a lifetime of workouts to define. My face, almost hidden behind dark hair streaked with sable, is a fusion of beauty and anonymity. Narrow brows beneath a high forehead, sculpted cheekbones running from the corners of wide chocolate eyes to moist beestung lips. Mocha skin makes a change from pale and interesting. The beauty mark above my lip is the only remnant of my last incarnation. It raises as my lips curl.

I know what you're thinking: vampires don't reflect in mirrors, you wannabe vampire bitch. That's bullshit. It would be a tragedy, having spent so much time and blood, shaping and refining, if we couldn't check out our look.

I break free, and open the door at the end of the corridor.

The studio is cavernous. A velvet shrouded cathedral, hung with feminine iconography. I recognise the heavenly blonde, and some have caught aspects of me, amidst a sea of the ultrafemme.

In the centre is the slender androgyne, Constantino Brunelli. He is clad in a dalmatic of shimmering silk, and a golden coverchief, from which his equally golden hair spills. A camera is slung over his shoulder. He directs a naked woman in a kaleidoscope pool of coloured light. Moving his hands as if he is sculpting her. When she is in position the colours begin to shift, as if she is floating through a fractured spectrum. He photographs her, circling like a predator, capturing her soul.

"Still studying the female form, I see, Constantino," I say as he lowers the camera.

"They all pale beside you, princess," he smiles, turning. "It has been a long time."

"Has it? I find it harder and harder to judge," I say, embracing him. "You have changed," I observe, feeling his emaciated frame beneath silk. "So far removed from the young dalesman whom I seduced in his father's barn."

"A work in progress," he replies. "So, why have you honoured me?"

"I'm in Paris on family business," I tell him.

"You know that the families respect my neutrality, princess," he says with a touch of concern.

"Do not worry, Constantino," I soothe. "I will request nothing of you that you would not freely give. There is no reason for me not to indulge in a little pleasure also. Besides, I like to follow the progress of my offspring. Like any good parent."

"I hope that I meet with your approval, Mother."

I laugh. "Of course."

He motions to the girl. "Can I offer you something?"

"Later," I reply. "First, let me ask you why you have never asked me to be your muse. I'm offended."

"You are in all my work, but I only use humans as subjects. They fascinate me."

"It is a contented man whose work is also his hobby and, in your case, his sustenance."

"Only if they allow it," he replies. "I gave up killing long ago. There are enough people willing to indulge in bloodsports to sustain me."

"Perhaps that is why you look so pale," I mock. "Our kind cannot live on scraps. You will be telling me that you raid bloodbanks next."

"That debate is older than both of us. Come, I think I can use you after all."

I watch as he positions his camera on a tripod.

"How do you want me?" I ask, as the light trip commences.

Constantino peels black skin from the firm meat within. His tongue strokes me, matching the slow clickety-click of the camera shutter. He begins at my throat, descending into the hollow of my shoulder, then climbs the swell of my breast. He bites my tit - just enough to hurt - then follows my grooves to my abdomen. Wetting every inch of my terrain. Passing over the part of me that yearns for his attention, he begins to kiss my inner thigh, spun gold arousing my skin. My hands entangle in his hair, gently guiding him between my legs. I cast a glance toward the girl to make sure that she is enjoying our performance, then to my partner. He has his fingers inside me. Leafing through my folds, engrossed in a forbidden tome. Our eyes fuse. We become one. Both giving pleasure, and receiving it.

I trace the curve of my sex. Teasing. My clitoris is sticking out like a lascivious tongue. Fingers spread me wider. I am dripping with honey, forcing deeper and deeper into myself. Caressing the outside of my pussy, then lashing my velvet walls with determined strokes. I can taste myself. An overripe blood orange, swollen with juice. My hips thrust against the squirming thing inside me, forcing it deeper, to explore my secret places. I am drowning in my own fluids, as I come in my face.

Brunelli whispers to the girl. "Come here. Come and play." She takes his hand, and he interlocks her fingers with mine. I kiss her, as he reloads the camera.

Her body is perfection according to the day's criteria. Large sculpted breasts flowing from a small ribcage, which narrows into a tiny waist. Wide green eyes, like a cat's, above an invisible nose and wide bovine mouth. Her labia are naked beneath a neat heart of hair. I forgo the foreplay, grabbing the firm globes of her backside, and forcing my tongue into her like a dick. The sharp taste arouses my appetite, as I tongue-fuck her. With a rapid downward movement I tear twin gouges in her vulva with my fangs. She screams, tries to pull away. She doesn't want to play grown up games any more. I tighten my grip on her firm arse, forcing streamlets of blood, and pull her into my face.

Blood floods me. I have to swallow repeatedly, like a machine, to avoid being overcome by her gushing cunt. As it is she splashes all over my face and chest. I pull back, and lap at the stream like a dog, before allowing her to fold.

Rapture consumes me, I fall to my knees, bracing myself against the curtained walls.

"I had high hopes for her," says Constantino, resting his body on mine. "She could have been my Mona Lisa, my Calliope."

"I'll buy you a Barbie doll. Forgive me?" I purr, as he massages her hot blood into my breasts. He uses his hair to paint with her vibrant redness on my stretched canvas.

"I will always forgive you, my princess," he sighs, raising my right leg. "You have given me everything, enabled me to quench all of my desires, and there have been many. I have enjoyed posthumous acclaim three times, and I have had the time to almost achieve my magnum opus."

I laugh, feeling his rigid cock finding its way inside me. Reaching over my head, I capture his throat as I ride him. The unearthly radiance of the gold tressed woman fills my vision from her position high above me. I imagine I am her, a devil playing angel, being fucked for the first time. My heavenly body being desecrated by the touch of man. My mouth tasting unknown pleasures. I feel myself rising, discovering new sensations, piercing hidden boundaries. Dancing rivers of iridescent luminescence engulf me.

The light's brilliance is muted. Pale spectres swirling across the stone floor like Universal mist. It seems to me that I have never seen anything quite as beautiful for a long time. Then I realise that the illumination is spewing from me. I am refracting the light above me with my perforated frame. A suspended waxwork. Somewhere in Haiti there is an effigy of me bent in agony. Still, the light show makes me smile. I have to pass through another gauntlet as the charred tunnels riddling my body begin to refill, slowly, from within.

Another visitor. It is the doctor. It must be Wednesday.

He ignores the selection on the rack, favouring the antique instruments in his stout black bag. The scent of surgical spirit wafts into the air and my nostrils. He looks me up and down, examining my body. His eyes are deep in thought. It is an act. Another ritual. The doctor is a creature of habit. They all are.

His surgeon's blade traces me, threatening my skin. I can hear his brain, reverberating with thoughts of what he is about to do to me. Sometimes I wonder whether he notices that it is the same subject that he goes to work on every week. The same breasts that he hacks away. The same womb he plucks from the same abdomen. The same face he peels like a fruit. I doubt that it concerns him, or even if he comprehends that there is a person within the body he butchers.

"Do you know what would make this perfect?"

He never talks.

"To hear you scream. I never get to hear you scream."

My heart bleeds.

"They are most insistent that I should never remove any of your restraints, especially the gag, but who will hear way down here?"

Just you.

"Apparently this will be my last visit for a while. It deserves to be memorable."

Precious.

"Their rules seem unnecessary anyway: don't remove any material from the room..."

The old man isn't sure of the extent of my recuperative powers. He doesn't want me escaping piece by piece.

"...don't leave any instruments inside the body."

That's a new one. One of the old man's assistants got a little surprise last month.

"I'm sure that they wouldn't object if I bent the rules this one last time. Would that be acceptable to you?"

I mask my excitement behind terror.

"I know that I'm not supposed to. You won't tell, will you?"

He reaches behind me and unfastens the strap.

Before the ball tip-taps on stone I have his hand in my mouth. Human blood. It has been an eternity. I feel my body ignite into life, blood racing quicksilver, synapses firing like an artillery barrage. My biology remembers its true nature, its true function. Incisors break free from their sheaths, locking into the hard flesh of his wrist, tapping the vein and rewarding me with a spurting torrent of life.

I raise him to me, and gently kiss his throat. I want to savour this, but I cannot hold back the hunger excited by his desperate screams. My teeth plunge into his neck, slicing sinew and piercing his carotid artery. I slurp like a peasant as I drain him.

I am done, he falls lifelessly to the floor. I revel at the energy coursing inside me. I begin to contort, inching towards each cord in turn, until I have all that are attached to my upper body gathered in my hands. Finding a rhythm, I apply more and more pressure. My walls erupt in sparks. The cords smack limply on the floor. Now it is a simple matter to carefully rock forward, and snatch the doctor's bone saw from his bag.

Two nights have passed since my emancipation. I must confess, I have overindulged a little. Drunk my fill of blood and passion. They're what I live for and, you must admit, I deserve it. It is true what they say; abstinence does make the heart grow fonder, and the blood taste sweeter. Descending the 836 stone steps, the awful feelings come again. Pain and perversion, the solitude of darkness. It feels like I'm coming home.

I'm not alone.

"Show yourself," I demand of the dark. "Let me see your face before I take it from you."

The darkness assumes female form. "Temper, temper."

"I know you," I tell the young woman, drinking in her angelic visage, and the catwalk figure beneath an ivory business suit. I recognise her, she seems displaced, as if she doesn't belong to this place or time. I have it, she is the beauty of Constantino's painting made flesh.

"Has it been so long that you do not remember me?" she says, with laughter that sounds like spring rain.

"Constantino?"

"Yes, my princess?"

"Is it really you?" I ask, allowing my trademark cool surface to melt.

"My final work," replies Constantino, hands following the shape of the body. "My masterpiece. Do you approve?"

"I don't know if it's art," I grin. "But I like it. Of course I will have to inspect it further. At close quarters." I pull her to me, resting my head against her stomach. Holding her for a moment. "I cannot believe that you are real."

"What troubles you, princess?" she asks, brushing my hair from my face. "You look as if you are about to cry."

"It's hard to weep with dead tearducts, Constantino, however great the pain."

"What happened to you? Where have you been these last forty years?" she asks gently. "I feared you had met your end during one of the conflicts we have suffered this century. I searched for you in all your favourite haunts but could find no trace."

"I was detained," I reply wryly. "I will tell you all about it in time." I ascend her step, tracing a kiss across her cheek. "For now it will suffice to say thank you."

I begin the descent.

"What is down here?" she asks, falling in beside me.

"A little matter I must take care of. A little matter of revenge," I say blankly.

"I remember you told me that revenge is a dish best served cold."

"That is true. That way you can serve it over and over."

We reach the steel door. I press my ear to its dull surface, enjoying the hollow silence.

"The city has changed, Constantino. You do still call yourself Constantino?" I ask.

"Some call me Angel, but I adore the way my true name spills from your mouth. Like a long wet kiss." I remember how to laugh. "It is true what you have said, princess, you should prepare yourself for how much the city has changed."

"The towers scratch the sky," I muse. "Teaming with new flavours."

"Behind the curtain too. Our blood has weakened without you to guide it. Your family has lost much of its influence. The barbarians are no longer at the gate, they have torn it down, and trampled it into the dust."

"We rise, we fall. It is the way of things. It is time to rise from the shadows again."

"They are strong."

"Trust me, everyone is susceptible to a little gentle persuasion, but first..."

"Revenge?"

"Revenge."

The door swings open, crashing into the unyielding stone. The old man is where I left him, suspended in my web. He stinks of fear, and his filth, which has showered the floor beneath him.

"He looks like a plucked game bird," comments Constantino.

"Then let's begin the game." I wave my hand, ushering the doctor from the gloom. A twisted stream of piss cascades from the old man, contorting above us. The doctor places his bag on the floor, flashing me a shark-toothed grin.

I look up. "First, old man, let me make it clear that I want nothing from you. There is no answer, no word I want to hear, that will end this. This is not persuasion, it is retribution, pure and simple, as old as time. When you have suffered pain and torment beyond that which any mortal could endure, then you will know that your ordeal has just begun. That is what I ask in return for my gift. The price of immortality. No need to thank me, your screams are payment enough." I reach up and tear the gag from his face. Then I turn to the doctor. "Have fun."

The doctor examines his new subject. Although it's not his preferred sex, it beats the alternative I gave him. "This could take a while. Don't worry, we have all the time in the world."

I feel Constantino's hand join mine. We watch. The old man screams, pleading for his life, mashing his lips to pulp with his new dental configuration.

"The irony is that I would have gladly brought him over if he had just asked," I tell my companion. "One as cruel and persistent as him deserves his place amongst the ranks of the damned. I almost forgot," I call to the old man. "You asked my name. I am Talitha."

We ascend the stairs, my name echoing behind us.

Carbon

Adrian Bott

That Carbon was bisexual was well known. What nobody seemed to know was who she was bisexual with. Like many other goths of the aristocratic, feline type, she was not given to public displays of affection and though she was widely lusted after, she met the attentions of her would-be paramours with the same sense of ennui and indifference, naïve and experienced alike.

She would stand like a caryatid in the corner of the Hellfire Club, a regular Wednesday fixture, and as much a part of the decor as the blistered black paint and the rotten sofas which were always full to spilling point. She rarely moved except to draw out another white menthol cigarette. The Guinness she drank sparingly seemed to have been conjured from the smoky air, or perhaps left for her as a votive offering.

To the students that came and went with the seasons she was a figure of myth. They would dare one another to go up and talk to her, to proposition her; but the realisation always came that the almond face and the outlined black eyes belonged to something unattainable. She walked through their sticky fantasies, if not their lives.

It is not certain if she was happy with this state of affairs. Whether her stark aloofness was the product of extreme shyness or some inherent notion of her absolute superiority is not known. She remained a glyph, a symbol; that however beautiful or desirable the conquest of the evening might be, the avatar of gothic perfection was always out of reach. It drove weaker men insane with frustration.

There was talk of spiking her drink, of getting her stoned, but this passed.

There were a few that Carbon deigned to talk to. Vincent was bald and built like a pasta chef, and owned the club. It would not have done for her not to have that passport among her assets. Martin was straw-blond and stammered a lot, and dribbled his drinks down his white T-shirt when Carbon spoke to him. He was possibly the most socially incompetent of the club's regulars, and it pleased Carbon's vein of cruelty to torment him with her attentions. The only man she viewed as a peer in any way was Krish, a pockmarked Asian leather boy, who had his own lovers in abundance.

She thus had an aura of the immaculate, a Virgin in black. A detonation of dark hair spread out and down like a negative halo around her. The leather jacket that she wore hung open at the front, where a semi-transparent material showed the beginning curve of her breasts quite clearly. Had her movements been less languorous, the leather might have parted that crucial couple of inches further, and revealed a glimpse of shrivelled nipple. The belt was of gleaming gun cartridges, the PVC of her jeans a liquid black mirror curved without a wrinkle around groin, thigh and calf, the thick plastic boots sharp-heeled and laced.

Her face was not remarkable in itself, fitting the ideal of the counter-culture; the cheekbones prominent, the eyes stylised, the ears small and delicate. Only the mouth, like a steaming slash of blood across the Arctic ice, brought a brutal sensuality to the whole, which was otherwise as sexless as a mask. It was moist with inner life, and had in itself an infinity of expression beyond the body to which it belonged. It and it alone argued that Carbon was a creature that had a sexual component in her nature, for it was as wanton as her bearing was cold and distant. Perhaps it was the lure in the lips which kept her suitors coming, convincing them that this ember could be nourished into an inferno, if only it could be caught and taken home.

As obscene as stigmatic blood on a plaster statue, Carbon's mouth twisted in amusement at the crowd in the club. The spotlights playing upon her corner were alternating their beams, casting her now in demonic scarlet, now in cryogenic blue. Wet beer lay in twinkling lakes and smears at the perimeter of the area.

Bodies on the sofas mouthed and clutched at each other.

The Hellfire Club was always busy in early October. The new batch of students had just about discovered it, drawing in their wake the other fairweather regulars who had shunned the place during the slow summer months. The bar was three deep in patrons and the light above moved over a sea of jostling heads.

Krish was sprawled three inches beneath Carbon's right elbow. A French student, his bandana long since gone and his shirt hanging open, was caressing the brown chest with a finger wet with saliva. The other hand passed a crumbling joint between them. As they sucked and exhaled, smoke rose before Carbon like incense, heady and earthy. She absorbed it; she was impassive.

A bright spark fell on Krish's bare skin and he jack-knifed up, swearing. His companion rolled away from him with a laugh. Momentarily distracted, Carbon watched them, and when she looked back to the dance floor she was suddenly aware of the music, as if the speakers had come on line in her skull without warning.

A boy was dancing alone in a ring of spectators.

The veins stood out on his arms and his face was a rictus of pain. The dance was something primaeval, more suited to skin drums and thunder than the electric wallpaper at the Hellfire. He warped and stretched under the lights, a figure in motion, a movement.

Carbon's glistening lips separated very slightly, with an inaudible sound.

As he span, there came the flash, flash, flash of lights reflecting off round mirrored glasses. His chest was bare but for the dark spatters of blood that decked it. As she watched him, she thought at first that his nose was bleeding; then she saw the cuts he had made.

He leapt and cavorted like a stag, and those that stood around him seemed to awaken, embarrassed, to their own normality. Muttering, they began to move away and resume more conventional dances of their own. He was oblivious to them, did not care whether they watched or not. An ecstasy higher than madness burned through his bones and cast him again and again into the spinning air.

Carbon realised she was moving. Her breasts rustled against the thin fabric, the nipples tautened and aching; her jeans creaked. Around her was the sound of Hell falling down. Her brain filtered it out, going into a kind of tunnel vision.

The young man struggled for a moment when she laid her hands on his shoulders. Her lips on his chest made him gasp. She was sucking at his wounds.

The blood was not fresh any more and had gone to a brown crust, but as Carbon's mouth worked on the cuts and her hands kneaded his sides, a little more began to flow. A faintly red liquid rilled down his stomach and into his hollow navel, blood and saliva commingled.

Some of the regulars at the bar had noticed the performance, and wondered if they would see - or at least get to hear of - the outcome. It seemed Carbon's unavailability was at last at a welcome end.

Hardly moving at all now, and in a different kind of trance to the one which had possessed him a moment before, the boy stroked Carbon's cheeks and felt her hair. She did not seem to notice, and began to run her tongue down the length of his smarting incisions. Then, without a word, she took his hand and pulled him from the club.

The city air made him shiver. His chest was beginning to hurt. He tried to tell her his name but she did not want him to speak. Memory was slow in coming; he knew he had left his jacket in the care of a friend, the same one who had sold him the wrap of whizz. He did not know the city, but felt strangely safe with her. They walked in a bubble of mutual heat through the streets.

In the middle of a derelict half smashed housing estate, where a burning car sent flames into the sky, she sat him on the cold ground and pressed her mouth against his. Petrol and particles of smoke made his nose run a little and awoke him to the urgent strangeness of it all.

She clutched at his groin and found him hard there, then pressed herself close against him, warming his naked skin. There was a final volley of deep kisses. Then she lifted him to his feet and took him through a tunnel of darkness into a half-lit house that smelt of damp and old carpets.

By now he was aching to have her. The stiffness in his pants was irritating, and moreover the rush of the speed in his system was decomposing into a tired, burned feeling. He lay on the sofa and tried to make himself comfortable.

In the bathroom, Carbon stared into the mirror. Her pupils were very wide and very dark. In the corner of her mouth was a mucky blot of blood. She was breathing fast, as if she were peaking on powerful acid. Tonight had broken the mould, a tangential smash to the usual round of things. This was change. This was the foreordained emergency she had waited for. Her imagination erupted like a volcano of black water, feeling feverish and high she splashed water on her face and went back into the room. She knelt by him where he sat and saw that his skin was so thin his heart could be seen beating through the ribs. He reached for her. She caught his hand and began to suck the first two fingers rhythmically.

The boy was vaguely afraid and choking with lust at the same time. She offered no resistance when he stroked her breast, through the netting at first, then working his hand under the seam to reach her. The nipple was hard as a nut against his palm. She breathed into his ear, deep and coarse, flickering her tongue inside until he squirmed away.

Breaking away, she sat on the bed and began to take her clothes off, and when she had finished she lay back in white nakedness. Her hand moved down between her legs, into the black delta, and despite the boy's urgent approach she did not let him near her. Her lips quivered; her middle finger danced on her clitoris, quickening in a spasm of urgency, then sliding down and in. Her whole lower body undulated.

The boy watched her masturbate, fascinated. He was not privy to this habit of women; of course he knew it must happen, but he had never seen it before. She let him look as the finger moved gently in and out, in and out of her. A gleam of moisture was gathering there. The sound was like that of a cat lapping at milk.

She impaled herself on her own middle finger all the way to the knuckle and churned her hand around, moaning. There was a naked heat in the room. The boy was dragging his jeans off, desperate.

When he reached her she was tasting her finger, experimentally. She looked at him, doe-eyed, and when he went to kiss her she caught his hair and forced his head down. Feeling a blast of the same energy that had stirred him at the Hellfire, the same reckless irresponsibility, he gorged himself on her cunt, rolling his tongue around the savoury depths and vibrating it against the pink promontory above. She barely moved, but her breathing was shuddery with sensation.

She worked a hand under herself and slid the slimy finger into the small opening of her behind, sliding it in and out slowly, feeling the peculiar ripples up her spine, the occasional queasiness, enjoying it. Her whole pelvic region from clitoris to asshole was one burning melt of stimulation. She began to scream, quietly, continually.

When he scrambled back up her, sticky-mouthed and breathless, she freed her hands and raked blood from his back. The pain brought tears to his eyes, and a sick feeling. Eager to finish this, he prodded her vulva with his penis and she arched upward and took him inside her.

She was clammy, clinging and hot inside, and he almost came immediately. He thrust wildly at her, she so awash with saliva and lubricants that he barely felt anything but a manic friction. His back was wet.

Slamming his belly against hers, he tautened all over and froze; there was a blissful spasm and the tide flowed into her, washing her immaculate womb in jets.

Her eyes were closed. He rolled away from her and stared at the ceiling for a while, then let his own eyelids fall. He felt cheated, defeated and ill, and wondered where he could get a taxi from.

He snapped back to reality when he felt a burning slash across his belly. Carbon was standing by the bed, bloodstreaked and smiling, a leather belt in her hand. She raised welts on him while he screamed and tried to drag his clothing back on. The bedspread where he had been lying was a mess of red-brown spots.

Carbon let him get to the door, then sank to the bed, laughing.

The Bones of Venice

Rosie Lugosi

I come out of the station onto broad flat steps; inhale the brackish air of the canals with a hopefulness I barely wish to admit to. There was no railway station when I was here last, but there was a small number of my people. So few, such a meagre community it seemed then; now opulent, luxuriant. They had become as insular as the semi-island people they depended upon. Inbred: the word is like stone. There may be someone here.

There are so many humans. I turn left away from the waterway and its hooting boats, find myself on a paved street packed tightly as a slaughterhouse with sweating bodies moving in a slow peristalsis from shop to shop. Motion; pause; motion; pause. I let myself be carried along, an indigestible item in their collective gut. I carry the heat of the south within me; watch them hug clothing close to their bodies, backs humped against the chill.

Sniffing, I make a wide circuit of the area round the ghetto stroking walls to stir up dormant aromas lost to my senses. I raise dust. We were here. I walk down the same street twice, three times, past the bakery dug into the walls, the old gateway, place my fingers into the gaping spaces where the hinges once rested. I met them when I was a child. They must still be here: I am not looking in the correct places. I simply need to turn the right corner, be facing the right direction. They will have sensed my arrival, are searching for me themselves, eager to greet their sister. We will fall into each others' arms.

I sit down, squat in the tight angle of wall and flagstone. Humans pass, peer at me, look away when I raise my head, scurry on. I could have waited here for one of us to pass by. I did not. I had a plan when I came here. It is difficult to remember. If I rest here it will come back to me.

I wake with a start. A human child is standing in front of me, his head level with mine. As I open my eyes he runs off, joins a group of similar children at the corner. They disappear down an alley, their feet pattering on the stone; faint, fainter, gone. They were laughing. Still, I am not hungry; the damp air sustains me. I should make myself feed. The thought makes my stomach rebel. I trace circles in the dirt to my side, feel the friable grittiness of sandstone on my palm. Sandstone. How do I know it is sandstone? What makes me think like this; that this is sandstone, this, granite? How has it ever helped me? I could have been like that idiot child of Mornacet's I helped to raise. Indifferent and content. Should have stayed in the south with the old woman. I could have buried her.

The church is like the belly of a ship, crusted over the centuries with holy barnacles, weeds, corals till the accretions have become the thing itself. I push open the door of this palace to the dead. The ceiling flies away, higher than the heavy sky outside. The floor is patterned with sparse groups of humans, subdued voices filling the air with the sound of the sea

Lining the buttressed walls are deep niches closed off with iron gates, flanked with candlestands, legs ribbed with tallow. The scent of fire pulls me along past the dark caves to one such side chapel, lit with rank upon rank of flickering wax tapers. Females hug the stone, rubbed by centuries of knees; wring their hands, whispering, heads bobbing, tugging lace scarves closer to their faces. Before them stands their god, a female like them but in white of impossible freshness, hands spread to reveal plaster breasts where she has been torn open, heart exposed and bleeding, pierced with thorns. Her eyes roll up, ecstatic. Beneath her layer of grime she is as pale pink as the inside of a mouth. Notices in four languages tell me she is the lady of sorrows. The earth seethes with their kind and they are sorrowful.

Saints twist in a rococo paso doble, on their knees to their torturers for more arrows in their flesh, more coals at their feet, greater agony so that bones protrude, flesh falls away, muscle, sinew melting in a passionate crucible, reducing themselves to the finest residue of... what? What have they discovered? Their eyes are blank, mouths gape, remain wordless. Hands held out to tantalise are empty. Humans huddle like beasts before them, do not see that their gods are behind bars; desire to be in those cages. Safe. Fed.

Then I smell her, unmistakable through the stink of cheap candles; rush to the rear of the church and the glass case my beauty sleeps in. I have found one of my people: a girl, dead over a thousand years. The card says her name is Lucy, her body snatched from unbelievers, the corpse already ancient. I am a little late.

I rest my brow against the window, whiten it with my breath. Her skin has dried to the hard shine of rubbed bronze, fingers crinkled with centuries of devout kisses so that the bones peep through. Her dress lies in stiff pleats, rigid with grime, tiny feet poking out from the skirt like two bunches of broken twigs, toes of an ancient brown. There is a faint rodent tapping somewhere. I see mice dancing around the body of my beloved: shall pluck them between my fingers, squeeze them like sores. A female in a dress the colour of mud approaches me tutting, mutters for me to step away from the saint. She stopped bleeding many years ago. I tell her in her own tongue that this child is flesh of my flesh and to leave me alone with her. She staggers back down the steps, smiling beatifically like they all do.

The tapping is more insistent. A drop of liquid condenses in the mist I am creating, gravity pulling it slowly towards earth, gathering moisture as it trickles, leaving a clear path through the fog. My eyes follow, as they fall I see my nails clattering on the pane. I try to make them stop and fail; they have become the hands of another person. I manage to haul them away from the glass, hold them in front of me, shuddering. I can still hear clicking.

My legs buckle and I fall to my knees, bone scraping against rock. My heart hammers high in my chest, migrating into the base of my throat; it stops me from speaking. My palms clamp together, fingers quivering. Is this prayer?

Through the rippled glass surrounding the desiccated body of the child I see the females in the church on their knees like me, hands together, heads bowed, squat grublike creatures with balloon heads and distended arms, grotesques to partner the carvings which necklace this building. My heart thunders, leaping uncertainly: each drop of moisture within me dances. I am more than four hundred years old and I am afraid. I breathe to calm the shaking, shake the air as it enters me. I must be on the ground. My face draws to a level with Lucy's behind its tarnished silver mask. At any moment the cheeks will dimple, neck creak as she turns her head to smile at me.

She lays her girl hands on my breasts like a lover then punches me once, hard, in the groove between, piercing the bone with clever knuckles, shoving inside and grasping my heart till it shudders, halts. I will die at the hand of my beloved. I am already on my knees so as my legs fail I have only a small space to fall. Lucy hisses a stream of words filling my head with deafening whispers. I cannot understand if she is saying farewell or ordering me to stay. I should be prostrate by now but she holds me upright, hand deep inside me, fisting my heart until it beats once more to her rhythm. At last she pulls away, hands red, empty: I am left without a wound.

Oh my darling girl, I want to hold you, crumble you to peaceful dust and cram my mouth with you; want to prise open your jaws, lift the tongue stiff as wood, find the hole I know will be there, raise your skirt and search for the signs that you are not merely human. You are mine. The storm you have raised was always here.

I can stand now. My face is wet; there is dampness inside my clothing. I must drink water soon. Her river of words rushes over my ears as I teeter down the steps.

The humans have noticed nothing, hugging the mosaic floor, maggot fingers squirming as they pray and pray for an ecstasy of new cars and sons who will send them money. Lucy smiles at me, her eyes on a plate. I can transport all of you, make you like these beautiful creatures whose eyes roll and bodies run with blood the colour of chocolate. I can do this for you, have begun already. You will be martyrs, witnesses to my love, my benediction. I will feed and leave you unspotted. Bloodless females crouch at my feet as I stride down the nave. I think of the bodies I have left behind me, the ones I have yet to transfigure. My heart rings like a bell.

Outside, I blink in the harsh, flat light. Shoes clatter on cobbles, the babel of a dozen shouted languages. The café facing the church door assails me with the crash of cups onto saucers: knives scrape plates, waiters scream at each other, bang coffee pots onto tables, slam glasses on silver trays, rattle coins in apron pockets.

A male jostles me and I fall back against the door, warm to my touch. A murmur of prayer reaches me from the interior. I look up; the walls bleed bile and ochre. I can sense blood surrounding me: still I'm not hungry. Thirsty. I take the few steps across the crowded square to the café, ask for water at the counter. Now. It catches in my throat. I brush my face and my hand comes away damp; heart still crashes against a wall of breastbone. I look at my moist fingers, watch them tremble. Why am I not hungry? The smell of fresh blood wafts through the swinging door to the kitchen at the rear, but I do not want her. I should: I have not fed for three days. My stomach is full. Behind the wooden bar a male operates a machine which fizzes and squeals, spitting a thick stream of coffee into a minute china cup. He stares at me throughout the whole procedure, hands working automatically, knowing each inch of the chrome. I tell him to ignore me, speaking louder than intended; heads turn, I am attracting attention.

I clamp my hands to my sides but the fluttering continues, communicating to the whole of my body through the skin of my palms. It is time for me to leave; they are looking at me. I want to scream at them to leave me alone: don't they know what I am, who I am, what I am here to do? Gripping the edge of the counter, I steady myself then push away like a swimmer, plough through the clustered tables to the door, hear glass break behind me.

I head northwest and after a few steps am free of the close press of bodies. I must continue searching. Lucy will guide me. The canals become narrower, the walkways thinner, barely wide enough in places to allow two bodies to pass. I find myself wandering down a small passageway which leads directly onto grubby water, have to double back. Some of this has the familiarity of a dream dreamt many decades ago; some streets seem new. The light falling on the canals makes them appear different. I recognise a turning which will take me back to the ghetto but find myself in a square bordered by creamy houses. Another path takes me between blank walls then spills me out onto a broad cobbled promenade facing the lagoon, a stretch of grey unmoving water beneath a low sky the colour of lead. But I was walking south: the lagoon was north of me. I inhale the stink of the water; millennia of piss, sweat, tears and blood diluted by rain; the sea a stranger here.

I press my forehead to the cool wall, look at my feet which seem to be those of another person: the shoes are shabby; I have no recollection of getting them. Raise my arm: the same feeling that it is a changeling, attached to me at some unknown point in the past. My fingers should be longer than these, the nails unbroken.

From a shop window racked with bottles of wine an orange cat peers at me, lowers its chin and squeezes its eyes shut, having lost interest. I cross the space between us, usurped limbs unsteady; stare through the plate glass at the tawny beast, dozing now. As I glance up I find myself face to face with a short female, hunched almost double. She glares at me from eyes ringed with dark smudges, cheeks hollow, skin rough, scratched by the cat, perhaps. She looks ill. Feeling pity, I smile at her, she snarls back. For a shop owner her clothes are dirty, her pale hair matted into filthy lumps. I reach out and my knuckles hit glass. Inside the cat purrs in peaceful solitude. There are drops of water between my feet on the pavement.

Lucy dances behind me: her reflection catches in the window next to mine, laughs through her tiny yellow teeth, her excited clapping the rustle of leaves on a treeless island: she is gone when I turn. I try to take a deep breath, find myself bent over, unfold myself. An ageing male leans against the doorframe and assesses me meditatively. I tell him I am beautiful, watch his pupils dilate; he coughs and disappears behind the ranked wines.

They ignore me. I am the angel at the gate of Eden: could you let me back in if I choose, the only god left in this garden. The only one there ever was. I could have saved you, but that was so long ago. I wanted to, far south of here. Is it the cold which makes me lose the desire to help you any longer? It has pierced my marrow, my mouth; my tongue is sluggish; I no longer wish to feed from you. You disgust me. I will not drink your slime while you suck the goodness from me, howling accusations that it is me who drains you.

My gums are dry, all my saliva now in you; healing you, cleansing your filthy human blood: you've been crammed with dirt ever since we pushed you out of the trees, shoved you blinking out of caves, shading your eyes, supporting each stumbling footstep. You would not have lasted without us. We have carried you. Now only I remain, sword raised to hold back each sickness, each disease gnawing my shoulder. I am tired of protecting you from the contents of this garden, this hell we saved you from, tired of being blamed for keeping you out of paradise. Paradise will find you soon enough when I drop the sword and let the garden come to you. It is already beginning.

I cross the great canal, feel bones crunch beneath my feet, hear voices talk of the stink of the water. I breathe in and all I can smell is their decay, the rottenness of human waste. I walk through their crumbling bodies, see my hand sweep through them as they fall into putrefaction. I would kneel and lick them from the stones. Oh glorious virgins, martyrs at my right hand, let me feed and keep you unspotted.

I pass them, choosing postcards of gondolas. She chooses scenes of night, sparkling coloured lights to match your eyes my sweet, runs her fingertips round the edge; takes two, three of the same picture; holds them as if she would have the image sink into the skin of her palm and journey through her bloodstream to her heart. Her other hand wanders to the arm of the male next to her, prods him through the bright fleece of his jacket. Yes, he's still there. Waves the cards before him: he smiles. He strokes the metal display stand; will not touch the cards. They toy with their glossy visions of canals while I hover at the edge of their dreams. She is freshly pregnant, scarcely a week, but the scent hangs on her. She does not know.

"I am your friend," I breathe into their ears. They turn, eyes misted with happy recognition. I accompany them to their hotel, wait in the lift while they collect their key, my fingers leaping. I have so much to tell them, to explain. "I am so glad I meet you." Their heads nod. I clasp their hands in mine, smile till my cheeks ache, we are so pleased to be together. "A drink!" I cry, throw open the minibar, cradle their shoulders and tip the pretty bottles down their throats; tell them to remove their clothes. I am not ashamed. They struggle with buttons, tight sleeves, zippers which catch; he hops from foot to foot as he removes his socks; her tights have left deep indentations around her stomach. They stand before me, hiccuping, pink faces and bleached waspish bodies, her breasts long cones pulled vertical by their own weight, his balls swaying in their loose sack.

I will have her now. He will watch, learn how to be a lover. His eyes are leaden as I lead her to the pastel bed, stroke the triangle of reddish hair at the meeting of her thighs, kneel and enter her. He is still fresh inside her; I taste so many couplings: this morning, yesterday, the day before. Unaware of the fattening of blood around the minute egg. My dear, I sip your quickened blood: the child not yet a child will fall from your body. You will never know. You are my forbidden fruit, so ripe I choke on you; a banquet to tempt me: the fat of animals, bones boiled down to greasy stock, meat rubbed with salt and roasted, dripping when cut, blood and offal stewed in vats, spiced and pounded into mash, the oily feet of pigs, the tender breasts of birds, a broth of brains and ox's tongues, a sticky soup of marrowbones.

"It is time to write your postcards now," I tell her as she brings her knees together; hand her a pen. She scrawls on the back of The Rialto Bridge By Night. "Today is the feast of Saint Lucy" I suggest.

She is here with me now, holds out her platter. I stand, take the chair under the mirror, swing it, catching him beneath his left ear. He falls to the floor in a tranquil arc. I bring it down upon him, slamming a carved leg into the wound on the side of his head. The delicate bones in his temple collapse inwards, the space filling with a dark viscous gravy. He draws up his right knee, kicks spasmodically, halts. The female's hand falters; I tell her to continue. He did not love you. He hated the cards you chose. You can write them in peace now; "today was such a special day."

I bury my face in his shattered skull; wash and wash and come up bloody. Thrust in my fingers, snake damp trails around his nipples, down to his navel; drive in the nail till it pierces the skin. Still warm inside, dead but as warm as a glove. How long will this one take to cool? With my other hand I enlarge the hole, draw the curtains of his belly. He gapes at me, quailing like aspic. His bowels have emptied, the ropes of his intestines quiet, peristalsis a thing of the past. I loop my fingers in the coils; cannot undo the knots. There is nothing here for me; I unlace my hands. He seems so small now; something has gone. Where did it go? I step into the gaping body, feel his organs settle around my ankles. I am the dragon rising from the body of the virgin. "Me," Lucy cries. "Me now."

I will take all of you with me. I have what? Seventy? One hundred years left? I have time. I will take you one by one, without ire or anger. I do not confuse killing with hatred. I cherish each one of you. You are all dead. Wait.

Moonlight Seductor

Stephen Lewis

They sat on the bed and looked at each other, neither of them believing that they had only met a few hours ago.They joked about something she considered to be meaningless and finished the last of their champagne. He tossed his glass to one side and made a cheap advance for her that she swiftly ducked away from. She stood up and looked out of the window at the beautiful moonlit sky, the stars, the people in the streets below, all so unaware. She breathed on the glass and drew patterns in the steam. He came up behind her and slid his arms around her waist, but she glided away and he stumbled after her; turning round she loosened his tie and pushed him backward onto the bed. She slowly unbuttoned her silk dress and he tore at the buttons on his shirt in a half-drunken haste. She let the silk item fall delicately to the floor as she stepped out of it, she wore no underwear, only a pair of silk black stockings. He shifted himself farther back onto the bed and beckoned for her to come to him, she obliged. As she stepped out of her shoes and climbed onto the bed with him, she playfully crawled around the bed as he reached out to grab her. Catching her ankle he pulled her to him and began to kiss her shoulders and neck, she didn't really want to do this but knew she had to. If she didn't do this one she wouldn't be able to stay alive.

"One of the requirements" she had been told. He guided his hand along her leg to her hip as he continued to grope her. She wanted to get this over with, never been one for staying around too long. She prided herself on that, was proud of the fact that she would never remain in a place long enough for people to hurt her when they found out what she was like. She grabbed his arms and rolled herself on top of him. It was a good thing he was slightly intoxicated; that way he didn't notice her excessive strength. Brushing her hair from her face she shot a quick kiss at him as his warm hands ran down her spine, she pulled away from him and began to undo his trousers. He grabbed at them and tried to rip them off, but she stopped him with a quiet shushing sound as she teasingly fingered her lips.

"Slowly," she whispered with a voice as gentle as a summer breeze. He did as he was told and let her do the rest. Tossing his trousers on a nearby chair she pulled him to his feet and kissed him again.

"Close your eyes," she sighed soothingly as she ran her hand softly over his eyelids. She left him with his eyes shut, as she went over to switch off the light. She knew he had opened them, but she moved too fast for him to see her. She crept along the bed behind him and grabbed him round the waist; he let out a quick breath of surprise and she pulled him down with her. The moon illuminated the room beautifully, casting gentle playful shadows around the walls and ceiling. His hand on her breast brought her back to the business at hand and she forced a sweet smile to her lips as she kissed his forehead, then his eyelids, cheek and nose. To his lips and chin and softly round to his throat and neck, she looked up and caught a glimpse of herself in the mirror and saw her piercing blue eyes cut through the room. She thought of how far she had come in such a short time, at how much she had learnt and grown. A slight twinge of loneliness crept into her, but she fought it out as she had done many nights before now... it was time to play. She sank her teeth into his pale smooth skin and his neck yielded to her touch. She knew he was afraid, knew she had to make him want this. He wasn't special, not special enough to be turned, no one had ever been... yet. She gently removed her teeth and stroked his neck with her hand, dabbed a finger in his wound and licked at his blood, just a small taste to keep her going, keep her in the mood. His head sank into a lulled sense of pleasure and she knew he willed her to do this, that he wanted it to happen more than anything in the world.

His hand moved from his side and stroked her lips with one lone finger, then felt her sharp teeth knowing it would be the last thing he did, the details etched in his mind yet he accepted it freely. She teased him, softly licking his fingertip and gently nipping at it, just enough to draw blood. Feeling a shiver go through his body, she knew she had caught him, that he was handing his life to her on a silver tray. She decided to toy with him for a few moments longer, in a way to prolong his death and perhaps also to extend the pleasure this was giving her, it had been a long while since she had been with a man, longer still since she had... played. She took his hand and placed it on her breast and he squeezed at it as she felt his crotch, he sighed in pleasure and slight laziness, he felt half asleep, numb and very relaxed. She lowered herself to kiss his lips before she licked at the wound on his neck, teasing, playing. She helped him slide out of his boxer shorts as he lay back on the bed, he laughed quietly to himself almost trying not to let his excitement show. She felt excited at this game she was playing, it was a new one to her, so often she had just killed and left. But this time would be fun for her as well as a meal! She took his penis in her hands flicking and darting her tongue at it, he let out a cough of surprise as she began to lick his scrotum, letting her moist lips settle for a while before teasing them away.

He clapped his hands on his forehead in ecstasy and she looked at him under hooded eyes as she took a little bite into his groin, he sucked in a breath of pleasure and pain mixed in a dark sexual cocktail. She crawled up him rubbing her body along his and making a trail of blood up his chest from the new wound in his groin. He opened his mouth to speak but she put a finger to his lips and silenced him. Moving backward to his chest she bit down hard on his nipple and tugged away. He writhed in a split second of pain but she kissed him to keep him quiet letting their saliva and his blood mix in their mouths. Sliding him into her and settling herself on top, clawing her hands on his chest as she rode him in perfect rhythm to her own racing heartbeat, the nails made small cuts in him as she clawed, but that was tough on him. He sat himself up and took her hands in his, kissing her breasts and tasting his own blood as he did so. Her grip tightened on his hands as she forced him back onto the bed and stretched him out along it. She licked at the open wound on his neck again and felt her senses explode in a mixture of want and rage. Again she looked at herself in the mirror, her red eyes glared back at her and she knew it was time, she must take him now... and she did.

She bit down hard onto his neck, a lot harder than any previous bite she had given him, his whole body tensed as he came and he remained in a light state of shock and submission as her teeth stuck fast to him. His blood was warm with a salty taste, it was pure and full of life, if slightly tainted with the alcohol in his body. She craved more, and drank deeper. She felt the blood pulse from his heart, past her teeth, down her throat and into her being. Her heart started to beat in rhythm to his so she was him in thought and feeling. She milked him dry until there was no more energy left. She felt tired, full and for once she felt satisfied. She knew she had given him pleasure of a different sort, the kind you only experience once and your whole being yearns for it so much you'll give anything for it... even your life.

He'd given his life to her.

She knew he had felt his blood being drained from his body to be replaced for just a few seconds of pure, oh so pure, ecstasy and then... nothing, who knows?

She got up off the bed and dressed herself looking at him as she did so and with a wry smile of satisfaction on her lips she left him there in the darkness of the room with the moon as company, and only the stars bearing witness.

As she left through the open window, she wondered how long it would be until she felt blood trickle past her lips and into her mouth with that delicious taste? How long would it be before she felt pleasure like that again? When would another man give up his body and soul to the darkness of the night? Perhaps one day she would let one into her world, perhaps she would let one care for her, maybe fall asleep in his arms till the breaking dawn woke them. But that would be another day... perhaps! Tonight had been too much fun.

Red Wings

Zane Black

"Look, all you got to do is suck a woman's blood," said the President angrily. "It's easy. What is the problem?"

"I dunno..." I said, shrugging and looking past him so I didn't have to look into his angry red blister of a face. "My stomach gets upset easy. Like, you know, I can't eat meat unless it's real well done."

"Well, ain't that a shame!" jeered the President of the Satan's Saints, leaning closer until his hairy sneer filled my vision. His breath assaulted my nostrils: booze, cigarettes and marijuana in about equal measure. "Listen, kid," he continued in the same angry tone. "If you want to ride with the world's toughest motorcycle club, you're gonna have to earn your Red Wings. And the only way you're gonna do that is to go down on some woman when she's on the rag and scarf up her blood like it's tomato juice!"

He leaned closer still. "You got that?"

I nodded. I felt like a kid in first grade getting bawled out by the teacher for wetting his pants. It's hard sometimes being the youngest, newest member of the Saints.

"It's club rules, kid, same for everybody!"

I glanced down at the colourful badges on the front of his denim vest. Our club 'patches'. One of them held my attention. The red badge in the shape of bat wings. All the guys in Satan's Saints have them.

All except me.

"You didn't raise such a fuss when you got your Brown Wings," the Prez added, grinning. The guys standing around watching chuckled knowingly.

I didn't say anything. I was still trying to forget that.

"Okay, who am I gonna do it with?" I asked, anxious to change the subject.

The Prez glanced around the crowded club house. "Well... how about Mary?" he suggested. "She's always ready to lend a hand." That got another laugh from the guys.

At the mention of her name, Typhoid Mary turned and looked towards us, a question in her eyes. Somehow she managed to do this without letting Dirty Dogg's prick slip from her mouth. She didn't even stop her pumping action. She swept some greasy hair out of her face, looked straight at me and winked. Then her fat cheeks bulged as Dirty Dogg shot her a hot load.

"Are you kidding?" I almost choked. "I don't want to catch..." I didn't say what I was afraid of catching from Mary. There were too many possibilities to choose from.

"Well, if you're afraid of catching something, you just better find yourself a virgin," said the Prez. "Only make it fast - because if you ain't eaten bloody pussy by Sunday, I'm gonna rip them club colours off your back. Then I'm gonna fuck you up real bad!"

He turned and stomped away to take his turn with Mary. The grinning horned devil on the back of his denim vest looked like it was giving me the finger.

A virgin? Right! Only where was I going to find myself a virgin that friendly?

"How 'bout Angela Redmund?" suggested a voice so close to my ear I almost jumped. I looked up into Snake's lean mean face. I hadn't even heard him approach.

"Angela Redmund," he repeated in his slow drawl. "You know, that high school kid, the one they call Blonde Angie. I hear no-one's popped her cherry yet."

"Thanks, Snake," I mumbled gratefully. "Good idea, man."

Well, it seemed like a good idea at the time. You see, strangely enough, I knew Angie Redmund. She was at the same school as my younger sister, Kelly. A very attractive girl, a real looker in fact, with long blonde hair, blue eyes and the kind of full lips girls in porno movies always have. I knew her family was strict - her folks were religious weirdos of some kind - but I couldn't really believe she was still a virgin at age sixteen, not with her looks. I told myself I'd ask Kelly about her later.

Kelly bit her bottom lip and screwed up her face as she finally came. When she was through making animal noises I rolled off her and reached for a pack of cigarettes. My sister and I have always been real tight.

"Tell me about Blonde Angie," I told her when we'd both lit up. "Is she really still a virgin?"

"She says she is," said Kelly, flicking hot ash off her left breast. Then she told me Angie hated being the only virgin in her class. Maybe in the whole school. The thing was, her wacko father and three brothers never let her go out alone. They kept her on a real tight leash. Like they were afraid she was immediately going to run off with the AntiChrist or something.

All Angie needed was an opportunity, said Kelly.

"Talk to her tomorrow," I said. "Tell her her time has come."

Mine too, I hoped.

I parked my cycle half a block down from where Angie lived and walked quietly up to her father's old house. The place looked like it ought to have had a 'Museum' sign up outside. It was gone midnight and all the lights were off, just like she'd said.

I rapped softly on Angie's window. At least I hoped it was her window and not her old man's. She'd told Kelly she slept on the ground floor at the back of the house. A long moment passed and then Angie's excited face appeared behind the curtains. Slowly, very slowly, she eased open the window.

"Come in, quick," she whispered, adding "Quietly!" as my motorcycle boot scraped across the window-frame. I climbed inside, careful not to knock anything over. All around me was a girly clutter of china dolls, fancy mirrors, glass animals: everything guaranteed to break noisily when dropped.

Angie was looking sexy - dead sexy - in a silky white nightdress stretched tight in all the right places. Everything about her was perfect except for the worried frown on her face.

"I hate to tell you this," she said hesitantly. "But I've got my curse."

Which was just what I wanted to hear. Of course, I wasn't going to tell her that. Instead, I shrugged and said, "It's a piss-poor soldier never fought a bloody battle." I'd always wanted to say that.

Then I pulled her to me and we kissed deeply, our tongues dancing together wetly. My hands glided over her soft warm body, wanting to hold every part of her at once.

In no time we ended up over by her bed. I reached down and her nightdress whispered off her body. She stood before me completely naked. Her young girl's bush was reddish golden in the light of the candles she'd put by the bed. Again our bodies pressed together hungrily. I was already hard, my prick beating its head against the inside of my jeans in eager anticipation.

But that wasn't what I'd come for.

Angie stepped back and lay down on the bed, arranging herself for me like an offering. I noticed she had carefully spread a red towel on the sheet beneath her. Good thinking. No need to get any blood on the cute funny animals or her pink sheets.

I knelt on the end of the bed and looked down at her. In the candlelight she looked both innocent and inviting at the same time. I leaned forward and kissed her hard on the lips. Then I kissed her pink-tipped breasts. Then her red gold bush. As I pressed my lips to her soft furry mound, I caught her scent: a spicy mix of female arousal and the sweet butchershop smell of blood.

She still had her legs pressed together tightly. Sitting up, I took hold of her ankles and slowly pulled them apart. Her white thighs opened up, baring her sex to my gaze. At its meaty centre a liquid ruby glinted moistly in the candlelight. Blood.

I didn't feel disgusted like I thought I would. Not much anyhow. I was too excited. Excited by Angie's body spread open before me. And by the thought of the Red Wings that would soon be mine. The Red Wings that would make me a full-fledged member in good standing of the Satan's Saints.

Leaning forward again, I slid my palms under her hot little buttocks, raising her virgin vagina towards my mouth. I licked at the inside of her milky thighs, worming my tongue upwards until I reached that soft sweet spot where her thigh met her body. Then I switched my attentions to the inside of her other thigh, again working my way tantalisingly upwards. The little breathless noises Angie was making as my tongue did its work told me she really liked what I was doing.

This time when I reached the top of her thigh, I trailed my tongue lightly across her golden bush, then probed her fur with my tongue tip until I tasted her moist womanflesh and the sweet coppery tang of her blood.

The moment of truth had come.

Sliding my hands upwards, I gently thumbed her labia apart. Opened up, Angela's pussy lips looked like a pair of red wings, stretched ready to soar like a butterfly.

Between the meaty wings, the delicate flesh petals of her cunt unfolded to my touch, revealing the deeper, darker cavern below; it was leaking red jewels.

Above the poppy flesh sat her 'little man in a boat', the engorged stub of her clitoris. Angela squirmed beneath me as I kissed her clit, then circled it slowly with lazy flicks of my tongue.

There was no backing out now. I couldn't put things off any longer. Shit, what was I worrying about, I told myself: she's a goddam virgin!

I reared my head back like Dracula about to take a bite, then stabbed my tongue into her red wet crevice and began to lick. I licked her blood up like a cat happily tonguing a plate of cream. And the more I licked, the more I got to like the taste: sweet and salty and metallic, spiked with the sharper tang of female sex juice.

I lapped it up like I was afraid of missing a single drop. I licked the inside of her cunt and the sides and all around it. If I'd had a piece of bread, I would've used it to mop up the gravy.

If only the Prez was here to see me now, I thought. If only all the Satan's Saints were here to see me...

I felt Angela's blood overflowing from my mouth, all mixed up with her juice and my saliva, and dripping down my chin in red streams onto her thighs. I could imagine what my tongue and teeth must look like – all red and stained, like I'd just eaten a whole big bowlful of raspberries.

As I licked at her, Angela continued to make enthusiastic love-sounds and writhe her buttocks against my hands. I felt her own hand reach down to stroke my hair, then to press my mouth harder against her. A tremor shook her body and I wondered if my licking and sucking had made her come.

"I want to feel you inside me," she suddenly urged in a throaty whisper. "Come inside me..."

I didn't need much urging. My prick felt like it was burning a hole through my jeans. Wiping my mouth, I raised myself up and unzipped. Instantly, my prick sprang out, as tall and thick as I'd ever seen it. Fluid was already dribbling from its tip. This wasn't exactly safe sex, but who was worrying at a time like this?

I'd never had a real virgin before. I'd often wondered what it would be like. Now I was going to find out.

I shifted my weight to my hands, positioning myself so the head of my blood-swollen prick was pressed hard up against Angie's bleeding cunt. She gasped out loud as I pressed harder still and pushed a little way into her, making a smooth liquid entry. I expected to come up against an obstruction, a thin wall of skin, but there didn't seem to be any. I wondered if she'd been lying all along about being a virgin. Right now I didn't care. I pushed in deeper and deeper, filling her inch by delicious inch.

When I was five inches into her, I felt something unexpected. Something hard. Hard as nails. Hard as teeth.

Then the pain, excruciating as it was sudden, clamped down hard on my prick!

My screams brought the rest of them running, her father and her brothers. Suddenly the room was filled with them. They must have been still up because they were all already dressed, all of them in their old-fashioned black suits.

Urgently, they pulled me - *tore* me - shrieking off Angie. They must have thought all that blood was hers, because they started shouting and punching and kicking me. I screamed back at them. Couldn't they see what she'd done to me? Couldn't they see her - that thing on the bed - lying there, *feeding*?

As I fell forward, fainting from loss of blood, they caught me and held me up by my hair. They started chanting something, words I couldn't understand. Beyond their fevered faces I glimpsed Angie, standing tall up on the bed now. *Too* tall somehow.

She looked down at me, spread her red wings wide and laughed.

A Personal View

Michaela Bisiker

I've been a prisoner in this room for what seems like centuries. Strange how long a day can be when one is confined with nothing to do, no way of filling the weary hours except staring at one's captors. Since it's impossible to make mischief in a glass cell, they've at last given me a notebook and pen so I can set events down on paper to while away my life.

It's still a mystery in my mind how I, who have lived for generations, could fall into so simple a trap, although it shows how even my formidable powers are no match for astute female intelligence. Now I am imprisoned inside this glass box, an exhibit, an experiment, on display to the swarm of awe-struck mortals who have suddenly become my masters. And there, amongst the scurrying technicians, she sits at her desk, watching me over her monitor, trying to fathom my existence. I wish her luck. In over four hundred years it is a feat I have never accomplished.

I cannot recall seeing her before the day I realised she was stalking me. In the few hours immediately following sunset, it was my habit to sit at the window of my garret flat and gaze down at the busy thoroughfare below. I have always been fascinated by the frenzy that drives mortal men and women, the rush to meet, marry and mate before their hasty little lives run out like so much sand through the fingers. It was during these evening reflections that I gradually became aware of the same figure, night after night on the street corner opposite the building, looking curiously up at my window. At first I dismissed her as a common prostitute, but when one night, whilst out hunting, I caught her following me, it occurred to me that I might be discovered. I had made a number of kills recently and in some cases had been careless. With age comes complacency and I had been remiss of late. Since I was well fed, I elected to solve the mystery and approach my pursuer.

I turned abruptly and marched straight up to her. "Are you following me?" I asked, bold as you please.

"Yes," she replied. "You interest me. Can I buy you a drink?"

I have made a huge effort to move with the times, but I still cannot adjust to being propositioned by women. Masking my bafflement, I accepted her offer and presently found myself seated in a local bar, a bottle in front of me and this curious woman opposite. I sipped the beer slowly - I can process human fare in moderation - and listened while she told me about herself. She was unlike the majority of mortal women I have known in that she exuded a love of life, an enthusiasm for living that is rare to see. She was no pale, waif-like insect, being curved in all the right places with just the correct amount of fat required for proportion. As I watched her, eyes asparkle and hands gesticulating as she spoke, I felt a stirring within me that was out of keeping with my kind. A mortal stirring of lust, the kind I had almost forgotten. At that moment I craved more than just the juice of her veins and the final spasm as she collapsed cooling in my arms. How I wanted her!

She told me she was a research student studying human behaviour and its peculiarities, such as the weather, seasons and tides. I listened to this with some amusement. It seems that humans are completely self-obsessed, needing to know all the answers before they can live their life at ease. Perhaps this is why I have always found them such easy pickings - they're too wrapped up in themselves to smell danger until the blood-letting has begun.

We talked away the evening, and when closing time came, I realised I had drunk - and probably said - much more than was good for me. Rising slowly from my chair, a sick, poisoned sensation washed over me, reminding me that alcohol was not my normal refreshment. Out of charity she offered to see me home, and driven by inebriation and impure motives, I accepted.

In the cool darkness of my bedroom I yielded to her brazen advances, forgetting my masculine pride and savouring the sweetness of submission. In my day, she would have been married young, or married to God, either way a virgin or as good as. On her flesh, however, I could see the imperceptible fingerprints of countless lovers, each leaving his invisible signature on breasts and buttocks. In the perfumed valley between her thighs I tasted the spilled seed of others, an intoxicating cocktail of welcomed pleasures bathing my tongue with the products of her desire. With the moonlight as my witness, I plundered her fertile valley and in turn left my mark in her gallery of vice.

All night I lay beside her, watching her sleep until the first pale fingers of dawn stole across the sky. Tenderly I kissed her brow before hurrying to the narrow compartment in the eaves which had become my daylight retreat. My emotions drained, I lay down in the box of earth and closed my eyes, knowing nothing of what was to come.

Even now shame fills me at the ease with which I was subdued. A sprig of mountain ash placed upon my sleeping form rendered me immobile. As if this were not enough, my devious mistress draped a wreath of garlic over the lid of my coffin to ensure I could not escape. All of this I witnessed through the eyes of my subconscious, how I was bundled into a van by four young men and driven through the town centre at speed. That is how I came to be a prisoner in a laboratory, to be studied like a rat in a cage.

Their first experiment was to expose me to sunlight. Directly above my transparent cell was a shuttered shaft that opened onto the roof. Over several days this shaft was opened for increasing periods of time until my flesh was burned and smoking and my sensitive eyes almost sightless. Finally my tormentors realised that I could not be conditioned to withstand the sun's rays and they gave up, making the most of my incapacitated state to open the cage and fan away the stench of my roasted body.

It was now almost a week since I had fed: I was now so weak that the healing of my wounds had slowed almost to a human rate. Every movement caused me more pain than I ever thought I could feel, though it didn't come close to the pain in my heart that stung me every time I saw her. There are those who say a Vampire has no emotions. There are those who say we cannot feel the same physical love as mortals. The myth surrounding the Undead has swamped the fact; we are not totally obsessed with the search for blood. Vampires make skilled and truly uninhibited lovers, but it is a sad truth that our self-control is poor. One sight of a pulsating vein, throbbing with the heat of lust is often too great a temptation to ignore, thus many of our willing partners do not survive to sing our praises. I wonder if this was also a matter of research, or whether she truly cared for me. Perhaps I shall never know.

Night has fallen. I do not need to see the moon rise to know that it has done so. My inverted body clock can sense the change from day to night, even in this tiny room without windows. It also helps that the laboratory staff have all gone home, leaving me with my thoughts.

Footsteps in the laboratory - I am obviously not alone. A desk lamp illuminates the face of my beloved; she stands at her computer staring at me. Are those tears in her eyes? Does she feel regret for having imprisoned me thus? I rise slowly from my narrow bed and meet her at the wall between us. Her hand rests against the glass barrier and I match it with my own. I smile gently at her and she weeps, glistening rivulets trickling down her cheeks into the corners of her mouth. I know how I must appear - face still burned, cheeks hollow, gums shrunken from my teeth like withered meat - but this is not what she sees. To her I am a dumb animal, tortured and suffering from her cruelty, and remorse now racks her mercilessly. At last I notice the bag she is carrying, and from it she takes a sealed pouch of fluid. Saliva rushes into my mouth at once for it is a bag of blood, processed and prepared for transfusion into the needy. At this moment in time, there is none more needy than I. She unlocks the door of my cage and holds out her gift, which I seize hungrily, my teeth neatly lancing the polythene and allowing the contents to flood my parched throat. There is something vaguely sterile in the flavour of my feast, but in a state of starvation I am no gourmet. Having swallowed every drop, I sit back on my bed, closing my eyes as a degree of strength returns. A movement of the mattress reminds me of her presence, and I open my eyes to find her sitting beside me, her eyes still full of sorrow. "I'm sorry," she whispers, and I shake my head and embrace her, holding her close enough to feel the beat of her heart. Her lips are parted and I press mine to them, exploring her mouth with my tongue as she lies back on the bed. Moving my lips to the soft skin of her throat, I press my fingers between her legs, and as the long unused fangs pierce her throat, twin rivers of hot fluid begin to flow. Her breath is stolen by the sharpness of my kiss and she gasps in silent horror but still her hips lift against my hand even as the life floods out of her and into me. When her movements have all but stopped, I rise from my meal and study her on the brink of death, her lips as blue as the ocean, and I am moved. Still she tries to breath, tries to cry out, prevented by the weakness from blood-loss but nevertheless still fighting. It is this strength, this desire for life that moves me. Growing stronger with every passing second, I bite open a vein in my wrist and press it to her mouth against her feeble struggles. I force her to swallow and the sudden expression of dread on her pale face shows her comprehension of this act. Pausing once to kiss her lovely cheek, I leave the glass cage, lock it behind me and pocket the key, exiting the building as quickly as possible. I should, by rights, have killed her, but I thought it more fitting for her to complete her research from a more personal viewpoint.

Death Becomes Her

Jami Stirling

Fernando plunged his hands into the dark chasm of the woman's cleavage and felt his expert way around the heavy white globes of her breasts for the erect buds of her nipples. Roughly he toyed with them, twisting and wrenching the hard buttons of flesh with his long fingers. The woman lay unresponsive beneath him, her flesh cold and white, a start contrast to the dark wood of her coffin in the black pit of earth.

She had been beautiful and popular while yet alive, but now all that beauty was for Fernando alone to enjoy. Her long red hair cascaded over her shoulders, her eyes were slightly sunken already by her two days in the ground. Her skin was pinched at the corners of her mouth, the mortician's last attempt to disguise the agony of her death. A narrow white scar tracing her throat from ear to ear marked the cause of her untimely demise under the knife of a maniac with rape and murder on his mind.

Fernando's tastes had never strayed to rape. The idea of a woman struggling to be free did nothing for him - far better to have them quiet and unresistant, without a thought of flight. Helen Falconer was at peace now, and her pain was over. Fernando liked to think he was redressing the balance of her life by giving her pleasure after her death. Plus there was of course the bonus of getting pleasure for himself in the process.

His cock was rigid and swollen already; it had been so since he'd prised the lid off the freshly-buried coffin and set eyes on the latest victim of the Hamdale Ripper. She had only been 16 when the Ripper had struck her down. Fernando was glad of some young meat after his feasts earlier in the year, following the maniac known as the 'Granny Slayer'. Fernando had taken advantage of the man's prodigious death toll, but it was always preferable to use the young flesh of dead virgins and children than the wizened skins of the elderly. What he did was about life really, not death. The younger they were, the more full of life, the better.

Helen Falconer was far more his idea of what was right. The death scar on her neck, the suppleness of her pallid skin - so slow to decay when they were young - thrilled him. His fingers sought lower down her body, pulling apart her blouse to expose the lightly bruised ribs and flat belly. So ravishing in death's serene calm, so tantalising and pure.

Fernando leant closer to her, breathing in deeply the scents of formaldehyde, jasmine and earth. The scent of the dead, the scent he loved above all others. He nuzzled between the large globes of her tits, tongue racing lasciviously over her nipples. His cock sprang into life again, straining keen and eager beneath his robes.

One hand slid down to her skirt, gently hitching it up over her stockinged thighs and hips. The flavour of her cunt was strong in his mouth already; he could anticipate the thrill of her cold dryness, that so familiar sensation that always made him so anxious to come. Just to lie there, drinking imaginary juice from her dead lips, licking at the bloodless clitoris and half expecting a shudder of response from the corpse! Every body was the same at that point, every one seemed about to recover life to offer him a pearlescent tribute - but none of them ever had or would.

He snuggled between her legs, making himself comfortable against the crook of her knees, his mouth almost upon her softly downed lips. The first gentle lick, his tongue sliding cautiously into the crack of her pussy, and he clutched at his throbbing cock as a delicious spasm rocked through him. He licked harder, his fingers closing into a fist upon his rigid tool, as more spasms rippled through his cold body.

The rhythm took over - his tongue sliding into the dead girl's slit, his hand pulling back the foreskin over his rampant cock. His ears were full of the rhythm, washing his senses away on a tide of deafening blood.

His saliva was all over her cunt now, making it slick and moist and faintly warm. She felt alive, but not too much that she would push him away and run screaming to the authorities. Not even his dog collar would give him immunity if he were caught defiling a corpse, one of his own parishioners whom he had buried on Saturday.

The danger spurred him on to a greater sense of ecstasy and he clambered to his knees, holding his robes up as he admired the pallor of her cunt and the stiffness of his inflamed cock.

With a cry of feral delight the two met, hot rigid meat forced hard and deep into the gently decaying flesh of her cavity. He withdrew, pumped again, withdrew, sank in deeper, withdrew, pumped and came explosively.

The body shuddered away from him as the jet of his spunk filled up the narrow tunnel. His senses numb and ecstatic, Fernando reached out to touch the cold tits again and felt a pulse beneath his fingers.

Impossible! - an hallucination again as had happened with others sometimes when the orgasm was so monstrously intense.

But then he felt her belly and finally her face, and the truth was inescapable. She was growing warmer! With terror clawing at his heart he scrambled to his feet and reached for the coffin lid to force her back into the world of the dead. It cannot be, he told himself urgently, panic consuming him. Cannot, cannot, cannot.

"Father Fernando."

The voice struck horror into his very soul and he turned his gaze upon her face. She lay in repose, no sign of life or motion apparent in her white form.

"Father Fernando." More insistent now - stronger.

He sealed the coffin frantically, pouring earth on top of it to hide his crime whilst scrambling to get out of the pit.

"Father Fernando."

"Stop it!" he shrieked aloud. "Leave me alone." He quit the grave, tumbling more earth into the hole to bury her evil voice.

He fled into the safety of the church, falling down prostrate before the altar and the bleeding Christ on the enormous wooden crucifix. How lifelike the blood seemed to his demented eyes, how real the pain on that plaster face. Words of a prayer began to tumble out, senseless and confused.

Suddenly a hand clamped down on his shoulder and he leapt to his feet, paralysed with terror. Turning round he saw the friendly, open face of his bishop, a curious expression of compassion or understanding on his face so out of place with Fernando's sin that he fell away from him, blood searing his face with agonies of shame.

"Father Fernando."

Fernando stared wildly about, before fixing his eyes on the bishop's face. Surely he could hear that spectral voice too. Then the bishop's lips moved and spoke. "Father Fernando." His grip on Fernando's shoulder intensified and he brought him closer until their faces were but inches apart. "Father Fernando," he said again, a sinister smile edged with razor sharp teeth splitting his friendly expression apart. "I always knew you were fit to be one of us." The Hamdale Ripper smiled wider, fangs gleaming, and descended on the exposed throat of the priest.

Road Kill!

M. E. Warner

She walked along the frost crisp track. The small-framed twirly girl. Breathing in the surrounding air. Like the ground, it was cold and hard, and it tickled her nose and throat like a flutter of razorblade butterflies. She giggled, twirling, raising her open face to the deep black blanket above. There were holes in the blanket. If she squeezed her eyes real tight, the holes got bigger. But, no matter how hard she tried, she couldn't make the blanket disappear completely.

The throaty 'Budweiser' chorus of frogs caught her by surprise. Her laughter merged with the night sounds. The frogs, the erratic cacophony of crickets and a distant owl. Her joyful exaltation wove itself into the rich fabric. It was as if it had always been there.

She twirled again, her dress merry-go-rounding, as if the earth was a continuation of the air. Her clunky shoes hardly disturbed the petrified ground.

She dropped with a delighted squeal.

Another instrument had joined the symphony.

The girl pressed her ear to the cold earth. She had seen someone do it before to get a better listen, perhaps on TV.

It tickled, making her mouth fall into a trembling grin.

"I'm telling you, Jimmy, we just hit somethin'," said Billy, flicking Pearl Jam from the radio with a grease-grubby finger.

"It was just an animal, that's all," replied Jimmy, taking another beer from the cooler wedged between them.

Billy ran his fingers through his slick mop of jet hair. "I don't think so, Jimmy. I saw a flash o' white. And pink I think."

"Pink you think?" said Jimmy in his practiced hillbilly retard voice. "It was just a 'coon or a rabbit, Billy-boy."

"There ain't no harm in takin' a look-see, Jimmy. Maybe we can fix it up all right."

Jimmy, the older and larger of the two men, looked at Billy. Billy smiled as he felt the pickup relax from its salt flat speed.

"All right, Billy, we'll take a look. If it is a critter we'll cook it up Tex-Mex style. What do ya say?"

Billy smiled again, Jimmy usually relented if he pestered him long enough. "Sounds good, Jimmy."

Jimmy swung the truck around, picking up a bumper full of camouflage from the roadside.

"Told you," grunted Jimmy, clearing his throat and shooting an arc of mucus brule into the road. "There ain't nothin' here. Not even a rabbit. Not even a fuckin' possum. Looks like it's beans, beans and more beans for our first meal in the cabin. Some start to our huntin' trip."

"It was further back, I'm sure of it," said Billy. He jogged down the dirt track, his breath ectoplasm escaping into the night. "Right back there, by that fat old tree stump that looks like your momma."

"What's that you said about my momma?" laughed Jimmy. He whipped Billy's buttocks with his faded red baseball cap, running after him toward the stump.

The smile fled Jimmy's pitted face. There was something still and pale beneath Billy.

"Oh my God," breathed Billy. "Is she dead? Please say that she ain't dead."

Jimmy scratched the wiry stubble on his jaw. He removed his cap again. This time he did it as he had on the three occasions he had been in church and the twelve times he had been in court. He knelt down by the small girl curled up on the cold earth. He thought that she looked like she was sleeping. He brushed some loose strands, escaped from her ponytail, from her teen queen face.

"She sure is pretty," he uttered in hushed tones.

"But is she alive, Jimmy?" Billy whispered as if afraid to wake her from slumber, falling into Jimmy's solemnity.

"She's cold. Cold as a witch's titty," said Jimmy. "I can't feel any breath. And I can't feel no pulse either." His fingers crawled, skinned and stunted serpents, along the girl's statue neck. "Wait, there it is. It's slow, but she's alive alright, Billy."

"Thank the lord," sighed Billy. "What are we gonna do now, Jimmy?"

"I don't know, Billy. You know we can't tell no-one."

"We have to get her to a doctor or somethin', Jimmy. We can't leave her out here. She'll freeze like a Popsicle."

Jimmy stood. "We ain't takin' her to no doctor, Billy," he said firmly. "They could get a sample of paint from the truck off of her. That's what did cousin Earl. Then where would we be, Billy-boy?"

"There's no paint, Jimmy. There ain't a mark on her. Besides the paint's hidden by six coats of dirt and horseshit," said Billy. "We can't leave her, it'd be murder. I know we ain't no angels, but our mommas didn't raise no killers."

Jimmy became fixed by chilled resonance.

Billy turned into Blue, the 'coonhound pup his father had given him one birthday. It was the only present his daddy had ever given him. It was the only birthday on which his daddy hadn't been in prison.

"I guess we can't," he relented. "It wouldn't be right."

"Can we look after her, Jimmy?" asked Billy excitedly.

"Help me get her to the truck," came the reply.

The two men lifted the girl. She's got no weight at all, thought Billy, helping lay her on the tarp in the flatbed of the pick-up. He thought the girl smiled at him. Just for a second. But her face was deathly still.

All skin and bone, he said to himself, but his eyes accepted the things she showed him. Pert breasts, the almost imperceptible swell of her hips beneath the gossamer skin of her floral summer dress.

Jimmy held the girl in a Karloff stance while Billy tidied the bed. Billy pulled back the red and black check blanket, it smelled of stale sweat and Nachos. The caravan rocked as Jimmy walked to the bed, releasing the girl as if she were a dead leper.

"Careful, Jimmy," blurted Billy. "She could have a subdural haematoma. You don't wanna aggravate one of those."

He tenderly positioned the girl on the bed.

"How old do you reckon she is, Jimmy?"

"I don't know, maybe seventeen or eighteen, maybe older. Ladies these days try real hard to hang on to their youth. Lil' Mary-Lou told me that one of them there Spice Girls was in her forties, so I guess you never can tell."

"Should we undress her?"

"No, Billy, you leave her be," said Jimmy firmly. "We'll see how she is in the morning. Decide for ourselves what's what."

The caravan mimicked the Tilter-Whirl, taking almost a minute to settle after the men had jumped down.

The caravan was in a small clearing - about twenty feet square - in the middle of dense forest. It stood alone about fifteen feet from a chunky log cabin which was complemented by an outhouse and a charred barbecue pit. The lantern above the cabin door barely illuminated the van's gunmetal flank.

"Are you sure she'll be alright in there, Jimmy?" asked the concerned Billy. "I mean it's awful cold. Shouldn't we bring her in with us?"

"We discussed this, Billy-boy. There's only one bed in the cabin, and I don't see why we should waste it on a perfect stranger who probably can't feel nothin' anyways."

Billy ran from Jimmy's side to the cabin, then back again. Jimmy had only moved a few paces from the trailer.

"I feel like Superman, Jimmy. Like I'm on PCP or somethin'. I haven't felt this way since..."

Jimmy slapped Billy. "You know you ain't supposed to talk about that, Billy," he said sternly. "You're just over excited is all. You'll calm down when you've had somethin' hot inside you."

"'Scuse me," grunted Jimmy following his third rumbling fart. He was sitting on a moth-eaten recliner in front of a spitting fireplace and a gun rack. Two stools acquired from Burger Boy, a table and a low double bed, were the only other pieces of furniture in the cabin.

"That was good eatin'," said Billy as he put the pots and plates by the door for the morning. "It wouldn't have been no better if we'd had a rabbit. Or a possum neither."

"Reckon so," concurred Jimmy from his throne. "You know what would make the night's entertainment perfect?"

"I know," smiled Billy.

Jimmy got up from his seat, brushing crumbs from his chest hair. He removed his light blue short-sleeved shirt, and stood before Billy. Jimmy's torso was constructed from rigid muscle, the kind you get from working on the road gang rather than in the gym. A pot belly rose from the lean sinew of his frame, swelling over his thick belt like a balding man's head.

Billy knelt before Jimmy, licking the sweat that melted down his body like butter. Gently, he toyed with the General Lee belt buckle hung low on Jimmy's snake hips. He unfastened it, then unpeeled the other man's once-black jeans. Jimmy kicked the pants away and stood naked, swimming with the fire's amber waves, while Billy playfully licked his balls. Billy savoured the salty tang, feeling Jimmy's excitement grow and nudge his forehead.

Jimmy's cock was something to behold. It was at the top end of average length, but its girth would bring tears to even a working girl's eyes. It was thick and gnarled like a chunk of heavy driftwood. Knobbled veins encircled it like blood-bloated leeches slithering to feast on the fat swollen head. Billy began to flick beneath the head with his tongue the way he knew Jimmy liked, then pressed his lips to the purple monster. They parted, gently allowing Jimmy to ease inside Billy's mouth. The first few times with Jimmy, Billy swore he heard his jaw crackle like bacon.

Jimmy grunted his approval as Billy deep-throated him (Billy having a genetic lack of a gag reflex). After ten minutes he tapped Billy's shoulder. He was ready. Hard and proud like an oak.

Billy quickly removed his clothes, and crouched facing the armchair. He gripped the fabric, feeling the heat, and smelling the damp musk, of Jimmy behind him. Jimmy's coarse, work-roughened hands caressed Billy's slender frame.

"Did you bring the KY?" asked Jimmy quietly.

"Damn, Jimmy, I left it in the pick-up," answered Billy. "I'll run and get it."

"Don't do that candy-boy. It'll just ruin the mood. I'll just butter this bad boy up." Jimmy walked to the table and picked up a half patty of butter left over from dinner. He returned, massaging butter into his cock as if it was an athlete's limb. When his appendage was Thanksgiving basted, he slipped the rest of the butter between Billy's cheeks. The young man stretched like a tired old dog as Jimmy's slick, thick fingers inched inside him, finding his sweet spot.

Jimmy wiped his hand on the chair, then grasped a mane of thick black hair. The first time Jimmy had fucked Billy he may as well have buggered him with his ten inch hunting blade he'd bled so bad. Tonight, after almost two years together (including spells in prison), Billy's puckered hole welcomed Jimmy's dick like a hungry little mouth. Billy cried out, like he always did, as Jimmy rodeo-fucked him.

The girl opened his mind's eye. Alive, eyes closed, twirling in a shallow stream of consciousness. He tried to see beneath the clinging liquid cotton of her grandma dress.

He felt himself growing hard. Let his hand find himself.

It was the first time he'd ever thought of a girl in that way.

When Jimmy's hot load splashed over his back, it was Billy finding release.

Inside her.

Billy scanned the clearing. He had washed away the residue of last night's meal from the plates and utensils in the creek, and had left Jimmy there fishing. He tiptoed to the caravan, which was displaying its oxidising glory in the mid-morning sun. Slowly, like a bomb squad officer on Friday the thirteenth, he opened the door. Some of the water in the corroded pail gripped tightly in his hand splish-sploshed onto the ground. Its icy stream transferred chill to Billy's spine. He leaned in, a child opening the cookie jar twenty minutes before dinner, and could see the girl deep in oblivion.

Sleeping angel.

Billy looked over his shoulder before entering the van. He remained still, transfixed. Watching her. She didn't seem as pale as she had in the milk moonlight. Perhaps she was getting better. The merest trace of sunlight was able to weave itself through the heavy red curtains, causing a blood red half-light to wash over the van's interior.

He moved closer.

After sitting on the bed for a thousand quick heartbeats, he drew back the blanket from the left side of the girl's Lenin still body. His hand moved toward her arm, fine silken down rose.

He pulled back.

He repeated the action four times before allowing his awkward fingertips to kiss the flesh of her arm. She was soft, warm like a puppy's belly. Touching her made Billy feel like he'd ridden the Cyclone twelve times straight. Not breaking the connection, he leaned over her, bringing his face close to her hair. It filled Billy's nose and throat. It occurred to him that she didn't smell like Jimmy, nor any of the men he had shared himself with. She smelled like his mother's lavender soap and bubble gum.

He liked it.

It stirred him deep inside.

In his blood.

Billy felt the need to wash her. To make her clean. The lifeless body on the bed. It seemed like the natural thing to do. Comfortable. Familiar. He tried to remember, back to the time before the doctors in clean white coats took his dreams - his bad, bad dreams - from him.

His mind was flooded with her.

Silently, moist tongue between teeth, he disrobed her. Carefully unfastening buttons one at a time along her length. When he had freed her, he peeled open her dress. Dizzy with anticipation. A child at Christmas.

Open eyes took her in. Her stomach was flat, rippled like the beach at low tide. It needed to be touched. Billy laid his hand on her abdomen. His fingers pulsing, as if each tip bound a racing heart. Her skin was velvet. He explored the shore, each slight ridge, each swept slope. Billy's fingers manoeuvred themselves beneath the waistband of her panties. Soft spirals ensconced his sweat-moistened digits. The underwear was removed, so that both hands could stroke the neat mound of chocolate hair. He traced her sex, a little afraid that it might bite him, then allowed his hands to travel the electric flesh of her torso. He reached her bra. It was the kind with the lace around, and a little pink rose between her breasts. He had to lift her to unfasten it. It took several attempts but, finally, he freed her.

Her breasts were a new wonder. They were just small mounds of flesh, but they captivated him. He touched them. They weren't hard muscle as he had thought. He pressed them, stroked them, entranced as they returned to perfect pertness beneath his over-eager hands. Now he knew what other guys saw in girls.

Water flushed into the bucket as Billy squeezed out his flannel. Tentatively, he lowered it to the girl's naked body. Droplets diffused on her skin until the sodden cloth embraced her. He bathed the girl's stomach, making her glisten like caramel.

"What the fuck are you doing?" roared Jimmy from the doorway.

He slapped Billy across the face, sending him scurrying to the floor.

"I was just..."

"You can't take advantage of a girl like that, Billy, you know that. Don't you realise that you're sexually harassing her?"

"I'm sorry, Jimmy," whined Billy.

"Get out," ordered Jimmy.

"I'll fix her up, Jimmy. I'll take it back."

Jimmy pulled the cowering man to his feet, and hurled him

through the door. Billy's shoulder grazed a rusty hinge, which tore into his shirt and his flesh.

He watched Jimmy roughly dress the girl, his hand held to his weeping injury.

"Promise me you'll never do nothin' like that again, Billy," said Jimmy after he had jumped down from the caravan."You know we just can't afford no more trouble, don't you?"

"Sure, Jimmy. I was just curious I guess. I'm sorry."

"That's ok, partner," said Jimmy softly."Here, let me see that."

Billy removed his hand. His palm was wet with blood. Billy instinctively raised it to his mouth and licked it from his skin, while Jimmy gently examined the ragged tear in his shoulder.

"Is it bad?"

"Nope. It's nothin'," replied Jimmy.

Billy fingered the dressing that Jimmy had bound around his upper arm. He wanted to touch it. To feel the sticky red stuff on his fingers, but he knew that if he picked it it would never heal.

His mind turned to the task in hand. Billy had to collect some firewood – good burning logs not sticks – while Jimmy cleaned the two big catfish he had caught.

He had six good sized pieces bundled in his arms when he was distracted by a fast-cut of fluorescent orange.

Two men, wearing bright orange hunting tabards, stepped from the tree line. Both were in their mid-forties, and about forty pounds overweight. Both were cradling hunting rifles with comically large targeting scopes.

"Hoo-eee boy," called one of the men."You nearly had yourself an unscheduled lead injection. Thought you were that trophy buck we've been chasing all over the state."

"I ain't no trophy buck," said Billy.

"I can see that, boy. But it's a sure bet that you scared him away."

"Good," replied Billy."A buck's too much to eat. Jimmy says you should only kill what you can eat."

"Is this Jimmy a fucking communist or one of them hippie tree-fuckers?"

"No, Jimmy's my friend." Billy was suddenly captivated by the sweat slick red skin of the second man.

Six sticks fell.

It took a moment for the first man to register what had happened to his companion. His mind couldn't comprehend that the handle pressed to the chest of his friend by the young stranger meant that the rest of the knife was inside him. As the man crumpled he saw the silver shark tooth. Then the blood came. A gushing flow of oil-like blood erupted into the stagnant air.

Billy had just wanted to see what would happen if he stuck the man with Jimmy's best hunting blade.

Just curious, that's all.

He liked it.

He liked the gurgling bath draining gasps. The shock swollen eyes. But most of all he liked the steaming river of hot, thick blood.

He pulled the knife out with a soup slurp. Thrust it back into the man's face. Features and structure collapsed around the sharp intruder. A single, detached eye stared back from dripping steel.

"Son of a..." The living hunter could find no words. He levelled his gun at Billy, but lost his footing as it was wrenched from him.

The butt of the gun turned flesh to pulp as Billy hit a succession of home runs on the folding hunter.

The water was cold. Liquid ice. It streamed over Billy's naked chest, deadening skin. It took away the bad stuff.

The dirt.

The sweat.

The blood.

He was tired after doing what he had to do to the two hunter men. Tired but good. Like all you can eat at Denny's, sex with Jimmy, and the first two Star Wars movies mixed together.

He felt like melting into the creek. Drifting away with the current.

There was no time for dreams. He traced the bloody knife across his tongue, before giving the last of the blood to the water.

"Where are you goin', Billy-boy?" called Jimmy when Billy walked past him with a vacant lot stare.

Billy turned. "I have to see her, Jimmy. To tell her. To show her."

"No, Billy. I told you," chastised Jimmy. "Leave that girl be, she's sick." He caught up to his friend. "Come and help me cook the fish. No-one can make catfish taste as good as you."

"No," said Billy abruptly. "I have to see her. She wants me to."

"Listen Billy, get her the fuck out of your head." Jimmy grabbed Billy's arm. "I ain't goin' through this shit again."

Billy knocked Jimmy's arm away. "Then don't." Jimmy came again. He was used to restraining Billy during one of his episodes, but he had never seen him as spaced as he was this time. Billy caught

Jimmy's right arm, twisting it hard behind his back. Forcing him into the barbecue pit, he pressed his knee hard in Jimmy's back. Jimmy spat out the thick black dust as he was shunted down.

"It's Billy's turn to drive now. Why don't you ever let me drive, Jimmy?" Billy tugged down Jimmy's blue jeans, then unfastened his own. He stabbed Jimmy's ass with his cock. Again and again. Jimmy stayed silent. Not making a sound as Billy fucked and grunted with all his being.

Billy smiled when he made him bleed.

When he was done, Billy crushed Jimmy's skull with one of the stones lining the pit.

"It's me," said Billy quietly, moving closer to the girl. "I came back. Like you wanted."

The girl's face remained still, a broken clock.

"I'm the new Billy now. The real Billy," he told her eagerly. "Now we can be together. I wanted it to be you, me and Jimmy, like one big happy family. But that can't be now. No Jimmy. No doctors. No nothin'. Just you and me forever."

Clothes fell from him.

He followed the familiar road of buttons down her body. He opened her, desperate for the reward of sweet young flesh.

It didn't disappoint.

It made his blood course through him, bursting down dams and bridges.

He straddled her. The charged skin of her belly tickled his balls. He felt, saw, her essence rise up to him. Open, a cactus flower, to swallow him. He began to stroke his fledgling erection, massaging it into bloated hardness. He moved his hand faster and faster, furiously, feeling every fibre, every ounce of energy yearning to break free of the flesh.

His fluids spilt over her. He gasped as his own essence coated her stomach and breasts. Falling in beside her, his hot flesh melted into hers.

The twirly girl's eyes slowly blinked open. She stretched bonelessly, a lazy cat full of cream.

The sound of men and dogs filled her ears. Above there was another sound, maybe it was a whirly copter.

She swallowed a spontaneous giggle.

Closed her eyes in comfort.

She knew that someone would take care of her.

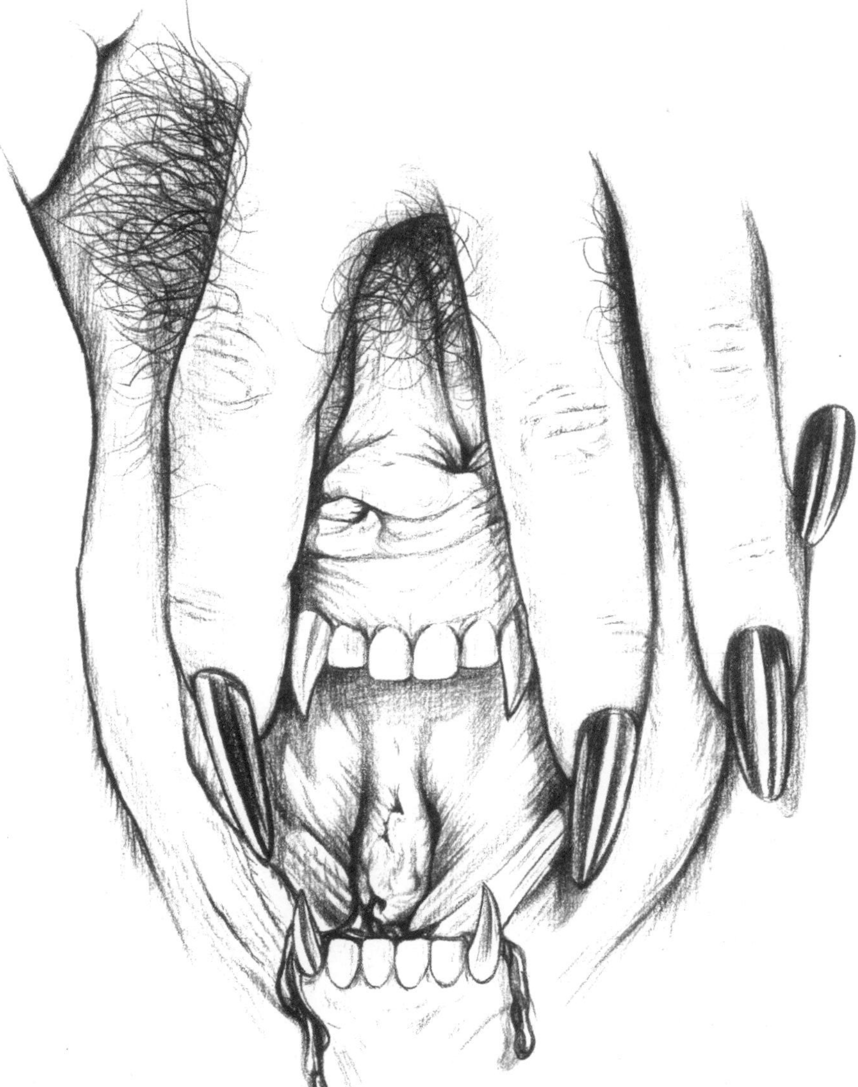

Hungry

Louis Ravensfield

Lust. Sorrow. Silence. Power. Sexy. Pain. Joy. Anger. Ecstasy. Violence. Alert. Desire. Fulfilment. Sex. Blood. Hunger. The Darkness. The Gift. The Curse. The Hunger. Hunger. Feed.

The daylight once again succumbed to the dark, as it is destined to for all eternity, a never ending battle of which there can be no victory for either power. Light will always disperse darkness just as darkness will always blanket the light.

The darkness in the large airy room was penetrated only by a solitary candle which stood in a far corner. Shadows flickered, licked and lapped, dancing on the plain wall as the candle sputtered slightly in the stillness. Impossible to see the windows, for the curtains allowed no light in and none ever escaped. The only visible item of furniture in the room was a huge square structure, hardly perceived in the blackness of the room. A structure of long dark mahogany posts with slats at the top connecting each post dominated the room. Heavy drapes hung from the slats, obscuring any hope of making anything out.

Time. It was time. They would be here in one hour. The bright yellow flame jumped as the still air was jolted by the drapes around the bed being swiftly pushed apart. One hour. Hungry.

The doorbell was just audible over the heavy bass which beat from the speakers. Time. It was time. Excellent. They made it. Terry and Samantha stepped into the brightly lit hallway as they were ushered through the open door. Excellent. Both were young, well, early 30s. Young. She was tall, elegant, neither slim nor large, very pretty, confident, sparkling. Her eyes were blue, bright, sparkling. Smiling. He. Terry. Smiling. Warm, loving, fun. Both. He smart, slightly nervous, attractive, slim not skinny. Hunger. Coats removed and carefully hung up. Samantha. Short red dress, stockings not tights, class. Shoes - sensible, sexy. Hair long, straight, dark brown. Make up - light, complimentary. Terry - clean-shaven, short hair, white shirt, dark grey trousers. Shiny. Shoes are clean and shiny. Relaxed. At ease - drinking - talking - laughter. Relaxed. Two males. One female. Sexy. Lust. Power. Desire. Hunger. Terry. Samantha. Hunger. Fantasy. Samantha. Naked. Bound. Light. Bright. The room is filled with candles, brightness. Terry naked and bound to an X-shaped cross, wrists, ankles bound by leather straps. Facing a double bed covered in white satin sheets. Bright. Light. Lust. Sex. Desire. Hunger. Samantha - fantasy. Terry - fantasy. Samantha to get fucked. Terry to watch. Naked. Bound. Samantha - kissing. Tongue probing, lashing. Hot. Sexy. Lust. Desire. Hunger. Mouth on mouth. Fingers on neck. Caressing. Back of neck. Sensual. Hands moving. Down spine. Stroking thigh, inner thigh. Clawing. Stockings. Dress zip down. Shirt off. Terry watching. Lust. Desire. Hunger. Dress gone. Panties, tiny, damp. Trousers gone. Stroking, touching, feeling. Samantha. Hungry. Bra removed. Tits, firm, round, soft, warm. Squeeze, gently. Nipples, squeeze, pinch. Pain. Lust. Hunger. Nipples pinched, hard. Cock, hard, solid, engorged. Blood. Two cocks. Two stiff, hard pricks, one quivering, untouched, one being stroked, rubbed. Sucking, Suckling. Nipples, pert. Knickers down, pussy shaven, wet, hot, fingers caress clitoris. Hunger. Mouth on cock, mouth on cunt. Licking, sucking, foreskin pulled back, engorged swollen cockhead. Blood. Rubbing, sucking, stroking. Ecstasy. Pussy lips spread, fingers - two - penetrate cunt hole, tongue flicks clitoris. Clit swollen. Cunt wet. Terry, hard cock. Frustration. Turn-on. Legs spread wide. All fours. Samantha. Tongue licks anus, fingers fuck cunt. Samantha wants cock. Cunt wet, slippery. Cock hard, thick, long pierces tight cunt, pushes deep. Terry delirious. Ecstasy. Samantha delirious. Cunt stuffed full of cock. Muscles clench, cock gripped, vice like. Cock thrusts harder, Samantha cries out. Ecstasy. Hunger. Terry begs. Samantha wants to suck cock. Terry's cock, while her cunt is ravaged. Terry, very stiff. Horny. Hungry.

Dildo. Large, black, thick, long. Too long. Too thick. Too large. Cock leaves cunt, cock to mouth. Samantha. Bitch. Suck. Lick. Taste cunt juices. Suck. Harder. Terry. Begs. Harder. Too long. Too thick. Too large. Dildo pushed into hot wet gash. Ecstasy. Cock, wet with saliva, cunt juice, head pushes tiny bud of anus. Pushes. Pain. Ecstasy. Dildo. Cunt. Anus. Cock. Pain. Ecstasy. Hunger. Screams of pleasure. Fucking. Terry, helpless, frustrated, hungry. Starving. Samantha, cumming. Convulsions, cock gripped – fucking anus, cunt gripping dildo – fucking. Fucking. Ecstasy. Pain. Cumming. Cock spurts, pumping anus with fluid. Samantha, screaming, pleasure, fucking, cumming. Dildo, cunt, fucking. Samantha, screaming, pleasure, pain, fucking, hungry. Hunger. Tearing, pleasure, ripping, pain, screams. Samantha, screaming, dildo out of cunt, liquid flows from cunt. Hunger. Blood. Sharp blades, cut pussy lips. Blood flows. Blood. Gushes. Mouth to cunt. Screams. Samantha. Terry. Drink. Fulfilment. Pleasure. Ecstasy. Blood. Hunger. Samantha. Cunt. Hunger. Blood. Gushing. Life. Lust. Power. Torn. Ripped. Bleeding. Blood. Pouring. Drink. Screaming. Pain. Screaming. Terror. Pain. Blood. Hunger. Sobbing. Screaming. Red satin sheets. Terry. Screaming. Samantha. Dying. Terry, cock stiff, dribbling slightly. Samantha. Dead. Lifeless, dragged to Terry's feet. Cock – wanking. Tight grip. Samantha. Dead mouth open. Terry sobbing, screaming, cumming. Ecstasy. Pain. Cum spurting into Samantha's mouth. Arse full of cum. Mouth full of cum. Fantasy. Cunt full of blood. Body full of death. Reality. Candles burning low. Traffic outside.

The room is bare, except for satin sheets on a bed, white spattered red. A naked man is tied to an X-shaped cross, sobbing. A dead woman lies at his feet. And somewhere outside a battle is won for a few hours, as the light of a new day disperses the darkness of another uneventful night...

The Gift

Louisianax E. M. Caliban

It would be a white Christmas, it seemed. The air outside was laced with snowflakes, and a thin coating had already begun to cover the rooftops. From the dark night sky it fell softly, resting on the window-sill and melting slowly.

The room was warm and comfortable, the air heavy with the blended aromas of sandalwood and musk. Incense cones stood on every available shelf, and the only light came from a small oil lamp which cast eerie shadows into the depths of the ceiling. The bed was large and soft and square, draped in black satin sheets which were cool and slippery to the touch. The pillows were a feathered dream to die for.

Into the room walked a man, his shoulders fallen, at ease, his long dark hair framing a face which told a thousand intimate tales. His eyes were filled with lamplight and dull fire. His lips were wet and stained with red wine; his large hands still held a crystal goblet, empty now but for a drop of blood-like liquid, thin and bitter-sweet. His clothing was loosened: his shirt fallen astray from his waistband and his belt open. With an apathetic glance he surveyed the world outside, delicate patterns of snow spattered against the window framing the view like a picture postcard. Come tomorrow, the snow would be thick enough to play in, and the kids would be out screaming and laughing, torturing each other with handfuls of ice. His lips curled derisively and he turned away to face the room.

His eyes focussed on the lamp for a moment, and then strayed to the darker corners of the room where tiny pinpricks of smouldering light picked out the edges of books and statuettes in a curious bas-relief. This room held many memories, most of which he preferred to keep hidden away where they caused him the least pain.

He sank down onto the bed and set the goblet onto the floor. The satin sheets whispered beneath his weight and the pillows subsided under his elbows. The cloying taste of the wine, the warmth of the room, and the heady perfume of the incense lulled him into a dream state, and thence into a swooning sleep. As his eyelids drooped somnolently, and his breathing slowed, a vision came to him, a vision made more real by the presence entering the room which he could neither see nor sense...

It was her! With the certainty of the entranced he knew it. He could sense her presence, could feel her closeness. She was in this very room, and he knew what she wanted. Intimacy. Blood. He could almost taste her lips before she touched him, and although he feared it, somehow the expectation had roused him to a state of almost unbearable excitement. He could feel the hot blood rushing to his cock, could feel it swollen and engorged with lust and need and urgency. He wanted to cry out, but she would come to him soon enough, he knew. There was no need to beg her, for she would come. "Please..." The word came out anyway, his voice high and breathless with the contemplation of what was to happen next.

"Patience, little one." Her voice was like a choir of angels, so why did he feel so afraid? What was it about that innocent little voice which struck terror and desire deep into his heart and soul? "You know the rules."

"Oh Goddess, yes, I know, I know..." His eyes peered into the velvet darkness, but he could see nothing. It was as if he had been struck blind. "Show yourself, please." He was almost whining, but he no longer cared if he sounded pathetic. Let her but come close enough and he would prove how strong and virile he was. That thought made his balls tighten, and he feared that he would come too soon. But no, she would not let that happen. She was somehow in control of him, even when she was not even touching him. In such complete control...

Suddenly she was there, and he could see again the pale, luminous beauty of her body. She was naked and perfect. The gown of raven black had fallen down around her tiny feet, and she stood exposed to him in all her glory. His eyes burned with the sight of her, and his mouth was suddenly hot and dry. Her face he scarcely looked at, it hardly mattered at all, but her body...The texture of her skin was flawless, its colour so pale as to be almost deathly. The globe of her shoulders was smooth, her breasts firm and round, though not so very large. The dusky rose of the areola looked so damned inviting, and he wanted so much to kiss her there, to make her tremble with desire. Her stomach was slightly rounded, and the dimple of her navel was decorated with a tiny amethyst stud. In the angular contours of her hips he could see the veins, thick and blue and hard against her skin. Her arms and legs were long and willowy, giving her an impression of great height, although in reality he knew she was far shorter than he. The elvine petiteness of her hands and feet merely accentuated the illusion of height, giving her an air of something otherworldly. When he looked too long at her face, he felt convinced she could not be real, so he shied away from doing so. There was something in her violet eyes that could kill passion before it had even begun, he knew that from bitter experience. It did not seem to anger her that he could not meet her gaze, that he stared only at her torso. She seemed to think it proper that way.

But, oh, the beauty of her was consummated in the most secret part of her. She was unlike any other woman he had ever known. Where women had thick, tangled, matted, ugly hair, she was smooth and naked and soft; where women hid themselves behind their hands or wrapped something quickly around themselves to cover their nudity, she stood proudly forward to be admired. There was an essence in her which drove the imagination wild. Even had she been fully clothed he would have wanted her, but naked she was worthy of nothing less than adoration. His Goddess. The mound of Venus, usually disguised under an ugly blanket of wiry down was unusually prominent on her, and its soft lusciousness reminded him of nothing more than a ripe juicy fruit, ready for the tasting. She stood with her legs slightly parted so he could see beyond the mound to the dark, blood-filled labia which curved inwards as though they were in truth lips puckered for a prim kiss. But demureness was not a quality easily associated with her, and if those lips were to do any kissing they would probably bite and gnash and gnaw with it. They were the Freudian shark's mouth encapsulated.

And then he saw it again, the part he always seemed to forget, the one element of her which startled him every time he saw it: the tiny ring which pulled the inner lips of the opening together. As she swayed her hips gently, the light caught the ring and the jewels strung through her labia sparkled invitingly. She was moist already there, and he could smell her fragrance now even though she still stood some feet away.

"Come to me," he whispered, trying to rise but feeling as though his body were weighted down with lead. "Please..."

Her feet made no sound as she approached him, and he watched in avid delight as her toes curled in the soft fibres. Her toenails were long and curved and painted a vivid scarlet, and they seemed to slice the material of the carpet at every step. Every movement she made seemed destructive in some way, but that only added to her dark yet pellucid beauty.

She reached the bed and bent over him so that her nipples were almost in his open mouth. The heat of his breath made them stiffen and grow, and he lashed out with his tongue to caress first one and then the other. She whimpered softly, a fragile, feminine sound which ill-suited her mastery of this situation, but which fed his masculine ego very well. But he knew better than to touch her, to try to embrace her, before she was ready. Like a cat, she would only allow such intimacy on her terms; like a cat, if he took things too fast for her she would spit and scratch and launch herself across the room and away from him forever. His tongue drew wet circles around her nipples, provoking the same soft cry. Inclining his head gently he enclosed one of the firm peaks in his mouth, and applied a slight pressure by sucking. This seemed to be within acceptable boundaries, so he tried it again, a little harder. The sound which escaped her lips this time was louder, wilder. She twitched subtly away from him, her lips parted and moist.

"I won't hurt you," he promised. "I swear on my life." Somehow her silence made him think that if he offended her that would indeed be the price she demanded of him. "Please come closer. Lay next to me." He felt wretched without the closeness of her, cold and alone.

She climbed onto the bed and curled up close to him, a curiously passive motion, as though she were ready to sleep. She wrapped her limbs about herself in a mock foetal position, and huddled against him. Her cool knees rested against the raging hunger of his stiff cock and he cried out. The temptation to fling his arms around her, to throw her onto her back, to make mad, wild, abandoned love to her helpless body was so strong that it threatened to tear him apart. And yet he knew the rules, and he would not dare offend her. She might be passive now, but he knew she had a much wilder side, a feral ferocity which was terrifying to witness.

Her body seemed so cold and he drew the covers up over them both. She smiled slightly, seeming to like this attention. He risked a gentle touch on the shoulder. She moaned gently, her lips apart. If something didn't happen soon he wasn't going to be able to control it. He felt about ready to burst and he wanted so badly to come, inside her, all over her, soon it wouldn't matter. That locked cunt of hers would be so warm and so wet inside, and it would be simplicity itself to ease his large, swollen cock into her, to feel it sink inside her right up to the hilt, to feel her shuddering and quivering, to feel the walls of her cunt tense and then relax as he filled her, to feel the snug closeness of her womb begging for his seed. If she didn't start it up soon, he would have to risk offending her, have to take her by force or just wank it all off over her cold, imperious face...

And then she was upon him. As though reading his impure thoughts she sprang to her knees and threw herself across him, straddling him with one leg either side of his hips. The huge red cock stood between them, thrashing and dancing with a life all of its own. She smiled to see it, and a knowing look came into her amethyst eyes. Without a word she sank upon it, her wide mouth opening to receive its swollenness. Her lips were painted the same scarlet as her nails and the sight of that bloody mouth eating up his firm cock nearly drove him out of his mind. He felt once more as if he would come, but she gripped the base of his cock so hard with her hand that the desire to let go fled him. The pain was over instantaneously, and he thanking her silently for stopping the eruption. It was far too soon. She always had such wonderful control over what he did, how he reacted. As though she could tell when it was getting close, and when he could no longer control it himself.

She began to move once more, her red lips sliding up and down his monumental erection, sometimes licking around the head and gently under the foreskin, sometimes taking the whole of the shaft into her mouth and deep into her throat. Several times he felt the climax coming, forceful and resolute, but each time she grasped him tightly until the urgency subsided. He damn near wept to keep coming so close, and never actually spurting. It was a wonderful feeling, the sensation of her lips and her tongue all around him that way, but it was also incredibly frustrating to be stopped just before the peak like a recalcitrant schoolboy getting caught slipping a quick one off behind the bike sheds. White anger began to build inside him and he begged her to put an end to his misery, begged her to allow the orgasm.

But she would not. The more he pleaded, the more she squeezed and licked and mastered him utterly. And then, when the anger began to break out, she pulled rapidly away from him and sat back on his thighs, her eyes dark and baleful, glaring thoughtfully down at him. His face was suffused with blood, and his lips were trembling with thwarted passion. His cock throbbed and ached, the veins standing out like blue ropes under the roseate skin. His self-control was remarkable, but he was losing it fast. His hands were clutching at the sheets, trying not to stray to his cock and finish it off himself. She knew what had to be done now, that the moment had almost come to end it.

With one swift movement she clambered up the bed to rest with her distended labia right over his perspiring face. The tiny ring which held her inner lips together was tantalisingly close to his mouth, the string of jewels which swung from it tickled his chin. The anger crested in him and he longed to tear it from her, to rip her labia to shreds just so he could force his huge cock right up inside her and laugh at her screams. "Do it," she murmured, her voice gentle and caressing as silk. "Please do it. Set me free." His teeth reached out for the end of the jewelled string and he tugged viciously. With a loud shriek somewhere between pain and delirious pleasure the ring came out, slicing through the delicate skin of the vulva and letting loose a thin stream of hot blood which spattered onto his face. He spat out the ring and lapped at the blood. Reaching up closer to her he enclosed the clitoral wound with his mouth and took the blood directly from it. How delicious she tasted! It was nectar: the blood and the lubricant juice of her freed cunt mixed together into a heady cocktail which exploded on the back of his tongue and burned all the way down to his stomach. Good Goddess, nothing had ever felt this good before!

"I want you now," he whispered, slipping his tongue up into the warm sticky passage of her cunt. "Please don't deny me. Let me fuck you."

For a moment she seemed to hesitate and then the decision was made. Before he even had time to catch his breath she had sunk down onto him, swallowing his cock deep inside her cunt and holding it there with all her strength. She began to move against him slowly, oh so slowly! Painfully slow for him, finding her own pace and rhythm. He was losing control again, but the pressure of her labia closing on him worked as well as the pressure of her hands or her mouth, and the stress flowed temporarily away again. He was astounded at the way she could control him, at the way she kept it going for them both. She was an incredible creature, more real than any dream.

When she was ready for it she released the pressure on his cock and he felt the climax building up yet again. Seizing the initiative, sensing that to do so now would not be unwelcome, he clasped his arms around her and rolled her over. She lay still, looking patiently up at him with a passivity which threatened his control once again. She gave no indication of it, but he could feel the tension rising in her body, in company with his, and this time when the climax approached she did not seek to withhold it from him, but rather let hers swell with his. He came with an explosion of starlight, a shattering cataclysm of ecstasy which seemed to go on forever. For the first time in his life he actually felt the spunk spurting from him and burning its way inside her. Each individual seed seemed to have a psychic connection to his brain, and he felt each movement with a clarity which literally blew his mind. The moan that escaped his lips was long and feral and exhausted.

And then she felt it too. Her body arched up against his, the rich warm spunk flooding deep into her womb, and her whole cunt contracted around his cock. She seemed to be crushing his weakening cock, striving to extract every last drop of maleness from him, and as she milked him so aggressively the climax came to her, and everything inside her tensed and convulsed in delirium, once, twice, thrice... and then she fell away from him, spunk and sticky cunt juice pooling with the blood still leaking from her clitoris.

With no more than a vulpine smile she murmured a brief blessing, and was gone...

The man awoke with a start. It had been so real, the way that dream always was. But this time it had been different. This time he had actually got inside her, actually penetrated her. And this time he had looked into her face as she said goodbye.

With a shock of pleasure he noticed the cool stickiness of his spunk all around him. Yes, know this sensation well. The dream always did this for him. But he had really made love to her this time, really pushed his cock up inside her and fucked her. He sighed heavily and slid his arms behind his head. I fucked her, he thought happily. Fucked the mystery dream woman, after all this time of being denied. He'd been having that dream for years, and never before had it been this vivid, this real...

Then his fingers closed around something beneath the pillows, and a gasp of terror clutched at his throat. Something cool and round, with a thin thread of smooth stones hanging from it, something which was warm and fleshy at the other end. Unable to stop himself he drew the object forth and stared at it. Yes, there was the ring, and there were the jewels, and there, still dripping blood, was the fleshy fold of skin he had torn from her cunt in the dream. And as he fell in horror into a dead faint, he realised that the flesh was still moving...

Crucifixation

Craig Giles

He sat in a large dark oak chair. He was totally alone. The silence in the room, indeed the whole house, was almost deafening. It was dark and dim but for six candles standing in the centre of the huge dining table at which he sat. The candles flickered gently in the silent air. Everything else was still and calm and such a contrast from the tormented visions spinning through his twisted and hurt mind. His heart was broken, but more still than that. It was shattered beyond belief and totally irreparable.

He leaned forward to a glass resting next to a half full bottle on the table. He took up the glass and sipped slowly at the dark red liquid within. He drained the glass, poured himself another, downed it in one swallow, refilled the glass again and set it down by the side of the now nearly empty bottle. He glanced around the room but did not take in much. Partly because it was so dark – although his nocturnal sight could easily adjust to this – but also because there were other things on his mind. The once roaring fire to his right was struggling to stay alight, through lack of attention. He just sat there alone and totally disconsolate.

He thought of the day the Witchfinder General and his scum cronies had dragged his only love, Richelle, from her bed while he slept in his crypt below. Oh, how he cursed his vampire nature which made him helpless as they took her kicking, screaming for their so-called trial. He heard her cries of pain and heartbreak as she was beaten and tortured then burned at the stake. A sweet innocent who had fallen in love with an immortal; that was her only crime.

The huge door at the back of the room creaked open slowly behind him. A slight draught eased through the room like a deathly ebony sigh. The candles flickered more violently and regained their composure.

The door had been closed behind the intruder, who was now leaning back against it lasciviously licking her lips, as she stood in the dark looking longingly at him.

He sat there knowing, but unconcerned by her presence, for he was still encased in the private hell of his own complex mind. He knew what she wanted but he knew that he had ultimate control over her.

Although he had baptised her into his vampiric way of life or un-death, and therefore prided himself on knowing her thoughts, desires and aspirations, she did have her own feelings. They were always kept well hidden, so well hidden that not even he could sense them. He knew her feelings of lust for him - and indeed many other men both mortal and immortal. Of course he did. After all what is lust but basic and carnal. The need to fornicate can be felt and experienced by anyone whether alive or undead. Mortals indulge and practice but never truly experience, not fully... like a vampire.

Yet deep down inside her darkest inner self, she knew she loved him utterly. She so wanted to be his, instead of his brother's - the Neanderthal, Jacob.

She moved from the door now, stepping ever so slowly towards him, her long purple skirt trailing along the floor around her bare feet as she glided effortlessly through the room to where he sat motionless in the candlelight at the table. When she finally reached him, she raised her elegant hand and rested it on his shoulder where his long golden hair lay. She eased his hair from his shoulder and the side of his face and gently whispered his name. "Janos."

He gave no reaction at all, he did not even glance. He just stared straight ahead into the flames of the candles and the melting wax dripping down their length to the tabletop.

"Janos?" Again she spoke, but more questioningly and a little more forcibly.

"What do you want?" he mumbled quietly in a broken voice hardly befitting one of his stature and capabilities.

She moved around to his left slightly to stand at his side, almost but not quite in front of him. Still a little unsure.

"What's wrong, my Lord?" she asked in her softest, most innocent velvet voice, her large brown eyes searching for some or any kind of emotion in his pale face. But all she could see was some sort of grief or loss in his eyes, and also in the air about him in this half-light. She peered down deeper into those eyes. They stood out even more than usual tonight. He had always had amazing, hypnotically amber eyes, but now they were bordered by a glowing redness which contrasted greatly against his oh so pale skin and dark eyebrows.

She must be mistaken, a trick of the light she guessed. But no, she could be mistaken no longer. This great and powerful vampire, master of all he surveyed, beast of the night, he who could have anyone or anything his black heart desired, sat alone in a room crying like an infant. He could be vicious, ruthless, cruel and heartless. No-one but Richelle had ever got close to him, and she so desperately wanted to. And yet here he was with the unmistakable pain of spent tears in his eyes.

"Richelle? Surely you must have known it would only be a matter of time before they came and took her from you. You should stick with your own... kind," she said with an almost mocking tone in her voice. A very dangerous game.

He glanced to his left where she stood, and looked up only briefly at her half gloating, half concerned face. She was a very beautiful creature in spite of her nasty streak (or maybe that just made her more alluring!) Still with the look of a twenty year old as she was when he turned her. Long dark hair in curls, hanging down over her shoulders, pale skin even paler than his own. Yet she somehow always had, or seemed to have, the youthful, embarrassed blush of an innocent young girl in her cheeks, though she was now well into her second century! But this just explains the ease with which she found willing young men to seduce... and then kill.

"Leave me alone. I don't want to hear your taunts, Emma."

"No, I want to stay with you." She smiled with the most erotic look in her eye that she could possibly manage.

"I said leave me!" His brow furrowed as he became angry at her intruding on his private thoughts. He raised his left arm between the two of them as if to stop any intended approach. She took hold of his arm and held his broad hand in her much smaller, slender hands. She stooped her head to kiss his knuckles lightly, and stroked the back of his hand against her smooth silken cheek.

She straightened herself up a little and uncurled his loosely clenched fist, turning his hand slightly to face her and placing his palm on her breast as she begged: "Take me tonight, Janos."

He gazed at her, squeezed gently on her breast as she just sighed, then he released his slight grip and withdrew his hand. She looked down at this intense creature and she now considered this as a bizarre challenge.

"Let me take her place. I will give you all the pleasures of the flesh you could possibly desire," she purred.

"You are not worthy to be mentioned in the same breath as my beloved Richelle, and you never will be," sneered Janos.

A moment of hurt crossed her brow, then undaunted she took a step back and unbuttoned her creamy white blouse, pulled it from the waist of her skirt and let it slip over her almost moon-silver shoulders. As she stepped forward again she let it fall to the ground. Her hair looked even darker as it cascaded down onto the glorious naked flesh of her ivory skin.

She knelt down by his side, the candlelight dancing beautifully on her ripe, slightly upturned, firm breasts. Still he looked into the nothingness ahead of him. She leaned forward now towards him and her right breast rested gently on the back of his hand. He waited for a second or two then pulled his hand away again. This time he rested it in his lap. She felt that in his hesitation he must be succumbing to her obvious charms, and so a small victory was hers. With this in mind she pushed a little harder. She had seduced a great many men in her time, and she knew exactly and instinctively how to please and tease male and sometimes female flesh to amazing heights of both ecstasy and pain.

She stood up again, this time unlacing the side of her skirt and letting it drop on the floor. She had an absolutely stunning figure, lithe and elegant, not a hint of excess anywhere on her wonderful physique. Long graceful legs with strong firm thighs, up to her hips and slim waist. A perfect, flat, taut stomach and smooth abdomen which she was in a way proud of because Janos had many times remarked upon how beautiful he thought it was. Especially when he was kissing her from head to toe then back up again as he made his way to the thin stripe of pubic hair at the centre of her femininity, which he could spend an eternity kissing, licking, stroking and caressing. He took such pride and joy in sending her into spasms of delight and rapture and then near fits of orgasm: oh! how wonderful he used to think it was to have her writhing around inflamed with passion above him at his merest touch or caress of his tongue. But... then Richelle.

But that was a lifetime ago it seemed, too long ago she thought. Now she just had to put up with the pathetic fumblings of his younger brother. But what could she do? Janos would never love her the same way she loved him. Once upon a time maybe, who knows, but not now, not after Richelle. That bitch Richelle.

So she just pretended that the occasional lust filled encounter between them meant more than it really did. It had been a long time since their last coupling, yet here she was in his great hall naked.

She stepped out of her discarded skirt and sat on the edge of the great table. She swung her long legs around the end of the table and positioned herself directly in front of Janos. The tips of her fine porcelain breasts stood about two feet directly in front of his face, nipples erect.

She continued her attempted enchantment by placing first her left then her right foot on the huge arms of the chair either side of him. He avoided contact with her eyes, she knew she was now winning this battle of wills. Her hand moved up to her mouth where she licked a couple of fingers, moved them down and stroked her right nipple until it was as hard as stone. Then she moved her hand slowly, ever so slowly down to her sex, lazily sliding her fingers up and down her moistening entrance with her head tossed back as she moved her fingers occasionally inside herself.

Now he finally looked up at her and into her eyes. She smiled dreamily at him. He stayed expressionless as she continued to masturbate slowly until he could stand no more.

"Enough of this, whore!" he snarled.

He jumped up suddenly, pushing back the enormous heavy chair with such force that it flew across the room. Having rested much of her weight on the chair's arms she fell forward into his arms. She held onto him thinking he had surrendered to her. But this was not what he wanted. He grabbed her forcefully by the arms and pleaded with her one last time with yet more tears in his eyes. "Just leave me alone, Emma. Please." His voice was almost at breaking point now.

"But I can make you feel better, just like I used to. Please won't you let me try?" She smiled and tried to stretch up to kiss him, but he was too tall for her to reach.

His patience finally snapped, he could take this no longer. The beast within him broke free and showed itself. He glared at her as she stood helplessly in his vice-like grip. He snarled at her and bared his murderously vicious teeth, his fangs fully developed and ready to rip out any throat he so desired.

"If that is what you so crave, then who am I to deny you?" he bellowed at her. He threw the bottle and glass from the table, then lifted her effortlessly and threw her onto the table. She lay there naked and trembling, a little scared, a little nervous but also a little excited. She was pleased that she could still provoke such passion in him. He ripped off his own clothes and climbed onto the table above her, then paused over her, face to face, then tenderly he kissed her eyes, cheeks and lips. Next he worked slowly down her body, over her fine body, as he had done so many times before.

He gradually moved over her supple flesh, exploring every possible inch, kissing and moulding the pliant flesh of her breasts, leaving pink scars in the wake of his sharp fingernails. She writhed and panted, more breathless with every touch. Lower still he moved over her soft belly and taut abdomen, which he loved so much, to inhale the inflaming musk of her sex. The more she moved the deeper he probed into the hidden depths of her cunt, her inner flesh, wet and warm like freshly slaughtered meat. Hungrily he ate.

She moaned, she panted, but more - much more - was still to come. His tongue like a frenzied cobra seemed to seek out every hidden delight within her most secret place. As she was at the pinnacle of climax he stopped, and moved back up the table and kept moving until he sat astride her breasts, his erection of cold solid flesh just in front of her face.

That lascivious smile returned to her face as she lifted her head and took him in her mouth. As she did so he was leaning over and behind her on the table to where the candlesticks stood in the middle of the table. He picked one up and snapped it easily in half. Emma lay unconcerned, giving all her attention to the beast in her mouth, not aware of the horror about to befall her. Janos took her hand and pulled it back to the table, from where she had been stroking him, then plunged the sharp end of the candlestick through her palm and deep into the old oak table. Pain seared through her hand.

She released his cock at once and screamed in agony, just as Janos jumped off the table and took another candlestick. He repeated his vicious actions on her other hand on the other side of the table. Again she howled like a banshee.

So there she lay pinned to the table by two broken candlesticks still fully lit! A twisted crucifixion. Still the rage in him did not cease. Still naked and more erect than ever he climbed back onto the table between her alabaster thighs and plunged himself into her to the hilt. She yelped again as tears streamed down her cheeks. He pounded away at her and moved to kiss her throat. He grazed skin with his razor sharp fangs then pushed firmly to puncture the flesh. He fed on her.

'Ah!' he thought. 'The blood of a vampire... nectar. A fitting end for you Emma. For you test the patience of a saint.'

She lay there helpless at this double penetration as he slowly drained her unlife down his throat, knowing she would be nothing now but a lifeless husk. He raised his jaws from her throat and let her final mouthful of existence rain down onto her now motionless body in a crimson flood. As he withdrew from her sex he looked down at her as she lay, pinned to the table.

A female vampire posed as a naked, blood-soaked crucified messiah.

He got down from the table and stepped back looking at what he had done. As her life ebbed away he retrieved his fallen chair and sat back as before, the grotesque scene still displayed in front of him.

"I vow from this day forward that I, Lord Janos, will avenge the murder of my beloved Richelle. I will destroy any witchhunter, priest, holy man or mere mortal that stands in my way. Until I find the Witchfinder General himself who took my love I will bathe in the crimson blood and tears of all those who oppose me. I do this for Richelle and all the innocents who have suffered beatings, torture and abuse in the name of their so-called merciful God. From this day forward, and ever more, so be it!"

The Gentle Art of Betrayal

Beverley Lee

I saw him the moment I entered the bar, sitting in a corner alcove, absentmindedly turning his glass around in his elegant fingers, watching the ice cubes float in the amber liquid. Southern Comfort, I guessed. What else would you drink on Bourbon Street?

Checking my reflection in the mirrors behind the bar I eased my way through the crowd. He knew I was approaching but didn't raise his eyes until I was standing by the table.

"Amias, how are things?" he enquired politely. Treading on eggshells, Jordan, why?

"Things," I replied. "Are very good indeed." I flashed him my most charming smile. This seemed to have a calming effect on him and he relaxed visibly.

"May I sit down?" He moved along the seat, creating an empty space.

The waitress appeared and placed an ice-cold bottle of beer in front of me. I gave her a $5 note, stating no change. I didn't want any interruptions.

"Did you and Marco have an argument?" I asked him.

"No, nothing like that. There's only so much digging about in ancient relics a guy can take." He grinned sheepishly.

"Of course, Marcus is there too." I instantly understood. Visions of Marco and Marcus enthusing for hours about a Renaissance painting. Poor Jordan, he was just a 20th century boy.

And quite delectable, I pondered...

I watched as he moved his lips in time to the words of U2, strumming his fingers on the table, his pale hair glowing, almost white under the lights. Marco's only child and Marco was thousands of miles away in a dusty cellar with Marcus. Not that Marcus wasn't beautiful too. Of course he was, I made him.

The tempo of the music changed, a haunting ballad.

"Dance?" Jordan stood up and reached out his hand, his eyes locked into mine, dazzling orbs of amethyst light. I took his hand and he led me onto the dance floor. Shocked is not an emotion I am used to feeling, but at this moment in time, it summed up my feelings completely.

The music was soft, seductive, it wrapped itself around us as we moved into each other's arms. Jordan pulled me closer and now we were together, our bodies pressed tightly as the dance floor filled with other couples. This was a gay bar, so our togetherness provoked nothing more than jealous glances.

Jordan's hands found their way under my leather waistcoat, just a thin cotton covering between them and my skin. "You're very forward," I whispered into his ear, noting the way his hair curled into the nape of his slender neck.

"I like your company, Amias," he replied. "Why take all night when we both know why we agreed to meet?" His honesty impressed me.

"Marco will have me burnt at the stake if I molest his precious fledgling." I ran my lips softly over his cheek. I heard him gasp.

"I believe you have someone at home, a few blocks away from here, who will be none too pleased to see us together like this." Jordan said. "At least Marco is on the other side of the world."

Stefen... for the first time tonight I thought of him. He had declined Jordan's invitation, preferring instead to watch a re-run of an old film on TV. Stefen would never have been seen in this bar, would never have made the first move, he shied away from mortal crowds.

But in my arms tonight was this new born vampire of the times, my dark brother Marco's child, and the way he was pressing his hips into mine and digging his fingers into my back I knew he was more than willing.

The music faded out gently, Jordan pulled away slightly. "Come on, let's hunt, I'm starving!"

The look on my face stopped him in his tracks. "Amias?" A faint frown creased his face, his skin was still mobile, still human, the marble visage of the older vampires was a long way ahead of him.

I slipped my arm through his as we headed for the door."I'm just used to hunting alone," I answered."Stefen is not one who enjoys company at his meal table." Jordan nodded, understanding immediately.

It was a clear, beautiful night, myriads of stars twinkled above us like tiny ice chippings on a black velvet carpet. Quickly we made our way to the edge of the Quarter, Jordan's face held an air of expectation, and his lovely eyes were gleaming fiercely. I could hear his heartbeat quicken as we slipped into an alley on Esplanade.

It wasn't long before dinner arrived in the shape of a young boy about 18 years of age, a native of New Orleans, taking a short cut all the tourists are warned against. His mind was full of a recent disagreement with his flatmates; he had come out to clear his head. Bad move.

I stayed in the shadows watching as Jordan stepped out in front of him. The boy jumped back in fright and then as his eyes met Jordan's the colour visibly drained from his face, his mouth fell open, his body seemed paralysed. Jordan had obviously decided to introduce himself in the true manner of the vampire myth. His fangs were bared and he snarled at the boy, "Welcome to your worst nightmare." In a split second he had the victim pinned by his throat against the alley wall."Dinner is served, my Prince," he said, as I stepped out from the shadows. The boy uttered a guttural moan as he realised there were two of us. I watched fascinated as Jordan severed the boy's jugular with one bite. Immediately the scent of the blood hit me like a tidal wave. Jordan's mouth was over the wound and I could almost feel the sensation as the hot elixir pumped into his mouth. Then he held out his hand and pulled me towards the boy.

I lowered my head to the boy's neck and as Jordan broke free I closed my mouth on the still pumping wound. As the blood filled my mouth I had my eyes on Jordan who was leaning against the wall with the most contented expression on his face. This cat had had his cream.

The boy's death was quick, I think he died of fright. My appetite was satisfied as I had fed earlier on in the evening. Quickly we disposed of his body in the murky depths of the Mississippi, it would not be found for weeks and by then no one would know how he had died.

The streets were almost deserted as we cut through the Old

French Market, I knew our steps were leading us to Royale and my town house. I also knew that this was when Stefen went to feed, the house would be empty. A question was burning away in the back of my mind, 'Why are you taking him back to the house you share with Stefen?' And the answer came back each time as loud and clear as a bell, 'Because you want to, Amias, that's why, and isn't it a little exciting that maybe you might be discovered?' I pushed this thought away. God and the Devil help me if Stefen found me in Jordan's arms.

The house was in complete darkness; I scanned for signs of life, and found nothing.

"You have a beautiful home," Jordan said, as we entered the drawing room. He walked silently across to the window overlooking the patio, pulling the lace curtains aside, he seemed to scan the darkness.

"Let's go outside, Amias. I want to feel the night air on my face." He raised his eyes, looking at me with a strange expression on his face. I went to him, putting my arm around his shoulder.

"Something bothering you, Jordan?" I asked.

"No." He rested his head on my chest. "I can't quite believe I'm here with you and you're all mine tonight." He ran his fingers softly over my cheek. I shivered in anticipation of the night's sport. "No regrets, Amias, what we do tonight is to live for the moment." As our lips touched I felt him tremble, his skin still warm from the kill. Jordan, the forbidden fruit, and mine for the taking.

I ran my tongue over his lips. They tasted slightly salty, a remnant of our midnight feast. I could feel my desire for him rising. "This is pure lust, my child," I murmured. "Pure physical, animal attraction. You are delicious." Again I licked his lips. He seemed frozen; his voice came in a whisper. "And you're such a beautiful beast." His arms were around me then, his hands roughly tangled in my hair, but the pain was like a drug.

"Outside," he panted. "I want you outside!"

I gathered him up in my arms and was through the back entrance in seconds.

Putting him down on the rough-hewn stones, I thought I sensed a presence. I held my breath. Nothing. Just the sweet, warm air moving in the magnolia trees.

"Now, where were we?" I questioned, a wicked smile on my face.

Jordan was standing by the wrought iron rail that ran up the side of the house, to the upper balcony.

"Come and get me," he growled, his eyes smouldering like

embers. Needing no other invitation, I approached him menacingly. I made my face emotionless. "You're playing with fire, Jordan, and vampires shouldn't get burnt."

My need for him was growing; the ache in my groin had become urgent. Steady, Amias, you're not thinking straight tonight.

Pressing him against the railing I ran my hand up the inside of his thigh, stopping before I reached the top. His breathing was coming in short bursts; his eyes had a deeper shade to them, almost sapphire. I felt his hands unfastening the front of my shirt, then the belt on my jeans.

I groaned out loud. This was one hell of a roller coaster ride.

I kissed him again. Immediately he opened his mouth, inviting my tongue to explore. I could feel the points of his fangs grazing my tongue as our passion increased. He had one of my hands in his, and he had turned and pushed my back into the railings. Why Jordan, you want to be the dominant one tonight, does Marco let you take the lead?

Suddenly I felt a cold bracelet encircle my wrist and in a second a sharp click. Jordan pulled away.

I found I had been handcuffed to the railing.

"This is the start of my game, Amias, do you still want to play?" His voice was rough. I knew I could free myself if I wanted to, but how would I explain to Stefen how I had wrecked the railing?

No, I wanted to play this game as well.

He stood before me, glorious in his passion, his face flushed, his hands on his hips. The night breeze played with his hair. Baby hair, so pale and soft.

"You do realise, Mr. Wilde," I told him. "That when I'm free from here I'm going to fuck you senseless." I flashed him my most alluring smile.

"That I am in no doubt about, Monsieur!" He laughed. "But first…." He produced a black scarf from his jacket pocket. "We're playing my rules, yes?"

I let him blindfold me without uttering a word. My mind had gone into overdrive. If these were the kind of games he played with Marco I was stunned. But I knew from Marco, that when Jordan was mortal, Marco had made him act out sex with men and women, so I knew Jordan was very much a child of the sexual revolution. I felt a twinge of jealousy, how warm my nights would be if my dark angel were so bold.

"Don't say a word, my Lord," he whispered in my ear. "Death is for living, and there's so much to drink of." The scent of blood. Then his wrist against my mouth. Temptation, and I took it. "Slowly, slowly," he soothed. I relented a little, my senses were swimming, and the act of being blindfolded had heightened them all to a point where I felt like I was drowning.

I felt his other hand on the zip of my jeans.Then he slid his hand inside. Gently he took me in his hand, stroking me to a full erection. He pulled his wrist away from me, and I hungrily licked the remnants of his blood from my lips.

I knew he had knelt on the ground before me, he had freed me from my clothes and was running his hands expertly up and down my throbbing organ.

"Jordan," I moaned, almost losing my voice I was so aroused.

"For once in your life, Amias, quit talking and enjoy the ride." Then his lips were around me, hot and moist and he ran his tongue down the length of my organ. I had started to move my hips in motion with his foreplay. I threw my head back in ecstasy, hitting it on the wall, a sharp pain to add to my arousal. I lost all track of time; it could have been seconds or hours that passed, every time I thought I must reach my climax, he held me back. Playing the submissive, I mused had certain advantages. I clenched my teeth as his fangs dug a little too sharply into the tender skin of my groin. Suddenly I realised that I had to be in control.

"Jordan, a moment," I said breathlessly. "Now we play by my rules, take off the blindfold." I hope you can deal with pain Jordan, because my need is so strong, there will be no foreplay.

I felt his hands unfasten the scarf, the fabric slipped from my face and I found myself looking into two glowing silver-grey eyes.

Jordan was sitting on the old trough at the edge of the patio, a rueful grin on his face. But if Jordan was there, then, oh sweet fires of hell, it was Stefen who had just given me the most expert head I had experienced in a long time!

I tried desperately to think of a plausible explanation, but what could I say? If Stefen chose to leave me now I could not blame him. A lump had formed in my throat as I nervously raised my eyes to his, expecting the venom to meet me razor sharp.

Stefen had turned his back to me, I knew Jordan and he were communicating silently. My mind was too confused to try and read Jordan's mind. It puzzled me that Stefen had shown no anger towards Jordan, but then Stefen could always control his emotions when he wanted to. Marcus' influence, I suspected. He turned around, folded his arms and looked at me. My God he was stunning tonight. His recently washed hair fell waiflike around his shoulders and he had dressed in a pair of black leather trousers with lace up sides, black ankle boots and a soft white silk shirt, which accentuated his colouring. If ever an angel walked on this earth, it was my beloved Stefen.

I watched spellbound, as Stefen approached Jordan. His slow, seductive walk held us both enthralled. Raising Jordan's face with one hand, he slowly ran the back of his fingers along Jordan's cheek, caressing it lovingly. Stefen turned to me, shooting me an expression of pure lust before he lowered his lips to Jordan's and kissed him very gently. Still with his eyes on me his kiss became deeper, more wanting. A low groan escaped Jordan's lips and I knew he was at the edge of surrender, and about to fall.

"Stefen, for heaven's sake!" I yelled jealously.

Breaking the kiss, Stefen retorted. "So it's perfectly justified for you to cheat on me Amias, but when the tables are turned..." He paused. "Do you remember, one night last week you accused me of being boring, staid and frigid, I think was a word you used?"

Flashbacks of that night - it had been a terrible argument - started over nothing of any importance, and heated words between us, ending in Stefen storming out and not returning for two nights. I had been frantic.

"I went to Jordan that night, Amias," Stefen confessed. "We had an interesting conversation concerning our vampire makers. Jordan convinced me I could prove to you that I wasn't boring." He emphasised the last word. "Did I surprise you, my love?" Stefen chided.

I admitted defeat. "Stefen, you have astounded me. I promise I will never call you boring again." I felt the colour rise to my cheeks, in the game of one-upmanship Stefen had triumphed. I did not like being beaten. I wrenched my hand free, tearing the iron railing viciously. Adjusting my clothing, I licked my wrist where the handcuff had made an angry red gash.

"So all this was a test, Stefen?" I was finding it hard to believe that he could have thought of such a scheme.

"You could say that. But I knew Jordan would seduce you. I just wanted to see the look on your face when I took the blindfold off," he added with a grin. My heart turned over.

"You are depraved," I said.

"That's an Amias word."

"But you earned it tonight, Wicked One," I answered.

A movement in the shadows. "Jordan, don't you dare try to slink off!" I ordered. He looked at me sheepishly, exchanging a quick smile with Stefen. "I'll wait for you inside," Stefen said softly. I waited until I heard the door click softly behind him, then I knew we were alone.

"It seems that I underestimated you, Jordan," I stated.

"The hardest part was blocking my mind to you." Again, that smile, how had Marco managed to wait years for him?

"As I recall, reading your mind was not one of my priorities," I grinned.

"I guess you could say I got full marks in this charade." His eyes met mine.

I moved closer to him. "Is that all it was, Jordan?" I couldn't stop the hurt in my voice.

Jordan put his arms around my shoulders and embraced me. "No, Amias, it was a game at first, but then the game intensified and I knew I had two choices. To quit and confess the whole scheme, or go with my feelings..." he paused.

"How far would you have gone?" I questioned. I had to know. If Stefen had not been there, how far would this pretence have gone?

Jordan pulled me closer and whispered, "All the way, Amias." My heart missed a beat. "I found you irresistible. The thought of making love with you was the greatest temptation."

"Another time, another century?" I asked, smiling; my pride had been restored a little.

"I'll keep that in mind," he said, softly.

"Will you tell Marco?"

"Probably. We don't harbour many secrets." Marco's reaction would be interesting to witness. I made a mental note to tread carefully next time we met.

"Good night, Amias." Jordan kissed my cheek chastely. I watched him gracefully leap onto the wall and disappear silently into the darkness.

Slightly wearily I made my way into the house, and up the stairway, crossing the darkened landing. I pushed open the door to my bedroom.

The whole room was bathed in candlelight. At least a dozen candles, some perfumed, were burning, illuminating the room with soft, and flickering shadows. The white, cotton sheets on the antique four poster bed had been pulled back invitingly.

Sitting on the window ledge he was a breathtaking image. The candlelight played on his skin; his eyes were so trusting, so sorrowful.

I opened my arms to him. He almost threw himself against me;

we held each other tightly. I kissed his hair, his face, a lump had formed in my throat and I tried very hard to force the tears back.

"I love you, Stefen," I whispered. "Please remind me of that when I'm such a bastard."

"Let's go to bed," he said simply.

We lay down together, contented in each other's arms. "I thought I'd gone too far when I saw you with Jordan," Stefen said, as I nuzzled into his neck. "You seemed so right together. Your passion was very arousing." A wicked smile lit up his face.

"Why, Stefen, don't tell me you have become a voyeur?" I teased him.

"But I'm not boring?" he challenged.

"And certainly not frigid," I said, as I slid my body on top of his. His body felt so right beneath mine. I knew the curves of him intimately, but the feel of him never failed to thrill me.

"Do you think Jordan will be alright?" Stefen said, a look of concern on his adorable face.

I grinned. "Shall I go invite him to join us?" Stefen rolled his eyes and playfully nipped me on the neck.

"I think we've both learned valuable lessons tonight." Stefen said, suddenly serious.

"Stefen," I said softly, as a wave of self doubt ran through me. "Do you really love me?" Sometimes I could not believe his unquestioning devotion.

He answered me with a voice that was a little unsteady. "You are reckless, arrogant and stubborn, but loving someone with all your heart means accepting their faults," he paused. "We are two sides of a coin, Amias, one cannot be without the other, they are moulded together forever. Fate flipped us together all those decades ago. We have been spinning in eternal darkness ever since, but a coin can always catch any ray of light that penetrates the dark. Your love is that light."

I buried my face in his hair so he would not see the tears in my eyes. A devil I may be, but I had been truly blessed with the love of this exquisite creature, my beloved companion, my demon with the grace of an angel. And mine for eternity.

Abandonment: The Deadliest Virtue

(Sequel to 'The Gentle Art of Betrayal')

Beverley Lee

I lit the candles and glanced around the room. Perfection. The covers on the bed were pulled back, the room was lit by the unearthly glow of a dozen virgin white candles, but would he come? I had flung down the gauntlet to him last night as he sat leaning against Marco's legs, dozing in the aftermath of the hunt, I had sent out my ultimatum. "Care to finish what we started, tomorrow evening?"

Now I waited. Stefen was out prowling for food. This time I had told him of my intentions. Remarkably, he had taken it quite well, get him out of your system, Amias, and make your conquest, he had told me simply, his eyes understanding. So there was no guilt, just a fear of being refused.

I sat down on the bed, smoothing the covers with my fingers. Why was I here tonight? Just to fuck the most delectable vampire of this age or something more? I knew the reason: revenge. The sweet taste of revenge. Marco had rebuffed me cruelly when I had confessed my love for him in the heady days of the French Revolution. I hope I wound your heart tonight, boy demon.

A movement in the shadows, a slight rush of air. I stood up and smiled. "Good evening, how kind of you to accept my invitation."

He moved towards me, gracefully, how well he had adapted to his new form. Marco had taught him well. A shiver of delight ran through me as I realised that tonight he would be mine completely, no games, no deceit, just lust. I did not veil my thoughts. He picked them up and grinned sheepishly.

Standing before me with his head cocked to one side, an impish grin on his face; dressed in the denim uniform of today's youth he stirred the very beast in me. To possess him would be a very sweet experience and one I meant to savour.

I opened my arms to him and he willingly came, and I pulled him closer. No resistance. "Did you think I would refuse you, my Prince?" he whispered, deftly unfastening my shirt.

I smoothed the wisps of hair from his forehead and caressed the back of his neck. He pushed his head back to increase the pressure of my fingers.

"Lust is a heady emotion, and a deadly sin," he said, his voice low and hypnotic. His eyes were half shut; I could see the ice-blue fire slowly kindling.

I moved my fingers to his neck and began to massage him there. He caught hold of my hand, and playfully nipped the soft flesh at the base of my thumb.

"I don't need much foreplay, Amias. I could come just thinking of you fucking me." His eyes met mine and I marvelled at his honesty.

I swallowed hard; his words released the hunger inside of me. I could feel my own erection straining against the rough fabric of my jeans.

He ripped the shirt from my back, pausing for a moment as I freed my hands from the sleeves. He began to kiss my chest, licking my nipples until they were hard.

His moist lips sent shivers down my spine, each stroke of his tongue like an icicle of fire. I struggled for control and lost.

With a fierce cry I pushed him face first against the wall and tore the clothes from his body. The candles flickered in the draught, casting dancing shadows on his firm, smooth skin. Pressing my body to his I pulled his head back and growled, "No escape this time, Jordan. Can you take it?" Even Marco flying in on the wings of one of hell's angels could not stop me now.

I noticed with a smile that he was standing with his legs apart, a willing victim. I peeled off my jeans quickly, keeping the leather belt in my hands. Dropping to my knees, I ran my tongue over the skin of his buttocks. I heard him gasp as I firmly parted his cheeks and darted my tongue over that most delicate area of passion.

Standing up I took the belt firmly in my hand and flicked the end sharply across his back; a gasp of surprise from Jordan.

"Begin your descent into hell, my child, and know that tonight you will belong body and soul to me alone."

Again I flicked the belt, teasing his skin, and again, harder this time. The weals from the belt marked his pale skin, each kiss from the leather adding to his arousal. I ran my hand through his damp hair, the sound of his laboured breathing made me want him even more. "Beg for me to continue, Jordan. Not that it matters, I just want to hear you plead." My voice was trembling with sexual longing.

Jordan's face was pressed against the wall. His reply came as a muffled cry. "I want you… I want you inside of me, now!" His last word was a scream that accompanied the final thrash.

I licked a few drops of blood from the edge of my belt; it tasted of leather and pain. I loved the sensation as it melted on my tongue.

With one hand I picked up the small brown bottle standing on the bedside table and taking the cap off with my teeth I covered my fingers with its oily contents.

"Face the wall!" I snapped as he turned his head. Then without warning or foreplay I inserted a finger inside of him.

"Amias..." he moaned loudly as he tensed against me. He was gloriously tight, and as I moved my finger inside him I could almost smell the unconditional need that arose from him. His body was shining with a faint blood sweat. I lapped at it as it gathered in the small of his back, glistening on the delicate hair that grew there.

"On your knees against the bed." I ordered. He needed no other encouragement. I reached between his legs and cupped his balls in my hand, fondling him gently. He shuddered violently. "Now, Amias, now," he murmured. He leant against the bed and grasped the covers tightly.

"Not quite yet, Jordan." I mused. I ran my fingers down between the damp crack in his buttocks. And this time with two fingers I entered him, exploring deep within, expertly playing him like a musical instrument. He was my violin, I was the bow, and the reckless cries of his pleasure were like music to my ears.

The intimacy of my touch and the sounds of rapture from Jordan brought back mortal memories of my first time with Antoine. The rats scurrying in the corner of the darkened room, their claws scratching the wooden floor, and the roughness of the straw against my skin, my hands clutching the empty wine bottle. Then the white hot pain as Antoine took me, and the burning pleasure of having him inside me. I remembered the sudden wetness and the realisation that I was bleeding, and then the brutal ecstacy.

"Lean back, my darling, I know it hurts but the pain always comes before the pleasure," I coaxed.

Slowly he obeyed me but he stopped as the pressure of my fingers was obviously too painful.

"All the way, Jordan," I said softly and I forced him back against the harsh momentum of my fingers. A small whimper as I pulled his hair back and exposed his throat. The white soft flesh beckoned me and I shut my eyes tightly. Not yet, Amias.

"Please, Amias..." His words came as a plea. I caught his eye as he said the words breathlessly. His pupils were dilated, his eyes glazed and wisps of hair clung wetly to his forehead. He was ravishing.

I removed my fingers from him and delicately stroked the downy hair on the inside of his thighs. I was already wet with anticipation. I positioned myself over him and spread his legs further apart with my knees. He buried his face in the bed covers and tensed his body. I smiled devilishly before I plunged into him roughly.

"Don't fight me, Jordan," I whispered. "It hurts more when you fight, or do you enjoy that pain?" I ran my nails down his back drawing blood and then licking it from my fingers. "Can you bear the suffering before the ecstasy. Stefen does," I whispered alluringly. A shudder of delight ran through him and I scanned his mind as he imagined Stefen in the same position.

A feather light touch on my shoulders, soft breathing in my ear and a heartbeat I knew so well. His arms were around me then as he spoke in a voice that was so elegantly seductive: "Fuck me softly, for you know I need the pain. Bleed me gently, before I go insane."

"Stefen, my love," I whispered. I saw him from the corner of my eye, his arm around a mortal boy of some 17 years of age. The boy was high on alcohol, his thick, dark gold hair dishevelled over his shoulders. I noticed a bite mark on his neck. Stefen had already tasted his wares. Stefen tried to take his arm away and the boy swayed dangerously. The boy laughed and moved forwards, collapsing on the bed in a fit of giggles. His shirt was unfastened, as was the zip on his PVC trousers.

I gave Stefen a look of amazement and he smiled innocently back at me, displaying one fang and looking totally delectable. Stefen pulled the boy into his arms and whispered endearments to him in old colonial French, as the boy fumbled with the antique gold buttons on Stefen's lace shirt. The boy peeled the shirt from Stefen's body as I watched. I found it totally amazing that Stefen could hold my attention whilst Jordan writhed beneath me. Since the episode with Jordan a few weeks earlier he was using his new found sexuality in everything he did, and he was driving me to a state of nearly permanent arousal.

Deftly Stefen removed his trousers and gazed at me. He took the ribbon from his hair and as it cascaded onto his shoulders in an ebony waterfall, I felt a low growl escape from my throat.

Stefen knelt down beside Jordan and licked the blood sheen from his face. He moved round until they were face to face, body to body, their cocks pressed up against each other enticingly.

"Didn't I warn you he was rough, Jordan?" said Stefen, a note of manipulation edging his softly spoken words."Give yourself to him fully, abandon your reserve and let him make you scream."

Stefen's hand was on Jordan now, stroking the end of his cock. Then he carefully inserted his sharp thumbnail into the moist opening.

Jordan cried out in feral abandonment. Stefen smiled provocatively at me over Jordan's shoulder and moved to the side. Stefen's dazzling eyes were spiced with sexual hunger and I could see the reflection of the candle flame dancing within them, and his nostrils flared slightly; my making out with Jordan was arousing him more than I could have imagined.

As I pushed Jordan back onto the bed I felt him open to me like the unfolding of the petals of a flower. He had surrendered finally, small sobs of distress drenched with rapture coming from his mouth.

"Submission is one step from possession," I whispered to him, as triumphantly I sent out images of Jordan's surrender to Marco. I would cope with his wrath later; I was living for the moment. And besides, I adored Marco when he was angry. He was like an eagle with ruffled feathers, beautiful with a deadly bite.

I let my senses go into overload. I could hear the wax as it melted and slowly ran down the candles. I smelt the wild lust tinged with fear from Jordan, and I saw myself mirrored in Stefen's clear, jewel like eyes as I plunged into Marco's child, each stroke making him mine more completely.

All this time the boy had been watching. He had removed his clothes and was content to be a voyeur. Stefen held out his hand and beckoned to the boy to join him. He slid from the bed and into Stefen's arms. I could smell his passion as Stefen french kissed him slowly, his adrenaline pumping through his veins. All the boy's inhibitions were lost in the haze of alcohol that clouded his reason.

Stefen motioned for the boy to turn around and then he pressed his body tightly against the boy's back. He groaned out loud as Stefen ran a finger down his body and took hold of his erect cock. With his other hand Stefen took a firm hold of his neck and pulled his head back. It was spellbinding to watch Stefen, a master of the vampire act. I heard his fangs slice cleanly into the boy's throat. A stream of crimson ran slowly down the boy's chest and dripped onto the polished wooden floor. The scent of the blood drove me to my climax and I released myself into Jordan with a sharp cry of conquest.

Roughly, Stefen entered the boy, relinquishing his hold on the boy's neck. The boy winced in pain as Stefen drove deeper, dominating him completely. Stefen's mouth was smeared with blood; he made no move to wipe it off. His fangs gleamed in the candlelight as the boy cried out beneath him.

Leaning across I wiped the blood from his mouth with my fingers. Jordan took my hand and guided my fingers to his mouth, sucking the blood from them hungrily. His eyes were gleaming thirstily and I realised he had not fed before he came to me.

The boy was now sobbing uncontrollably; the drink had overcome him finally. A blessing really, for he was surrounded by a trio of vampires who were to show him no mercy. Lovingly Jordan swept the boy's damp hair from his neck. He stroked his throat slowly, Jordan's eyes met Stefen's, and they exchanged silent words.

Jordan took hold of the boy's slender wrist and offered it to me with a calculating smile. Stefen threw his head back in a frenzy of excitement as Jordan viciously tore into the sweet white flesh of the boy's throat, rapidly satisfying his other hunger. I allowed myself the luxury of watching Stefen climax before I severed the main vein in the boy's wrist, gasping as the hot metallic taste hit my tongue and he lapsed into unconsciousness.

In the glow of the rapidly dimming candlelight I drank his death, full of youth's sweet dreams, with a sigh. Jordan and Stefen were cradled in each other's arms, Jordan's head resting on Stefen's chest, Stefen languidly running his fingers through Jordan's baby soft hair. A look of contentment graced both their faces.

What a splendid sight we made, three immortals living death as it was meant to be, exploring the night with everything our heightened senses had to offer, and unafraid of losing control.

Stigmata

A. J. Barron

He hangs uncomfortably on the ominous cross as sunset arrives and shrouds the hill of Golgotha in a bloody red-purple light. I watch the body of my friend Jesus writhe in agony, his limp torso suspended on the jagged wooden crucifix.

He tries to hold his pain at bay, his grimace receding and his body ceasing its struggle against the sharp flesh-piercing bonds. He manages to look down at me, his face now calm and incongruous against the bruises on his cheeks and around his eyes. He smiles at me with anticipation, revealing his longing for me to drink from him. He wants me to empty his body as we both did Mary Magdalene's. He wants me to leave not a drop spilled in vain. That's why he agreed to such a death, for me.

His face looks so beautiful with its bleeding wounds. The crimson streams of pain which run down his forehead from the well-crafted crown of thorns are magnificent. What a sensational touch that makes. How it gives him the appearance of being the king. The king of blood, pain and torn flesh.

The blood gushes generously from his injuries where the long rust encrusted nails have severed the tender skin of his palms and ankles, small droplets falling to the white stones below and marking them with his life.

I've been here all day. I watched Jesus ascend the hill laboriously on weak thin legs which near gave out under the weight of the cross which he carried diligently on his aching shoulders. I watched as the centurions took the cross from him and put it to the ground, leaving Jesus standing there shivering with fatigue and exhaustion, his body lank and skinny, giving him a definite look of emaciation. Uncontrollable fear was painted over him in the form of perspiration which flattened his usually luxuriant mane of blond hair to his tender head. This light shade of blond is now drowned in the red liquid that poured evenly from the cuts which have been inflicted by the still steady crown.

Other people were there then, and they shouted abuse and insult at the pathetic looking individual. They couldn't wait to see him crucified, and neither could I, but for far different reasons. I want to see him fulfil his promise to me. He wants to die amidst the sexually heightened pain-filled experience of blood drinking, and I am here to grant his wish and take my own pleasure from it. The pleasure of sinking my own teeth into him and drinking as he died in the intense enjoyment of vampirism.

And it is going to be soon.

I observed unflinchingly as the centurions laid him upon the cross, spreading his hands out to fit the shape of the well-carved wood. They tied his arms first with strong rough rope which began to instantly cut into his flesh. Jesus watched me as all this went on beseechingly, begging that all of his suffering would not amount to nothing. It won't. I'll make quite sure of that.

Then his serene face turned immediately into an expression of the utmost pain as the spikes were driven in with a splatter of blood that flew in all directions. I felt the cold drop of a single speck as it hit me lightly on the cheek. I wiped it off with my finger and for a moment observed the scarlet redness before placing the stained index fully into my salivating mouth, scraping it along one of my long clean fangs. I tasted instantly the sweetness. The sweetness that would increase so much with the later high doses I would intake.

The centurions looked at me with glances of uncertainty as they saw me looking over their shoulders to get a good view of the injuries they had inflicted on my friend. But they had no real interest in who I was so they continued in their task diligently.

They hoisted my friend up precariously, burying the lengthy stem of the cross in the hard earth so that it had no need for further supports of any kind.

The girl I stood with, Martha, and other spectators who had come to watch the crucifixion asked me: they said, "Judas, do you not feel ashamed for what you have done to your companion Jesus?"

And my answer was always the same: "No, I don't feel ashamed in the least, he asked me to do it."

It was not always just I and Jesus who used to drink together. In fact, until quite recently there was a third party in our little blood-letting pack. We were a triangle, and I was the sharpest of all the points, for I was the only real vampire. I was the only one for whom the transference of the bodily fluid was necessity. It was only I who needed it to live. For Jesus it was spiritual. He claimed it assisted him in doing the work of his Father. The blood was the force behind him which helped him establish himself as a Messiah. He said it was what fuelled him to perform his miracles. And perhaps he was right. I don't know, not being one of his followers myself. I travelled with him, yes, but only because he begged me to, so that we could continue our own pleasures. I, Jesus and Mary Magdalene.

She was the third member of our party. She, I have to say, was far more passive than Jesus. He was insanely jealous of my permanent fangs, and he sometimes became aggressive because he was unable to break skin as easily as I. Mary, on the other hand, loved to drink any way she could; it made no difference to her how it was spilled. She loved it however it flowed. She loved us, and we loved her.

We would meet on regular evenings at my secluded home. It was there we preferred to commit our wonderful travesties. Mary and Jesus always knew that at my dainty bungalow the candles always flickered demurely, and a pot of spices always boiled in the centre of the room, filling the heated air with an intoxicating scent that each of us had come to associate with sex. In the corner would sit the pale and flaccid body of Lazarus, whom Jesus had resurrected from the dead as a favour to me. Now, Lazarus acted as a blood supply for me whenever I was in need. His dead characteristics made him seem adverse to pain as I discovered whenever I sank myself into him. Not a flinch. Sometimes the three of us would use Lazarus, but not often. I was grateful to Jesus for that man servant. I think that's why I adored Jesus' blood so much. It was filled with astonishing magic which seemed to illuminate my entire immortal being with light that cannot be described. A light that filled me with such sexual energy that I was able to weaken Mary greatly with my strong pelvic thrusts. Energy that would force me to make her scream with unbearable pleasure. Thrusts that would make her bleed, that would make her sleep for hours on the reddened blankets of my bed. Jesus' blood was soon something I felt I needed. It was a liquid that Mary knew would help satisfy her extremely.

On the night of our somewhat sad separation from Mary the night air was unbelievably humid, bathing I and Jesus in sweat as we sat naked against the wall, awaiting Mary's entrance.

Jesus picked up the sharp knife I kept close by for our evenings. He scrutinised the sharp blade with his calloused thumb, slicing the tough skin not deep enough to make it bleed. He ran the cold steel over his arms and protruding ribs teasingly, knowing that he was subjecting me to insane torment. He was well aware that I watched him out of the corner of my eye, wishing for him to venture far enough to cut his flesh for me. But he wouldn't, he simply meant it to drive me wild with hunger so that I would perform more satisfactorily for him and Mary. He knew that by doing this I would drink so much deeper from each of them. By doing this he was sure that I would feast on their very souls like an enormous leech, sucking away their life almost. I really wished I could have.

The truth is that Jesus wanted so much for me to turn him into a vampire also, but, alas, it was impossible. I am unable to do that for anyone, although I would have liked to for either or both of them. But it's a matter of birth. A matter of ancestry As it is possible for two people of pale skin to produce a child of black, so too is it possible for two non-vampires to spawn a vampire if there has been blood-drinkers somewhere in their lineage. That is what I came from: two mortals who had the vampiric cells pumping somewhere deep in their black-centred hearts. Neither Jesus or Mary had this. Or if they did it had not been fully embodied in them, more's the pity.

My sultry pondering was broken as the door swung open and Mary entered wrapped in a thin black cloak. She stood for a moment framed in the opening to my meagre abode before coming in and eyeing both of us hungrily. Lazarus sat as usual, oblivious to our antics. He would always just sit there within his cracked loose skin, unfeeling, unneeding, unknowing. Probably.

There was no need for words, we had done this so many times before. So many times we had all embraced in our blood lust, I and Jesus working on Mary to send her to the heights of sexual awareness. And this time was no exception, or so we then thought.

Mary let the black cloak fall to the floor revealing her nakedness which had previously been concealed underneath. Her voluptuous body was a canvas of razor cuts and bite marks. The curves of her thighs were marked with protruding scars that appeared whiter than her tanned flesh. Some of the lines were fresher than that though, like the ones of her large brown-nippled breasts that were still red and scabbed with blood. She was so attractive to us in this marked frame.

I was the first to approach her as Jesus stood by the spice fire and watched eagerly. Her large green eyes closed delicately with sexual electricity a split second before my hand came into contact with the mound of fat that was her breast. It was as if the animal lust that hid slyly within my aura had already taken her. I took her in my arms and kissed her deeply, her experienced tongue probing my own expertly. As we continued our oral bond I led her gently to the bed where we both lay facing each other as our kiss ended.

We looked into each other as we lay comfortably. All else in this world had been banished for a few moments, and we neglected Jesus for a while as our rapture began. She ran her lips over my neck playfully as I massaged and pinched her breasts with increasing ferocity, until she eventually shouted out in glorious pain. She wrapped one of her long shapely legs around mine and began to pound gently against me as a prelude to our ultimate bond. I tried to be passive to this but failed as her smooth skin enveloped me completely.

I put my hand over her neck and pushed her lightly, turning her over so that she was facing away from me. I could not remove my gaze from Mary but on the other side of us I could still make out the waif-like form of our third member, as he gripped himself with a firm fist and began to excite it with gaining speed. He stood on his toes and assaulted his member feverishly until finally he spent his semen on the floor below, his body convulsing under the spell of the amazing spillage. His mouth was open in awe of the supreme energy that ran through him and left as he panted in a post-masturbation glow. I managed to take my attention away from the awaiting female and motioned for Jesus to hand me the knife. He shook himself out of his hypnotic state and brought the blade to my hand, where he placed it firmly. I gripped the handle tightly and brought it towards Mary, my eyes now firmly fixed on Jesus as he watched with trembling lips. Mary's eyes were closed as she awaited the cut. I balanced the sharpness an inch away from one of her nipples and sliced, causing her to flinch as the blood began to run. It flowed steadily from her in a crimson line. She went to touch the opening but I stopped her. It was for Jesus.

"Drink," I whispered to him.

He lay himself down beside Mary and, hesitating for a moment, enveloped the wound with his lips, nuzzling into it and sucking stealthily.

Now it was my turn to begin.

Mary was gasping under the heavy suckling of Jesus so she did not notice my fangs teeter expectantly on the soft meat of her perfectly rounded shoulder. My member was dangerously erect and it steadied itself by the slim hair-lined opening of her tender anus. She kicked the air with her legs erratically. She was ready for me also.

I pierced the smooth flesh of her shoulder with exquisite ease as I also led my penis into her muscular ring simultaneously. Her intense groan was very audible in both pain and so much pleasure as I broke into her. I continued to enter her with slow and methodical timing, my hip movements fluid in their aim. And along with this I continued to sup on the dense red plasma of her body. Her life force was glorious to my taste-buds.

We kept on for a time. I assailed to another plane as I still pumped myself into Mary. She took the painfully exquisite sex without objection. Her eyes simply remained closed to the excellence of our bond. Jesus continued to feed ravenously from the cut until he could take no more blood from her. When he had finished he moved himself up onto the top of the bed and placed his stone hard erection between the lips of Mary, who took it thankfully, bathing it in lubricating saliva. Jesus groaned emphatically as she worked faster.

I worked faster also, causing Mary to emanate near shrieks through her oral fullness. I took more blood and concentrated on it diligently, marking its journey as it slithered so smoothly down my gullet. I was so charged that I could no longer contain my sexual fluid. I came like a thunder storm and lined the wall of her colon with my semen, removing my stained fangs from her red-dripping injury. She screamed as the orgasm took her, the seed of Jesus immanently spraying itself over the back of her throat.

We all slumped into exhaustion for a moment, my eyes closed. When I opened them again I noticed Jesus watching me intently. I returned his gaze with a 'what is it?' expression.

"It's not enough any more," he whispered.

Mary did not hear him, her mind was still elsewhere, shrouded in euphoric bliss.

I knew what he meant. I felt it too. This was good, but that's all it would ever be from now on. Eventually our worst fears would come into reality and this would become monotonous.

"I don't just want to be inside Mary any more," he continued in hushed tones. "I want to really get into her, to investigate her further."

Yes, I thought. That's right. That's what we'll do.

The knife still lay next to me and I picked it up.

"What is it?" Mary asked, as she felt my grasp on her wrist, preventing her hand as it approached her vagina.

"You can't go there," I replied with a smile. "That's a place for – us!"

On the word 'us' she screamed in an echo of the utmost pain as I rammed the blade into her genitals ferociously. It wrenched itself into her further than any penis had ever gone, stabbing at the spirit of an unborn child lying dormant in her womb. Her eyes shot open widely, her mouth gaping, now unable to scream.

I grabbed the knife-handle between both hands and brought it upwards, breaking, with a snap, her pubic bone and continuing to rip towards her throat. Her stomach cut like the soft flesh it was, her chest was harder to cut through but by mustering all the strength I had I did it, until Mary was nothing but a pool of blood surrounded by severed flesh. She had torn like a sheet, and the sound was not dissimilar. Jesus could only stand back and watch, flying lines of crimson liquid hitting his chest.

He looked at me with shocked eyes so I told him that it was what he wanted, in order to reassure him. Still, though, he could not move. So I took his head in my hand and guided it slowly to the massive gaping hole of Mary's once vagina. He was reluctant, but against all of his better judgement he allowed me to put him inside of our dead blood companion. He stayed motionless in that womb of redness for some time before its overwhelming power overtook him and he began to move. He caressed her cooling flesh tenderly and then moved his drenched head upwards to the torso where he resided for a short time. He began to investigate the soft intestines that crushed beneath his probing face. He lapped at her empty stomach, over her pink lungs and black looking heart which no longer pumped. It was all so perfectly organised in there that Jesus almost felt guilty for distorting such inward beauty; for searching an area that was never meant to be infested by human hands. He almost felt guilty; but an animal thirst had taken control of him and it made him take her still heart in his hand and grip it strongly like a child with a favourite toy. In that one hand he held Mary, and he would not let go. He drank like he never had before, in large greedy gulps. When he removed his cranium from her beautiful body he looked at me and smiled, his white licked clean teeth incongruous to the scarlet dripping face. He beckoned me in with him and in I went.

All evening we played with Mary. We caressed each other with her blood, greasing ourselves with the still plasma. We drew indistinct shapes on each other's bodies, serene in the memory of Mary. We knew this was what she would have wanted in the end anyway. And believe me or not, in those last moments before she fell lifeless I'm sure there was a definite hint of overwhelming pleasure in those agonising screams of hers. I'm sure of it. We drank her completely dry, at intervals even eating previously unseen pieces of internal flesh. How high it made the two of us feel.

Bless you Mary.

"I'm jealous," Jesus said morosely as he gazed on the blueing corpse.

"Of what?" I asked.

"Her."

It was then I suspected that that was my cue to do something quite similar to Jesus. My theories were confirmed only a few nights later when I sat with Jesus and all of his gathered disciples at supper. Jesus held his shaking fist above a goblet and with my own blade - the blade we had used on Mary - he cut his forearm, targeting the dripping blood into the wine.

"This is my blood, drink it," he then said and handed me the goblet.

I knew then that he wanted to die so that I may drink from him. He wished his death to be my responsibility, and that's exactly what it is, for now he hangs on top of Golgotha.

As evening falls and Jesus is near enough only a silhouette against the backdrop of a perfect purple sky the jeering gleeful spectators have left. Now it is only I, Martha - who is the sister of Lazarus - and Jesus in the company of two crucified thieves who are close enough to death to be ignored.

Martha looks at Jesus lustfully, as I have guided her well in the ways of blood-drinking.

How amazing a moment can be. When you realise in a precise instant that it is time - that single second of knowing what is to come. What will flow so copiously. This magic thought fills me with such transcendent bliss that I simply ascend up to him like a butterfly, stopping only when our hungry gazes meet. I slap his face lightly to wake him. He looks at me with glazed blue eyes, his lips dry, the blood encrusted on his face. He's beautiful - such an image of agony.The perfectly symmetrical lashes on his back from the whip drive me wild with thirst. They have dried in the hot desert sun too, though, so I'll have to make some fresh wounds. Below, Martha is beginning to remove his loincloth, dropping the bloody rag to the ground. I watch her eagerly, my eyes darting from her face to that of Jesus, as she swallows his member skillfully, making it more erect that it ever had been before. The pleasure washes over Jesus in one uncontrollable shiver. And the intensity of this is increased to an incalculable degree as I sink my fangs deep into his neck. He struggles vainly and needlessly against his iron bonds as I drink from him, Martha continuing to massage his penis with her soft lips.

After this I know I'll move to my friend's stigmata and drink from that. I'll drink until every ounce of life has seeped from him and he is motionless against the splintered wood of his cross.Then I'll take Martha and I'll split her like I did Mary underneath the corpse of my friend (I have the blade under my cloak). His shadow will hide us as I take all she has, leaving her barren. And we'll all carry each other to a sumptuously dark oblivion where we'll reside until the break of the new dawn.

"Thank you, Judas," Jesus says wanly through his dry mouth. "Thank you."

Only £1.99 Per Min.

Darran Heath

A day after the phone call and Saul sat drunk on his smooth leather couch, a dying bottle of Absolut glued to a lazy hand, a just-lit cigarette dangling between the jellied fingers of the other, listening to Morrissey's velveteen voice painting rainy, grey Manchester clouds over the lamp-lit walls of his roomy, fifth storey Soho flat.

So alone, and - horny.

'But hey, aren't you always?' Saul thought, taking a messy slug of vodka; clear, liquid fire that was doing its 40 per cent proof damnedest to numb every last nerve in his GQ body, kill every last memory of her in his brain.

But still, images of Jayne and him hung heavy in his hazy consciousness: out of focus, good-time colour prints, past which his mind stumbled boozily asking 'Me, a sicko freak?'

"Shit honey," mumbled Saul, taking a long, slow drag on his cigarette. "You showed me a few moves." As he exhaled, smoky halos rose above his head, that shimmied, and quickly burst.

It had only been a month-long thing, but for Saul that was commitment. A declaration of love. And like one of the skeletal homeless he passed on the way to work each morning, begging for breakfast change, he was already violently hungry for an evening spent in Jayne's Chanel-scented company.

Cigarette in hand, Saul lifted the butt-scattered ashtray that rested on his lap, and leaned forward to place it on the coffee table in front of him, then firmly stubbed out the half-smoked Marlboro into the crystal round, spitefully imagining it was Jayne's pale, baby-doll face.

"So I bit you!" Saul yelled out, his angry voice cut with despair, and then gently complaining, recalling the coppery taste, and the way Jayne had psyched out."There wasn't even that much blood!"

'But enough to ruin the sheets,' Saul thought.

Finishing off the last of the Absolut, Saul arced the heavy glass bottle over the back of his head, hearing it hit polished floorboards with a satisfying thud, and then roll, and spin to a halt.

Unlike the flat, which rotated with merry-go-round jumps about Saul's blurred vision.

Glassy eyes that looked at the mobile phone lying on the coffee table he'd held to his disbelieving ear 24 hours earlier. He remembered Jayne's sweetened break-up line:"It's all over, Saul. It's just got too weird."And then, lemon sour, after a couple of down-on-his-knees, begging minutes later: "If you phone, or stop by, I'm gonna call the fucking cops, you sicko freak."'Which had hurt', Saul thought, recalling the way the insult had been bitterly thrown. 'More than the nip I gave you.'

The Smiths CD played to an end, leaving Saul's ears privy to the muffled sounds of a city held firmly to the shaking bosom of a Friday night tarted up in a slinky, low-cut party dress.

And somewhere out there, without him, nestled deep, was Jayne.

'With someone else?' The thought hammered a nail into Saul's heart.

Made him reach to the coffee table for the pornography he'd picked up from a sex shop on the way home from a moody day at the office.A fetish magazine he'd bought purely because the cover girl had resembled Jayne, and not, he'd assured himself as he'd handed over a crisp twenty to the knowing shop assistant, because of any S&M kink that needed a firm, steam-pressed ironing.

Saul lay back on the couch and flicked through the pages of the magazine until he came to the spread that featured the woman who'd caught his eye inside the sex shop.

Up close and how-more-personal-do-you-want-to-get, she was even more like Jayne than he'd earlier realised.

From lilac painted toenails, up a curvy, creamy body, to an oval face about which fell sheaths of raven-black hair – the model was Jayne's double.

But whereas Jayne had adored the gentle, silky caress of lacy lingerie the model, page by glossy page, was in to, and out of, skin-hugging, shiny black PVC, her alluring green eyes inviting Saul to feel the crack and sting of a ropey, leather whip, held with explicit ease.

And oh, there was another difference too, one that Saul thought at first was the vodka playing fucked up mind games with him; but each photo of the model revealed her with the same studded, scarlet lips, bearing - the same sharp fangs.

Savage-looking, snowy-white canines the woman had found the decency to cover up on the front of the magazine.

But not inside.

Inside, the fangs seemed to cut through each colour page like a razor.

Seemed real - and deadly so.

'But they can't be!' Saul thought.'It's just a cheap vampire gag for submissives.'

Yet Saul also felt excited by the vivid images he saw starkly laid out before his widening eyes. Poses that had made his cock grow hard. His heartbeat quicken. His skin hot. Signs of lust not only for the woman's heavy breasts, curvy ass, and pierced cunt. He was even beginning to like the idea of cold, cracking leather against the run of his muscles.

But more than all that - Saul found himself longing for the woman's bite.

Her fangs in his flesh.

'Would it be as good receiving, as it was to give?' Saul silently asked himself, smiling wickedly, looking at a phone ad beneath the last photo of the woman: one of her on all fours, fangs snarling at the camera.

An ad that read: "I WANT TO SUCK ALL YOU NAUGHTY CHILDREN OF THE NIGHT DRY. For the ultimate in eternal pleasures, call LUXIA on: 1-801-398-VAMP NOW!!! Only £1.99 Per Min. No CC reqd."

'Well, it's only fantasy,' Saul thought, looking at Luxia's sparkling, come-on-ring-me eyes. 'A sicko freak fantasy, but hey Jayne, you brought it out of me.'

Sticking out an arm, Saul grabbed the mobile phone from the coffee table, and raising his knees to support the magazine at a readable angle, pressed in the numbers on the phone that would connect him to the model vampire.

Saul placed the phone to his ear, and listened to it ringing out. Each ring heightened his anticipation. Fuelled his desire.

On the fifth ring, the phone connected.

Saul pressed the phone hard to his ear, his heart skipping a frantic beat.

"Hello, this is Luxia," came the sultry voice on the other end of the line, as soft and drawn out as satin bedsheets.

Then nothing.

Having expected a recorded message, Saul suddenly found himself stumbling for words to say. "Er... yeah... I saw the ad... the photos in... er... 'Chains & Whips'," he said, and then, cooler, trying to regain his composure. "And I thought I'd give you a call."

A moment's silence.

"So you liked the photos?" asked Luxia, teasing.

Saul let out a gentle breath, relaxing. "I like you," he replied, picking up on Luxia's playfulness and leisurely batting it back down the phone line.

"And what about me turns you on?" The question was returned fast and with spin.

"Your body," answered Saul, leafing through the magazine photos of Luxia, forgetting Jayne. "And..." His voice backed off, scared, embarrassed.

"And?" asked Luxia.

Saul looked at the teeth flashing before him, glistening with spit.

"And?"

"Your fangs," said Saul timidly, tonguing his own puny teeth, not believing his own voice, what he was doing.

"And would you like me to bite you?"

Saul cast the magazine aside. "Yes," he whispered, lowering the zip on his jeans, freeing his pulsing cock, and taking it into a rocking hand.

"Are you sure?"

"Yes!" replied Saul anxiously, his breathing louder now, as heated as his ardour. "I want you to bite me!"

"Then close your eyes," said Luxia, her tone breathy, commanding. "And think of me."

Saul did as he was told, and for a brief second he saw nothing but darkness behind his shut eyes. And then out of the oily shadows, he saw Luxia, her black PVC catsuit keeping perfect hour-glass time with her voluptuous body as she swayed closer, and closer toward him, until all he could see was a face as white as chalk dust, shifting to show off eyes that danced with jade fire, and silver-decorated ruby lips that split to reveal fangs as pointed and curved as ivory-bladed knives.

"Where do you want me to put my fangs?" asked Luxia; but the question Saul heard sprang from the lipsticked lips he saw with his mind's eye, and not from the crackling ear piece of the phone. "Do you want them around your cock?"

Saul gasped, marvelling at the life-like image he'd conjured in his mind, his rapid hand stalling on his crotch, before continuing its sweet pleasure giving movements - slow, then fast, then faster. "Oh yes, there! Put them there!" he answered with effort, concentrating on Luxia's fangs.

And as he did so, Luxia's mouth came into close-up, so all he saw was that mouth, those lips, those fangs, and the pink, moist hole behind.

Imaginings from which began sensations as if Luxia's warm, wet, toothy kiss was actually upon him, around him, joining his hand - firing off tiny, rainbow-coloured fireworks of ecstasy throughout his writhing body. Sending him swirling speedily over the edge.

As he came, feeling the sticky spray of his excitement spatter onto his shirt, his hand, Saul went to open his eyes - but couldn't.

His eyes remained tightly closed as if they'd been glued together with his own sweat, allowing him only the sight of a tongue licking lipstick-smudged lips clean.

A mouth that opened wetly and said: "Now that you've had your fun - it's time for mine."

Saul dropped the phone from his ear, tried to get off the couch; but he found he was kept there by a fleshy-feeling weight that straddled him, vicing his body still. Though as he swung out his fists in panic, all he struck was nothing, thin air. "Leave me alone," he screamed, trying to free his mind of the vampire's mouth that hissed cat-like in widescreen against his blinkered eyes.

But the feature presentation continued, with no intervals.

No mercy, but the feathery fall of brief kisses that Saul felt on his neck, like the touch of falling rose petals, and then - a plunging bite, sharp and clean. Incisions that made him yell out in perfect pleasure and pain.

A cry he'd once heard Jayne dispense, had wanted to experience for himself.

And in his head, Saul could see Luxia's blooded lips, between long, deep sucking sounds, moan: "Oh yes... caller... oh yes... OH YES!"

Faith & Fear

Michaela Bisiker

The sun is slowly setting in a halo of crimson and gold as I rub the sleep from my eyes and set to recording the events that uprooted my life and twisted my soul to the very core of my existence. My world is forever changed by a power stronger than any mere religious conversion; faith itself would quake and crumble in the face of my new inner-strength. I am no longer merely me, I am myself and more.

I owe my transformation, as all young girls owe their formative experiences, to my beloved and erudite father whose wisdom and fine judgement are truly a gift from God - although from which I am not certain. I will thank him for all eternity.

It was mid-September, mild and dusty autumn when my father received an urgent message from the Royal Art School in London. In his younger years, Sir Edward had enjoyed a great deal of critical acclaim for his works of art and had now, in his later years, devoted himself to the encouragement of young talent. My father was not surprised to find the letter a plea for help on behalf of a student.

I was both excited and alarmed at his unexpected request. Though I relished the thought of fresh company in our quiet, secluded home, I was also a little afraid of having a stranger in the house. Since my life had been a solitary one so far, I'd had little contact with men, especially from educated society, and my emotions were thrown into turmoil. I was shy, reclusive, introverted even, and the whole concept of an unfamiliar man under our roof filled me with thrilling nervous energy. I stood transfixed at the window, letter in hand, very much afraid.

My father granted the request, allowing this esteemed pupil of Sir Edward's to reside with us for a number of weeks, and hurriedly despatched his reply.

Sir Edward was overjoyed to receive my father's reply so promptly and hastened to arrange the event. My apprehension grew as the date of arrival became imminent, although I later discovered that my fear both was and was not justified. An entire facet of my being was shattered into fragments the day he arrived.

The morning began with a springtime sun warm enough to thaw the heart, but, once melted, the thunderous masses that swamped the brilliant blue sent a fatal chill into all that lay vulnerable below. A deathly calm descended and by midday all was unnaturally quiet and still in the path of the oncoming storm. The air became heavy and humid as the afternoon passed, gradually building into a dark, oppressive silence.

A carriage burst from the woods accompanied by the first booming peal of thunder, the team of horses shying and rolling their eyes in sudden terror. The wheels of the carriage churned up clouds of dust that thickened into mud as the downpour commenced from black, brooding storm clouds. Hearing the sound of riotous hoof-beats, my father and I followed the servants to the front door which was almost wrenched from its hinges by the furious wind. The carriage had stopped at the foot of our steps, the footman trying in vain to quiet the whinnying horses as well as open the door for the passenger within.

I stood waiting in the portico, clasping the cold, grey marble column, hiding behind it, watching as my father extended his hand to the figure stepping down from the carriage. He was a little taller than my father, neatly turned out in black and carrying a large portfolio case. He was slender with long, unruly dark hair that contrasted with his pale, oval face and matched his dark brown eyes. He shook hands with my father who welcomed him warmly and led him up the stairs towards me. I backed into the lobby as they approached, and one of the servants passed me to collect our visitor's bags.

"Sir, may I present to you my daughter, Theresa." My father took my hand and offered it to the young man. My trepidation shone clearly enough to him, for he took my hand gently in his long, pale fingers. He looked into my eyes and I felt the walls in my mind I'd built over the years had been crushed to powder in those delicate artist's hands. The smile came to my lips easier than I expected, and he returned it, a slight raising at the corners of his ruby lips. "I am honoured, my lady." He kissed my hand.

"Theresa, this is Sir Edward's most favoured student, and our guest, Philippe DeCheance."

"I am pleased to meet you, sir. You are very welcome in our house." He released my hand with the barest hint of reluctance. Again, he smiled at me and then turned to my father. "I truly appreciate the favour you have granted me. I hope I haven't caused you any inconvenience."

"Not at all, young man, I'm very pleased to assist you. Johnson will take your bags and show you to your rooms. Please make yourself comfortable. Dinner will be served at seven o'clock." Our visitor bowed elegantly and followed Johnson upstairs to the rooms we had cleaned and freshened for him.

Dinner was interesting. My father eschewed the head of the table in favour of the seat beside the young artist. I took his place and had an uninterrupted view of Philippe during the meal. My father discussed with him the merits of his artistic training.

"I recognise the great historical importance of the classical masterworks, but I feel that it is now time for a darker, more passionate approach to art. I am a great believer in passion." I caught his gaze across the table, but the expression in his eyes was unreadable. Suddenly, I found my tongue.

"And what, sir, is the ideal subject for your passion?" I asked him, watching the candlelight sparkling in his eyes.

"I prefer to work at night, capturing the nocturnal beasts about their business. The play of the full moon upon the fields and trees has a foreboding beauty seldom matched during daylight hours." Philippe watched my disturbed expression before returning to his meal.

Over the next few days, we discovered the phenomenon of the 'artistic temperament', something Sir Edward had alluded to in his letter. Philippe rarely rose before dawn, even then keeping to the privacy of his rooms. On the most beautiful days, he would remain aloof until dusk, and yet on grey, overcast mornings he would accompany my father on horseback through the local countryside, observing the rocky terrain with interest. I greeted them returning from one such expedition and Philippe asked – rather slyly – if I would oblige him by posing for a portrait amongst the granite crevasses. He felt certain that the harshness of the environment would contrast with my refined, ethereal beauty. I turned to my father, and he nodded his assent. "I would be honoured to sit for you, sir."

One evening the next week, after dinner and conversation had ended further into the night than was usual, Philippe warned us that he would be out late that very night, and that we should not be alarmed to hear the door closing behind him in the small hours. He thanked us for our indulgence and assured us both that the servants need not wait up for him before ascending the stairs to his rooms.

I didn't hear him leave, but I awoke suddenly in those grey hours that formed the hinge of the coming day. I couldn't recall hearing a sound or any dream disturbing enough to rouse me. I drew back the lace bed curtains and wandered barefoot to the window, my night-gown rumpled and caught up about my thighs. Still half-sleeping I regarded the three-quarters full moon and the unhealthy yellow light it shed upon the woods. My attention was drawn to a figure striding across the open ground towards the house. His movements were hurried and erratic, and he appeared almost drunk. It was undoubtedly Philippe; no-one in our service had such long, lustrous hair and bone-white features. He seemed to sense my presence at the window, watching him, and pointed at me, his teeth bared in a cross between a smile and a snarl. A cold-clawed hand gripped my heart and a shocking tingle of excitement lanced through me.

I heard a door at the back of the house close and I froze, staring at the door to my room in terror, expecting at any moment for it to burst open. Of course, it did not and I returned to my bed almost regretfully, noticing in alarm that I was trembling and my night-gown felt damp with nervous sweat. I nestled beneath the blankets and spent the remainder of the night in a fitful, disturbed sleep.

Next morning I awoke much later than was usual and the events of the night returned to haunt me. My face in the mirror betrayed my shock; a shadowed, anonymous skull set upon my shoulders. I dressed hurriedly, all the while attempting to fabricate an explanation for my troubled appearance. Frantically, I left my room in search of my father, but my headlong dash halted at the stairs leading up to the attic and I was caught as if in a web. Against my better judgement, I obeyed the insidious voice deep inside that urged a naïve, innocent girl ever closer to the spider at the centre of the web. My needs to be with family and to pray were overridden by an eagerness to follow my curiosity. I climbed the stairs to the second floor, grasping the thick, wooden banister as if it were my only link to the real world. At the next landing I began to ascend the narrow stairs to the attic, my trepidation subsiding and a nervous fever replacing it. The panelled door at the top was slightly ajar, tempting me inside.

The room within had once been a study, but we had arranged it as a studio for our guest. The smell of linseed oil assailed my nostrils, accompanied by the sharper tang of turpentine. The surfaces were littered with dozens of sketches, all of local views except one. Executed in white on black paper was a portrait of me. Philippe had given me a sardonic smile and a malicious glitter in my eyes that hinted of untold longings. Was this how he saw me? I shuddered at the sight of this thoroughly evil picture.

The door to the bedroom was closed but not, as I discovered, locked. It opened silently onto the darkened chamber and its sleeping occupant. I approached the bed, my heart hammering hard enough to wake the dead, though Philippe slept on. I drew back the curtain to reveal twisted sheets, draped across his lower body in careless modesty. All evidence pointed to a restless night; he lay oddly on his back, head thrown back over the pillows with his long hair tangled and matted about him. Other than the sheet, he was naked, and my girlish innocence brought a blush to my cheeks, but the treacherous voice in my head guided my eyes in their guilty appraisal. I had been brought up to think nudity shameful, but no-one had told me that mortal sin could feel as natural and healthy as breathing.

He was not particularly muscular; his torso was formed like a classical Greek sculpture. His skin was a pale, creamy white, his chest and stomach covered with soft, dark hair that clung to his body. I traced a line along his breastbone with my fingertip, entranced by the strange, alien feel of his flesh, my guilt overcome by a sense of discovery. I reached for the sheet that lay across his waist and thighs, and lifted the edge, raising my eyes to his face as I did so. His eyes snapped open and a welcoming smile parted his lips to reveal sharp pointed fangs. To my horror I saw patches of dried blood at the corners of his mouth, and the true reason for his nightly excursions became terrifyingly clear. His eyes locked on mine and I felt a sudden influx of strange and unholy desires that both disgusted and aroused my senses. The source of these myriad feelings and impulses could only be Philippe subjecting me to a barrage of mental intimidation. Having thus enlightened me, he turned away and slept once more. The horror and revulsion within me boiled to a peak and I fled, pounding down the stairs to my room, slamming and locking the door. I collapsed against it with my breath coming in gasps, my mind reeling from the shock of his thoughts in my head. What manner of sin had I committed? I could only think of hurrying to the chapel and pouring out my shame.

My father found me an hour later, knelt in front of our humble family altar, soundlessly mouthing every prayer of repentance I had ever learnt. He sensed my distress when I jerked violently at his hand on my shoulder. I was hurried into the drawing room and fortified with a large brandy whilst father set about extracting my story. The lie was ready on my lips and I stammered out a muddled fear of a terrifying beast approaching our home, approaching my room, ever threatening, never entering. Father assured me of my safety. "I imagine you heard Philippe returning late last night and formed a dream around it. There's no harm in Philippe."

This I heard and shuddered at. Our guest's first appearances of eccentric reclusiveness had - for me at least - been shattered. I was truly afraid of him, yet attracted to the mysterious, seductive air he possessed with those knowing, mocking glances I repeatedly caught. The thought of dinner with him set my nerves alight.

I returned to my room to wash and change for dinner. I looked through my wardrobe and felt myself drawn to a linen dress cut lower than my usual attire. I held it before the mirror and noticed that my hands were shaking and realised I was dressing to tempt the Devil himself, deliberately trying to provoke a reaction. Disturbed by the changes taking place inside me, I left for the dining-room.

Philippe was most apologetic when my father recounted my experience. I flinched and waited for him to denounce me but his face betrayed nothing. He smiled gently. "I must have disturbed you, my lady. I'm very sorry." He held my chair as I sat and returned to his place opposite me to eat. Throughout the meal I was constantly darting glances at his mouth, trying to catch a glimpse of those wickedly pointed teeth. Surely father must notice them? Or perhaps he had shown them to me alone and the only reason I had seen them was because it had been his wish. He made no reference to my morning visit and I relaxed, indeed, I felt more comfortable with his presence than I had in the chapel amongst the saints and in the sight of God. I could find no reason for my loss of faith other than the enormity of the sin I had committed, and I finished my meal in guilty silence.

I spent the evening alone in my room, criticising my wardrobe. I was filled with a sense of waiting, but not knowing what for. My bed was covered with discarded clothing, all of it old and designed, so it seemed, to smother and repress. My choice of gown had arrived in a parcel with a number of others as a gift for my seventeenth birthday. On first sight I had consigned it to the back of the wardrobe as fit only for a courtesan, but now I realised how well it suited me. Fashioned in a bloody shade of silk, the dress was cut low across the bust in an immoral flourish. It was now, as I admired its contrast with my white flesh, that I heard Philippe leave, heading for the woods with grisly purpose. I watched him disappear, then returned to my bed, a wave of sleep suddenly washing over me. I lay amongst priceless fabrics, my mind haunted by dark dreams as I drifted away.

The shriek of an owl disturbed my rest. I saw the night was paling and rushed to the window, knowing I would see him. Without hesitating I ran from my room down the stairs and into the ballroom. I stood at the ornate French doors, watching him approach, then opened them wide, admitting the warm breeze to ruffle the curtains in welcome. As he came closer, I could see that taunting, fang-revealing smile on his lips. I backed away as he entered, fighting the urge to flee, the voice of reason screaming at me to run from this personification of evil. But I didn't run. He stood before me, arms outstretched to hold the door-handles and swing them closed behind him. Standing in the open doorway, he was a blasphemous picture of the Crucifixion, arms wide, head bowed with an expression of peace on his face. A perverse tableau indeed with his long hair ragged and his shirt - usually so neat - ripped to his waist exposing the lithe body beneath. Philippe raised his hand and wiped his mouth, smearing a thick bloodstain across his chin. Moving slowly towards me, he smiled invitingly and this time I stood my ground, extending my pale hand in submission. Philippe took it and kissed it, leaving a rusty print of his lips that burned my skin.

"Are you afraid of me?" he asked.

"Yes," I replied honestly. His smile broadened as he examined my attire. "You are very beautiful. There are so many things I want to teach you."

"I want to know what you are," I stammered. He laughed aloud, a thin sound that echoed into silence. In one fluid motion he slipped his arm around my waist, holding my lower body tightly against his. I gasped and made a token attempt to struggle, knowing that I should fight him off and scream for help, but the warm feeling pervading my body was too pleasant to curtail. He placed the palm of my hand on his bare shoulder through his torn shirt and clasped the other in his. We danced across the black marble floor of a room that should have been silent, but my ears were filled with the music of a discordant orchestra.

"What do you see when you look at me?" Philippe inquired, his mouth close to my ear. I looked once more into his eyes and felt the immoral tide of emotion flood through my mind. I struggled to find words to adequately express the strange conversion taking place within me.

"I see a source of evil so great... so depraved... and yet twisted by bizarre nature into desire... so pure... entrancing..." Overwhelmed by his presence, my head sank forward against his chest. I felt him lean forward and his lips brush my neck, the fleeting touch of a butterfly's wings. Perhaps I gasped in surprise, for he whispered "You must not fear me," before kissing my lips and neck with rapidly increasing passion. I tipped my head back, baring my throat to his teeth as our dancing slowed to a standstill before the great, gilded mirror on the wall. My reflection stood alone in solitary delirium, the only evidence of my ghastly paramour was the movement of my bodice as his slender, artist's fingers unlaced and parted the fabric. He pressed his fingertips against my trembling virginal flesh and followed them with his moist, burning mouth, festooning my body with bloody kisses. An intense sense of burning suffused my loins, a feeling I had never before experienced in my tender youth and my knees buckled as the heat enveloped me. I collapsed into Philippe's arms, his face haunting me as the darkness came.

I awoke in my bed with the lace curtains drawn about me, covering the immodest disarray of my clothing. Sunlight streamed in through the casement, bathing me in its scorching rays unable though to cleanse my sins. The guilt had passed to the back of my mind now, along with my childhood religion that still protested against my licentiousness. As I stood before my mirror with my dress discarded on the floor, I recalled each and every touch feeding the furnace inside me, driving my desire to the point where I thought it would surely kill me. Upon my milky breasts I bore the ruddy marks of his lustful attentions, though not one of these blemishes was a puncture. He had made no attempt to taste my blood and I knew now that he did not mean me to die along with his victims. Despite my skin remaining inviolate, I could feel the transformation progressing. I remained uncertain of my future but my fear had become eager anticipation.

A sharp knock on the door startled me. I snatched up my negligée to cover myself and opened the door a fraction. My father stood in the hallway bearing a tray of salad, fruit and sweetmeats. "I suspected you were feeling unwell so I've brought something to tempt your appetite." I took the tray from him and set it on the bed. From the light outside, I guessed it was early afternoon. "I am feeling a little poorly, father. I'll not be down for dinner this evening." He kissed my cheek. "Get plenty of rest, my dear and send for anything you want."

I closed the door behind him and returned to my bed, tossing the negligée to the floor with my crumpled gown. I tasted the food and, to my disgust, discovered every fruit to be soft and pulpy, the aromatic, lightly oiled salad bland and flavourless. This confirmed my suspicion that there was now only one form of sustenance that would assuage my hunger. I sat alone in my room, whiling away the hours as I waited for night and the darkness I sought in human form.

The sky darkened as evening approached and I stood before the looking-glass in a flowing gown of flawless linen and lace. As a nervous bride on the eve of her wedding's consummation, I trembled, my apprehension returning. I jumped when I heard the front door slam and, driven by the demon possessing me, I hurried down the back stairs and out through the servants' quarters.

Philippe disappeared into the forest as I rounded the corner of the house. Twilight had advanced rapidly and I risked losing him in the gloom. The woods beckoned with seductive evening birdsong and velvet leafy shadows. Nervously I entered and was instantly swallowed up by a world of trailing boughs and long rustling grass. As I stumbled through the trees guided only by the full moon above me, I encountered other creatures of the night already bloodied by the kill. A distant cry drew my attention back to my quarry and I struggled through the undergrowth towards it, shreds of my dress hanging from the thorns in my wake.

In the depths of the forest I rediscovered the old barn, drawn onwards by the sounds of pursuit and death. I detected movement inside and I crept through the decaying wooden door to be greeted by a sight that almost provoked a scream. Sprawled across the floor, pale and drained, was the body of a woman, her face frozen in a rictus of terror. Her throat had been bitten open and retained the bruising from the pressure of a hungry, sucking mouth. Soft footsteps on the floorboards above betrayed the perpetrator of this gruesome crime and I climbed the narrow rotting ladder, torn between terror and rapture.

He stood by the glassless window, silhouetted against the sky with his clothes torn and his hair in disarray. His eyes were half-closed and he appeared satiated from his meal, for the time being at least. He turned his attention to me as I clambered through the trapdoor into the hayloft.

"You followed me. Some might call a shy, aristocratic virgin foolhardy for such an act." He walked slowly towards me and I was rooted to the spot, unable to move or speak. He cupped my face in his hands, licking the traces of blood from his lips, the moment dragging on forever in the still, silent atmosphere.

"I had to come. I needed to see the truth," I stammered.

"And now you know the truth?"

"I want it."

At once, he gripped my waist and flung me into the mound of hay at the rear of the loft. I could not stifle the scream and sound echoed from the eaves until I felt his weight holding me down and he stopped my mouth with his own. I tasted blood on his lips and tongue and it spurred me to respond with my new-found passion unchecked, my fingers curling in his tangled mane of hair as sinuous as snakes. His nimble fingers unlaced my gown and spread open the folds of lace. My conscience whispered its evil thoughts; I would be damned for this. He would abuse me, humiliate me and God would not forgive me for permitting this desecration of my body, and yet the expression on the demon's face was not one of triumph, but of purest love. His tender fingertips spread warmth into my belly as they investigated the parts my virtuous youth had preserved intact, his touch both calming and inflaming me. Abashed, I closed my eyes as he paused to strip off his torn clothes, re-opening them when I felt his kisses upon my breast to see him knelt between my thighs. His weight forced me into the hay and I sensed a burning pressure, followed by a sharp twinge of pain as my innocent flesh yielded to the firm thrust of his manhood. The cry of pain died on my lips as his movements within me drew forth a strong, focused ecstasy on the shady border between pain and pleasure. My spine arched in delirious abandon accompanied by Philippe's hoarse groans. He gripped my waist tightly, growling deeply as he pressed still further into me. Then I felt his teeth.

Those vicious fangs slid into my throat with the same moist ease as his member pierced my loins. I dug my nails into his back, groaning as he drew my consciousness out of my veins and pulled me into sleep.

I awoke with the failing rays of the moon in my eyes, a brightness my brain wanted to rejoice in. I rose from the hay, proud of my nakedness, and walked to the window where Philippe sat, lost in his own thoughts. What was he thinking? What did a vampire feel for a mortal whom he himself had sucked dry and drawn across the barrier between life and death ? He sensed my presence and reached for me, resting his pale cheek against my stomach and permitting me to stroke his matted hair. A thin dribble of blood stained my thigh, a testament to the loving violation I had suffered at his hands and he bent his head to lick it away, following it to the source until my breath quickened. Dawn was almost upon us and we had no more time to dally. Hurriedly donning our tattered clothes, we ran through the forest to the house where my father and the servants still slept. We regained our rooms unnoticed after a passionate farewell and closed the curtains to keep the dawn at bay.

Once again I stood naked before the mirror, examining my wounds. The bite upon my neck was fading already, given as it was in love and not the rage of hunger. At last I felt no shame, my downtrodden Christian conscience squirmed and finally expired, leaving me excommunicated and finally free. With a sardonic smile, I retired to my bed to sleep the contented sleep of the damned.

The sun has finally set after losing its crimson and gold halo and slunk disconsolately below the horizon. I am nearly finished with the past and my pen grows dry.

All day long I have heard my dear father's desperate attempts to rouse me from my slumber. Now I will go to him and prove my love for him by satisfying those earthly needs he has for so long repressed. Then I will use his failing flesh to feed my own before my vampire lover leads me on the road to paradise.

I lay down my pen and stretch my limbs. My hunger is for blood, but it must first give way to the irresistible compulsions of lust.

(A Little) Death in the Harem

Jami Stirling

The gossamer drapes fluttered in the balmy summer breeze as the Maiden slept in her silk-covered bed, a naked savage fanning her prone body as she lay in the sultry embrace of the Egyptian night.

A full moon hung low over the palace, the sticky air punctuated by the distant cries of tonight's lucky recipient of the Pharaoh's lustful ardour.

The Maiden turned in her sleep, one hand absently cupping her blossoming breast. Despite the heat her nipples were taut and firm, stiff peaks of delight to be one night devoured by the mouth of her captor, the Pharaoh. Her smooth skin glowed with a faint flush of pleasure as her other hand sought lower, finding the smooth swell of her mound, one tapered finger slipping deeper between the hairless folds of flesh.

Her eyes flickered, a tiny moan escaped her lips, as her finger found the hard nubbin of flesh within its protective hood, instant drops of pearly liquid running from deep inside her. She turned again, her legs falling apart beneath the transparent veil of her bed-sheet.

The savage stood seemingly impassive to the scene, but the stiffness of his huge black cock belied his disinterest. His hand closed tighter about the long stem of the fan, the other touching the swollen hardness of his naked manhood. While the Maiden still slept, such liberties were possible, but the punishment for getting caught committing such sacrilege would be severe indeed. Sometimes a risk was worth taking.

The Maiden cried out once more, her hips arching up as though to meet the thrusts of some phantom lover's cock. One hand balled into a tight fist in her ebony hair, she ground the other hand against her cunt lips, shuddering in open-mouthed ecstasy as the waves of delirium coursed through her virgin body. "My Prince," she breathed, her voice softly aspirating a frenzied gasp of rapture. "My Prince, come to me now. Let not the Pharaoh taste my virgin blood."

In a silent flurry of movement at the open window a figure appeared, eyes penetratingly black, round and soft-lidded, skin pale ebony and flecked with silver moonlight and deep black shadows. A cloth was bound about his head in the Egyptian manner, but this was no Egyptian. His lips were parted, dry and hungry to feast on the sleeping Maiden. Such a rare beauty she was, her flawless body smooth and untainted by the corruption of mortal man.

Soundlessly he entered the room, passing one hand swiftly in front of the face of the wide-eyed savage. "See nothing," he said in an accented whisper, and the savage's eyes clouded over as he stood, motionless, a mute statue cast in ebony.

"Awake, my Princess," breathed the intruder, tracing the outline of her bare breasts with one gentle hand. "I have come as you bade me come."

The Maiden's eyes snapped open, moonlight flooding those brown depths. A soft sheen of perspiration patterned her body, evidence of her self-pleasure, her guilty passion. Her mouth widened into a smile of pure lust, all hint of the virgin subsumed in her desire for this invader of her private chambers. "Joshua," she sighed, his name a breathless mantra on her lips. "Joshua, Joshua, you came to me. You found me at last."

"Of course I did." He leaned over her, pulling back the sheet to fully expose her perfumed nakedness. "Perfection incarnate, do you think I would let a mortal fool like this barbarian Pharaoh touch you?"

She gasped as his fingers found her wetness, rose up to meet his hand and push it harder against her pussy. Her silky lips slid apart beneath the force of his fingers and he buried two digits deep inside her, stifling her cry with a kiss. She clasped her arms about his body for a moment, before letting one hand trail over the waistband of the loin-clout he wore. She could feel his rampant rigidity already straining to be free, and she massaged the thick length of it with an eager hand.

He groaned and pulled at the knot of the clout, anxious to be rid of it that she might pleasure him further. It fell away from him and her hot little hand was upon him, uncoiling the engorged serpent of his cock and licking her lascivious lips in anticipation.

"Let me kiss it," she begged, her eyes wide and anxious. He knelt closer to her on the soft bed, straddling her naked body as she wriggled up against the bank of pillows.

"Oh my gods, yes," he responded, pushing near to her so that the wet tip of his cock nudged against her pouting lower lip. "Kiss it, kiss me."

She opened her mouth in a broad smile, her long dark tongue curling out to flick across the glistening head of his stiff weapon, to lick the salty tear that hesitated there. Then, aroused at the taste of him, she plunged down hard on him, devouring his length and taking it deep into her throat. A low growl of pleasure formed in her throat, came out stifled and flat through the flesh in her mouth. She sucked vigorously on his rod, feeling him grow even harder, even longer, as she mouthed him. More pearlescent tears fell upon her tongue, and she yielded her juice to his probing fingers.

Frantically he started to pump inside her wet mouth, and then equally frantically pulled away, wanting it so much to continue, but knowing that to continue now would be to end it all too soon. She groaned with her need for him and reached out for him, but he drew back. "Not yet," he admonished.

"Then kiss me," she sighed, putting up one hand to restrain him when he bent to meet her mouth. "No, kiss me... there." She arched her hips up to show him where, showing him the golden lips out of which ran rivulets of white heat, flowing over his fingers. The heady scent of her arousal made him dizzy with hunger for her. It had to be tonight - he could wait no longer to thoroughly possess her.

He knelt in adoration before her shaven slit, the long smooth curves of her legs either side of his head. "So beautiful," he whispered, bowing down to lick her warm wetness. "You cannot imagine how long I have waited for you to be ready." His eyes glittered, crimson fire burning in their depths. "Are you ready - for death?" He nuzzled his face against her, tongue probing deeply the secrets of her virginal sex.

"For life," she replied, paroxysms of pure ecstasy tumbling through her. "Give me back my life." She cried out as the first orgasm bled into the second, as his mouth closed firmly about her swollen clitoris. "Grant me my freedom from this earthly bondage."

The Prince drank deep of her, draining the hot elixir of life and her passion from her heaving, spasming cunt. She was more than ready for the bite, that deadly kiss that would reunite them for once and for ever. "Sheba."

"Joshua."

As he moved away from his feast, she turned her head to one side, exposing the pulsing artery to his view. She felt his hardness slip between her legs, felt the wet globe of the head of his cock brushing against the opening flower of her cunt. "Yes, my Prince."

Pulling her roughly up against him he drove deep inside her, impaling her on the rigid serpent of his adoration, feeling the virginal bond tearing beneath the force of his lust. He sank deep, thrusting slowly but firmly into the warm cavity of her, lost in the sweet sensation of her tight wetness.

The Maiden groaned to feel his spike piercing her, reached up to clasp her arms about his neck, to touch his silvery face. "My love," she breathed. "My Prince." The slow, deep rhythm of his fucking ran in time with the thumping pulse of her heart, her blood washing white hot in her ears. Defenceless beneath the questing hunger of his massive cock she abandoned herself to the urgency of her own mounting desire, descending into the pit of his violent need to face the devil she knew only as Joshua.

In the heat and desperation of their coupling they writhed, twin demons locked in a frenzied coital spasm that seemed endless and inevitable. From the moment he had found himself in the land of his country-woman's captors, it had been inevitable that they would end up on this silken bed.

He could smell the rich salt of her blood as he bent closer to her throat, tracing the line of the pounding artery with his long hungry tongue. Thirst cast a dry grip on the back of his mouth and his belly hungered for her life essence.

"Yes, Joshua," responded the Maiden. "You know it is time." Her cunt open to his rapine, her legs locked in eternal bondage about his waist, she plunged ever further into her own damnation. Her whole body aflame with the desire he had inspired, she soared up to meet his frenzied thrusts, to force his cock even harder, even deeper, inside her - harder, deeper, until she thought she would die of it.

His balls tight, the Prince felt the dense tide of salty blood-spunk rising in his shaft, tried to stem the flow, but unable to control it, came in vast shuddering waves of ecstasy. His rich spunk jetted deep into the Maiden's cunt, burning towards the deepest, darkest part of her. She screamed out to feel this unfamiliar sensation, her entire body trembling on the cusp of yet another climax. She came with a breathless gasp, a choked attempt at his name as he sank down over her and plunged his fangs into the raging fever of her throat.

Crimson fire exploded against the roof of his mouth as he bit into her, bubbling fountains of it shooting down his throat and into his hungry belly. She clung to him, her nails digging deep furrows in his shoulders, her body paralysed, back arched in pain and pleasure. Another stream of wetness gushed from her cunt, his spunk and her blood conjoined.

Blackness descended as her strength ebbed away, her eyes singing a final farewell in the moonlight to the immortal saviour of her soul.

And then, inevitably, came the sunlight, and she rested and slept and died and was buried. And as the evening moon once more drenched the balmy night in silver, her eyes re-focussed on a world reborn, as the Prince took her hand and enveloped her soul in the eternal shroud of erotic nightmare.

Blood would be nice!

Holly & J. Flaxton

I ran and ran until all my breath was gone, my heart pounding. Alas I had arrived too late. Throwing myself behind a small bush I could only watch the scene before me, my heart slowly breaking. I had always been so very diligent, I just couldn't understand it. I had been away but an hour.

I watched the two men drag my dearest beloved from the resting place in his tomb into the strong evening sun like he was a rabid beast. He fought so very bravely but he was just too weak to fight free. With the sun burning into his skin he was no match for the two thugs. Damn them for the cowards they are! Hate began to fill me, horror consumed me, yet somehow I managed to remain silent, stifling the screams of despair within me.

My dear beloved had prepared me for this. To love a vampire I had to be prepared to see him snatched away from me like this. He had made me promise that no matter what happened I should conceal myself, or I too could be attacked, even killed. Even so, I so wanted to help my love, wanted to run to him. My darling had assured me that should this ever happen he would feel no pain, but even so it looked horrific. He looked so horribly burned and he cried out so. Was he calling to me?

It was all happening so quickly, the stake found its mark and it was all over, my dear sweet beloved was dead! I just could not believe it! Tears burst from my eyes and I screamed inwardly with grief. An awful emptiness consumed my soul and I felt numb with horror.

I think I must have fainted, for when I regained my senses the two attackers were getting into a white car. One of them shouted to the other that they must be at the blue bridge before 7pm. Almost instinctively I looked at my watch. It was six-fifty. And then they were gone.

I rushed over to my beloved, unable now to stop myself from crying out to him. My legs felt shaky and I fell to my knees beside him as he lay dead on the cold hard ground. They hadn't even had the decency to place him back in his resting place or even to cover his body. Hot tears streamed down my face as I leaned down to kiss his cold lifeless lips.

In my grief I begged his forgiveness. I had only been away such a short time, only to return to this horror. I knew it was my place to stay beside him, to watch over him as he lay in vulnerable sleep, to guard and protect him, and yet I had deserted him at the very time he needed me. But I was hungry. I needed to eat! He knew I always felt weak after he had fed upon me. And now he will never again feed from my breast, nor shall we ever again consummate the perfect love we shared. I, who had never known another man, had given my all in love for him, in lust for him.

And now he could never fulfil his promise, to take me into his world, to give me the bite of immortality. Who would now sate my body and soul as he did? Why, oh why couldn't I just bear my hunger until nightfall, just a few short hours away? And now, because of my selfishness, my one true love lay dead.

Tears were almost blinding me as I touched the stake that still protruded from his chest. I swore to him that he would have his respect, have his dignity, even in death. It took every last ounce of strength I had in me to pull the stake from him, hurling it as far away from me as I could. The face of my beloved looked peaceful now, and he could now take his final rest. I fell to the ground in utter despair. I no longer wanted to live without him. They had killed my darling, my own true love, and now I wanted to die too. I felt such grief, such loneliness, such guilt. My love, my life, my hope – all were gone!

I sat up abruptly, startled by my own thoughts. Blood! His blood! Yes, I had to drink my darling's blood, just as he had drunk mine. I craved the power I felt in him as he drank from me. And then the sweet bliss as we made love, as I let him take his pleasure from me also. I could deny him nothing. I reached out and rubbed his cock through his trousers, but there was no life in it now. Oh but how I had loved his cock, loved to feel it in me, loved to taste it, loved to worship it. I licked my lips, for a moment I almost fancied I could once again taste his semen, and for a moment the hot burning lust that we had shared coursed through my loins, making me cry out.

Yes, I would swallow his blood! And then he would be alive, alive in me, and in me always. Yes I would take him in me, and then we would never be apart. Images flashed in my mind, the ferocious lovemaking that always followed his feeding from me. I felt those same feelings through my loins as I leaned down to him.

I took as much of his precious life-giving fluid into me as I could. It was still slightly warm, thick and sweet, and I sucked avidly just as I did when I sucked his thick sweet semen from him. I felt his strength in me then, the strength to do what I had to do. And then I could swallow no more and I let my darling rest. I kissed again the lips of my beloved, I just couldn't bring myself to kiss his cock as I had done on so many previous occasions, the thought that it would not respond and grow to fill my mouth would bring me despair beyond anything I could endure. So again I kissed those sweet lips, and as I did I vowed that the evil scum that had driven that awful weapon into his sweet body would never again know comfort or mercy. If I could no longer have the love of my dear beloved, all that was left to console me was the thought of revenge, and I promised on the body of my beloved that I would have that revenge in a manner and at a time that suited me!

With an effort I managed to drag the body of my beloved back into his sleeping chamber. New strength helped me to accomplish what would hitherto have been an impossible task. With a final kiss I bade him rest, then I closed the tomb, vowing to return only after I had exacted my revenge. Now would my search start in earnest, a search for a white car and a blue bridge. But where to begin? All I knew was that they had to be at the blue bridge by 7pm.

I had to work out a plan of action. True, 7pm had been and gone, but I only had one lead to work on. The blue bridge had to be in the next town, they had driven off in that direction. And according to my watch at the time they only had ten minutes to get there, which meant it must be quite close. I trotted back to where I had parked my car, a little way from the tomb.

It didn't take long to get into town, and the rest was down to just asking around. I discovered straight away that the blue bridge wasn't a bridge at all, but 'The Blue Bridge' public house.

I stood outside the pub for quite a while, just looking at the white car. They were in the pub alright! With a last solemn promise to my dear beloved, I went into the pub. It was fairly small inside and there weren't many people, so that as I ordered a drink at the bar I could plainly see the two assassins sat together in the far corner of the room. I took a seat where I could keep an eye on them and watched with utter revulsion and contempt as they actually celebrated the killing of my darling. How I loathed and despised them for the cowardly attack on my beloved. Vampire he may have been but he was the most caring, loving person I had ever met, and those two low lives weren't fit to lick his boots!

The one who had stood by and watched as his friend had killed my beloved (and so ended my life too!) spotted me and smiled at me. He then said something to his murderous friend, who then also looked my way and smiled, before turning again to his companion. In fact he kept on looking at me and smiling. I drew breath to spit my contempt at him, but just managed to control myself. No, I must stay calm, I must not betray my true feelings! It was revenge I wanted, and I had to draw them to me by whatever means was necessary. If they walked out of the pub now I might lose them forever. I would do anything, anything that enabled me to avenge the murder of my darling.

I smiled back at them, and it was all the encouragement they needed. The first one came over to me and invited me to join them to celebrate a successful venture. I agreed to join them, but as they celebrated the death of my dear beloved I celebrated the revenge that was soon to be mine!

The first one, Jeff, was drinking very heavily and got steadily more drunk whilst Colin, the murdering bastard, remained sober as it seems it was he who was driving the car. Strangely, neither of them made a pass at me, my task would have been easier if they had. I could have used sex to lure them on, until the time was right to exact my revenge. I'm a fairly attractive woman with a nice body, and using it to trap the scum wouldn't have bothered me.

By closing time Jeff was absolutely legless, Colin had to literally carry him to the white car and throw him into the back seat. Colin turned to me and asked me if he could drop me off anywhere. Of course I said yes, I needed to keep in contact with them, and I hadn't worked out a plan yet. I had spent all that time in the pub watching them and loathing them when I should have been thinking of how to get even. I felt despair creeping over me. The thought that I was so close to avenging my beloved, only to have the chance snatched away from me, only brought tears of grief again flooding from my eyes. Colin put his arm around my shoulder and asked me what was wrong. Strangely he seemed genuinely concerned. My mind was racing, what could I say?

With a sob in my voice I blurted out that I couldn't go home, that I'd had a blazing row with my husband and that if I went home he would fly into a drunken rage and batter me senseless! Colin said he could either take me home and give my husband a good hiding, or I could stay the night at his place. I almost laughed when Colin said he knew something was wrong because he thought my mind had been elsewhere all night. But I didn't laugh, I begged him to let me sleep at his place. I even blurted out that I would be ever so grateful and promised to make it up to him somehow. Colin never so much as blinked, so (inwardly asking my beloved for forgiveness!) I told Colin that I would be grateful enough to sleep with him. Still there was no reaction, so I softly kissed his lips, at the same time sliding my hand down to his groin and gently rubbing him. Nothing, his manhood never even twitched. Shit, surely he wasn't gay?

As Colin started to drive us back to his place I pretended to sob, saying that he didn't like me. He said of course he liked me, I was a very attractive and sexy woman, but sometimes he had a need for other things. Other things? I felt my pulse quicken, if I trod carefully I might just find out something to my advantage, something I could use against him. So I carried on sobbing (even louder) and said that he was only saying that he liked me and that he was just like my husband and that he hated me. Colin was by now getting a little flustered, he didn't quite know what to say. So I sobbed some more. And then he came right out and said it, and it was far more than I could have ever dreamt of. I could almost picture my revenge in my mind's eye. Inexplicably I began to feel quite aroused.

Colin said he was into S&M and could only get it off if he had someone, a Mistress, to dominate him and sort of torture him. He asked me if I knew what he meant? Lying through my teeth I told him that was what had started all the rows with my husband, that he had caught me and a man friend indulging in a little S&M, and had found me whipping his bare arse. Colin laughed loudly saying that was kid's stuff, that he was into real pain and torture, real advanced stuff. Smiling, I told him that sounded really exciting and that the thought of it was really turning me on. He asked me if I thought I could do it to him. I laughed and said that I would love to torture him, and this time I wasn't lying!

By the time we reached Colin's house he was quite excited, and I rubbed his erection through his pants. He practically begged me to be his Mistress, even if only for one night. He even offered to pay me! I said we could always give it a try and that doing it would be payment enough. He smiled. I smiled. But I bet we were smiling for two very different reasons.

Colin carried Jeff into the house and dumped him on the sofa to sleep off his drunken stupor. He suggested we just leave Jeff where he was, so he could show me his special room downstairs. He took me down into the cellar and there we entered a strange room. I can honestly say that I had never seen anything like it. The walls were painted black and all manner of weird looking stuff was hanging from them. The whips and manacles I recognised, even the chains and masks, but most of the stuff was really alien to me. There were what I could only describe as harnesses and strapping, even what appeared to be a full leather body suit. There was a sort of big wooden cross in the shape of a large letter X fixed to one wall. Just the thing for a crucifixion! And there were wooden trestles with chains and anklets, obviously to bend someone over for whipping. Along the longest wall was a bench, also painted black, with a lot of small bits and pieces on it, though I didn't look closely at what they might be. In the corner was a full length mirror on a swivelling stand. I couldn't begin to imagine what that was for. I didn't need anyone to tell me that this was a torture chamber... I mean, a real torture chamber! And the thought of inflicting some real torture was making me feel so wet.

Colin expectantly asked me what I thought about the place. I smiled and said I thought it was wonderful. He moved closer and kissed me, his right hand rubbing my breast. Don't ask me why but suddenly something just snapped inside me. I guess I wasn't used to anyone but my beloved touching me like that, I just couldn't help myself. I sprang back and slapped him hard across the face. Colin looked puzzled, god what had I done? I had to think quickly. I just laughed and asked him if that was the sort of thing he liked. The puzzled look left his face and he began to laugh, long and loud. In spite of the fact that it was rather warm in the cellar I shivered, it was the same laugh I had heard as he left my beloved with a stake through his heart. It was a timely reminder not to lose sight of why I was here, and to keep my mind on the task ahead of me.

I again silently begged my true beloved to forgive me, and then I kissed Colin, asking him did he want to get sexy tonight, then maybe I could indulge him in his more perverse needs the next day. I told him that if he wanted I would make love to him, right here in the cellar, or if he preferred it I would suck him off. He smiled and said that whilst the thought of filling my lovely mouth with his cum was a particularly attractive one, he preferred me to spend the night with him in the cellar, punishing him for his sins. Now it was my turn to laugh. Oh yes, and I knew what the sins were, and believe me, I intended the punishment to end just like the crime... in death!

I told Colin that although I had some small experience I would have to rely on his guidance if we were to both derive satisfaction from the night. He grinned and said that if things worked out he would fuck me like never before. As if to reinforce his statement he slid his hand up under my skirt and rubbed between my legs. To show my willingness I lifted my skirt and pulled the crotch of my panties to one side so he could feel how wet I was. I blew out a lung full of air as his finger penetrated me. The excitement, the thought that I could be about to torture Colin to death, was just too much for me and to my shame I found myself begging him to do it to me more.

I looked him straight in the eye and told him I would kill him for touching me like that. His response was to rub me even harder, he laughed and said he loved the way I was getting into the spirit of things. As the words left his lips I had the most amazing shuddering climax. I was crying for mercy and at the same time begging him to do me harder. My legs were shaking and I felt them buckling under me. I was puffing and panting as his finger rubbed me to ecstasy. In my mind all I could visualise was Colin dying slowly at my hands, and it turned me on like nothing ever had before. I wanted his blood! Not just to spill it, but to rub it all over me, and then to drink it! Then I would own him, his life would be mine, to give or take as I wished. Mine to destroy!

I felt so fucking horny, it was as though I had to let him defile me to justify punishing him to exact my revenge. My legs just wouldn't support me any more and I fell to my knees in front of him, his fingers pulled from inside me. My orgasm still had me trembling, so just as I had done so many times with my beloved I opened Colin's pants, pulled out his semi-erect cock, and forced it into my mouth. It tasted slightly salty as I sucked it hard, swallowing its entire length. As with my beloved I sucked and rubbed it, faster, faster. I wanted him to cum in my mouth, that last, final, total act of defilement. Then I could kill him!

And then the effects of my orgasm subsided and I was snapped back to reality like an elastic band. I spat his penis out of my mouth, god the thing wasn't even hard! I clamped my eyes tight shut and prayed to my dearest beloved... watch me! Watch me! Now he trusts me. Now he dies!

I got to my feet, wiping a smear of seminal fluid from my lips, and asked Colin did he want to start now? Colin was stripped naked and on his knees in front of me almost before the words had left my lips. He was begging me to punish him, to hurt him. How could I deny him? He was like an expectant child waiting for a present. Or was it a lamb waiting to be slaughtered? I laughed, I don't know why, I just felt so exhilarated. I felt very warm, I was toying with the idea of taking my clothes off and making him do things to me, maybe lick my slit, or make him fuck me, I was just so damn horny. Then I laughed out loud again, how could he fuck me, he couldn't even get a hard on! Oh but killing him was going to be the ultimate turn-on, better than fucking, better than anything!

I had him on the large wooden cross in two minutes, his hands in manacles, his feet in ropes, spread-eagled before me. As he hung there naked I looked down at his limp cock. Whatever had possessed me to take that thing into my mouth? I hated that cock for not even having the decency to go hard. I wanted to hurt it, I wanted to punish it for insulting me. I looked round, looking for a weapon, anything I could hurt him with. I saw a cat o'nine tails hung on the wall and grabbed it down. I was surprised at how heavy it felt. It was made of hard leather and each of the nine tails (yes, I even counted them!) had a small weight at the end, a tiny metal ball. Colin nonchalantly said that the cat was for more advanced punishment, and that I should probably start more gently, so to speak.

My answer was to lash the cat across his stomach as hard as I could. Colin yelped like a chastised dog. He yelled at me, asking me what the fucking hell did I think I was doing? Well, I was punishing him, wasn't I? He asked me to, didn't he? Very ungentlemanly to speak to a lady like that, so I gave him another, right across the stomach. I told him that if he spoke to me like that again I would really punish him. The bastard just laughed saying that I was really getting into the part. So I gave him five more, real hard ones. That shut him up, in fact he seemed to be having difficulty catching his breath. The weals were livid, raised like red tracks over his stomach, like so many veins turgid with blood. I was getting horny again.

Then the thought of blood. Yes, blood would be nice! Lots of it, enough to drink and get real fucking horny. It was hot in the cellar, unless I was just getting all steamed up and red-hot horny. I went over to the full-length mirror and looked at myself. Yes, I did look a bit hot. And then I thought of the blood again, lots of blood! I thought maybe I'd better take some things off – if there was going to be blood splashed around I didn't want it on my clothes. Besides, the thought of warm blood splattering on my naked skin was making me feel really wet.

I turned to Colin, who watched me silently as I first took off my blouse and then my skirt, before folding them neatly and putting them behind the mirror out of the way. I posed in front of him in just my bra and pants. Nothing, his prick didn't even twitch. So I hit him again with the cat and I felt an electrifying thrill shoot through my groin, so powerful that it made me clutch myself. I never knew that hate and pain and sex went together so well.

God, I felt so fucking horny, so I gave him about another twenty strokes of the cat on his belly. It could have been thirty, it could have been fifty. I don't know. I just hit him and hit him as hard as I could until my arm was too tired to do it any more. Colin was screaming, begging me to stop. Oh yes, it felt so good. The vibrations from his screams went straight to my crotch, like having a vibrator in there. This was fantastic. My dear beloved was a wonderful lover, but this was something else. I was panting with lust. One or two weals on his stomach were bleeding. Colin was sobbing and whimpering and... Jesus, his cock was starting to go hard! I leaned down and licked some blood from his belly, it made me feel even hornier. His cock brushed my cheek as it began to harden, I turned and took his cock in my mouth and as it slid between my lips it went harder. Long, smooth and hard, I thrust my mouth down over it, trying to swallow it all, but it was too big and hard. I allowed myself an inward smile. That's better, I thought, I was beginning to think he didn't like me!

But no, his cock did nothing for me. It didn't excite me like when I took my beloved into my mouth. So I did the only thing I could do under the circumstances, I stood back and lashed the cat with all my might across his cock and balls. Colin screamed, his body twitching in pain, and for the first time I thought I saw fear in his eyes. I asked him did it hurt? He began sobbing again, begging me to set him free. So I lashed him again in the same place. Colin screamed again. His scrotum now had a small tear in it, and his cock had several small cuts. But it was still hard as a rock.

Blood! Blood oozed out of the cuts on his cock, and it dripped slowly, oh so temptingly slowly from the rip in his ball sac. I quickly got to my knees and licked his scrotum, tasting the blood. As I began to suck at the small tear, almost instantly I felt a power well up in me, the power I had felt when I drank the blood of my beloved. Other feelings, wonderful feelings, surged through me. I felt so horny I pushed my hand down into my pants and began to masturbate. I wanted his cock then, so I took it into my mouth and sucked hard. I could feel the blood being drawn from the cuts and into my mouth. It was just so incredibly erotic. It tasted good, so good, and it made me so horny. I suddenly realised that I still had the cat in my hand. I turned the handle round and, pulling the crotch of my pants to one side, I forced it into my vagina. I fucked myself hard and rough. That's what I wanted, what I needed!

I reluctantly took my lips from his cock and looked up at Colin. With quivering voice I told him what I was doing. I told him how I felt so sexy from sucking his blood that I was fucking myself with the whip handle. I told him how good it felt, how it was like a big hard prick fucking me, how I was all wet and slippery, how I was taking the whole handle up me, how it was better than any fuck I had ever had. Yes, it was working, his prick was getting visibly larger. So I began to suck it again, to draw the beads of blood out of it again. Oh the sweet blood! It was exquisite, so sweet and so warm.

Someone once told me that semen is constituted from the man's blood, so drinking spunk was like drinking blood. They said that was why women love to suck cock, to drink spunk, because it was the same as drinking blood, because most women are natural vampires. Stupid statement really, but it's one I've always remembered. It came to my mind now because that's what I wanted to do. I wanted that final, total, act of defilement. I wanted Colin to cum in my mouth. I'd drunk his blood and now I wanted to see if it was true. I wanted to drink his semen to see if it really was the same as blood. I had to know! I had to make him cum and I bobbed my head up and down his shaft for all I was worth. I sucked hard as though trying to draw his spunk up his cock like it was a drinking straw.

Colin cried out... and then I got what I wanted! His spunk pulsed into my mouth, like blood pumping from a vein. My orgasm hit me like a runaway train, Jesus I could hardly stand it. My whole body, my whole being shook and I tried to scream, but I couldn't make my lips let go of his cock. His semen was thick and hot, salty, just like blood. Just like blood! There was so much of it I had to swallow hard and fast to stop myself from drowning in it. Mixed with his blood his spunk tasted fantastic. I almost felt cheated when he was spent.

I was still crying out with the ecstasy of my orgasm as I let his limp cock fall from my lips. Colin just watched as I slowly drew the whip handle out of my vagina and flung it away from me. I was still panting, it had been fantastic, better than anything. I had imagined that it had been my beloved fucking me, but it was oh so much better. Colin started to say how wonderful he thought I was, but I told him to shut up. He did! I wiped some of his spunk from my chin with the back of my hand and walked over to the bench of equipment. I looked along it, there was all sorts of weird and wonderful things, clips, clamps, pins, hooks, and... a craft knife. A small razor-sharp craft knife. I picked it up and took it back to Colin, showing it to him. I asked him where he wanted the cuts, but he just laughed, he didn't think I was serious. So I thought I might as well tell him.

I told him how I had seen him and Jeff murder my beloved, how I had seen him drive a stake into my dear one's heart. Colin stared at me as I told him how I had drunk the blood of my beloved and how I had vowed to never rest until I had avenged his death. Colin just looked bemused, and then he seemed to suddenly realise that I was serious. He started yelling and protesting, but I wasn't in the mood to listen. He had committed his last act of defilement. He had murdered my sweet beloved and in doing so had shattered my life. And what of my personal defilement? I told him of my disgust when he had put his fingers in my vagina, and his cock in my mouth, and when he had made me swallow his cum. And now, I told him, it was my turn to do the defiling, and I was going to start by defiling what he had defiled me with.

Two quick strokes with the craft knife and I had all but severed the fingers of both his hands. Blood seemed to spurt everywhere, and Colin fought frantically against his restraints, but he was well and truly captive. I looked down, my breasts had splashes of his blood on them, and a stray spot of semen. God, I felt good! So strong and so horny. Colin screamed out that I was a vampire too! I pondered that for a moment. Yes, I suppose it was true, I did drink the blood of my beloved. Perhaps that is why blood makes me feel so damned horny and so fucking powerful! Anyway, who cares?

What next? Oh yes, his prick! Colin screamed when I told him what I was going to do. He was really scared now, he knew who I was and I had convinced him that I would do anything to avenge the murder of my beloved. I took hold of his prick in my left hand, and amazingly it started to go hard. Jesus, what a pervert! He was asking for it, in his own way he was asking for it, so I did it. A neat slice, four inches down the length of his prick and as deep as the blade would cut. The whole thing seemed to explode with blood, and Colin screamed yet again. Or was that a prayer I heard? I felt so fucking horny, I just couldn't help myself, I just had to have blood! I took his bleeding cock in my mouth again. Colin squealed and squirmed as my mouth filled with his blood. I gulped it down avidly, and it was hot and sweet. It would have been nice if he could have cum too, but I guess he wasn't feeling particularly sexy right at that precise moment.

So what now? Kill him I suppose. Trouble is, I got a bit carried away with the craft knife and Colin would die from loss of blood from his hands and cock if I didn't kill him soon. I didn't want to be cheated of my chance to kill him, not now, not when I was so close. I told Colin that I was going to kill him. He went quiet, and I do believe he would have got a hard on, if his prick had been capable of holding blood... but I guess it wasn't!

I told him that he had murdered the most important part of my life and that was why he had to die. I told him it would have to be soon, as he was already getting pretty weak from blood loss. So I told him I had decided to use the craft knife to cut his throat. He might have been weak but that didn't stop him begging, pleading, screaming for his life. God, it made me feel so horny! So what the hell... he screamed, I masturbated. But it just didn't feel the same as before. I would have to kill him to get horny enough.

I put the knife a couple of inches under his left ear. Colin clamped his eyes shut and sobbed. He was trembling with pain and fear. I asked him if this was sexy enough for him, I couldn't help myself, I had to laugh. I told him to listen. Listen! Listen! I wanted to hear it, wanted him to hear it. Amazingly he went very quiet and very still.

That's when I did it. There was a soft soughing sound as I cut through the vein under his left ear. He never moved, so I cut through the vein on the other side. Jesus, I had never seen so much blood. I didn't know a person had so much blood in them. As the blood bubbled and dribbled down his body I lapped it up, just like a cat.

After only a minute Colin began to twitch, with what I took to be his death throes. He slumped motionless against his restraints. The blood still pulsed from his neck, but it formed just a slow trickle now. I looked around, there seemed to be gallons of blood splashed everywhere. I lifted Colin's head and his eyes fluttered open weakly. I felt a surge of arousal in my groin. I cupped my hand under his neck until it held a small pool of blood, then I pushed my hand into my pants and rubbed it into my sex. And then Colin closed his eyes for the last time, he was dead. I forced two fingers into my vagina and rubbed myself to the most unbelievably fantastic orgasm.

I finished up on the floor, lying in Colin's blood, finger-fucking myself like crazy. It was incredible, I had orgasm after orgasm, I loved it, loved the blood, loved the power, loved how it made me feel so fucking horny!

It was early morning by the time I had showered and washed the blood from my hair. I even masturbated in the shower, it turned me on watching all the blood being washed off me. My bra and pants were ruined, so I stuck them in my hand bag and just wore my blouse and skirt. Time to go home.

It was then that I remembered, and pangs of loneliness stabbed my heart. Even if I went home my beloved wouldn't be waiting for me, instead he was lying in his sleeping chamber, never to awaken. And with him died my hope, my reason to live. No, wait? There is a reason to go on ... revenge! That was a good reason to live, revenge upon all those people who had ever hurt me or my beloved. That could take years. Yes, years! I felt my groin tingling, but only blood could satisfy me, only blood would make me horny, make it all worthwhile. Blood, cum, death, sex, it's all the same thing, isn't it?

I stood looking at Jeff, he was quite good looking really. Time to wake him up I think. I shook him until he roused. He moaned that I should leave him alone, but he was soon wide awake when I told him I was feeling horny. In fact his eyes nearly popped out of his head when I lifted my skirt and he saw I was naked underneath. Judging by the size of the bulge in his pants it wouldn't take long to get him interested.

I asked him if he had ever been tied up. He said Colin did it all the time and yes, he wouldn't mind giving it a try. When I asked him would he like to be tied up naked whilst I sucked him off he practically jumped out of his clothes. When I produced the rope I had brought up from the cellar, he obediently let me secure his arms and legs so he could hardly move. And when I took my clothes off, saying I didn't want them to get stained, his cock swelled in anticipation.

I knelt beside him and promised him that if he managed to cum in my mouth I would have a real surprise for him. He was so excited I knew it wouldn't take long.As I slid my lips over his knob he closed his eyes. I felt his cock go big in my mouth and I knew it would happen very soon. He lay, eyes closed, oblivious to everything but his own pleasure. I reached into my handbag with one hand and got hold of the craft knife. My other hand moved down between my legs. My lips could feel the veins in his cock filling with blood. God, I was starting to feel horny again!

Blue

Rachel P. Kendall

In the dimly lit bathroom Faye was preparing herself for a very special night. The ash from the cigarette between her lips fell unnoticed onto her moist skin where it remained, staining her breast a dusty grey. Flakes of it floated around her body and stuck to her like jetsam in a murky sea. Working the razor along one white, skeletal shin which stretched up out of the water, her painted toes reached for the dark of the window. Between each stroke she paused to admire her work. It made her tingle with excitement, and each nick, every tiny speck of blood on her leg was simply a pleasurable presentiment of the night ahead. Pleased with her efforts she reached over the side of the bath and pressed play on her remote control. Trent Reznor's melancholy wail sliced through the steamy air and then dipped below the water to reach Faye's ears, to send a message to her brain. Taking a deep breath she screamed out her hysteria and revelled in the anticipation of the unknown night. There seemed to be a sting of electricity in the air which rained down on the body in the bath and made her skin crawl delightfully. Lying back in her plastic womb, the cooling water played with the tendrils of her hair which encircled her jutting cheek bones and mercury eyes. The music lulled her. With one hand between her legs and the other on the edge of the bath she arched her back and fucked herself with eager fingers before she was to become the harbinger of death once more.

The girl she was planning to murder tonight worked the night shift at the local cinema. Usually, after she had shown the customers to their seats she would linger around till the end of the film. This had made it easy for Faye to watch her, to follow her home and to make her plans, which had been beautifully unfolding like a rose since she had first seen the creature. Every time she had looked into those endless black eyes something new had opened up; a different game they could play, or some new device to be introduced. The tying, the cutting, the choking, the searing of flesh. It was planned up to and after death took over the body. Death was not an end to the games, it was merely a detail, and often it was a whole new challenge.

This girl with the waist length black hair, the perfect curvature and the pale skin, had excited Faye the most of all her victims. She was flawless and Faye was almost breathless at the thought of digging her nails into that face and leaving an open wound, a fresh orifice as sensual as any other.

Faye did not kill her girls because she was lonely. She was not one of those sad cases who sought love and companionship from a cadaver. She could get what she wanted from live flesh. She killed simply because she loved to kill. She loved to hurt, to maim, to rip beauty to pieces and to bathe in new-found death. Faye never ate her victims. Neither did she sleep with them for nights on end till their blackened flesh separated from their bones. What she did enjoy was the feel of fresh skin and fresh gut, fresh blood and a still warm pussy. But the thing which gave her the most pleasure was to look into the eyes of a beautiful girl as her new gashes flayed and her blood splayed; to not lose contact with those eyes as she thrust her fist deep into the girl's shattered pelvis and licked the last of the spittle from the corners of her cooling lips.

On the corner of the dark street whores were tapping their feet to the music which played in their heads. The lethal heels of their boots gave their fleshy thighs a feline curve, and stretched the muscles of their calves to give the supple look of a cat's hind leg. Faye knew if she were to walk over to them on the other side of the street they would stink of sex and secretion. Occasionally cars would slide by, driving slowly in the drizzle, looking closely at the women. The men in the cars were just like Faye. They too liked to indulge in the female form. Only they left their victims alive to re-live the rape a hundred times over.

Two men stumbled out of the cinema, laughing like children.

Faye watched them look over at the women, who looked back, tapped their toes, hitched up their skirts, played games. It was fun to watch the ritual. Soon these men would no doubt be injecting those women with their own brand of happiness and would pay them for the honour. But Faye had no time to watch this comedy. Soon her girl would appear and so would begin another night of watching and waiting. But tonight she would watch pain. And tonight she would wait for death.

Faye backed away from the glow of the neon cinema sign, and nestled herself into the wall, into the shadows which bathed her in the chill of the night. She felt relaxed, washed over by a calmness which she could only feel before a murder. She could not feel nervous; she rarely panicked. Just the thought of seeing a pair of beautiful eyes turn from the bright blue colour of life to the grey marbling of death soothed her. She was excited too, excited about evoking emotions. She wanted to see pain and fear, grief and finally death in this girl's eyes. This was the greatest gift a victim could offer.

She had felt nervous once, when one of her victims escaped her and ran down the street shouting and screaming. In the end though, it had been a perfect death for Faye when she finally got the little bitch back into her clutches.The fear in her eyes had been remarkable. She had been role playing that night, Hallowe'en, just two months earlier.The girl had not been chosen beforehand, but she had turned out to be the perfect host at her own death. Faye had met the stupid young thing alone in a club dressed up as a vampire.As soon as she had laid eyes on the girl, who was perhaps just seventeen or eighteen, it was obvious she would be an easy target. Like so many others who plagued the midnight streets and night clubs dressed in black, dancing to music that penetrated their searching souls. These people had nothing but their music and the constant longing for suicide, like a déjà vu in their drug infused brains. These young people who made themselves up to look like the dead invited it and would embrace it when it showed itself.At least, this is what they liked to think.

The girl on this night was the same. Dressed in black velvet and lace, talons filed to the extreme, lips as red as fresh scars and her whitened epidermis as soft as cotton candy. She had tasted almost as good as she looked. On this Hallowe'en night she had been surrounded by others who liked to dress as the dead and macabre – zombies, mummies, ghastly images taken from the empty world of the media. It always amused Faye the way people would play the role of the dead, but when offered to them it was always turned down. The girl, who Faye had named Elizabeth, had tuned herself so wholly into the role that Faye decided she would do a little role playing herself. What could be more pleasing to a girl who so obviously desired to be a vampire, than to be seduced by one of the immortal dead for real? It had worked beautifully at first. The girl was pulled to Faye's outstretched arms like a pretty little magnet and had happily taken off her clothes in an offering of flesh for the combining of juices. Even when Faye had pulled out a knife and made a tiny incision in Elizabeth's belly she had only whimpered and arched herself towards the blade. Her arms and legs already had the signs of self-inflicted knife wounds so Faye knew the girl was not afraid. But what fun is it to kill someone who does not fear? What is the solution? A little mental torture could always turn a reaction around. To be told that her skin would be peeled from the tissue beneath, with a sound not dissimilar to that of tearing velcro; that her neck would be sliced from front to back, leaving a delicate necklace of bleeding life. The girl ran. But she did not get far. Running through a forest of oaks which lined the street, she had fallen over tree roots and Faye, strong and pumped with adrenaline, was right behind her. Holding her down she did what she had to, to make Elizabeth's release from life meaningful. She bit hard into her neck. Without fangs she had to tear madly at the skin with her blunted teeth to get a hole big enough to drain her, but it was not a problem. Faye had found it all very erotic and had made love to the girl repeatedly until her husk had been left bruised and torn.

Tonight's victim would be different. This would not just be a biting ritual, there would be variation. Things had to be done differently every time to avoid losing the thrill. It usually depended on the girl. This one had been singled out for special treatment. This was going to be the best. Thinking of the girl now Faye realised how like Elizabeth she was. Sitting in the cinema week after week she had watched silently as the film played blue shadows onto the girl's face, bathing her beauty in angelic light. Faye had named her Blue, for her flesh was paler than a silver haloed moon in the cover of sky.

Faye rolled up a cigarette as she waited. It seemed that she had waited for hours, although the whores were still scrounging for men, like starving rats in a sewer. As she clicked open her lighter to inflame the cigarette, she heard voices just inside the cinema entrance. Snapping the lighter shut and throwing the roll-up to the floor she leant back and was deathly quiet, hidden from the street. Seconds later Blue hurtled out of the door and onto the pavement, her long legs seeming to fly in every direction at once. She stood outside the cinema door and looked around, her feral eyes darting in every direction. For one moment, as Faye stood with eyelids melted shut, she felt Blue look straight at her. Then the feeling was gone. When Faye opened her eyes Blue had walked on and was half way up the street. Faye peeled herself from the brickwork and followed, the girl's swaying hips and ribbons of black hair securing her attention.

Faye's silent footsteps traced the clicking of Blue's heels. Blue's black coat was tied around her constricted waist and her legs stretched below for miles, with black knee length socks giving her a little girl sensuality. The rain blew horizontally into Faye's face, making it difficult to see the girl ahead. It soaked into her hair, turning it to strings of brown, and poured into her half closed eyes. Blue kept up her pace and the hunter continued to follow.

After the seemingly endless walk Blue stopped outside an old warehouse. This was not her home, which Faye had seen many times over the last month. The boarded up windows and blackened stone made this the perfect setting for the Reaper. Faye casually watched from a shop entrance nearby as Blue turned the handle and opened the heavy wooden door. She watched the girl's powerful back slink through the tiny gap and saw a last flash of a white leg before she was gone from view. Swiftly Faye followed her into the gloom and found herself in a large hallway. In this empty room she took deep breaths and gathered her thoughts. Blue had disappeared, obviously up the staircase in front of her which was the only way to go. Against her left breast she could feel the tip of her knife as it pressed through the skin of her inside pocket. The feeling was violently erotic, and when she bent over with hands on knees to let her hair drip a puddle onto the concrete floor, it pressed deeper. She remembered the whores from the street and wondered whether any of them were being fucked right now.

Standing up straight she was ready. Her wet hair hung limply to her cheeks now and her skirt was sticking to her legs. She did not mind. Reaching into her pocket she blinked once, twice, and pulled the knife out. A drop of water fell from the web of her lower eyelashes and coursed down her cheek. With one hand she brushed it away and made her way up the stairs. Reaching the narrow door at the top she knew this was it. With the knife in one hand she eased the door open with the other and stepped into madness.

"I knew you'd come."

The voice was deep, almost gravelly, and it came from the girl at the edge of the room. Blue was standing with a large church candle cradled between her hands. There was a soft glow emanating from a mass of candles on the floor and a large window at the opposite wall let in some dirty orange light from the street. Apart from this, the room was bare, and very heavy. Something, somehow, was causing the air to feel heavy, so that Faye had to drag each breath in through the tiny well of her throat. And there was a smell. It was pleasant, like incense, but there was something riding beneath this, something sinister. It was the aroma of flowers carrying the scent of a freshly dug grave; or the sweet sickly smell of a still-born baby. She stepped forward.

"You've been expecting me," she whispered. The voice was supposed to be laced with poison. Instead, it sounded like a cry for mercy.

"Oh yes," replied the beautiful Blue. "Now come and claim your prize."

Placing the candle at her feet she began to untie her boots. As she bent over, rivers of black hair spilled down towards the floor, like a hundred moths to the flame, and Faye was powerless to do more than watch, like a voyeur at her own funeral. Boots were flung to one side and then the girl snaked her hands up her legs, to the waist of her short black skirt. She looked up and Faye was able to see her face for the first time in the warmth of a candle flame.

Where the eyes before had been whirlpools of black liquid, looking into them now was like experiencing near-death. The black was still there, but now it surrounded a bright silver ball of ice. The lashes lining her lids curled upwards like the legs of insect corpses and the lower lashes could almost have been drawn onto the skin in ink. Her narrow nose pointed down towards a large mouth, where at this moment crystal pink lips were stretched over teeth in a smile. Dragging her gaze down to the neck Faye saw blue veins pulsating with life all over the skin in a network of intricacy. As Faye watched Blue ease her skirt down over her thighs she saw how prominent her veins were. As the girl lifted her sweater over her head, Faye watched as they appeared to pulsate and radiate a blue brilliance. She provided a new silver sparkle to enhance the golden glow of the flames.

Blue was naked, except for white knickers which covered her

hips and the flat of her belly. They were adorned with tiny blue flowers, like a pair Faye once had when she was a child. When Faye looked at these knickers she saw them blood-stained. It was the way she saw everything, such was her fascination with the draining of this red sap.

Blue was offering herself to Faye, unaware that she was to be a human sacrifice; a quench for her thirst, a drug for her addiction, a canvas for her creative mind. Soon her pain would be all too real. It was time.

With a glint in her eyes and a sardonic grin scarring her face she raised her left hand in an arc. The knife sailed high and stopped above her head, blade pointing towards the naked flesh in the corner. She moved forwards, fast, dipping the knife, slanting it, aiming for the soft skin beneath the ribs. She brought it down in a swoop but suddenly it was knocked from her hand with force as Blue punched it from her grip. It landed with a clatter amongst the candles, a sacrificial blade to a make-believe god. Faye watched it spin for a couple of seconds before coming to a slow stop. Turning her head around she looked at Blue who, with hands on hips and weight resting on one leg, looked like one of the whores from the street. She was laughing.

"Ha! What do we need a knife for? That's not a test of strength. It's not a fair game if you have a weapon and I do not."

Reaching out, Blue extended her fingers and placed the tips on Faye's shoulders. She leaned her face in and kissed her first on one cheek, then on the other, while unbuttoning her blouse. The kisses left ice-cold moist circles on Faye's cheeks which made her skin rise in goose bumps. Blue slipped the blouse from her shoulders and began to remove the rest of Faye's clothes.

Naked and without a weapon Faye was vulnerable. Yet she had been in this position before. She had killed Elizabeth with just her teeth and could always rip flesh with her nails. Her confidence remained and this erotic stranger continued to entrance her. She decided, as Blue eased down her own knickers, past jutting knees and over bare feet, that she could plunge into this girl. She could take her alive, enjoy her warmth, and then kill her. She placed a hand on each of Blue's shoulders, but in one swoop Blue had brushed them off and Faye was on her back, her wrists held down by strong hands, bare buttocks sitting on her stomach. The girl was so light Faye could hardly feel her. Yet she could not push her off. Right now she could do nothing but submit. Still, her ravaged mind created images she did not want to miss. As Blue's hair like black asps hissed threateningly towards her eyes, Faye saw the scalp as it should be, ripped into clumps of skin and hair, each piece scattering the floor like a bloody, decaying rat. In a flash, her slender body was lifeless, cauterised wounds and bloody tracks in her diaphanous skin, a rip joining her pussy and the hole in her neck where blood still poured.

But here and now the body was still alive, and she was strong. Most definitely she was unafraid and this caused Faye some concern. She began to struggle madly, but was caught in a trap. Blue bent her head to Faye's ear.

"Shhh," she whispered. The sound came from somewhere deep inside her cavernous body and seemed to calm Faye a little as it came to rest inside her ears. Dipping her head slowly Blue's mouth touched Faye's; their tongues embraced and their moist lips gliding skilfully and hungrily. Until Blue sank her teeth into the corner of Faye's mouth, biting off a chunk of her lip. Faye gasped and Blue yanked her head up, a thin line of blood sloped down her chin and dripped onto her left breast where it stayed. Faye could taste her own blood, it was on her teeth. She did not like it; the taste or the consistency. She drew the back of her hand over her lips and tried to push the girl off her. But using all of her strength she could not do it; she was locked between her thighs. The girl was giggling.

"You are my victim now, my darling," she hissed. "Do you like it? Does it make you hot?"

Faye struggled and began to thrash about. Adrenaline was coursing through her limbs now; her blood was speeding through her veins as her saturated heart beat double time to keep up.

"Who the fuck do you think you are anyway?" Blue yelled angrily, though there was a tinge of playfulness to the voice. "Ha! Do you think you're some kind of serial killer? An assassin?"

Leaning down she shouted into Faye's ear: "Do you think you're fucking immortal?"

With her knees Blue spread Faye's legs wide and held them in place with her elbows. Faye saw her nails, each one a double edged athame, pierce the tender skin at her wrists as the girl held her in place, captive. She had known pain before, and she had known fear. But at this moment she was more afraid than ever. Turning her head to the side she could see the window. The soft rain was caressing the glass, leaving streams of orange light down the pane. She closed her eyes and let Blue's icy tongue wash over her body, lapping up the rain water and the cooling sweat.

Faye's eyes snapped open as she felt cold air between her legs and a tongue on her cunt.The girl was looking at her, watching her as she drank. As her tongue moved rhythmically over her clitoris, Faye wanted to arch her back, to push herself towards the girl's face, even in her pain. Now the girl's tongue was deep inside her. So deep. Faye felt she was going to shatter. But just as she felt her orgasm was about to grab a hold of her and rip her in two, the girl stopped. She raised her head, glanced once at Faye and then with incredible force dropped her head and sank her teeth and face into Faye's pussy.

All of Faye's senses exploded in a shower of pain, blood and saliva.The walls between her and the girl had come down and she knew she had lost all control.Though she fought and wrestled and tried to kick out, Blue would not loosen her grip.The sensation of losing her life overwhelmed and weakened her. Submitting to the pain and the pleasure within, she watched, eyes transfixed on Blue's lowered lids as she greedily sucked and swallowed. She was swallowing her blood, letting out little whimpering noises through her nose as she suckled. When she had her fill she paused and lifted her head.

"Do you know what I am?" she whispered.

Faye's eyes widened, the pupils dilating to cover the streaky blue. She could not believe this vision in front of her.As Blue's face floated inches from her own, the pink mouth, now stained with blood, was open wide.Two fangs sloped down from her upper jaw, like icicle stalactites from the roof of a deadly cave. Faye's blood dripped from the points, it collected in the corners of Blue's mouth and she hurriedly snaked out a tongue to retrieve the luscious liquid.

"You taste so good," she whispered.

"What are you? A vampire?" Faye kept her eyes locked onto Blue's silver hosts.

"I am an Angel of Death." She leaned in further so the tip of her nose was just above Faye's ear. "I reign supreme over your soul. I bring death and I gorge myself on your blood, you stupid little bitch."

As she sat back on Faye's stomach, her talons still securing the girl's wrists, she began to withdraw. Her fangs still protruded, her breathing was shallow and fast. Silence could have shattered the air between them like the thunderous end to a stifling summer heat. Blue raised her chin and stretched her neck where electrical currents throbbed in her raised veins. Two dark lumps had appeared on her back. Faye could see them as they appeared over

Blue's heaving shoulders, while she continued to stretch and writhe on top of her. The vampire's eyes were shut and her mouth twisted into a half smile of ecstasy and pure agony. Her veins throbbed, the lumps began to grow and unfurl. Like hide they looked hard to the touch. Steadily the thick growths expanded, rolled out until they stretched into two huge bat-like wings, which touched the walls on either side of Faye as she lay on the floor in disbelief. The expanse of these flaps of skin was enough to block out the light from the window and knock over some of the candles. The room was thrown into further darkness and covered Faye like a death shroud. At the delicate points the wings trembled slightly, opened and closed rhythmically, as if Blue were about to take flight. She had become one pulsating energy, moving in time with the universe; the raising of her breasts in time to the beating of her heart; the constant shuddering of the wings to the throbbing rivers of blood which would be a needle user's dream. She was beautiful and Faye, slippery in her sweat-glistened skin and the blood from her wounds, knew that she would die.

Crawling backwards to rest on her muscular haunches Blue opened her eyes and smiled. Easing one nail at a time out of Faye's wrists she left large black puncture marks and a little spurting of blood. Faye could not move as Blue lifted her hands high above her head. She could barely breathe any more in the heavy air which weighed down on her limbs and ate its way into her throat. And as Blue brought down her hands and smashed them into the succulent meat of Faye's belly, she did not have the air in her shrivelled lungs to scream.

Taking the red painted edges of the lacerated skin in each hand Blue tore the honey flesh apart and sank her face deep into the hole. This was her destiny, to fill her starving body with the life of her dying victim, as Faye lay silent and without gratitude on the wooden floor of her grave.

The Strange Client

Leo Cores
(Translated from the Spanish by Annie Velo)

I found myself walking about the streets near W–. Cemetery, in Earl's Court, as at that time I was in the business of prostitution, after having left my village town in Wales to go to a dreamt-of London. What I am about to tell you next was the most notable reason for my abandoning such an occupation, therefore the experience of which I am about to tell you overturned my life in many ways, what is more, I was never the same person again.

It was a little after eight on a winter's evening, it had stopped raining a short while ago and the pavements were still wet, when I heard some heavy footsteps behind me which sounded dry despite the humidity which covered the asphalt. I drew near the bright light of a street lamp to show my pursuer what I was in case he was a prospective client, now that the night appeared cold and rainy, it would prove most pleasant to be able to go soon to some warm hotel room; and who knows if perhaps not spend the whole night in that very room, if my client was generous. The footsteps did not take long to reach me, but they lingered at about two metres from where I found myself. The figure I had before me represented a man of tall stature and strapping build, elegantly dressed from what little I could observe at that moment, as he stood in the semi-darkness where the light of the street lamp grew more tenuous.

"Are you what I think you are?" said a voice with a grave and pleasant intonation, which made the little fear I could shelter disappear, already accustomed to this type of situation in the last few months; but I had not destroyed my defence wall because of this as you never know who you may encounter, at worst with a policeman who are the strangest ones.

"I am what the gentleman desires me to be," I replied with half a smile I doubt he managed to see.

"Good, well let's not talk evasively. There's a hotel on that corner which I believe accepts these kinds of visits."

"Ah, the C–.! Yes, it's very nice there, but a bit expensive."

"Don't worry about that. I'll also pay you well, how is two hundred pounds?"

"Perfect, sir."

That was three times as much as what I usually charged. I could either go to my room soon, or else devote the rest of the night to my client, who seemed most pleasant.

He put his hand inside his blazer which he wore under the thick overcoat and took out a magnificent black leather wallet out of which he pulled a few notes without counting them, and stretched out his hand to me. Avidly, I took them and put them away in my handbag. Once again he stretched out his arm with a gesture for me to take it, and so I did. I felt the strength of his arm and his height at once, I hardly reached his shoulder. He started walking at a quick pace, well I did, since he seemed to fly so that we were before the Hotel C–. right away.

We climbed the few steps up to the threshold, he rang the bell. Under the door light I was able to see his face well for the first time; thick, black eyebrows joined a perfect Greek profile, his eyes were also either black or very dark, his hair, also dark, and slightly greying on the sideburns, was long reaching his shoulders and he wore it gathered in a pony-tail above the nape of the neck although a few stubborn locks stuck out which gave him a more juvenile air; he was about forty-five.

Impatiently a few seconds later he rang the bell once more, then I noticed his gloved hands, they were enormous, giant-like. He bent over me, with an expression which attempted to outline a smile but was unable to; his well-shaven face seemed of white porcelain under the light. My first thought was: "He is very handsome, we'll have a good time." The door opened by the action of a half balding, potbellied man who wore a badly adjusted tie.

"Sir... madam," he said, looking firstly at my host and then in a more contemptuous fashion at me.

"I'd like a room for the night."

That voice arose again, and once more, its magic took effect, since the receptionist fell in amazement before it and was all reverences.

"Please, sir."

He opened the door, moving away and allowing us both to pass into the corridor which was carpeted in grey and with high white-washed walls which correspond to those Victorian buildings. The receptionist directed us towards the end of the corridor where there was a small counter and the staircase to the upper floors.

"Would sir and madam like a room with two single beds or a double bed?"

"Double, please."

"Good, it's number twelve, at the top of the stairs on the first floor, the second door on the right," said the receptionist, stretching out his hand to give a plastic key card to my client, who made a courteous gesture of gratitude while adding a thank you with his habitual intonation. He looked at me and motioned towards the first steps, as if inviting me to initiate the ascent first. I had never had such a pleasant and handsome client in all those long months of walking about those streets of London, I thought.

I climbed the staircase and paused before the door which had the number twelve, he was already behind me. He introduced the card in the slot and as if without any effort pushed the door, which opened slowly and completely. We entered the room almost at the same time, I switched on the light while he closed the door; I contemplated a spacious and well-furnished room, papered in a not very pleasant pastel colour (I do not recall if green or blue) with a fitted wardrobe in one of the walls, a bedside table on each side of the ample bed, opposite the latter hung a small television set from the wall, there was also a beautiful dressing table made of fine wood, and a door which must have led to the bathroom; it was most welcoming.

I turned round, embraced my client at the same time as I attempted to take off his overcoat. He lightly rejected my embrace saying: "Turn on the lamp." What lamp? I thought. Yes, there was a small lamp on the right bedside table, I approached it and turned it on while I felt the light in the room decrease, after turning off the switch of the spider lamp on the ceiling. He likes being in the dark, I pleasantly thought.

"Yes, it's much more welcoming like that, more intimate, you're right."

"Undress yourself," was his reply.

And so I did and I stretched out on the bed, his dark, black eyes pierced mine, they had an enchanting shine. He took off his burgundy silk tie, took both my wrists in one of his still gloved enormous hands, and he lifted my arms above my head; with the other hand he tied both my wrists to the headboard.

I smiled obligingly, it was not the first time that I had faced these kind of games, sometimes it was the actual client who wished to be tied up. While he did this I noticed a strange smell, thick, perhaps dampness. Yes, it was like the smell of houses that have been closed for a long time! It could not have come from that clean and tidy room. That smell began to engross everything, and came from him or from his clothing.

Once he finished doing this he moved backwards, and standing next to the bed he began to take off his dark grey suit, dropping it without caring about how and where it fell.

His chest was strong, wide, although not with those artificial muscles of today's young men; no, it looked more like the chest of an actor in old films. Strong, wide and lacking chest hair. But what most surprised me was the extreme pallor he had, he seemed sculpted in white marble like a statue of Michelangelo, I had the feeling it was also as hard.

His shining dark eyes did not stop for one moment to lay on mine, hypnotising me, while he undressed.

Finally, he removed some rather old-styled underpants, and, oh, good heavens, my eyes did not believe what they were seeing. His member was monstrously big, it must have been at least two spans long and another half a span wide. The idea of him penetrating me with that filled me with dread, but I was unable to pronounce a single word, such was the power his shining eyes held over me.

In view of my astonishment his face seemed to be filled with satisfaction and pride, conscious as he was that the cause of my expression was that thing which raised itself above his navel.

His whole sex was bereft of pubic hair, as if it were shaven, but no, that was not it, it seemed as if there had never been pubic hair there. Now I realised that excepting his dense head of hair his eyebrows and eyelashes, the rest of his body completely lacked body hair. This did nothing but increase my dread, to which my strange client said: "Whores, you're my favourite dish, easy to find and nobody worries if you don't reappear."

While he said this I was able to look at something which had passed unnoticed. In his mouth, two small, sharp canines protruded from between his teeth, which he now treacherously displayed when he talked perhaps with the intention of increasing my astonishment even more.

This made me let out a muffled moan, which was all I could do, such was the point of amazement which his gaze and that nauseating smell had me submitted to.

Upon saying this he pounced on me, forcibly opening my legs, he penetrated me with a single blow with all his member.

The pain I felt was indescribable; it was as if I had broken on the inside, I felt how my vaginal walls had burst, I still do not know how I could have contained that inside me, but I do know that thing had reached my intestines in such a way that it made me vomit everything that was in my stomach all over my chest - none other than a dark gruel with small pieces of meat - the leftovers of my dinner which was not totally digested after a few hours. This did not seem to worry him in the least, I rather think it even seemed pleasant, since he lay down on my body, without ceasing to frantically move his member into my innermost parts, and began to lick the vomit that slithered down my neck, clean, he then sunk those small canines as sharp as pins into my neck until they made two wounds from which he began to suck, while he groaned with pleasure like a wild animal.

His body crushed mine with its weight, he must have weighed a ton, not only was it cold and hard like a marble statue, but it also weighed like one, even the bed seemed about to come apart at any moment given the noise it made beneath his brusque movements.

My raving moans died away before those raucous grunts of pleasure he made. It felt as if all of my blood flowed forth to the area of my neck from which he sucked.

Then I lost all notion of time, I could not specify if two hours or ten minutes had elapsed. The monster I had upon me would not stop penetrating me nor would he cease sucking my blood. I elapsed from a state of hypnosis to one of catatonia. But he suddenly stopped, raised himself on his knees and took out his enormous bloody cock from between my legs. While the penetration lasted, my pain had grown stable, now, with his member outside of me I noticed the pain of those wounds that monstrous cock had provoked with greater fierceness.

I felt I was losing blood from between my legs, that sensation made me feel an incessant faintness. Anyway, I felt that weakness due to the lack of blood cushioning my pains. They had only just started.

On his knees, on the bed before me the monster smiled for the first time raptured with pleasure, flashing his small, but very sharp canines while my own blood, slithered down the corners of his mouth. Suddenly, a very thick, milky liquid began to gush forth from his member, falling on my chest and belly, provoking spasms due to how cold it was. A multitude of shivers ran down my spine, as if someone had thrown a bucket of ice-cubes over me.

And that fountain did not stop emanating its content, which resembled pus more than anything else, to the point of soaking all my thorax, cleaning off the leftovers of my previous vomit and dragging itself in surges down to the bed sheets which were starting to become soaked, between my blood, the vomit and his disgusting milk.

The wild beast hurled a new raucous grunt and the thing, as if obeying him, stopped spitting. Ipso facto, and without even giving me time to batter an eyelid, he gave a small jump on his knees falling on my stomach. The terrible impact caused me to vomit blood and to piss myself at the same time. The contact of urine caused a tremendous stinging of my vaginal wounds.

The beast prepared to lick the blackish blood I had vomited, that made me cry with revulsion and impotence, which was his greatest pleasure from what I could understand from the expression he showed on his marmoreal face.

The smell of my hot urine reached his senses, he raised his face from my blood-stained neck and turned to look at my aching sex. Another new jump on my belly and he placed his face between my legs; this time, a respiratory arrest joined the bloody vomiting which I was almost unable to stop, only his unintentional aid allowed me to. So, what happened next made me release the only scream I was able to make during the whole night (I never found out why nobody came to the bedroom to my assistance after that yell) and this allowed some air to enter my lungs once more, while emptying my throat of the coagulated blood which blocked it.

Attracted by the smell of my urine, the beast had extended one of his enormous hands over my cunt, with a swift and blunt movement he plucked out all its hairs; or at least I thought as I screamed, but could not have been so, since he repeated the action various times, but I had already lost my strength for subsequent screams.

Little dots of blood started to appear from the pores of my pubic hairs which the beast undertook to savour with his tongue that scratched like a cat's as well as the blood from the wounds produced by his hieratic cock, not caring if they were wet with the urine I had shed.

Tired of this game he sunk his canines into me once more, on the inside of my left thigh. This new blood suction was too much for my weakness and I lost consciousness.

When I regained consciousness a dim light was coming through the window, it illuminated the room, the day was breaking, there was no trace of the killer beast.

I was untied, but had no strength to get up. My whole body ached, but what I felt the most was an intense thirst, without a doubt due to the loss of liquids.

I still bled from between my legs, and made an effort to get up, and put the pillow between my legs to block the haemorrhage.

I looked around me, no, he was not there, he had switched off the lamp and had gone, probably leaving me for dead. I made a supreme effort, got up and headed towards the bathroom, with the pillow still between my legs. After opening the door I began to drink from the washbasin tap, once my thirst had been quenched, I looked at myself in the mirror. Good heavens! I actually looked dead. I washed my face and chest from the traces of blood and vomit, but, oh!, there was no trace of the sickening pus, no!, I had not even noticed any on the bed. As quickly as I could (with the pillow between my legs and feeling weak) I went towards the bed. There was blood everywhere but not a single sign of sperm.

It was as if he had never been there, if it wasn't for the horrible state I found myself in I would have sworn that it had all been a macabre nightmare, he had been there, and he was the cause of my present malaise, I looked like a genuine skinny weakling.

I did not like looking at myself in such a state, so I prepared to dress and to rapidly leave that horrendous place. I placed a small tablecloth which covered the bedside table in my panties to serve as a sanitary towel, something to hold back the haemorrhage until I reached my room where I could cure myself and freshen up at ease.

My mind only thought of quickly fleeing from there, it did not respond to other stimuli. Now dressed I approached the window and a shiver ran through my damaged body, in such a way that I almost fainted again. I had to grip on to the curtains with such strength that I almost pulled them down, all this because from that window I could observe W. Cemetery where it had all begun. That image made my thoughts about what monster had attacked me pound in my head. That wretched bloodsucking beast must have been the devil himself, I am sure of it. I turned half round, I quickly went out of the room and the hotel.

I never walked the nearby streets of that cemetery again, not by day, nor by night; whatever attacked me that night came from there, and from what he himself had said, he had already done that on other occasions, and it is certain that he was still doing it. That time I was fortunate enough to come away from his encounter alive, but I would not wish to meet him again, not for anything in the world; even now as I write about this after so many years it makes my stomach turn, my legs tremble only remembering this.

This was my experience and this, from my present-day comfortable position, my way of telling it; I hope that by doing so I can help somebody. My advice would be, avoiding, as far as possible, to pass through that wretched place.

Gothboy

Mark A. Henderson

"Pretty little Gothboy."

Simon Greyling was pretty, it's true. His hair was a fine, natural black, framing a smooth, pale face. One look from his huge, deep brown eyes could melt the coldest heart – if he were to make eye contact.

But Simon was quiet also, carrying his luminous beauty beneath dark cloth, smearing his perfect skin with a clown's mask of black eyes and white skin. He moved with inconspicuous grace, concealing himself from the very people by whom he wished to be accepted. If people mentioned him at all, the conversation would always steer to the fact that Simon looked like he could burst into tears at any moment. Then no one can recall actually seeing Simon cry and they laugh, suddenly uneasy, and change the subject. Cold hearts indeed.

Little wonder she found him then. She, the coldest heart of all.

It was goth night at Rock Central and the place was packed. Dim lights strobed over peeling paintwork, as poorly applied as the overdone make-up daubed on the faces of the black-clad dancing figures.

Simon sat in a corner, peering in quiet despair over a glass of red wine at the sea of heads, some swinging in contemplation of the rhythm, most thrashing with wild abandon. These were reasonable people, thought Simon. What then makes them act like such animals? How can they look at themselves in the mirror afterwards, all flushed and dripping?

He shuddered and sipped his wine.

"Pretty little Gothboy."

Simon looked up, startled. This never happened; someone was sitting beside him.

She was beautiful; a goddess come to life, a goddess in this sweaty, beer-soaked night-club, a goddess who reached up elegant, white fingers to brush his cheek.

"So sad," she crooned. "Are you lonely, little Gothboy?"

Simon disliked being made fun of and tried to be indignant, but she lifted her eyes to meet his, her gaze seeming to stroke his other cheek, and he fell silent for a moment before simply saying, "Yes."

More than ever, he seemed ready to burst into tears, but she just smiled, took his hand and led him through the exit into the warm night.

"Good," she whispered.

"Silly little Gothboy," she laughed.

He had tried the 'your place or mine?' line, trying to sound like he was used to this. She just sat back in her taxi seat and laughed. He tried to be annoyed, to say "don't call me that!" but he couldn't. One touch of her hand or eyes and he fell still.

"My place," she mused. Then she smiled again, though this time the audacious mischief in her eyes was replaced with a look of sadness. "You wouldn't want to be in my place."

Then she brightened again, a luminescent full moon in an otherwise empty night sky. Simon stifled a sigh of utter longing.

"Your place then," she grinned.

Simon's flat was like him, attractive enough, but draped in such soul-stilling darkness as to deny the life within. It seemed a dead place, a deliberately contrived tomb, suitable only as a place to lay at rest.

"I like it," she nodded.

"Really?" Simon asked. "I'm hardly ever in here myself."

"I know," she said. "I've been watching you. Pubs, clubs – they are your particular haunts. The places where people like you go to become the animal selves they deny all day; to trade their dark meat with sweat and alcohol."

Simon was unable to speak as she crossed to him and gently held his face close to her own.

"But you," she whispered, her breath like a winter breeze across his cheek. "Sweet Gothboy. You're not buying, are you?"

Simon just stood with his mouth slightly open, until she released him. He shook his head a little, as if he had just woken up.

"Um," he started. "Would - would you like some wine? I mean, I have a bottle of red in the cupboard."

She took a step back and, narrowing her eyes with an ironic smile, said "I never drink... wine."

Then she collapsed back onto a velvet chair in peals of laughter, a musical, tinkling sound that somehow lacked soul, the laughter solely for her benefit.

Simon merely stood in dumb bemusement, looking confused almost to the point of tears. Then she stopped laughing, her mood changing. A darkness dropped over her eyes, a look of dangerous passion couched in cruel hunger.

"Kiss me," she said, staring into his eyes. It was an order, a command, not for affection but for proximity.

Simon didn't disobey; he couldn't. He moved with his usual natural grace and knelt before her.

"Kiss me," she repeated, this time revealing hints of a passionate need. However, his lips barely brushed hers, as if he feared he might defile this beautiful goddess, with the base touch of a mortal kiss.

"Kiss me," she said, one last time. She touched a clasp and her thin dress whispered off her shoulders, revealing ivory-white breasts. Simon pressed his head against hers. Her chill lips against his own seemed to melt what remained of his will, yet still he did not cry.

When the kiss was broken, Simon lifted his head to stare into the eyes of this impossible creature.

"What are you?" he whispered.

She pulled his head down onto her slim shoulder.

"A traditionalist," replied the vampire, and bit his neck.

I'm dead.

He's dead. I'm...

I'm hers. She took what she needed to live and so I died and now we're...

We're going out.

I'm sat before my mirror in my bedroom and she's reconstructing my dead face with kohl and white powder. I can't see her in the mirror but I know that she's there. Her fingers caress every inch of my face and I'm dead and gone to heaven. If she wasn't there I couldn't cope. I couldn't exist. I'd be dead.

But I am...

She bids me stand and I stand.

One kiss and we're out, into the night. It's colder now, the air bites with tiny teeth.

Did I think that or did she tell me?

Now we're at Rock Central again and she's laughing and I laugh with her though I can't feel my face smiling. But of course I'm smiling because she is.

Faces flash by us in the club. Eyes deader than mine I think see my face and turn away. They can't look at me and I don't understand. Is this my first time here or my hundredth? Then I know. I've been here many times and always with her. Always with her. Then why won't they look at me?

I look to her with questions but receive no answers. She doesn't look at me either. She just looks around and laughs and laughs. Laughs at people stupider than me. The ones that won't stop for her. Why won't she look at me? But then why do I care? I don't care. She's with me and she's holding my hand and she loves me and I love her. Yes. Why should I care?

I'm dead.

"My little Gothboy," she purred as she stroked the silky hair from his neck. "My pretty little pet."

Months had passed since that first night, when Simon Greyling had died, and the first snows were just now beginning to brush past the windows.

Inside the flat, given now to dust and indifference, Gothboy sat in mute adoration at the feet of his beloved mistress, gazing up at her pale naked body.

"Yes," she said. "You're mine now," and bent to his neck.

Gothboy did not even wince any more when she penetrated him. He knew now that she only nipped him, drawing just enough blood to sustain her. Just enough to keep her from needing anyone but him, he hoped.

And how he needed her. Over the months, a glamour had seemed to overcome him, like a blanket of fresh snow over his sense of self. Only her carefully placed footsteps through his mind revealed what lay beneath. What she wanted to uncover.

He watched as she settled back into her chair, the same chair in which she had killed him and claimed him. He watched as she closed her eyes and licked a single drop of blood from her lips. As she relaxed to enjoy the rejuvenation that fresh blood seemed to bring, Gothboy regained enough of himself to dare to reach out and touch her, sliding his hand up her bare thigh.

Quicker than mortal thought, she grabbed Gothboy's wrist and threw him across the room.

"How dare you!" she snarled. "Do you think I'm just one of those mortal girls you can grope and fuck?" Gothboy winced at that curse from the mouth of his angel.

"You still haven't the faintest idea of what I am, do you?" she yelled. "I drink from you every night, bind you with enchantments, and you still think I'm just one of those fuck-whores from the club. A purveyor of dark meat!"

She laid her glamour upon him again with contempt. "You're disgusting. Get up." She turned away.

Gothboy stood, but then desperately jerked down his jeans, revealing a rising erection. He struggled to muster what remained of his will.

"Please," said Simon.

She turned, startled. "Sorry?" she whispered. She had recognised the altered timbre of his voice and knew that her Gothboy was, temporarily, banished, and she was stunned.

"Please," Simon repeated, gesturing pathetically at his groin.

She sighed, sounding disappointed. "How mortal," she sneered. "How male. You must have used supreme force of will to break my glamour. And why? Because you just can't go without cumming!"

"Damn you, witch!" howled Simon. "I loved you! I want you. I..." He broke off, exhausted.

She stared at him, as if stung, then stood looking silently into his close-to-tears eyes for a few moments.

"Love...? Oh, Gothboy," she whispered, her arrogance dissolving into pity, for herself as much as for Simon. "I am sorry. I can't. We don't."

With her compassion rising, the enchantment eased, and Simon rose slowly to his feet.

"I know... what you do," he whispered hoarsely, "And I know what you want."

Simon reached out and took the vampire's hand. She did not protest when he moved her hand over his erection, but her eyes said it all. "I would. I can't. I wish..."

Simon squeezed her hand around his cock, tighter than must have been comfortable for him, then, without warning, pushed it away quickly, drawing her long, sharp nails along the shaft.

He stifled a gasp of pain. "I know what you want," he repeated through tightly clenched teeth.

"Simon," she pleaded, softly, as she watched the blood well up in pulsing waves, running red rivers through his pubic hair and down his legs. "Oh, please, Simon. No..."

But the scent of blood was upon her, inside her, and she was already sliding to her knees.

Simon's breath came in ragged gasps as she slid her cold lips down his cock, over the ragged wound, and began sucking hungrily.

For almost half a year, she had been his world, and now that world seemed filled with smooth ice, jagged pain and mounting pleasure. And her. Always her. She would be his entire world, forever.

Her hands caressed helpless apologies along his thighs, the ice-cold needlepoints of her fingernails raising goose bumps. But still she sucked, drawing him deeper inside her, her hunger equalling his. Her tongue rubbed the tear in his flesh, sending shivers through both their bodies.

Simon fell to his knees, then slowly on to his back as she drained him, never letting him out of her mouth.

His feet and hands went cold, like hers, then numb, until he lay splayed on the floor, all the heat rushing from his body into his groin. His cock felt red-hot, her cold lips only making it hotter.

As the vampire's passion for blood peaked, Simon felt a prickling tightness around his balls, and then suddenly he came, his jism hotter than the blood, and she sucked on, swallowing both with equal hunger.

The last of his blood consumed, his prick went limp, falling from her gasping mouth.

She rose unsteadily to her feet and stared down at his lifeless, sprawled body.

Numbly, she noted the red stains covering his bare white legs. She saw the wounds on his penis, which seemed all the more ragged now he was limp. She looked at his dark hair, spread on the floor around his head like a halo.

But what she did not notice, as she called her garments to her and disappeared into the night, was a single, overdue tear, running slowly down his cheek.

The Last Train

Louis Ravensfield

It was four hours since sundown and this was the last train that would leave the station tonight. Four hours of fruitless searching, following and hunting, had left this slim tall figure wondering if he was ever going to feed tonight. But then that's what happens when you insist on hunting the same ground night after night. Waiting impatiently as a handful of passengers boarded the train, none of whom took his fancy, the whistle blows and he takes the decision to board in order to pick the best of a bad lot. Upon stepping into the carriage the sound of heels tapping the floor echo around the station platform followed by a stumble, a cry and an expletive curse. Turning he spots a woman tugging at her right shoe. A few swift long strides takes him to her side as the final whistle blows. Offering an arm for support he quickly assists her onto the train, closing the door, as it starts to slowly pull away.

Inside the deserted yet brightly lit carriage compartment she sits, holding a shoe in one hand, a heel in the other and curses again. She wears a short, tight fitting blue dress, low cut, revealing a deep cleavage and large heavy breasts. Stockings, the tops of which show as she sits, cover her long, slightly plump legs. A red jacket covers her shoulders on which long bleached blonde hair sits in a tangled mess. Looking up at her saviour she mutters a 'thank you'. Her heavily made-up thirty-something face looks the worse for wear. Crudely applied thick eye liner does little to cover her crow lines. The dark blue eye shadow, over-use of foundation and smudged bright red lipstick further confirm his suspicions. Catching his eye she lights a cigarette after her third attempt at striking a match. Exhaling loudly as the train rattles into the night, she starts to talk, bemoaning the hellish day she's had. A lousy forty quid for freezing her tits off all day. Three 'tricks', and two of those were only 'hand-jobs'! Then to cap it all she breaks the heel off her 'fucking shoe'. He smiles empathically at her.

She asks how far his journey will take - eternity, he thinks - the end of the line, he says. She asks if she can 'do' a little something for him? What did she have in mind, is the response. Hand job, blow job, full sex or anything goes. The price? £10, £20, £40 or £70. Reaching into his pocket and removing a wad of notes he counts out £200, handing them to her. Greedy eyes light up and whilst obviously a little flabbergasted she disguises it well and promises him the time of his life! Removing her other shoe she stands before him in stockinged feet. Slipping the jacket from her shoulders she pulls the top of her dress down to just below her large heavy hanging breasts. She massages her tits up and down, round and round, slowly swinging her hips from side to side. Pulling the dress down further, past her stomach, past her panties, letting it fall to the floor. Aroused by the sight his cock begins to stiffen. Though no ravishing beauty she was cute in a dirty slut kind of way. Requesting the removal of her knickers the whore obliges willingly, to reveal a thin line of dark thatched hair. The rest of her pussy is clean shaven. Sitting back down, her arse just on the edge of the seat opposite him, she spreads her legs wide apart to reveal her exposed pussy lips. Two fingers part the lips affording him a wonderfully explicit view of her wares. Slipping a finger into her mouth and moistenings it she slides it into her pussy hole, slowly finger-fucking herself. His cock strains at the material binding it and getting up from the seat he kneels before her. Burying his face between her legs the long tongue caresses her pussy probing her innermost regions, lapping at the moistness of her semen smelling juices. She pushes his head deeper into her pleasure zones. As his tongue flicks at her clit in rapid circular, and up and down movements she sighs deeply and mutters something incoherent under her breath. Pushing his tongue deeper into her pussy hole he then licks from her clit down to her anus, and back again. She breathes heavily, panting and gasping. She squirms as waves of pure pleasure course through her body. She verges toward orgasm before he draws back from the pink puffed lips of her pussy and engorged clitoris. She lays back taking a few moments to recover. The scent of her love juice permeates the stale aroma of the carriage, he can smell her blood in the air, such a sweet fragrance, especially when mingled with the scent of sex.

She moves over to where he has reseated himself and removes his jacket and shirt. Hands rubbing his naked chest before she slides them down to undo his trousers. Lifting his backside slightly from the seat so she can take them down and after slipping off his boots she removes them completely. Her hands gently rub the stiff shaft through the fabric of his briefs. Reaching for the elastic on either side of his hips she pulls the briefs right down, then off. Reclining back in the seat she uses her tongue to trace a line from his knees, up his inner thigh to the swelling sacks and hard throbbing cock. Lowering her mouth down upon the waiting cock, she licks its swollen head.Taking a bit at a time she takes the full length into her warm wet mouth. Sucking on the cock as he tells her how much it pleasures him. Her hands reach between his legs, one gently squeezes and caresses his balls, the other, using her index finger, probes for his anus. Once located she slips her finger into the hole, causing him to shudder and groan. He pushes down upon her head, making her suck him deeper and harder. She speeds up, wanking his cock with her mouth as he thrusts against her gradually gaining momentum Her head becomes a blur as she fucks him with her mouth. Passing the point of no return the spunk bursts from the tip of his cock in great powerful spasms, spurting and filling her mouth before descending down her throat. The spunk begins to seep from her lips as she tries to swallow in great gulps. Feeling his cock beginning to grow soft in her mouth she sucks on him again, flicking and licking the tip of his cock with her tongue.

The erectness returns slowly and she leads him back to her seat opposite where she positions herself once more with legs spread wide, as she lays back on the seat. Using her fingers she parts the lips of her pussy as the juices glint in the artificial light. Sliding his swollen tool into her warm waiting hole, she gasps as he enters her, filling her cunt with his cock. Drawing back he thrusts into her roughly, then pulls out before thrusting back in again. Her nipples swell standing pert and erect and to each in turn he lowers his mouth and gently nibbles before biting upon her heaving breasts. She starts to cry out softly as the mixture of sheer ecstasy tinged with a hint of pain as he bites her tits courses through her entire being. Gripping either side of the seat to steady herself he continues to pound her with his cock. As he fucks her harder and more intensely her orgasm begins to take a hold. She cries out for him to fuck her yet harder, fuck her cunt, fuck her arsehole, fuck her tits and mouth. The spunk rises the length of his shaft as her cunt muscles contract around it, she screams out as violent waves of pure pleasure course through her. He pulls it from her pussy, grabs her hand wrapping it around the shaft and she wanks it with rough, vigorous movements. The spunk bursts forth spraying her pussy, her stomach and her tits. Slipping three fingers into her soaking pussy he frigs her until the orgasm rips through her.

Using a tissue from her bag she wipes the liquid from her body and dresses quickly, keeping very quiet and avoiding his gaze. He remains naked, the lust satiated but not the hunger. Undecided whether to follow her home and take her again, before finally 'taking' her, or 'take' her here and now. She makes up his mind for him. As the train pulls into a station, she moves toward the door saying goodbye. The train grinds to a halt. Reaching for the door handle, she turns to him with a wry smile saying she forgot to tell him that she was HIV positive and apologises. As she steps down through the open door he grabs hold of her and pulls her roughly back inside the carriage. Covering her mouth with his hand to prevent her from screaming, he pins her down. Attempting to fight him off he slaps her hard and viciously across the face. As the train moves off he rips the front of her dress open as sharp teeth tear open the flesh of her neck, piercing the thick vein. The blood flows freely and he drinks hard and long, greedily consuming great gulps of the warm nectar. Though HIV cannot affect his kind, it was the principle that so enraged him. He was mortal once, a long time ago, and this fucking whore thought she was signing his death certificate. Now he was signing hers. His cock grows hard again as her blood courses and charges through his body. She loses consciousness and he ceases the relentless feeding to tear the rest of the dress from her body. She is helpless to resist as he rips the underwear from her. She is dying. Spreading her legs open he rams his cock into her cunt, and slowly fucks her whilst draining her blood. She dies as he continues to pump her lifeless corpse. Shooting another load of come, deep inside her dead torso, the pleasure is divine, beyond compare. He shudders and screams out his spent passion. Leaving her lifeless body bleeding all over the carriage, he departs from the train at the next station. His lust is now fully satiated, his hunger too, and disappears swiftly and silently into the darkness of the night.

More than a one night stand

J. Flaxton

So what if all her friends thought she was a tart, Sharon didn't give a shit! Saturdays were for fun, and Saturday and sex both began with the same letter. She spent an age getting ready, carefully choosing her clothes to show off her sexy figure, the short, short skirt to reveal her long shapely legs, the low cut top showing plenty of cleavage. She knew she had the kind of body that drove men wild, so why not flaunt it? And then maybe at the end of the night, just maybe, she might pick out a guy who could take her to bed. With her figure and good looks she could pick and choose. She was smiling to herself as she applied the last touches to her lipstick, and touched the stray strands of her long blonde hair into place.

The Golden Pearl was the place to be on a Saturday night; they said if you couldn't get laid there on a Saturday night then you never would. Most Saturdays Sharon did. That's why she came here, that's why she didn't mind paying the £10 it cost to get into the most exclusive disco in town. So what if it cost her a tenner, it was worth it if she got bonked senseless at the end of the night.

It was as she sat alone at a table sipping her drink that she suddenly became aware of a guy sitting across from her. She was a little startled for a moment because she hadn't noticed him join her at the small table. She looked him up and down. Not bad! In fact he was quite a looker, young, dark hair, slim, and he definitely had that look that said this guy has money. "Hi." He leaned forward towards her. "Ever been shagged by a vampire?"

Sharon smiled. She had heard every chat-up line in the book, it was refreshing to hear something different. Let's face it, that's what they all wanted when you got right down to it, every guy in the place wanted to shag her and she knew it! "Well, actually... no, I don't think I have." She looked him unashamedly in the eye. "But if you are asking would I like to be, well it so happens that you have hit on one of my last remaining ambitions. Do you happen to know a vampire?" Oh yes, this was the one, this was the guy she was going to bonk tonight. Somebody who at least tried to be different always turned her on.

When they left The Golden Pearl at something approaching 2am she was aching to get him in bed. Him? She smiled, she didn't even know his name. What the hell, he was a pretty interesting guy, sex was going to be fun with him, deep down and dirty! She liked him, yeah she would do little special things for him, the things she knew men went crazy for. As she slid beside him into his expensive German sports car she thought to herself that maybe this was worth more than a one night stand, more than a quick bonk and her taxi fare home.

When they arrived at his place she could hardly believe it, the place was enormous, a mansion. He smiled at her comments and said he hoped it would be the place of her dreams Would it ever! It could hardly have been more perfect. He led her into the house and through a darkened hallway, into a huge room. He turned on the lights and Sharon gasped. The room was so big, with the most gorgeous thick carpet in her favourite shade of blue. Strangely there was only one piece of furniture in the room, a long coffee table perhaps seven feet long by three feet wide in beautifully polished mahogany. He pulled her against him and kissed her. "Ever been shagged by a vampire?" he asked again. She kissed him back and gazed into his dreamy blue eyes. "No," she smiled wickedly. "But I sure as hell want to be!"

Sharon began to frantically pull at his clothes, in fact he had to smilingly tell her to calm herself. He helped her to undress and she just threw her clothes out of the way. She didn't mind standing before him naked, she was proud of her body and the way men wanted her. She watched him undress and as he stood as naked as she was Sharon couldn't keep her eyes off him; his body was in perfect condition. Without a word she dropped to her knees and took his penis into her mouth, letting the silky smooth tip glide between her lips. Even that felt perfect.

"There's time for that later," he said lifting her back to her feet. "First, you get shagged by a vampire!" She laughed as he picked her up and laid her on the table. She giggled as he leaned over her and kissed her breasts. She splayed her legs wide, invitingly pulling his head down. Then she stopped laughing. Something didn't seem right. She felt strange, lightheaded. Perhaps she had drunk just a little too much to be indulging in sexual acrobatics. But no, it wasn't that, it was a feeling she hadn't ever felt before. She felt heavy, unable to move, like she was being pinned down. She looked up at him. His eyes! God, his eyes were red and his black hair had turned grey. And he was a decidedly ugly bastard! Shit, what am I doing here, her mind screamed. Jesus Christ, he's a monster, a fucking monster! She couldn't speak, her mind was screaming out but she couldn't make a sound. Shit, no, no please!

Sharon felt something rubbing against her sex. His knee? Her legs felt as if they were being forced apart, she just couldn't pull them together. Then he shifted his body slightly and she realised that it couldn't be his knee rubbing against her. She managed to raise her head to look down her body. Sweet Jesus, no! There between her legs his erection bobbed up and down, rubbing against her. A huge misshapen thing, thick and knobbly. It was as thick as her arm and seemed to be covered in warts. Her breathing became rapid in sheer panic, and yet she felt powerless to do anything. Strangely, as his huge knob rubbed against her it felt very erotic, she could see the end of it glistening with her juices.

Then he stopped rubbing and he nudged it against her open vagina. No! Her mind was going frantic with fear. No, Jesus Christ, no! It's too big, no, please don't hurt me. Help me Jesus, help me! Her breathing was now so rapid that she almost felt faint, almost in danger of passing out. She was rapidly brought to her senses as he jabbed the end of his gross knob into her. She was trembling now, she knew it was going to hurt. She gritted her teeth, trying to brace herself against the pain. Please Jesus, please sweet Jesus! And then he pushed into her, slowly and forcefully, the entire length. Her eyes widened as she watched it slide into her. God, it wasn't possible, no way could she take all that. And yet, as she watched, he buried himself deep into her.

Oh God, oh God, oh God! It felt so good, so fucking good. Yes, oh Jesus it felt so good. Her mind screamed in ecstasy, she felt so full of him, this was better than ever. Oh God, fuck me! As if he could read her mind he started to rock slowly backwards and forwards, his shaft slowly withdrawing from her and then slowly plunging deep into her. Oh yes! Yes! Come on, please, fuck me please! Read my mind, fuck me, please!

Still rocking slowly, he leaned down and bit her left breast. Sharon winced as his teeth tore into her, but there was no pain, just sweet bliss. Oh yes, one night of this is not going to be enough. More, I want more, do me harder. As if in answer to her silent wish he began to increase speed until his cock was ramming in and out of her. Yes, yes, it's so good, do me all the way! Oh please, please!

He raised his head from her breast, her blood dripping from his mouth and then stopped. Her brow furrowed in puzzlement. He smiled, and then his orgasm ripped through her. Oh shit! As his thick semen spurted into her it felt hot, it was so hot it burned. And Sharon screamed out, the first sound ringing round the room as she growled in the throes of her own orgasm. "Oooh, yes! Do me, do me! Oh Jesus, don't stop!" He raised himself and she watched his long cock slide from her. She was almost disappointed to see it leave her body. She wanted to be nice to it. She sat up and held it in her hand. She rubbed it lovingly and the last drops of his semen dribbled from it. She leaned down and took the big knob into her mouth, tasting his semen. "Yes!" he said quietly. "Now you are mine. Now you have tasted me you can never deny me!" Sharon looked up into his handsome face, to see his blue eyes and black hair. How handsome he looked. She let his silky smooth penis fall from her lips.

He bade her rise from the table and gently settled her down on the beautiful blue carpet to rest, and her eyes closed, and she slept. She awoke some time later and it was daylight. She looked around in bewilderment. She was lying in some filthy hovel of a building, a shed, a warehouse or something. She got up from amongst the debris and filth, her body was dirty, dusty, grimy, and it hurt. Dirt was caked on her slender feet, it matted her unkempt blonde hair. What the hell was happening?

Where is the mansion, the beautiful blue carpet, the polished mahogany coffee table? She turned around slowly. Oh shit, no! In the centre of the room where she expected the coffee table was a coffin, seven feet long and three feet wide. Oh God, she thought. I didn't get fucked on a coffin, surely? Jesus, I must have been pissed out of my skull! She shuffled around and eventually found a small piece of mirrored glass. She looked at herself, what a God-awful sight she looked, she was filthy. And she hurt. She lifted her left breast; bloody hell there was a big gash in it caked in dried blood.

Oh no, it will leave a scar! She looked down between her legs, to where it had started to get painful. There was dried blood on the inside of her thighs. She reached between her legs. "Ouch!" Shit, she was sore, what did that bastard do to me? She decided that she had to get out of there, get a bath and see what damage she had sustained. She looked around for her clothes, and spotted a pile of clothes and rags in the corner of the room. Sharon padded over to the pile and turned it over with her foot. Jesus, she stamped her foot, my clothes are in shreds. Shit, she thought, I paid thirty quid for that blouse! "Shit!" Sharon screamed. What the hell was she supposed to do with no clothes, she couldn't go outside naked. She cleared a small place in the dirt next to the wall and sat down to think. She sat with her back against the wall, legs splayed apart.

What was happening, what the fuck was happening? How can this guy be young one minute and old the next? How can he be so cute and then be such a dog? And this room? It was so nice, the carpet was gorgeous, how come it's a dump now? And the mahogany coffee table is now a coffin, complete with fucking handles! I suppose the Porsche was a bloody bicycle! If he hypnotised me into thinking all those things he must be good. Wait a minute, vampires are supposed to be good at that sort of thing, aren't they? Oh shit, he's a fucking vampire, a real vampire!

Sharon raised her knees and rested her arms on them. Nothing to do but wait. If the guy is a vampire he'll get out of his coffin at dusk, then he can bloody well get me back home. Sharon smiled and that old familiar twinkle lit up her eyes. That is of course unless he feels horny, in which case a good shag on the coffee table wouldn't go amiss. Sharon rested her head on her arms. Nothing to do but wait. She smiled again, Jesus he was fucking good, though!

Escape

JP

A few days alone in the countryside was just what I needed. Far removed from the hustle and bustle of the city, a chance to rest and relax, and that's exactly what I'd got. I managed to rent a cottage in a tiny village about 30 miles from the nearest major town. During the day I would walk, or sit and read in the delightful garden. It was late August and the sun was at its peak, strong and powerful for many hours each day. In the evening I would take long walks along the winding country lanes and pathways, invariably ending at the local village pub. My time was my own for once. The perfect opportunity for me to think and reflect on my life thus far, and plan my future. I knew I could not return to my former lifestyle. I needed a complete change from all that had gone before.

This particular evening I took a really long walk, some six or seven miles. I knew I had some serious decision-making to do about my future. I calmly considered my options as I strolled down a long deserted lane with shrubs high on either side. It was a beautiful evening, the sun was slowly beginning her descent below the horizon, the sky was a wonderful shade of red with tinges of dark orange. A light breeze blew gently through the air, cooling the warm evening and caressing my face and hair. I took a deep breath, the fragrant scent of flowers filling my nostrils as the air filled my lungs. As dusk fell over the busy chitter chatter of the birds in the trees I could hear the faint rumbling of a car engine in the distance.The sound drew nearer, and looking behind me I saw the vehicle approaching quickly. Stepping back against the bushes so that it could pass I watched as it followed the lane, drawing closer still. Finally just as the car was set to pass me by, the driver, slowed the vehicle right down, before coming to a halt right beside me.

The car was a magnificent black sleek affair, a limousine, perhaps a Daimler. Very expensive by the looks of it and immaculately polished. The windows were all mirrored, so I was greeted uncomfortably by my own reflection staring back.A few moments later and the rear passenger door opened with a faint click, over the gentle purring of the engine. I peered inside the gloomy dark interior, seeing very little for the sun was now sinking below the horizon. I took a tentative step forward towards the open door.As I did so a figure came into view from the black depths of the interior. I gasped slightly as a woman leant halfway out of the doorway.A vision of incredible beauty. Her hair was very long and raven black, contrasting strongly with her pale white face. Her lips were full, deep red in colour and so very kissable. Her eyes contained a glint, a twinkle; their colour I could not tell, yet I felt strangely delirious as I looked into them. They were made even more striking by the black eye liner which encircled them, again contrasting strongly with her pale complexion. She wore a flimsy black satin dress, daringly low-cut.The material clinging tightly to her skin, pushing her large white breasts together, revealing a deep dark cleavage as she leaned forward into the dusk. She beckoned me closer with a long thin hand, her nails very long and painted a deep crimson red. My heart beat faster, as a hundred thoughts fought for first place in my head. She smiled at me, teeth pure white, flashing against her red lips. She asked me in a slightly husky and very sexy voice if I needed a ride somewhere. A ride, yes, I thought, but not in a car! Refraining myself I explained that I was just out walking, taking the evening air. She turned her head briefly for a moment, and murmured something I couldn't quite hear to an unseen companion.Then turning back she asked if I would do her the honour of dining with her this very night. Well, who could resist? Not I, for one, if only for an excuse to gaze upon the deep dark beauty of this enchanting woman for a little while longer. I thanked her for the kind invitation, accepted and then she reached for my hand, drawing me gently inside the vehicle.

Once seated next to her the door closed behind me, and the car moved off into the fast approaching night. I spent a few moments taking in my surroundings. I could see very little at first, but gradually my eyes became accustomed to the dark. Her black dress ended high above her thighs whilst black stockings bridged the gap between her dress and the tops of her long leather boots. Sexy, very sexy.

Feeling a little ashamed by allowing my eyes to have feasted upon this delightful and highly pleasing sight I was startled as I became aware of this luscious beauty's companion, to whom she had spoken briefly only a short while ago, sitting to my right. It was a man, tall and thin, with long dark hair. His face too, like the woman's, was a pale white, with blood red lips and eyes that shone in the blackness of the car's interior. He wore a plain white shirt and black trousers. As my eyes wandered over him, he looked at me and smiled. I offered him my hand and introduced myself, he reciprocated the gesture. His hand felt icy cold in mine, and I could feel the sharpness of his nails dig slightly into my flesh. The minutes quickly passed as we exchanged words. The woman was called Anulka, the man Lawrence, they were good friends who had a house not too far from where we had met. I couldn't see where we were going, nor how fast we were travelling, but it wasn't long before the wheels of the car struck gravel and eventually came to a halt. The door on Lawrence's side was opened and he stepped out, followed by Anulka, and then myself.

A few short strides took us up to the large oak-panelled door. I glanced back briefly to the car, but of the driver there was no sign. I had precious little time to take in much of the architecture of the building we were entering. But I knew that this was the home of a very rich family due to the grandeur of the house whose door we had just passed through. The house was very still and perhaps a little too quiet. A great many doors appeared to lead to other rooms on the ground floor but all of these were closed. I was led up a giant, ornately carved stairway, which dominated the reception room. Reaching the top of the staircase I followed Anulka and Lawrence down a long narrow passageway, passing many more closed wooden doors. We entered a door at the furthest end and stepped into the room. It was huge, its centre dominated by the most beautiful four poster bed I had ever laid eyes on. Velvet drapes hung around it, and the sheets that adorned it were black satin, with pillows to match. My mind was working overtime, my cock swelling slightly in my trousers. All thoughts of the original dinner invitation faded quickly as Anulka led me to the bed and gestured for me to sit, which of course I did.

Anulka and Lawrence stood before me, tall, elegant, exquisitely beautiful and ever so sexy. They both smiled at me, telling me to relax. Then turning their attentions to one another, Anulka slowly and seductively undid each button on Lawrence's shirt. Removing it, she moved her hands over his chest, shoulders and arms, gently rubbing and caressing his taut exposed flesh. Her hands slid down to his belt buckle, undoing it, then unfastening his trousers, letting them fall to the ground. He lifted one foot at a time to remove his shoes, then socks, before stepping out of his trousers. Anulka knelt on the floor before him, her hands working their way up his legs towards his crotch. Her fingers caressed his cock through the material of his briefs. I watched as she slowly pulled them down, and off. His cock was long and very thick, it stood proud and erect as she took a hold of it, pulling the foreskin back over the glistening head. He shuddered his pleasure as she drew the foreskin forward, and then pulled it right back, repeating the process slowly but firmly.

She then slid her black satin dress from her shoulders and down to her waist, to reveal large firm white breasts, for she wore no bra, and erect dark brown nipples. Gripping one breast in each hand she knelt up and enclosed Lawrence's cock between them. She rubbed up and down, on either side of his shaft, as he pushed against her. My cock was stiff and erect as I watched this voyeuristic delight unfold before me. I longed to tear off my clothes and join the two of them in their coupling. Anulka turned her head towards me, had she read my mind? For she smiled, winked and gestured with her head for me to come forward.

I needed no further encouragement and within seconds stood before her beside Lawrence. Rising from the floor, and stepping from her dress, she stood before me in stockings, suspender belt and those luscious boots. A small triangle of black thatched hair adorned the upper part of her pussy. As I gazed upon this delectable temptress I was aware of two pairs of hands working quickly and efficiently on my clothes, removing everything until I stood naked before them, my cock jutting forward. Anulka took a hold of my hands and placed them on her near perfect breasts, whilst Lawrence knelt on the floor and began to fondle my balls, then caress the length of my cock with his cold strong hands. Anulka kissed my mouth and pushed one of my hands down towards her crotch. My fingers explored her pussy, gently parting her lips and delicately massaging her clitoris. My fingers probed further; finding her hole I slipped one, then two fingers inside her tight opening and slowly fucked her.

Lawrence meanwhile was flicking the swollen head of my cock with his tongue before taking my length into his hungry mouth. I had never had a guy go down on me before, but right now I didn't care. Anulka was too sexy for words and I longed to probe her depths with my cock, even if that meant having Lawrence suck deeply on my shaft, lashing it with his tongue. A few minutes of bliss passed before the three of us moved toward the bed. Anulka lay on her back, legs pushed up and spread wide apart, in the dim candle light the juices from her cunt glistened. I knelt before her on the floor, my mouth drawing closer to her puffed clitoris. My tongue probing her pussy, licking gently at her clit, as she placed her boots on my back pulling me in tighter. Lawrence meanwhile crouched behind me, using his tongue on my anus, whilst one hand squeezed my balls, the other pulled my foreskin right back over the engorged head of my cock. Anulka began to gasp as my tongue worked faster on her clit and cunt. Her legs forcing me to apply more pressure, licking her harder. I delicately nibbled on her clitoris and licked her inner lips with strong hard strokes. A few moments later she screamed, a long sharp piercing scream shattering the quietness of the house, echoing through the corridors. She commanded both Lawrence and I to kneel together opposite her, squatting on all fours she leant forward and took one cock at a time in her mouth before finally stuffing the swollen heads of both in together. Sucking like a woman possessed she took great delight in rubbing our cocks together.

With my desire and lust reaching an all time high and just when I thought I could hold back no longer she stopped her relentless pleasuring and lay back on the black satin sheets. Opening her legs she pulled her pussy lips apart for Lawrence and I to admire her inner beauty. She commanded me to take her, fuck her, impale her deeply with my cock. I wasted precious little time in positioning my body so that the head of my cock was pressed against the opening of her cunt. Meanwhile Lawrence positioned himself behind me, pressing the cold hard tip of his cock up against my arsehole. As I eased my hot rampant tool into Anulka's cool wet pussy, Lawrence in turn pierced my anus with his large throbbing icicle. We three moved as one together, impaling, pushing in, pulling out – fucking. the muscles around my anus relaxed allowing Lawrence's cock to penetrate me deeper. Anulka lashed around on the bed as my cock pumped her hard and deep, she squeezed her tits, pinching her nipples as I tore into her. I felt nails scrape my back breaking the skin in places. Then Lawrence's cold hands gripped my hips as he thrust harder and faster into me. I fucked Anulka violently as Lawrence assaulted my arse.

My cock felt massive, as if it would burst in a mixture of hot blood and burning spunk. I felt my orgasm rising like a torrent from deep inside me. Anulka began to convulse, gasping and panting. Lawrence groaned his obvious sheer pleasure, quietly at first then louder and louder. An ear-splitting high pitched scream from Anulka, and a deep growling cry from Lawrence, intermingled with my own screams of orgasmic carnal ecstasy, heralded the arrival of our orgasms. My cock spurted its spunk in great spasmodic gushes into Anulka's cunt, as she thrashed wildly upon the bed exalting a cry of pure carnal lust and overwhelming ecstasy as she reached a violent thundering climax. Lawrence pumped my arse to bursting point with his come, a seemingly endless flow of spunk coming from us both. Then with almost bestial cries of lust, both Anulka and Lawrence went for either side of my neck. Powerless to resist, sandwiched between my two lovers, they bit hard and deep, ripping apart my tender flesh and gorging themselves on my sweet hot blood as it sprayed forth from my deliriously satiated body. That was the last thing I remembered before passing out.

Dreams swirled through my head. I dreamt of the gorgeous ravishing beauty of Anulka, naked, her breasts rubbing against my face, my chest, my cock. I dreamt of taking Lawrence's arse, sucking on his engorged cock. I dreamt of us both taking Anulka at the same time, cock in mouth and cock in cunt, then cock in cunt and cock in anus. Sucking, fucking and the exaltation of triple orgasm.

I awoke slowly to a beautiful sensation. Gradually opening my eyes I looked around me and saw colours I had never seen before. A radiance seemed to come from various objects in the room around me. Everything looked different, and yet the same. I recognised the sensation that awoke me. But it was exquisitely more beautiful and pleasurable than ever before. I was floating in a new found ecstasy, the sensation coursed through my entire body. Looking down I saw the naked form of Anulka lying between my legs, with my cock in her mouth. Looking back at me she winked and continued sucking. A few feet away sat Lawrence, looking on approvingly. He turned, smiling, and said: "Yes, my friend, some dreams do come true. Welcome to an eternity of power, lust and satisfaction." Welcome indeed to my new 'life'.

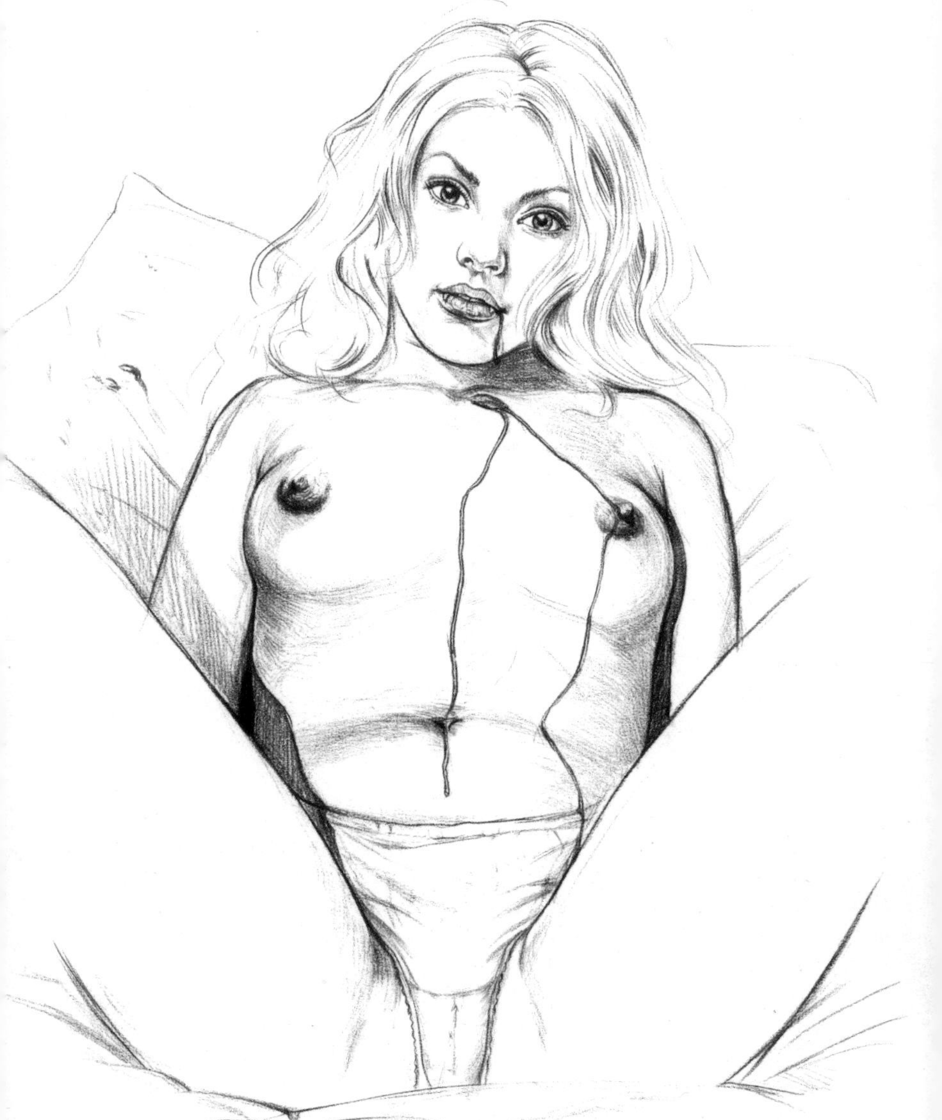

The Lamia Shall Not Age

Dean Aaron Geoghegan

'That is a doubtful tale from faery land,
Hard for the non-elect to understand.'

Lamia readied herself for the night's hunt by clothing herself in the flesh of a woman.

She slid into the body she had chosen and prepared herself by bathing and anointing herself with a selection of oils that she had found, through the many centuries of her existence, to be attractive to her prey.

In her past she had found such oils to be expensive and difficult to come by and had used the bodies she borrowed to barter for, or to earn, the coins needed to purchase them. In this time however she found the shops and stalls of the city to be filled with such items, no longer exotic but commonplace, and the need to endanger herself to obtain them long past.

Having thus prepared herself, and combed and teased the long blonde hair that belonged to the flesh she wore, she moved from her bathroom to the main room of the flat she inhabited.

Her room was almost bare with three items of furniture: a large old four poster bed draped with red velvet the colour of dark wine; a large chest (containing the clothes she needed to cover the bodies she inhabited); and a mirror.

It was in this mirror that Lamia examined herself. She ran her hands over the long legs, teased and stroked the large nipples till they stood proud in the centre of her breasts and finally she stroked the flesh of the soft parting between her legs and shuddered in the pleasure that this touch provoked.

Satisfied that the body would serve her purpose she moved away from the mirror, that would never show her true form, only that of the flesh she stole, towards the chest. The chest was old, in design much like many chests available in this time, but to the expert eye an item of truly great age, and the only item she had kept with her through the ages. Opening it she selected items that she would need if she was to feed this night, all of the clothing was black with only a touch of red or purple. Delicate lace underwear was pulled over her long legs and her female breasts were constrained and supported by a construction of lace and wire that pushed the large breasts together and upwards in a way sure to attract the eyes of her prey.

She had chosen well for the woman was, whilst not young, still firm and attractive to men in a way that Lamia could use. She had learned over the centuries that there was a difference between pure beauty and the voluptuous curves and fleshiness of the women men desired to bed.

She pulled on suspenders, fishnet stockings and then other garments of lace, leather and velvet. Some were a little tight for this stolen flesh was a little larger that her last host and she found the garments constricting and uncomfortable in a way that she also found pleasurable. The pinching of the leather against her flesh sent little tingles of almost-pain through her when she walked and moved.

Satisfied she looked around the room to ensure all was in order and then let herself out of the front door of her flat into the chill January evening, the coldness of the air sending an almost sexual thrill through her as it touched exposed flesh.

'Whither fled Lamia, now a lady bright,
A full born beauty new and exquisite?'

The upstairs bar was half-filled with velvet, leather and silk clad figures when Lamia arrived with, here and there, a few figures decked out in peacock splendour in a riot of reds and purples a sharp contrast to the almost uniform black of the Vampyre Club.

The members of this club dressed in the styles of times long past: Regency, Victorian, Egyptian and many other styles would be present later in all manner of combinations but all with vampires as a theme. All revelling in the caress of velvet, leather, silk and lace. Some members were dressed in this manner all the time as this was their chosen lifestyle, others dressed for the meetings only, the surroundings and the feeling of kinship with the other members an escape from the normality of their nine to five existence.

A haze of cigarette smoke hung in the air like some faint trace of ectoplasm and Lamia decided that she liked this place. There was a yearning in these people for times past that matched her own longing for the fields of her youth and she sensed in them a feeling of desire that she knew she could control or bend to her will.

She had collected a flyer for this club at a night club a month earlier when she had been after other prey and had kept the details for future reference as a possible place to obtain food.

Years had taught her caution and she was careful to ensure that her prey was selected from different places, cultures and social circles so that nothing would ever provide a way of tracing her. She had almost been caught and destroyed many times before but had learned her lessons.

She spoke briefly to the girl at the door, showed the flyer and was waved through with a smile. She took a position at the bar and ordered a drink by looking at the titles on the row of wooden handles in front of her. She cared little what she drank, the glass of alcohol would make it seem as if she had been drinking and would put her prey, when she found him, off his guard. The alcohol consumed by her host would not affect her.

Time passed and she chatted to a few of the others present: girls in corsets and wisps of lace finery or dressed in black flowing dresses of velvet; men in black T-shirts and jeans or like modern gladiators in the black leather armour of the road. None were suitable as they either had partners or were not interested in her and she could tell would not be prey for her though the blood was strong and warm in all of them. Whilst she needed to feed soon, centuries teach patience and the blood worth getting was worth the wait.

When her prey entered the bar she sensed it almost immediately: the serpent inside her shivered in its coat of female flesh. His eyes found her and she pretended not to notice the way they lingered on the swell of her breasts or the stocking clad length of her legs, she had selected a short leather skirt for tonight.As he approached she turned slightly towards him so that he could not help but notice the shadowed area at the top of her inner thigh. He started slightly and then asked her if she minded his sitting with her and introduced himself.

She made small talk. He was interested in films and she spoke of the many vampire and horror films she had seen from 'Nosferatu: A Symphony of Terrors', 'Dracula' (in its many, many versions) through to 'Vamp', 'Near Dark' and 'Interview with The Vampire' (one of her favourites). She mentioned casually that she enjoyed the sexual elements of these films and was satisfied at his reaction. They talked about vampire fiction and she thought of the Irishman she had met, over a century before, and how a glimpse of her true nature had sent him reeling away and left him with nightmares that had produced 'The Lair of the White Worm': poor, poor Bram she mused, working himself to death because, unlike his brothers with their civil service pensions, his works both literary and for Sir Henry Irving had not provided him with a means to fully support his family.

Now and again she would read biographies of the man and laugh at the accusations of venereal disease - if only the biographers really knew about Mr. Stoker.

The prey was a civil servant, recently divorced, and had come to the club in search of friendship and possibly a new partner. The need in him for a soulmate was so great she could almost taste it and it would make him a fine prey indeed.

She leaned towards him in a whisper of black fabric and allowed him to see a little more of her breasts, placing her hand on his leg as she leaned towards him and was satisfied to see the swelling at his crotch; he wanted her so much, her feeding was just a matter of time.

He was in his early thirties, younger than her host body, and slightly plump with short cropped brown hair and had come to the club a few meetings ago because of a love of horror literature and films and because his recent divorce, which had robbed him in short order of his home, his wife and his friends, had left him broken and with a void in his life that needed to be filled.

Lamia smiled to herself for all she needed to do was offer him the possibility of a future of sex and companionship and he would be hers.

She drank some more of the alcohol and allowed him to buy her more. She asked him how far he had travelled and then mentioned that she lived but a short distance away whilst moving closer to him and smiling.

He became nervous, not believing that this rather attractive woman was coming on to him. Obviously his experience was limited, and Lamia knew in his reaction that he was hers.

They talked for several hours, Lamia taking care to appear that she knew only a little of the subjects he mentioned: there was no greater turn-on to a man than to appear slightly more stupid than they.

Last orders were called and she took care to stay by her prey as he gathered his things together and prepared to leave the bar.

Lamia watched as he said goodnight to the few people he knew, pleased that he knew so few and had only been going to the club for a short time. If he had been an established member with many friends then his not-returning might arouse interest. As it was the other members would think he had just drifted away and she would be regarded as a woman who had tried the club once but decided not to continue.

He was slightly drunk and she supported him whilst suggesting that he might like to return to her flat nearby, coffee and a video were mentioned and quite a few other things were suggested. He agreed readily and she could see the hardly hidden lust in his eyes as his inebriated mind thought of the possibility of sex.

She guided him through the cold streets, his breath clouding in front of him whilst her own breath was invisible as her temperature rapidly cooled to that of her surroundings and she breathed through her host's borrowed lungs.

Reaching her flat she quickly opened the door and guided him inside. He looked around her room for a chair and then flopped onto the bed mumbling something about her not having a chair and that she seemed to have neither a video recorder or a television set.

She joined him on the bed and kissed him. He started, surprised by her coldness, and then eagerly responded, his hands moving to caress and warm her body and she allowing him to free her breasts and kiss and fondle the nipples which became as erect as earlier that evening.

She whispered that she wanted him and slid easily out of her clothes, so carefully chosen, so that he could see the naked body of her host. She then worked at his garments so that his erect penis was suddenly free and her lips played around its engorged tip, her tongue fluttering teasingly along its length, the scent of him and the closeness of his blood making her want to feed at once. But she had learned caution and using strips of silken material she gently tied his hands and feet to the four bedposts.

He started when he realised he was tied but she assured him that she just wanted to do things the way she enjoyed them and slapped him playfully before kissing him again and then fondling his erect penis.

She kissed him on the chest, teasing his nipples, and then sat astride him. Leaning over him she dipped her breasts to his face and allowed him to suck her nipples and then massaged his penis till he cried out to have her on top of him. She mounted him, her body rocking and bucking on top of him, his engorged penis rubbing up and down inside her and she felt the pleasure of her host body flooding through her as she prepared to feed.

The serpent inside her felt his erect penis enter the host and prepared to welcome him with its waiting jaws.

He gasped as he approached climax and as she felt the hot rush of his semen she bit down on his member, her venom swiftly coursing through his body as she sucked greedily at the part of him within her host and fed greedily on his blood.

He gasped screaming that he had never had such an orgasm or sexual experience like this before the last of her venom reached his vocal chords and silenced him forever.

Not all creatures have teeth in their mouths and Lamia drank deeply of his blood. Soon it would be time for her to bathe and sleep and then when she awoke she would feed many times on the paralysed body, mounting the erect member and riding her way to orgasm, before finally disposing of the empty husk and then seeking more prey whilst her current host body endured.

When the host was no longer of use she would find another female, with an appearance arousing to men, slide her serpent form from body to body and then feed on the remains of her previous host.

For now she ran a bath and stirred new scents into the water, her host body warm with the heat of the recent copulation and her true self, the serpent, bloated with blood. She lowered herself into the warmth of the bath and dozed as the scented vapours rose around her.

Lamia had existed for centuries – a serpent clothing herself in the bodies of women to drain her prey - and would continue for centuries more, but for now London was her home and she would hunt again soon.

'A serpent! echoed he. No sooner said,
Thus with a frightful scream she vanished;'

Sexy straight fun couple seek similar...

JP

Having scanned page after page it was this picture which had instantly caught his keen eye. Amongst the sordid array of photographs composed of women posing as bored housewives in order to elicit payment from desperate males and obese middle aged men seeking young women, some in drag, some dressed as schoolgirls he had found the one. "Sexy straight fun couple seek similar for hot adult games and friendship" read the advertisement below the black and white photograph. Perfect. It was made all the more so since the picture was of both parties. An attractive couple, late twenties pushing thirties perhaps. Perfect. Standing up from the table Steve tore out the relevant page and left the rest of the magazine on the vacant seat in front of his untouched coffee. Knowing that Jane would be thrilled he promptly left the all night café having mouthed a 'thank you' to the sleepy assistant behind the counter.

It didn't take Steve long to find her. Such a stunning and angelic beauty is never easy to miss in a crowd. This tall, slim, and elegant vision of ravenous delight with her sleek yet full face accentuated by high cheekbones and a gentle subtle chin was his maker. Jane's dark green eyes which seemed to him to twinkle constantly inside their frames of long lashes and shaped eyebrows peered devilishly at him. The soft yet sharp nose which complimented the contours of her face smelt him. Her full lips of crimson red over teeth as white as fresh paper smiled at him. The long straight dark brown hair covered her shoulders from which flowed arms ending in long slim fingers and sharp pointed nails, that reached for her pupil. Jane's perfectly formed breasts were squeezed against Steve's chest as she hugged him close. He could feel her small dark nipples in the chill of the night as they pressed hard against the material covering his flesh. They stood locked together for a while. As his hands rested on the shape of her hips he allowed his mind to wander briefly. Recalling their first time together he thought about those long, powerful legs ending in the most exquisite shaped feet wrapped around his back as he pounded her with all his might. Such a long time ago. He now knew every inch of his eternal lover intimately, there was not a blemish on her pale skin, nor a disproportionate part to her body beautiful. As he told her of his find, the vibrancy and energy tinged with a hint of excitement and anticipation exuded from her whole being.

They were the perfect beings, answerable to no-one, nor anything. They had but two rules which governed their continued existence. Avoid sunlight - at least to a degree - and gain sustenance through the consumption of warm fresh blood. Jane had taught Steve from the beginning to be at one with nature, so they fed on Mother Earth's most destructive element - humankind. For what fun there is to be had with warm blooded mortals!

Spending a while carefully choosing 'victims' had always added an extra dimension to the thrill of the hunt which was a turn-on for them both. Weighing up potential victims by a system of sexual cravings. One night it might be the large and beautiful breasts of the woman that were important. Another night Jane and Steve both craved the large cock of a man.

Following up the advertisement Jane had managed to flirt with, and woo, both the male and the female. Steve had simply stuck with what he was best at - making the woman damp between the legs following his own highly saucy but debonair conversation. Two nights later and the meeting was all arranged.

The doorbell rings somewhere deep inside the large house which had been divided into flats some years before. Steve, dressed casually smart in shirt and trousers, and Jane adorned in her current favourite red number wait patiently as the hallway light is switched on. She slips a hand between his legs and gently squeezes the already erect cock through the trouser material. With a smile Jane's white teeth flash in the darkness. They need not exchange words for both know what they want. The sound of two pairs of footsteps echo on the carpetless floorboards gradually getting louder.The door opens and a male some six feet tall, well built with short cropped hair, in casual, but tidy, dress stands beside a female of some five feet six inches tall with a slim build and long auburn hair. They nervously greet their guests. The tight figure-hugging clothes of the woman reveal ample breasts and firm round buttocks. Jane smiles at Steve with a glint in her dark green eyes which he knows to be the look that means she wants to have them both tonight. Steve returns the sparkle signifying that he feels the same way and they both turn and smile charmingly at the experience that awaits.

Once inside the couple lead Jane and Steve up to their apartment on the first floor. As soon as the door is closed behind them Jane makes a grab for the woman who cries out in shock as Steve swiftly pounces on the man knocking him unconscious to the ground. As the horror of what is happening begins to gradually sink into the mind of the mortal woman she starts to kick and scream as Jane drags her into the front room. Steve follows carrying the man's body into the same room.

Jane wastes little time in undressing the female, who has calmed down from the point of hysteria to a pitiful sob, down to a matching bra and panties set. Steve murmurs his approval at such an excellent choice and dumps the body of the male into a chair. Moving swiftly to his lover's side he helps her out of her red dress, to reveal long stockinged legs secured with a black lace suspender belt and matching black lace panties which just cover the small thatch of hair underneath. Jane's bared breasts are topped by nipples which stand proud and erect. Steve bows his head to her breasts and suckles gently on each nipple. His fingers slide slowly over the naked flesh of her lower belly and down to her crotch. The lace of her panties is damp and he pushes his long fingers upward, rubbing her lips and clitoris with the soft material. She pants and gasps loudly as her hands force his head up from her breasts so that she can remove his shirt, followed by his trousers. Steve's cock pushes forward, stretching the material of the briefs in which it is held captive.

They turn their attentions to the girl, who appears to be simultaneously hot and excited but scared half to death. Her bra and panties are torn from her by sharp pointed nails and the delicate fabric rips like fine paper. She stands before them, completely naked. Jane physically forces the girl to kneel at Steve's feet and orders her to remove his briefs whilst her continued sobbing and incoherent mumbling is met with a sharp crack across the face. She obeys and releases the stiff erect cock from its confinement. Pushing her head towards the swollen weapon Jane commands the girl to suck it. The warm mortal lips and mouth surround the head and Steve pushes forward, making her take more of his length deep inside, slowly fucking her mouth as Jane rubs her breasts against the girl's back, whilst fondling and roughly pinching those of the plaything.

The guy slumped in the chair slowly begins to recover, rubbing a bruised face as his eyes take in the scene before him. Steve pulls his cock from the girl's mouth as Jane forces the hapless victim onto her back. Squatting over her in a sixty nine position she pushes her tongue in between the girl's legs drowning her unabated sobs by grinding her wet pussy into the girl's face. Steve pulls the male from the chair gripping him tightly around his neck and orders him to strip naked. He tries to struggle but is warned of the consequences for both himself and his pretty girl. Once stripped the man is pushed to his knees and Steve stuffs his hard cock into his mouth ordering him to suck it. The licking and sucking continues as the dominant couple feed on the humiliation they have forced upon the innocents.

Jane ceases her oral assaults on the girl's warm pink pussy and picking her up, holds her head tight, making her watch 'her man' sucking Steve off. The two laugh together, revelling in the ecstasy of their enjoyment. Pushing the guy's head roughly away from his cock Steve turns his attention to the girl Jane is still holding and pushes his cock deep into her mouth, maintaining the hold on her head while Jane moves toward the trembling naked guy. Laying him down onto his back she proceeds to straddle him. Gripping his cock with her hands she slowly pulls the foreskin back and forth making him stiff before guiding the swollen tool slowly inside her damp hungry pussy. She squats down savagely, forcing his cock through the pure white lips of her pussy hole and beyond. She rides him hard, murmuring her pleasure as his red hot cock penetrates her inner coldness. Steve watches in silent fascination before twisting the girl around with her back to him down on to all fours. Kneeling on the floor and sitting back on his feet, cock jutting forward, he grips the woman's hips and guides her arse toward it, shoving his stiff cold cock into her warm wet cunt. She gasps at the coldness, like a spear of ice penetrating her depths. His hands reach round to her breasts, pinching the nipples until they stand out like little stalks. His cock pounds her cunt slowly at first, then gradually building up speed. By the sweet gasps that fill the room Steve is aware that Jane is fast approaching orgasm, thrashing herself wildly on the guy's cock until like music to Steve's ears she screams her violent orgasm.

Recovered, Jane moves to her pupil's side, leading the guy with her by his still erect cock, slowly wanking him off. She kneels beside him and both begin licking and sucking the male's cock as Steve's cock continues to penetrate the girl. Pulling out his cock and moving up a short space he pierces the woman's anus and she cries out in pain as he fucks her still harder. An unspoken message passes between Jane and Steve as their eyes meet. Grabbing the guy's buttocks and holding him completely still the frenzied pair sink their teeth into his cock; he screams as the skin tears easily and the throbbing veins are punctured. Drinking of the warm blood that flows the male shoots his load violently over the pair. Pulling him down to the floor they rip open his chest and gorge themselves on the blood that pours from his gaping wounds. The girl, unaware until now of what they have done, turns to see her now dead lover lying slumped on the floor. Screaming she tries to get away but Steve's hands grip her body, holding her firmly impaled on his cock. Jane kneels in front of her and sinks her teeth into one of the girl's breasts. Her anal muscles contract tightly around Steve's cock and he pushes deeper inside her, harder and faster, tearing the delicate skin with the force. He feels the orgasm rising through the length of his shaft. Fucking her harder he clamps his teeth onto her shoulder, biting and breaking the skin. As her blood fills his mouth he reaches orgasm, pumping her anus full of his liquid. ECSTASY! Jane and Steve devour the girl until her body slumps lifelessly between them.

Getting up from the floor Steve kisses Jane's hand, then her blood red lips. Running a finger over her erect nipples they smile. The night is still young they shall walk and talk under the stars, then make passionate love to each other before sunrise.

Until next time...

Lily's Blood

Luke McLelland Smith

I thrust my bloodied fist into my vagina with enraptured jubilation. It is smothered with the blood of the dead victim next to me. His body is quickly deteriorating and I can see the pallor of death gradually taking over his flesh. I work quickly, reaping the delights of his blood, seeing the signs of staleness and knowing that soon the cadre of joy will cease to give me the substance of my pleasure. I work with the music of Genitorturers in the background. I lunge for his penis with my sharp canine teeth in time to the music and bite into his sensitive flesh. I run my tongue along the still throbbing veins of his erection and pierce them with my fangs, sucking on his thick hot blood. It amalgamates with some left over pre-ejaculation sperm (I didn't let him ejaculate but as we all know, some always seeps out before) and the taste is electrifying. Like a slimy lizard his juices flow down my throat as I steal his red glow and bring euphoria and life to my once pallid parlour of a body.

I drain his penis as much as I can from its position at the apex of his body and in a frenzy of wanting more I then tear into it and rip it away from him with my mouth so that I can fully bleed it dry.The penis' veins expand until I rip them far enough and like a balloon they pop, blood falls over my face and into my mouth, covering me like syrup. I suck on his penis, it tastes as sweet as a toffee apple. I suck on it and watch it become whiter and whiter with each suck like an ice pop in a thirsty child's mouth. I then push the torn penis up my vagina, coating my warm nest with the remainder of the penis' blood and giving myself climactic pleasure. Blood splashes out onto my pubic hairs as I thrust his penis into me and I rub the substance into the metallic hairs, coating my forest with his sticky life force. I then work the blood further up and around my body and the puddle layered on my vagina spreads. I rub the magical substance into my breasts, watching them become pert as it touches them. I rub it into my anus, making myself look like I've been buggered and laughing at the thought, but I want more.

I bite further into his body, but the juices are disappearing. I rip into his flesh, into his cheeks, into his butt cheeks, into his elbows, into his feet, but all that is left is the mould of his skin. I get annoyed. I hit the body, smash its face against my head board and open up its anus with both my hands until an orifice like a black hole opens up in an attempt to get more blood. But that's all it is, a black hole, no blood and therefore no life. I push the body sulkily off my bed. He's been drained, he is nothing any more. I look at my red stained, once porcelain white, sheets. I suck on them, I rub my body into them, I shove them up my vagina in an attempt to be more satisfied, and with the sun beginning to spread its deadly rays throughout the city I go to sleep in the intoxicating now crimson coloured sheets, basking in my victim's blood until night rises and I can once again obtain some fulfilment.

I wake up with the fall of the sun, I look around my room. My bed sheets are covered with blood, my floor is covered with bits of my victim's body and clothes, and my head is hurting. I can't remember last night, I was drunk out of my face, and by the looks of things I was pretty rough with my victim. It's kind of sad to see what is left of what was once a stimulating individual. Last night when I saw him in the club, his androgynous qualities, his black lipstick and mascara and his pallid flesh, I knew I wanted him. He was once a beautiful creature but now he's just a layer of incoherent mess rotting on the floor of my room. But who cares at the end of the day, I now feel refreshed and alive.

The room is beginning to smell with the rotting, decaying and decrepit corpse, so I decide to get rid of it. I spread my reddened bed covers and place the corpse and all its clothes in it and roll them up into a cylinder the shape of a giant tube of Smarties. I place it in the corner of the room. I'll take it to the rubbish on my way out. Nobody will know what it is. I live in an apartment complex and the bins are gargantuan. The body will be like a piece of hay in a stack of needles. Lost in the prickly stench of people's rubbish. Lost in the gigantic load of everything else.

My victim's blood has dried onto my body and in between my legs and armpits. It's awkward to walk and it stings against my flesh, so I decide to take a shower before I go out tonight and find some more prey. I go into the bathroom, turn on the water and walk under its steaming rays. The blood dissolves off my body and once again becomes a liquid. I watch it flow down the plug hole and get annoyed and depressed at the substance as it spirals away into nothing. I decide to rescue the substance, so I get a cup from the sink and place it under my vagina. The red substance flows languidly down my body and from the hairs and orifice of my pussy and enters the cup. I drink. I taste the blood but it's weak, it's diluted by the water, my sweat and my juices. It still tastes fucking good though and fills me with a burst of energy. I leave the shower, dry myself and begin to get changed for tonight. Tonight I will dine again.

I put on some music. I choose Christian Death. I begin to get dressed. I go into my chest of drawers and pull out some black laced pants. I slip them up my perennial legs and cover my now clear and dry vagina. I then place on some black stockings. I toyingly run them up and down my legs, moving my hands over my flesh like a horny, nervous school kid would to a girl on his first sexual encounter. I then clip them in place. I then go into my wardrobe and put on a skirt, black latex skirt. I pull it up my legs and attach it round my waist and admire myself in the mirror. The skirt is high enough for the mesh frontier of the tops of my stockings to be manifest and I like it. I turn myself on, I know I will turn on all the horny males and females out there too, I always do. I like the way I look so much that I consider staying home and masturbating in front of the mirror all night, but I can't. Pallidness is beginning to creep over my face and I know I need more blood. I now put on a black bra. I always wear a bra. I've been on this planet for many years, if I didn't my breasts would probably have sagged down to my ankles by now! I then pull on a black, revealing tight sweater with a low neck that leaves the top of my breasts exposed, just enough to turn people on. Finally I put a pendant of Jesus Christ on the cross around my neck, it falls between my breasts like a stream through a mountain valley. Yes, I wear a cross, I don't shy away from religious objects. Don't believe everything you read.

I then parade in front of my mirror. I coat my eyes and mouth with a façade of black lipstick and mascara, my lips are quite pallid and they need covering and the oceans of my eyes need toning down in colour. I then paint my long nails with black nail paint and put on some perfume. I put some of the perfume inside my vagina. I am now complete. I look in the mirror, I look gorgeous. I watch myself, toy with my body, practice erotic movements, postures of elegant nature that will lure my victims to me. God knows why, I've had so much practice through the years that I know subconsciously how to lure victims. I run my fingernails across my skin, up my legs, through my hair and into my pants. My long sharp fingernails prick my clitoris, I become wet, but I stop playing with myself. People waste too much time in their own bodies, I want someone else's. On this thought I pick up the giant Smarties, leave my room, place the Smarties into the gargantuan bin of the apartment complex and hail a cab into the darkness of the rest of the city. I live on one of the busiest streets in the city, but it's taken ten minutes trying to hail a cab. I am enveloped in black, I am invisible against the dark, austere background of the city buildings. I get bored waiting so I close my eyes. I close them and open them again, opening the gates to the red glow of my soul through my eyes. The red pools are visible from miles off, I am picked up in seconds. Hopefully to go and obtain red pools of my own.

The taxi drops me off in the incandescent streets of the central city. People pollute the atmosphere. I can smell their blood, I can smell their sweat and I become excited. I want to just take victims here and now, drain each and every one of these people of their blood and leave them as rotting corpses, but I don't. The people in this neck of the woods are of a colourful nature, they bask in the sun, they wear bright coloured clothes, they go on holidays to sun baked coasts just to get a false pigmentation of their skin. I can do none of these, I wouldn't want to do any of these. There is a quality about the darkness which attracts me, its mystery, its ethereal qualities, its decadent but ever uplifting atmosphere. I've always felt like this, even before I was a vampire and thus the transformation was easy. I do not miss the light, the bright blue sky holds no interest to me, and because of this my victims must be of a similar nature, only children of the night can totally fulfil me. Others are taken only in desperation.

I make my way over to the dark side of the city. The place where shroud wrapped women sell roses at twelve o'clock at night, the place where every building has a secret waiting inside, the place where witches cuddle round barrel fires on street corners casting spells, the place where wannabe moribunds and vampires paint their faces with the colour of the night, the place where the taxi driver was too scared to take me. The place where I belong. The loud raucous roar of the others' voices quickly filters off and the lights become dimmer. The noise of death gradually seeps into my surroundings, I begin to see people hanging around on street corners smoking, shouting, fighting, screaming, chanting. I begin to see people covered in black passing by, always looking at my beauty, seeing in me desirable qualities that most others don't see. I then see the place where I obtain most of my blood, Innate Gloom. It's a night club. I walk closer, I hear the noise of Nine Inch Nails emanating from inside its walls. I draw closer and gradually the atmosphere envelops me. I become excited, I wonder what delights will be waiting for me within the club tonight, I become wet thinking of it, I begin dripping. A tear of juice seeps out of my pants and onto my leg.

I press the ball of my thumb against it and put it into my mouth, licking away the salty texture. I think of all the kids in there, I think of them dripping, I think of them dripping into my mouth and then I think of me ripping into their flesh, the surprise on their faces. Most love it, they want it, they want to become like me, but they never do. I don't let them become like me, there's only one vampire in this town. I arrive at the doors of the club. The people outside look at me in bewilderment, I look back at them, possible victims, but I want someone special, someone to make my body ache with delight. I enter the club optimistically.

I walk down the dark stairs leading to the main hall. People are making out and shooting up on the steps, boys and girls, boys and boys, girls and girls, and people so dark I can't even tell what sex they are. They all look up at me from their activities, whether they be in the realm of another's mouth, anus, or vagina. They look up at me with wanting eyes and stare. I walk down the remaining steps and into the club.

I look out onto the dance floor. Razed in Black come on the stereo with their gothic, industrial, dance floor mesh of sound. People cloud the floor dancing in time to the music and shying away from the beams of light that whizz across the floor now and again. I follow the beams into the far corners of the room where they light up the people in a less partying mood. Kids making out, kids having sex, kids sleeping, slitting their wrists. I see one girl's fingering herself while looking at some similarly dressed member of the opposite sex. She probably doesn't even realise the lights are making her actions manifest, she probably doesn't even care. I approach the bar and order a drink, a Bloody Mary: seemingly clichéd, but it makes for good visualisation. The barman knows me, forces a smile. He's never seemed to like me though, just grudgingly acknowledges me when he serves me and carries on with his work. He's gorgeous however, has a sort of androgynous glow to him with his thick long black hair and tightly woven flesh stretched finely across his face. I often think of picking him up but he gives me no signals of interest and he's too well known in this area to pursue forcefully.

As I am drinking my bloodied Mary a girl walks up to the bar. She has long blonde hair flowing down her back and pallid flesh to complement it, like one big fusion of colourless colour. She's beautiful and I know straight away that I want her as my victim. She nervously orders a drink. The barman smiles at her and she smiles back, turning her head away after acknowledging him in a nervous withdrawal. She turns her head to me, I smile at her, she smiles back but this time doesn't draw back her head. I look at her body with my red glaring eyes keeping her looking at me with their absorbing colour. I admire her white flesh and small moulds of breasts and she looks back at me in a similar but more submissive way. The barman walks off grudgingly at his defeat.

I look further. She has a slit on her left wrist, I examine it, the darkening flesh of its scar. As she sees me examining the scar she turns her arm over in a nervous action to hide her wound. I grab lightly at her arm and turn it over again. I rub the scar with my fingers, comforting her and stroking it with my nails. I imagine digging my nails into the scar and drinking her blood, but I conceal my desire. I play with it affectionately, reassuring her. She smiles at me and we begin to talk. She tells me of the bands she likes and how she hasn't any friends and why she slit her wrist and a million other pathetic but emphatic stories. I become absorbed into her words. I begin rubbing and stroking further up her arm from her lesion. I reach her bone white shoulder and caress it. I then move further round her body, running what little meat she has on her around in my fingers like putty. She will be easy to penetrate with such little flesh. She seems to like my actions. She begins touching the bottom of my leg. My pussy begins to get wet and my breasts become erect. I want her body. I want her innocent blood. I want to drink her innocent soul, her untouched beauty. I think she wants me to, her words mumble as her lips are wet, she moves her hand further up my leg, but I think she's scared. She stops moving her hand at the base of my thigh. I grab her hand, I push it further up, she smiles.

We decide to move over to a corner of the club where we can become more intimate, and so I grab her hand and lead her over to a place away from the lights of the dance floor. The corner is carpet covered and we sit down. I begin touching her lips with my fingers, fondling the flesh, and then I draw my mouth to hers. We kiss and unleash ourselves into the world of each other's bodily juices. I begin caressing her body. I feel her breasts, hand full sized moulds, and I move into her vagina. It's wet in there and I fondle the corpulent flesh. I can only fit two fingers into her, she's tight. I think she's a virgin. I smell my fingers, they smell nice, she probably purges her body every day, she is an angel. I feel her hands, they're cold but clammy and I can sense her nerves. I don't think she dares touch my body so I move her trembling, budding hands for her. I move her hands into my pussy. I make her rub it, caress it, she soon picks up the caressing action and I pull my hands away and concentrate on her body. I pull off her pants and enter her. I gradually weave more and more fingers into her as she becomes bigger with my pressure and more pliable as she becomes wetter like clay. She's now all over my body, over my breasts, into my pants, she even sticks her fingers into my anus. She wants me as much as I want her.

I continue kissing and biting at her lips with my teeth and tongue and looking into her eyes while playing with her body. I want to sink into her flesh now but I'm going to hold out. This girl is special and I want to get as much pleasure from her as I can before I drain her. Besides, there are too many people here. I will take her home with me, play and then kill. I can play for a long time.

Bands continue playing in the background. Chateau Royale, The Cure, London After Midnight, The Shroud, Ultraviolence. They all make our feelings more intense. I love music, nearly as much as I love blood, nearly as much as I will love this girl's blood. We continue playing, melting into each other's bodies like the caramel and chocolate of a Mars bar if left out in summer in the sinful sun, until the music gradually stops and people begin to leave the club. The club is closing. We are kicked out onto the cold street, we make our way back to my apartment.

On the way back we talk, I want this girl's body but I contain myself. The streets are cold, dirty and sordid and she deserves better. I hold her and we just walk and talk. She tells me of herself, she tells me her name is Lily. She tells me she is a virgin as suspected, I become wet at the thought. She then asks about me as most of my potential victims do before their inevitable draining and as always, I lie. I consider telling her I'm a vampire, wanting to tell her, but I hold back. I may tell her once she's locked in my house, but now she's too fragile and I think she's nervous enough as it is about coming back with me. I don't want to scare her off. I play the reassuring, caring partner like some over sexed, drunken, slimy, twenty something Townie, absorbing her into my body with false, kind, cajoling words which I actually begin feeling have some truth. Her cold shaking shoulders begin to become more relaxed as I tell her how I love her and as I lovingly fondle her hair. We arrive back at my apartment and we enter in, she smiles nervously.

I put on some music, Love Spirals Downwards, I tell her to sit down on the couch. I go and get us some drinks. I watch her from the kitchen, she's amazing. I watch her nervously scan my apartment looking at my possessions, I watch her pull her hair behind her ears, I watch her bite away at her nails. She's like a little wolf in a stack of giant lambs, everything overpowers her. A tear of euphoria runs down my cheek as I look at her, her white flesh and her boned face. I could look at her body all day. I go back into the room with red wine. She wraps both her hands around the glass like a scared homeless child with coffee on a winter's day. She looks into the wine, she seems to look for something inside its aesthetic glow, she seems to be looking for escape in its swirl. I remove the cup from her hand and stroke her hair, I kiss her, her tight lips. I kiss her until she becomes soft and warm as my passion spreads between us and her nerves decay.

I begin playing with her body, I undo her dress and pull it down, she has no pants on – I removed them earlier in the club. I move my face down to her vagina and begin giving her oral pleasure. Her lightly forested bush begins raining as I play with her clitoris and I hear low, noiseless, incoherent sighs of passion from her feathered mouth. She begins dripping beads of juice onto my couch. I stand up and pull myself away from her now wet orifice and undress myself. I pull down my dress, take off my bra and pants and then move onto her face. She licks my clitoris and I become aroused. I extend my fangs toyingly as I sink my vagina into her face, knowing she can't see them, practising for the big bite but quickly retracting them as I bounce back up from her and my mouth comes into her vision. She licks into my flesh and begins kissing my hard metallic pussy hairs, attaching her face to them like a magnet to iron filings. Lily is confident now, her nervous proclivity has taken a back seat to the passion of her budding youth and she elegantly toys with my body like a professional. I toy with her too, but I let her take the dominant role.

She licks for a while and then pulls her head up away from my vagina and with her lips coated with a thick lining of my syrup like lipstick she says something unexpected. She asks me if she can chain me up. I'm surprised at this. This innocent, unsullied child wants to chain me up. I didn't expect her to be so sordid and dirty. I look into her eyes, her innocent eyes, and see her pure flesh, body, mind and soul and I agree. This girl couldn't harm anything and I can drain her later. I will sleep with her and drain her harmlessly in her sleep. I will now let her have her pleasure. I won't even kill her when I suck on her blood, she can leave tomorrow with just two pin pricks on her throat and vivid memories as indications of our time together. She smiles at my agreement and walks over to her bag which is resting in the far corner of the room, and she takes out two pairs of handcuffs. She has handcuffs! I thought we would be using mine. She walks back and with beads of juice dripping down her leg she attaches one cuff of each pair around my hands and then using her initiative she walks over to my wall and takes down two hanging pictures, revealing two hooks. She pulls me over to them like a dog and attaches the other cuffs to them, stretching my body like Jesus Christ on the cross against my pale walls.

I stand there outstretched, she looks at my body and speechless she sinks into my vagina, she bites hard. I moan in ecstasy, she bites into my flesh with a now dominant passion. She continues biting until a knock sounds at my door. She pulls her face away and goes to answer it.

I lay there stuck like a fly in a spider's web as she talks at the door, I can't hear what she is saying. She then comes back, followed by the barman and dozens of gothic children from the club. The barman is holding Lily's arm. He holds her and smiles at me, sinister. He walks over to me, he unexpectedly begins biting into my flesh. Then he pulls down his pants and quickly penetrates me. I begin to cry as he soils my body, the children behind him laugh, they get undressed. I look around scared, I look to Lily, she is there playing with herself awkwardly. I look to the kids, they are playing with each other. I look into the once beautiful barman's eyes which now look evil, evil with passion. He comes into me and groans. He pulls out of me, wipes the sperm into my stomach and then signals to Lily. She goes back to her bag and pulls out a knife. I sense hesitation in her actions. He is speaking to me. He tells me he's been watching me, he wants what I've got, they all want it and they're going to get it. The children nod.

Lily hands him the knife. He caresses it and pricks the tip of his finger, it bleeds. He licks away the blood until more flows to the surface and then he places his finger into my mouth. I push it away with my tongue, I don't want this bastard's blood. I hang there motionless, I fear for what he's going to do to me. I fear correctly, he draws the knife away from his finger and close to me. He holds it up and presses it against my neck, and slashes a perfectly straight line as if done with a ruler across my skin. I feel blood ooze out of my neck like lava as he cuts my skin and he begins sucking. He grabs Lily and pushes her head into my neck, she sucks too, they suck together.

I hang there cold and scared, feeling my life run away from me like water as they suck. I look at the children, they move closer, hot with anticipation like a hungry pack of wolves. The barman waves them even nearer, and picks up the knife again. He pulls away from my neck and begins making lesions all over my body like I was an apple. He cuts my butt cheeks and I moan, he cuts my breasts, he cuts my vagina, my stomach, my thighs, he cuts me everywhere. […]

I become whiter and whiter as I watch the children stealing away my life, they suck on me until my body is nothing but a sack of flesh, an empty case of mangled skin.

I feel myself dying, I look at the kids, the barman and Lily, and they're all smeared with blood. My blood and a million victims' blood coated around their sticky faces. They look satisfied. They have what they want, they have an excuse to wear black, they no longer need to paint their faces white to get that look of death. They are their dreams, their hopes, their fears, they are what they read of, they are what they dress like, they are the myths, the fables, the tales, the nightmares, they are vampires.

They leave my apartment happy and fulfilled, they leave me hanging for dead like a plucked chicken. From my position I see them out of my window running for the darkness as the sun begins seeping into the city. I lick my lips, lick as much blood as I can from my face. I feel death coming soon, if not by lack of blood, by the deadly rays of the sun. I try to loosen the handcuffs from the wall hooks. They are solid but I feel maybe I could pull the hooks out of the wall. I begin shaking my body with what little energy I have, I shake my body like an epileptic. I feel flakes of plaster fall onto my face. I shake harder, chunks begin to fall off onto my body. As the sun pierces the window and onto me, I fall to the floor as the wall crumbles. I find the key to the handcuffs and undo them. I lick up the blood from the floor, desperate for life, I lick the blood that is drying all over my body. I push my hands into my slashed vagina and lick at that blood but I still need more, far more. I crawl across my floor into the kitchen, open the fridge door with senseless fingers, and grab at the bottle inside. My emergency supply. I strain to lift the bottle to my mouth but manage and drink, I continue drinking until the bottle is empty My head falls to the floor and I either fall to sleep or death, I'm too weak to know which one it will be.

I wake up, it wasn't death. I wake up six days later. I had enough blood to sustain my life, my lesions have disappeared and my body is now healed. I pack my belongings, grab my all important possessions and decide I am going to leave this town, away from all the vampires and the bitter memories. I ring for a taxi and it soon comes. I don't tell the driver where to go, instead I lunge at him from my back seat and quickly drain his blood. I do not even bother to look at his face. I drain him and kick him out of the car. I can drive myself. I drive past Innate Gloom, I look at it.

The place is swarming with police, kids are getting arrested. I know what for. I look at their natural pallid flesh, their white lips. They are getting put into cars. The whole place is full of vampires, I can always sense my own kind. They're moaning, they took their gift too far. I see dead bodies lining the street, drained of blood. I see hungry and scared children of the night, overpowered by what they have recently acquired, I see their hungry faces.

There were too many of them, they couldn't find enough meat, they got carried away, they didn't know what they were letting themselves in for. They drained carelessly and they got caught, let's face it, a club full of hungry vampires is quickly going to get itself noticed. I slow down the car and I see the barman in the back of a police car. He sees me and looks cold. I then see the beautiful Lily. She has no police chasing her. I look at her and see something in her, a girl who got carried away with the over-excitement of becoming a vampire and did silly things to gain it. I see myself two hundred and fifty years ago, when I first became a vampire, hating life, hating the light and wanting it so bad that nothing would stop me from getting it and I did stupid and nasty things. I stop the car and open the door for Lily. She looks at me with her angelic face and she smiles nervously. I wave her over to the car, she scuttles over mouse like, invisible to the police in her shy ways, she gets in and I close the door away from the rest of the world.

We drive off, the sun is beginning to rise and I know the rest of the vampires will soon die as the sun burns their souls. The police won't understand it; it will get written off as some crazy religious group. Maybe a few will escape to haunt the streets of this city, maybe not, but the majority will die with the rise of the sun. Lily and me, we'll just make it to the next town before the sun's deadly rays envelop us.

Lily places her head on my shoulder, I stroke her hair and face. I push her head down and let her bite me. She bites lightly so as not to do any damage and she bites with love as we drive on. I look at her bloodied lips, her long blonde hair, her beautiful eyes and her thin, pale flesh and as she pricks her wrist and places it to my mouth, I put one hand over her small, erect, cold breasts and fall into euphoria.

Obsessions with the Undead

Laura Phoenix

You don't know me, at least I don't think you do?

My name's Miranda and like my dear cousin Julia, I am so very beautiful! It is an unearthly beauty, for we are very unusual women. I do not think we were always this way, but then again perhaps we were. Our story is an obsession, a way of life, a dream

Shall I begin then, my darlings? With our story? How it all began, ah yes! You must listen carefully for my voice is very soft, come close then and I shall tell...

The winter sky was grey, it hung over the graveyard like a cloak and a cold wind blew against my face, biting my cheek with its wicked little teeth. I had been for a long walk with my sweet cousin Julia, and somehow we always ended up here amongst the tombstones. Of course it was part of our strange obsession, floating around in our long velvet dresses. Our faces pale as the moonlight, our long hair, mine black and Julia's crimson.

We loved the night-time, to creep around when everyone else was safe indoors. Prowling around that sleepy south coast town. We would walk down on the pebble beach, amongst the rotting seaweed and fish spines. It seemed that death was all around us, that the smell of decay clung.

We looked intently at the way the salt sea air corroded the iron railings and balconies. Would it rot the walking frames of all those retired people who crawled along the promenade each afternoon?

So many old, crumpled faces, did everyone come here to die? Julia and I watched. For we had nothing else to do. We had each other and our little games and fantasies, it seemed enough at the time.

We were living in a big house, its ironwork balconies painted blue, a crowded garden full of shrubs and trees around the back. It was a perfect, lazy life, for my uncle was living away in America and we were alone in that huge house. There was no need to work, you see Julia's father was rich and stupid, he gave us whatever we wanted. Of course what we really wanted could not be bought. The Undead, a vampire lover or two. Julia and I longed so much for eternal life, eternal ecstasy. At night we lay naked on our bed, our hair combed out and flowing over the satin sheets. We waited so patiently, the window open, even in winter, but they did not come. Julia and I were not lonely, we had each other and in our souls we were already vampires. As we lay on the bed, our hands between each other's legs, we fancied that we could change reality and so in a way, we did.

Julia stood in the red bedroom. Her crimson hair falling down over her shoulders to her waist. Her large hips were highlighted by the watery sunlight as it set over the sea. Her body was like the ocean, her movements always so fluid, her passion unstoppable. I had wanted her the first moment I saw her. Had dreamed of her soft full mouth on my skin, her large breasts pressed against me. I watched her as I lay on the velvet draped bed. She admired herself in the cheval mirror, stroking her nipples gently, her hands flowing down over her belly to her shaved pussy. She squatted down, her legs spread wide, her fingers opening out her pussy lips like a wet rose. Julia looked intently at her reflection in the mirror and smiled. She rubbed her finger over her protruding clitoris, watching in the mirror to see it swell with pleasure. Her fat pussy lips, glistening red cushions inviting you inwards. She opened herself wider, pushing two fingers up inside her cunt, moving them roughly in a circular motion to stretch her hole.

Slowly I slid from the bed, my black lace basque was wet with the heat of my lust. I crawled over to her, peering through my long black hair, growling like a panther. My whole body focused on Julia's writhing hips and parted thighs. I came behind her, my hands caressing her arms and tits. She pressed back against me, sighing. Her fingers thrust deeper up her tunnel as my own hand frotted her clit. I bent my head down, nuzzling her long sweet neck. I could feel the blood pulsing through her veins as I pressed my open mouth against her skin, oh to suck her blood! To be a real vampire! My lust grew at the very thought, I bit into her, bruising her flesh with my teeth. Julia moaned and lifted her wet fingers up for me to suck. I licked them slowly, the smell and taste of her sticky cunt juice exciting me so that I pressed even closer to her big round arse, my hips slamming hard against her, beating out a rhythm. I put my hand down to my stocking top where I concealed, like a dagger, our favourite toy. Carved in warm red wood, polished with use, an exquisite cock made to perfection and always hard for us. Its thickness stretched us beyond compare, its length filled us until we could take no more!

I pushed our phallic delight up into Julia's eager hole, her pussy swelled around it, clutching, hugging, devouring the wooden cock. Her body was rigid like an ecstatic voodoo priestess, her crimson hair damp and clinging to her body. I shoved the tool in and out of her cunt, her moans cat like and wild. I felt her body spasm and shudder, her muscles pulling on the dildo as her ecstasy reached its peak. She lay quiet against me for some time, the breeze from the window cooling us slightly. Her vulva still held the cock tight, refusing to let go. I pulled again gently until her muscles relaxed and freed it. Then I licked our wooden prick until there was no trace of love juice left on it. I tucked our treasure away in my stocking again. Its generous size made a swollen outline down my leg.

The cool night air was beckoning to us. The winter was the best time as it got dark so early. Time then to dress up and visit the cemetery again and maybe find a 'friend' on the way.

We put on our black leather corsets, lacing them tightly, our breasts pushed up over the top. Our stockings of black silk were held up with frilly garters finished off with long black thigh boots. We stood admiring ourselves in the mirror, our shaven pussies gleaming and starkly contrasted between the leather boots and corsets. Tight velvet mini skirts completed our look, our bare arses just above the hemline. Ah! how lovely we looked, our pale faces and black painted eyes, our red lips inviting, promising.

Down the stairs we trotted, our crippling high boot heels clicking on the polished wood. The hallway was decorated in rich reds and blues, fine paintings of unknown people stared down at us. Wicked ladies in powdered wigs, their plump tits peeking over frothy lace, their own painted eyes following us as we left, closing the door securely behind us. The night was ours for the taking!

The sea looked beautiful, a glittering relentless creature. The moonlight perfect for our cat's eyes and our slinky bodies. We walked arm in arm along the promenade towards the cemetery on the outskirts of the town. Not a soul in sight, they were all asleep for sure. We sat on a bench for a while, spreading our legs open wide to the cold winter night, stroking our clits and dreaming of our elusive vampire lovers.

The cemetery was deserted as usual. We picked our way between the graves towards the oldest part. No victims here! We sighed in unison, our breath hanging on the air in clouds of steam. Then from the corner of my eye I saw a dark shadow shambling towards us. We watched, crouching down behind a large headstone, trying not to giggle. There in the moonlight, a can of lager in his hand, came a man. He got closer and we could see he was young, his face was quite pretty with his hair drawn back in a ponytail.

I stepped out from behind the grave, smiling and tilting my head, my tits spilling out of my corset. I knew he would stop, he had no choice!

Julia stood next to me, her fantastic hair like a flaming halo. Her eyes blacker than pitch. Devouring every inch of that poor young man. He stared at us, a look of fear and hopefulness alternating across his face. We came closer, introducing ourselves, laughing, tossing back our luxurious hair, playing our silly games with him. His sweet face relaxed, just two silly tarts, he must be thinking, a bit drunk like himself. He followed us up to the old church where there were some big family graves with nice smooth tops of weathered, moss covered stone.

We sat on either side of him, our hands unzipping his leather jacket, up under his jumper to stroke his shivering flesh. So strange for even then we paid little heed to the cold, in fact we relished it. The man slipped his hand down between my legs but I hit him hard so that he fell backwards into Julia's arms. She held him tightly, her hands up under his clothes, gently soothing him. I heard her whispering in his ear, promising such a night of pleasure, but she didn't tell him that the night was ours alone.

I slid off the gravestone and knelt down between his legs. He was laughing now as I unzipped his jeans and helped to pull them off. I tossed his clothes away into the darkness, he wouldn't be needing them after all. Then I pressed in close between his thighs, my tongue lapping the tip of his cock like a hummingbird sipping nectar. My hand encircled his thick, erect prick as I slowly swallowed it, my mouth squeezing, my tongue massaging.

Julia held a strip of soft black leather, she stretched it over his mouth and nose. He could hardly breathe, I heard him gasping for breath, struggling as she tied it behind his head. Her laughter cutting the air like broken glass.

I sucked harder on his swollen cock and he relaxed against her again, giving in to our game, giving in to my mouth. I knew Julia had another toy ready, I caught the glint of it as I looked up. I felt the tautness in his body, heard his stifled ecstatic moans as he filled my mouth with his spunk. I swallowed it, sucking greedily, my cunt wet and swollen with anticipation. Julia slammed the knife into his throat, stabbing again and again, slitting him open. I looked up to see her wild eyes, the stiletto knife thrashing through the air. I felt the man's warm blood spattering over me, running down my body like a red river. The taste of his spunk was still in my mouth as I leapt onto his lifeless body licking up the blood. Julia lay across him too, smothering herself with blood, licking, biting, rubbing against him. We straddled him, sliding our wet pussies against his cooling flesh. Clenching our thighs, we came. Our hips spasming in our ecstasy, the victim's blood dripping down the corners of my mouth. My tongue hanging out and my eyes looking up at the stars.

Many months passed, we did not fear detection for we were never suspected. No-one spoke to us except the old vagrant that we sometimes gave money to. Harry Frieda was our only friend, he would smile with toothless gums, dancing and singing songs from old films we had never seen. He feared death, the unknown. He seemed vulnerable to us. We could not harm him. Like us he was searching, a fellow traveller on the road.

It was Harry Frieda who told us he had seen two mysterious people arriving next door, very late at night. We thought no more about it except that Harry seemed so afraid of them, as if death was finally after him.

The warm spring weather became the hot summer and we stayed out of the sun. Lying in the shade of our jungle garden. Coupling under the trees, our soft mouths searching out each other's doorways. I had been looking up at the house next door. It had been up for rent for over a year. The old man was right, someone had moved in. The curtains were drawn across the windows day and night. We had never seen the occupants, though we could hear them moving about through the walls.

Julia was playing with me, fucking me with her fingers, my legs were open wide. My eyes were still on the house, I stared at the windows and there I saw the curtains drawn back a little and a figure standing in the shadows, behind the nets, peeking at us. It looked like a man, very pale and thin, he watched as I noisily climaxed. I whispered to Julia and she turned to look up at the window. He had pulled the net curtain away slightly as if afraid of the light, his face looked directly down at us. We waved but he did not respond, so we opened up our legs to show off our pussies. He just stared at us and it seemed that his black eyes pierced my heart and I felt a strange thrill that I had never felt before.

All day I thought of the stranger in the window, Julia was curious too. Then at 8pm we found a note lying on the door mat, an invitation to visit our neighbours that very evening. So we dressed in our finest long flowing dresses, decorating ourselves with silver rings and bangles so that we rattled like jailers. Our hair was perfumed, our eyes painted black, ah, we did look lovely!

There were no lights on in the house next door. Just the glow of candles in the front room, making eerie shadows. The door was opened by a tall elegant woman who introduced herself as Fulvia. Her face was white and thin, her chestnut brown hair flowed down her slender body and touched the floor. She stared into our eyes, smiling, her tongue flickering slightly between her lips.

As she moved, her black taffeta gown rustled and it seemed she belonged far away in another country, another time. Julia and I glanced at each other, our hearts racing, faces flushed. Again I felt that strange erotic excitement as we followed Fulvia into the large drawing room.

Fulvia explained that she and her brother, Marcus, spent a lot of time travelling. That they had decided to settle for a year by the sea as her brother was in poor health and needed to rest. She told us he was sleeping upstairs and apologised for not seeing us.

We shrugged, trying not to seem disappointed, though Fulvia was entertainment enough. She told us that she lived alone with her brother and rarely ventured out, but she had so wanted to make new friends and had seen us from the window. Julia and I blushed, Fulvia must have spied on us also. She smiled at her effect on us, pulling her thick hair away from her front, so that we saw for the first time that her gown was cut away at the top so that her small round breasts could be viewed. Her nipples were very large and a deep plum colour, they were erect and so enticing.

She sat back in her chair, idly chatting, the low table in front of us was laden with sweet biscuits and cakes. She poured us thick red wine and drew our attention to the exquisite chocolate animals lying on a silver plate. They were perfect creations, almost lifelike in detail, some were white chocolate and some were rich black. We licked our lips, they smelled so good they could not be resisted. Julia bent down and selected a chocolate fish, each scale glistening in the candlelight. She sucked on its head noisily, the chocolate melting in her mouth. Fulvia leant forward over the table, her tits brushing over the cakes as she did so. She took a white chocolate rabbit, then sat back in her chair. Cream and jam smeared her breasts so she slowly began to wipe it off with her fingers. I could stand the temptation no longer, my pussy felt thick and wet with desire. I went over to her and kneeling down I began to lick and suck her nipples, rubbing my face against her, my hand slipping up under her skirts. She stopped me for a minute as she began to unbutton her clothes, slipping them off her body until she was naked before me. Julia and I began to undress, leaving our suspenders and stockings on. Fulvia sucked the erect ears of her chocolate rabbit, her pink tongue caressing it. Then she pushed it into my open mouth, screwing it round, pulling it in and out. I tasted the sweet chocolate on my tongue, I longed to eat up the rabbit but she wouldn't let me. Instead she pulled it from my mouth and shoved it roughly up her cunt hole until only its feet showed. She writhed in front of me, gasping with pleasure as my delicate fingers found her fat clitoris and began to massage it. Julia had pushed her chocolate fish deep into her hole, she squatted next to me, thrusting vigorously in and out, the chocolate melting faster with the friction. I could hear her breath coming in short panting gasps as she reached orgasm.

The white chocolate ran out of Fulvia's wide inviting tunnel, as if she had been filled to the brim with creamy spunk. I pushed my face into her pink pussy, my tongue licking up all the chocolate, poking up inside her hole, cleaning away the sweet nectar mixed with her own delicious body fluids. She came with a great wrenching spasm, clasping her legs around me.

Then she and Julia pushed me down onto the carpeted floor and began to fuck me with another, larger, chocolate rabbit. Its width forcing me open so wide that my pleasure was almost too great to bear and I reached my climax with a violent, urgent speed. I lay on the carpet, my body sensitised to every little touch, the melted chocolate smeared over me and between my legs. Fulvia straddled me, rubbing her pussy, with its soft brown fur, against my ribs and tits. Then she pushed my head to one side and I felt her hot breath on my neck. Her tongue licked at my flesh, my body filled with excitement as she bit into me, I begged her for more, to bite harder. She hurt me. I felt her sucking at my blood. Her own body racked with pleasure against me. Julia lay next to us stroking our bodies, kissing us softly, pleading with Fulvia to take her blood also.

The three of us lay together in tangled rapture, Fulvia sipping our blood at intervals, her ecstatic moans filling the room. As I lay in the dancing candle light, I noticed that the door was now half open. Marcus, the man I'd seen at the window, stood silently in the corner of the room. He had a clear view of us, his face was even thinner than his sister's. His long hair appeared darker as were his eyes, they seemed almost black. Standing there he looked like some ancient statue in a Roman garden. He was clothed in a black silk dressing gown that reached the ground and it fell open to reveal his naked form. He watched me as my eyes ran approvingly over his body, thin yet well muscled like a runner. Black hair growing in a line down his taut belly and framing his large thick cock, which stood out from his body like a spear waiting to impale us.

Fulvia sat up, pulling me with her, she wrapped her arms around me, nuzzling my wounded neck, opening the already healing wound again, to taste my blood.

I watched over her shoulder as Marcus slipped his hand down to stroke his prick. His black eyes never leaving mine, a strange hungry look on his face, almost like pain. Julia was close by, watching him too as he wanked himself off in front of us. His spunk shooting out like a fountain and falling in droplets to the floor.

We awoke to birdsong and early morning traffic outside. There was no sign of Fulvia or Marcus, the room looked dusty in the dim morning light. We left quietly, still in a dream state, not believing what had happened. Days passed and we heard nothing until another message mysteriously arrived from Fulvia. So we visited again and played our games with our new vampire lover. We shared our blood with her and she told us stories of long ago in hot Mediterranean lands. Of how lonely she and Marcus had been and that his strength was returning slowly. That they fed on the old people in our seaside town and that no-one suspected anything, for it was as if their victims had died peacefully in their sleep. Indeed, Fulvia promised that her gift of death was a gentle one and that they slipped away like the tide going out at sunset.

We did not see Marcus again and Fulvia did not offer us what we really wanted. Eternal life, to be like her, to be with them. If she suspected our ultimate desire she showed no emotion, and though we told her of our blood drinking murder, Fulvia was unimpressed.

And so the months of summer passed by and the autumn came. We waited and longed and finally made our decision. We would conclude our obsession with the undead. We would find Marcus and beg him to convert us.

That afternoon the rain came lashing against the windows, a cruel wind blew over the heaving sea as it dashed the life out of the sea creatures thrown up onto the shore.

We bathed in perfumed water and dressed in matching black satin dresses, our bodies naked beneath so that the fabric clung and shimmered around curved hips and breasts, the nipples clearly showing through the fabric.

We slipped into the house next door, prising open a back window. It was so easy, and we walked barefoot through the empty, dusty rooms until we came to the hallway. A twisting staircase beckoned us and we thought we could hear Marcus' faint breathing as he lay asleep upstairs. Slowly we climbed upwards, trying each door in the corridor, peering in. The rooms were all empty of course.

Then at the last room we tried the door swung open of its own accord. There he lay in the darkened room, a pale shadow almost whiter than the sheets on which he lay. We stood on either side of the bed to admire him, he seemed like a lovely angel, fallen from the skies. It would be dark soon and he would wake, we didn't think of his anger or remoteness, only that our soft bodies would placate him and that he would give in to us. We knelt beside him on the bed, our arms enfolding each other, making an archway over his body. We kissed. Our wet tongues tasting each other's mouths. Then we slipped off our dresses and began to stroke the object of our desire, running our fingers through his beautiful hair. We licked his pretty face like cats, kissed his cold lips, opened his mouth with our fingers to see his sharp fanged teeth.

We held our breath with fear and excitement as we saw his eyelids slowly open. At first his black eyes seemed glazed and far away, then he focused on us. His eyes drinking in our voluptuous bodies as he smiled faintly, lifting his hands to caress us and draw us down against him. We writhed against him, our hair smothering his face. We heard his sigh of pleasure as our hands explored his body, our fingers running through the soft hair around his cock. We stroked his balls slowly and felt his cock harden and swell in our hands as we rubbed it. We turned round so that our large round bottoms pointed into Marcus' face, our legs parted so that he could see our swollen, ripe cunts. We rubbed our faces against his throbbing prick, our tongues flickering over its tip, taking it in turns to fill our mouths with his generous tool.

How we savoured the taste of him as we pulled back the skin from its head to admire his cock better, licking at its juicy tip. Our hands holding his thick bucking prick, we tightened our grip as we drew our hands up and down its length, squeezing it rhythmically like our climaxing cunt muscles. We felt the shuddering passion of his body as his cock spurted its tribute over us, showering our faces and open mouths. We licked frantically, shoving each other out of the way, smoothing his spunk over our tits and bellies.

Marcus watched us with his wild black eyes, his pointed teeth showing as his lips drew back in a grin. His cock in stiff readiness again, he grabbed hold of Julia and pushed her down onto the soft bed. His body glistening with sweat. Julia pretended to struggle, trying not to giggle as he held down her arms, his teeth sinking into her neck. I smelled her fresh blood, saw her eyes filled with rapture as he shoved his cock roughly into her wet hole, his mouth against her neck sucking her blood. She spread her legs wider, grinding her hips against his so that he pushed further up inside her. Fucking her slowly as he savoured her rich blood, biting her again with a savage passion. He began to thrust vigorously, finally losing control and pumping her full of his thick sticky spunk. Julia screamed with ecstasy, her body spasming in rhythm to his own.

We writhed in passion on the damp sheets, Marcus licking our pussies in turn, his clever fingers pushing up inside us, playing with our clits until we were swollen and near to coming, begging for release. Then he would fuck us, his massive cock filling me so that his spunk ran between my legs and onto the already stained sheets.

He drank from us again and again, becoming stronger and more passionate with each drop of blood. Finally we lay quiet on the bed, our damp bodies relaxed. The smell of our love juices intoxicating. The blood and semen spattered sheets evidence of our night's rapture.

Marcus lay silently, as if thinking, his hands stroking us slowly. Then it seemed he had made a decision, and he bit into his wrist. Oh! at last, at last! We took our turns to drink his blood, our bodies filling with fire. We felt as if we burned from the inside out, our heads were spinning. Marcus cuddled us close afterwards, whispering words in Latin that we could not understand.

Then Fulvia came in, serene, in a plain black gown. She sat with us on the bed, watching over us, a loving look in her eyes.

And so, my dears, this story must end for now.

Julia and I have become the undead. We walk through the night with our vampire lovers, Fulvia and Marcus. For all our dreams and desires, we made them come to us, made it happen.

And we are so very beautiful, perfect in every way. You could not resist us, you would fall swooning at our feet. We travel far and wide, never stopping for long. Our life is much the same as our mortal one. Except that we no longer visit graveyards. For our interests lie in fresh warm blood and the dead have little to offer the undead, don't you agree?

Midnight Lazarus

Roman Suchyj

11.55pm Friday 31st December 1999

'Fuck,' thought Roseala. She didn't know why she had become a vampire. The dead priest couldn't tell her.

Five minutes to midnight her palmtop computer bleeped. The year 2000 would be here and she was clueless. The ankh tattoo on her arm itched. She scratched it and shivered because her flesh was cold.

She stood naked on the outside balcony breathing in the acrid air. Her head was full of butterfly thoughts and the industrial noise of the dying embers of the city. Car engines humming in the distance coughed and spluttered. Ghostly lights glimmered and faded like fireflies on the horizon. On the corner of the street, a street lamp flickered. The light created a strobe effect as if expiring before the millennium and the beginning of a new century. Everything was coming to an end.

The night heat mixed with petrol fumes was suffocating. A dusty coating covered her pale skin making it feel dry. She couldn't think straight. Her head spun with thoughts, colours, and a sense of time passing. She always felt like this when she'd just fucked. But this was the first time she had been turned into a vampire.

She knew she was a vampire because she had not put on her make-up and her face was still pale. She had an unbearable craving for blood when she looked at the dead priest. Besides, the fangs gave it away.

The blood had dried on his body and around his crotch. He lay entwined in the stained sheets of blood and semen, a sacrifice to an unknown god. His lacerated dick seemed vulnerable now. So limp. It was difficult to imagine it could become hard.

The smell of the blood was nauseating. There were speckles around the room and in his white hair. He lay in the crumpled sheets, a crushed angel.

She felt the desire for his blood and for him. She was tempted as she approached the angel priest. For old time's sake, she licked his flesh. She flicked her tongue over his body. The blood was dry, rough to her tongue and the flesh cold. It wasn't the same. She wanted his warmth again. She wanted him to hold her, someone to talk to. Someone to tell her why she was a vampire. But time had run out.

11.56pm Friday 31st December 1999

Her palmtop bleeped. She flicked the lid. Four minutes to go.

She had planned to spend the last minutes with her friends. Now it was too late. Besides how could she explain to Jake, Lara or Zilith that she was a vampire? Lara would say 'cool'. Zilith would say "I've never slept with a vampire". He would enter one of his depressive moods and curl the ends of his long black hair in his fingers. She would feel sorry for him.

To make Zilith happy, to ease his despair, she might sleep with him or give him a Clinton or hand relief. Zilith needed consoling; besides she liked sleeping with him.

Jake might try to help her. He was understanding and less self obsessed and had time for everyone. He was the intellectual with whom she talked about everything.

All of them had dressed in black and worn white make-up. They had spent their days pretending, wanting to be vampires. Now, she was the real thing. She had fucked a priest and she was a vampire.

She looked in the mirror. She felt strong and energetic even though her pale body was small and naked. Her body was firm. Her nipples pert and the rings dangled. Her bush vibrant black whilst her shiny black hair fell over her shoulders. Her green eyes glowed. Were it not for the paleness of her skin and its slight loss of elasticity and the feeling of strength, it would be hard to tell she was a vampire.

The ankh tattoo on her arm itched, which it always did when she was stressed. She scratched it.

'You jerk,' she thought. 'Maybe I should never have sucked him and drank his blood.' How could she have resisted when he had said in that rasping voice of golden syrup "Drink, this is my blood, and remember me." He offered on this balmy Friday night, so she accepted.

7pm Friday 31st December 1999 - The Bar
He shone like a burning angel in the darkness of the smoke-filled dinginess of The Bar. He, the priest, in his golden gowns embroidered in archaic symbols. A cerebus dangled on a long silver chain around his neck.

The Bar was a darkly lit cave. There were not many in. Roseala, her friends and a few others. Most sat in the alcoves. Jake, Zilith and Lara sat around a table. Roseala was at the bar, which was brightly lit with mirrors on the wall, highlighting the spirit bottles. They were talking or listening to the heavy music laden with doom, waiting for the first band to come on. The music would get louder later.

"A double vodka please, Alicia." She'd already had three because she felt sad. Time was running out.

Her palmtop bleeped. She pulled it out of her frock coat pocket. All day the palmtop had displayed the clock. There was a glitch. She couldn't access any information. She wondered if it was the millennium bug or just millennium lethargy. She was sure it was guaranteed against the bug but maybe not against the despair of a new century.

All day the black palmtop bleeped as if it were an electronic heart beating its last. It didn't even do it on the hour, just when it felt like it. As though it was warning her that everything was coming to an end.

The priest came at seven and began proselytising. Seeking converts to his Church of the Latter Daze of the Millennium. He swore his church was the true one. She had read that there were many converts to the religion of the Latter Daze. The theology was simple. She had discussed it with Jake.

"We're all doomed according to them, because we're confused. We live in a daze so we don't understand what we are doing. That's why the world is in such a fuck-up. The sole purpose of the church is to save people by snapping them out of the daze."

"The enlightened will be saved at the millennium?" asked Jake.

"Yes. I've heard that one way the priests do that is to fuck until both reach ecstasy and enlightenment."

"They're like shamen," Jake had said. "If it's going to end, it's going to end."

Part of her craved to find out if people really were in a daze. She wanted to know if the albino priest with his red eyes and shiny white hair had any insight. And part of her wanted to fuck the priest.

The intensity of his belief moved something in her heart. Perhaps, even in her soul, only she didn't believe in souls. Maybe she should because time was running out. He was cute. She wondered if he had a cute arse.

"This is the end. We are living in the days of daze, in confusion," the priest said. "Look how lost we have become. Leaderless leaders and visionless visionaries create confusion. Financial institutions fall. Corruption corrodes our governments. Money rules as the greedy drool. Look to the skies. They have darkened with pollution, choking all that gave life. The weather changes, storms and quakes. Now plagues spread. Fires and wars rage as famine hungers for victims. These are the signs of the end of time. We are living in a daze and are blind to the signs. We cannot see that these are the last days."

Of course, no one listened to him.

Prophets and priests were numerous, all predicting the end of time in their different ways. There was something different to this prophet.

Roseala watched his movements. The way he moved his arms, the passion in his eyes. Those red eyes that seemed hungry for truth, haunted by a need to convert before it was too late.

When he finished his speech he would have a drink, a Bloody Mary, then leave. This night she had decided that she would leave with him. She imagined his physique under the golden gowns. She wanted to fuck him. She wanted to know what he was like. Maybe they could talk some philosophy and find some meaning for the new century before it was too late.

The loneliness of living at the end of the twentieth century, of life itself, shadowed her wherever she went. She could never escape, whether she was fucking or with friends, or both, the spectre always haunted her. Whether fucking or talking she knew she didn't want to spend the night alone. She wanted to know she was alive. At the beginning of the new century she wanted reassurance that things would be fine. That it wasn't too late for anyone.

That's why she waited at the bar.

"These are the signs of the end of time. Only the converted shall be redeemed. The dead resurrected, as it is written," he said to her with intensity, his red eyes glowing. It was the best chat up line she had heard in a long time. Her palmtop bleeped at 8.05.

8.06pm Friday 31st December 1999
The memories were hazy; too much vodka and whisky always gave her an appetite for hot cock, the desire to fill the loneliness of the millennium eve.

"Do you want to convert and break through the daze?" he asked her.

"If it involves sex then yes," she said.

She waved goodbye to her pale friends, dressed in black, listening to the dark thumping music of despair. She left The Bar with the priest holding his cold hand. Somehow they ended up in his flat on the third floor, in a ménage à trois with a bottle of vodka.

8.30pm Friday 31st December 1999 - The Flat
When her palmtop bleeped again they were already naked. She was holding his cock in her hand and he played with her bush. They both knelt on the bed. They both came with the bleep.

"Drink, this is my blood." That's what he said and that's what she did.

She ran her blue fingernails down his flesh. He was slightly older than she was and his skin was not as taut as it could be. His white straw hair was covered in sweat as she passed her hand through. She went down his body and dug her nails into his pale skin. From his cheeks down to his belly the skin seared and she left a red streak of blood. He was so mild, lost in his world, and all he said was "Drink". He closed his albino eyes and left for the land of dreams.

10pm Friday 31st December 1999
In the heat of the night he woke her as he licked her pale skin and caressed her long hair. He kissed the ankh on her arm and nibbled gently. He explored the mysteries of all her crevices with his studded tongue and her body confessed its pleasures. He played with the rings in her nipples and the studs in her crotch.

Her mind entered a pleasure zone of delight, at other times she worried that her mascara would run. At the same time, she wanted to discuss religion and philosophy. She was panicking. What if the world ended and she died ignorant?

"Drink in my memory," he said and lay back on the bed. So she did. Moving her lips down his body to the throbbing vein where she bit gently at first and then harder as he became harder. And soon the vein burst. The blood spurted into a fountain spray that seemed to cover the entire room and all he did was groan with pleasure. Her head spun in a posy of red spots as she fell into sleepy timeless vodka stupor.

And when she woke up she was a vampire with a dead priest in the bed.

11.58pm Friday 31st December 1999

The palmtop bleeped. The millennium would be here in two minutes. The seconds were passing by.

The ankh tattoo on her arm itched. She scratched it.

She pulled on her black tee shirt and jeans, put on her frock coat and combat boots. She walked back to the balcony. The stars were pinpricks. There were no cars on the road. There were shadows on the street as people hurried to destinations ready to celebrate the millennium. From the distance she heard voices, prophets preaching. There wasn't much time left.

Roseala felt cold in the heat. Tonight things would be different. Would she find other vampires? How would she recognise them? What would she do? She felt alone. She would have to leave, find her friends. Perhaps, she could turn them into vampires. They would help her.

She knew no one would bother about the priest. He was just a local nutter. Nobody would miss him, only Roseala. Yes, she missed him. Their lovemaking had been deeper than just sex, for one night in her life she had felt loved. She had felt transcendence even though she had not reached enlightenment. She would never become a convert to the Latter Daze Church.

A new century was beginning and she would enter it as a vampire. Would everything end at midnight as the priest had said? Or was he just another sad eyed lunatic who happened to have been a good lay? Her heart pulled because she wanted to believe. There must be some truth as there were millions of followers of the Latter Daze. Maybe in the next minute they would all become disillusioned.

The bleeper went erratic. Seconds to go. The last bleep.

12.00am Saturday 1st January 2000

The palm top computer was dead. All her data was lost. A searing light lit up the heavens and the earth.

She could see her friends, Jake, Lara, and Zilith on the streets. They were pale. Their faces stained with blood. They were not wearing make-up. They waved to her. Instinctively, she knew that they were vampires too.

She heard a groan and turned. The priest like an angel was standing on the bed. He was naked, his gowns were over his shoulders, a golden cloak, and his arms were outstretched as if his golden wings were spread. His hair, a halo of bleach, shone and his pale body had no marks or scars, just dried blood.

His albino eyes looked at her as he smiled. "Drink and remember me."

He beckoned to her. She felt her crotch wet and warm as she noticed his erect dick throbbing. Her angel had returned and they would make love again.

Now she understood. She had been converted. She had been blinded in the daze and confusion of the chaos of the last days of the end of the world. Enlightenment had come to her. The dead had risen as was written and prophesied.

It was all clear now. The resurrection had begun. The vampires would inherit the Earth.

The Authors

Ryan Acheson

Ryan Acheson is a 19 year old student. This is his first published piece of work, but he hopes to be able to get more stories 'out there'. He writes mainly psychological horror, but occasionally, as shown here, likes to write something more visceral. Originality is his sole aim, drawing inspiration from nightmares and caffeine highs. More than anything he hopes he can make a living from writing.

A. J. Barron

A. J. Barron was born and lives near Newcastle and has been a huge fan of Vampire myth for as long as he can remember, buying into both film and novel fiction and 'true' legend. When all the other children were watching 'The Little Mermaid' he was indulging in 'Twins of Evil'. 'Stigmata' is A. J. Barron's first published work. The story is dedicated to Tracey - for everything.

Angélique Bessant

Angélique Bessant lives and works in Paris. She has had a passion for the macabre since her first visit to the Paris Catacombs as a child, and began writing about Vampires at around the same time. This is her first published work outside of her native France.

Michaela Bisiker

"The world insists that we be both young and beautiful, and by offering up our blood, our body, our soul, the Vampire will grant us these gifts. Who could resist the pale, seductive visitor who taps on the window pane at midnight? The bone-white smile, the glowing, hypnotic eyes. How can we resist so generous an offer? We can't..."

Zane Black

Zane Black has contributed fiction and reviews to magazines in the US and Europe. He was publisher/editor of 'XS: The Journal of Extreme Fiction' until it was suppressed by the British police and customs. Since then he has been lying low, mostly in Amsterdam and London. Recently he has been developing no-to-low budget horror movie projects. He is also currently researching and writing a non-fiction book, 'Does The Queen Know About This?: Princess Di's Gay Life'. Zane is an honorary member of the Satan's Saints Motorcycle Club of Santa Monica, California. He wears his Red Wings proudly.

Adrian Bott

Adrian Bott grew up in Sussex, moved to Manchester in 1986 and has been there ever since. He has been writing all his life. His first novel, 'The Necro-File', is presently being filmed. A practicing Thelemic magician, pirate enthusiast, lecturer, folk singer and (under the name of 'Cavalorn') net.goth, he spends most of his time managing a thriving occult bookshop/café. He has contributed articles to the pagan and magickal press over many years: his 'The Magickal Vampire' was the winner of a Baphomet Award from Talking Stick for the year's best article.

Louisianax E. M. Caliban

Louisianax, the proud owner of a hard earned BA Honours Degree in English Literature and Language, has been writing creatively for most of her life. She completed her first novel - an historical romp set in 17th Century France - at the age of 15, and has woven her love of history into her tales of Vampires and magick ever since. As sub-editor of, and regular writer for, Bloodstone, she has less time for creative pursuits now than she would like, but is currently working on a 'Highlander' spin-off novel and a tale of Pagan horror set around her beloved spiritual motherland of Avebury. When not writing, she is usually working on magickal projects. As a solitary

Witch and proud Pagan, she has been a walker on the path of light as well as darkness for many moons.

Leo Cores

Leo Cores was born in Villanueva de Arosa in a Benedictine rectory dating from the 9th century with an early Romanic style which at present belongs to his family. He obtained his degree in Philosophy at the University of the mediaeval city of Santiago de Compostela. Now he lives in the largest city in Galicia, Vigo, of Celtic origins. He has published some essays on pictorial surrealism, Marcel Proust, and the monster of Frankenstein in the cinema, in different magazines. This is his first broach of the theme of Vampirism "which especially interests me because it contains some of the most sought after desires from the beginning of time such as immortality, and not like the work of a writer, but obtaining eternal youth here and now; fleeing from man's fears, death, illness and age. Although this leads to anonymity, solitude, a tremendous melancholy and the death of his peers."

Holly & J. Flaxton

Husband and wife J. and Holly Flaxton have found some small recognition amongst Vampirophiles through their numerous contributions to the magazines and journals of various Vampire related clubs and societies, sharing their love of things Vampiric through their darkly gothic short fiction, poetry and articles, always with an underlying black humour and the greatest reluctance to take themselves too seriously. Sadly Holly passed away in June 1998 and her great passion, 'The Flaxton Papers', the novel she worked on for over five years, will probably remain unpublished.

Dean Aaron Geoghegan

Dean was born in South London and lived for a time in Jamaica where he learnt to appreciate the beauty of bats (and the cleavage of certain horror actresses) after sitting in an open air theatre watching Vampires on-screen and bats flying across the night sky. He now lives in Surrey where his life revolves around his lover, cats, horror films and rock music as well as murdering houseplants and collecting model gargoyles. He works, during the daylight hours, in an 18th century cottage haunted by the ghost of a Victorian businessman.

Craig Giles

Craig Giles lives in his home town of Bolton in Lancashire. Although he has had poetry published in the fanzine 'Black Planet', this is his first attempt at having one of his stories published. "I feel that the best Vampire stories, and indeed Vampires themselves, are a wonderful blend of fantasy, enchantment, lust, romance, passion, horror and darkness. How can anyone with any imagination fail but to fall in love with such an intoxicating cocktail?"

Darran Heath

Darran Heath lives in a verdant and violent suburb of Birmingham, renting an attic flat that is as cold as the grave, and maybe damper. 'Only £1.99 Per Min.' is his first published story, his first spill of fictive blood.

Mark A. Henderson

Mark Henderson lives and works in Glasgow and is an active member of the Scottish Vampyre Society, and a co-editor of its magazine, 'Nocturne'. "I feel that the Vampire in fiction sums up human experience. There is beauty, if you look for it, and when you find it - look, through Vampire eyes - you discover it's all around you. There is also sorrow and the feeling of being Outside, which everyone feels at some point. With this however can come a delicious voyeurism, as you become the observer of all the world's fictions. Pain, loss, love, longing: all can be found in Vampire fiction, described more fully and beautifully than in any other genre." 'Gothboy' is his first published work outside 'Nocturne' and "is dedicated to Hazel, my immortal beloved, and to Rose Lindsay, my first fan".

JP

"Late at night I prowl the dimly lit streets, ever watchful, ever waiting. Autumn is my favourite time of the year, yet I first struck during the summer. Few know me and most never will. They can, and will, continue to pretend whereas I do not. Never have, never will. I have written before but they were not my words. Four, five or six? More if you prefer. Only I know the real truth for I am he. The midnight bell chimes, it is almost time for me to depart. There are always victims out there for me. Be watchful as you walk the streets at night. Next time, the one who stops you for a light or the time may not be as innocent as he seems..."

Rachel P. Kendall

"Vampyre: Rising angelic from a burial womb, searching for prey as the vulture hungers. Elixir of sweet crimson wine. With the injection of fangs comes the ultimate penetration, blood drained and intravenous high like a drug, like an orgasm, like a shroud to cover the victim with elation and fear. Death wins. The Vampyre sleeps."

D. K. Korps

Mr Korps has always had a deep and dark interest in the macabre. He grew up in a remote backwater in the Forest of Bowland. With Pendle Hill, famous throughout history for its witches, rising ominously in front of his home, and extensive forestry and moorland to the rear, his childhood offered inspiration and settings for untold numbers of stories. He was able to get his first novel 'In the Sanctum of the Night' into print through Janus, a subsidiary publisher. And the undoubted pinnacle of his writing exploits was being awarded a Vampire Oscar at Vampyria II in 1998.

Beverley Lee

Beverley Lee lives in Berkshire, England. 'The Gentle Art of Betrayal' and 'Abandonment – The Deadliest Virtue' are her first published works. Her stories are mainly displayed on Internet sites where she has won many awards voted for by readers. "The Vampire is such an alluring enigma. A figure that haunts the night and a creature that needs the blood of the living to sustain an eternal life. There is something incredibly sensual about a creature who never ages but that has the wisdom of centuries. The Vampire is the dark side that lives in each of us."

Stephen Lewis

Hailing from Greek and Egyptian descent, Stephen possesses a dark and mysterious persona. Choosing to write about Vampires he feels he can express his feelings and emotions without mortal limitations. Hoping to portray the Vampire as more than just a stereotyped bloodsucker and show the seductive, amorous and romantic side. Having travelled Greece and its surrounding islands, Stephen is now taking time out to write. With other work in the pipeline he feels that this will be a very good beginning to his writing career.

Rosie Lugosi

Rosie Lugosi lives in Manchester, via London, Leeds and Sudan. She has an eclectic performance history from singing in 80s goth band 'The March Violets' to her current incarnation as dominatrix lesbian Vampire poet and compère. Her poetry has been widely published, and her short story 'Tears for Souvenirs' won the Queer Words Horror/Fantasy writing prize in 1997. She has just completed her first novel 'Nature's Favourite'. "I am fascinated by the idea of creating Vampires who could really exist - so I've dropped moonlight, flapping capes and crucifixes and have developed a separate species of biologically viable mammal, passing for human. Parasites who thrive on a liquid diet of menstrual blood. No bitemarks. Long-lived, but not undying. Believable."

Luke McLelland Smith

Luke is eighteen years old and lives in Borrowash. Although he writes frequently and has done so from an early age on an amateur scale, this is his first national publication. Previously he has won various regional and local competitions for short stories and poetry, and he has written for local magazines and fanzines. In the future he hopes to expand on this, produce more nationally distributed stories, and hopefully become an established and successful writer.

Laura Phoenix

Laura Phoenix is an artist who lives in London. Her paintings have been exhibited at the Royal Academy Summer Exhibition and are included in several private collections in the US and Europe. She is currently working on her first full length novel, with a Vampire theme.

Louis Ravensfield

During the summer of 1995 on the streets of London's East End a tall mysterious figure dressed in a long black coat and top hat carrying a skull topped walking cane prowled, taking tourists on a guided tour of the murder sites of England's most notorious serial killer - Jack the Ripper, culminating in a 'Midnight Walk'. Then this creature of the night vanished as quickly and silently as he had appeared. Then from the blackness of night he returned, created Dark Angel Productions and put on the highly ambitious 'Vampyria

– The Dracula Centenary Celebration' in August 1997. The launch of 'Bloodstone: The Magazine for Vampires' in 1998 was followed by the highly successful sell-out event 'Vampyria II: The Return of the Blood Sucking Undead!' in September. With the publication of 'In Blood We Lust' another dream is realised before the final part of the trilogy 'Vampyria III: Blood. Sex. Death. The Myth' unfolds.

Jami Stirling

"Vampires are the most exotic and erotic beings that live in the outer darkness. There is something inescapably sexy about the sinister lover who invades your bedroom at night and leaves you aching for more as the sun slowly rises. Who could ever resist such an exquisitely torturous desire as that which the Vampire evokes in all of us?" This is Jami Stirling's first professionally published work.

Roman Suchyj

Roman Suchyj has had poetry published in the small press and numerous anthologies, and has performed poems live. A short prose piece, 'Last Bite', appeared in 'Love: I Stand Infected' and a short story, 'Alicia's Raven', was published in 'Visionary Tongue' issue 4 in the summer of 1996. Roman has had a fascination and an interest in Vampires for a very long time, especially in the idea of life after death, eternity and of being caught between two worlds, that of the living and the dead.

M. E. Warner

M. E. Warner is a journalist. He is currently working on a contemporary Vampire novel set in a fictionalised version of his home town. He is also looking for a producer for a 40 minute script, 'Save Me', a darkly thrilling S/M love story which, he is proud to say, has been passed on by Channel 4 for being "too controversial".